DATE DUE

NOV 2 5	2002	JAN 2 8	2005
DEC - 2	2002		
		APR 1 1	2005
DEC - 9	2002		
DEC 1 8	2002	APR 2 5	2005
		SEP - 6	2005
DEC 3 0	2002		
JAN 1 0	2003	MAY - 3	2007
JAN 1 8	2003	OCLC 4-20-09	
		FEB - 3	2010
JAN 2 5	2003		
		WS 9 9-10	
		APR 3 0	2015
FEB - 5	2003		
FEB 1 3	2003	APR 2	2018
MAR - 3	2003		

Bad Faith

Also by Aimée and David Thurlo

The Ella Clah series

Blackening Song
Death Walker
Bad Medicine
Enemy Way
Shooting Chant
Red Mesa
Changing Woman

Bad Faith

AIMÉE AND DAVID THURLO

St. Martin's Minotaur ❧ New York

MYST
THURLO, A.

www.minotaurbooks.com

Design by Susan Yang

Library of Congress Cataloging-in-Publication Data

Thurlo, Aimée.
    Bad faith : a Sister Agatha mystery / Aimée Thurlo and David Thurlo.—
1st ed.
        p. cm.
    ISBN 0-312-29081-0
    1. Nuns—Fiction. 2. New Mexico—Fiction. I. Thurlo, David.
II. Title.

PS3570.H82 B33 2002
813'.54—dc21

                                                            2002069942

First Edition: November 2002

10 9 8 7 6 5 4 3 2 1

Author's Note

The Sisters of the Blessed Adoration are our own creation and thus fictional, but they were inspired by two cloistered orders that have special meaning to Aimée. The monastic practices described in this book are derived from horariums in common use. The details of daily life were taken from Aimée's memories of Ursuline Academy in Arcadia, Missouri, where she lived as a boarder for many years.

With special thanks to Diane Uzdawinis, who shared the details of monastic life with me, and never got tired of my many questions.

To Jane Piper, who always took time when I needed help.

To Jean Digerness and Mary Ann Woodland, who also helped by triggering my memory of our days at Ursuline Academy in Arcadia, Missouri.

And to the Ursuline nuns from Arcadia.

This book is dedicated to all of you with love.

Acknowledgments

With special thanks to the Corrales Fire Department, and especially to Tonya Lattin, EMTI, who shared her knowledge as a first-response intermediary with us.

Bad Faith

I

SISTER AGATHA STARED AT THE BLACK SMOKE AROUND THE tailpipe of the old Chrysler station wagon. This rusted-out bucket of bolts was what Our Lady of Hope Monastery graciously called transportation. Wiping her greasy hands on an old rag and grateful that her nagging arthritis hadn't flared up while adjusting the carburetor, Sister Agatha walked around to the engine compartment and reluctantly closed the hood.

The engine nearly died, then picked up speed again slowly, sputtering and knocking like a mechanical asthmatic running the marathon. With luck, she might be able to make it back to Our Lady of Hope without having to walk or catch a ride. This early in the morning, there were few vehicles on the road.

The Antichrysler, as Sister Agatha had named the ancient vehicle, needed major engine work again. Though she could do minor repairs, employing skills she'd learned from her brother years ago, an automotive specialist was needed now.

Getting back into the car, she continued her journey back to the monastery with the spools of thread for a quilting project the other nuns were rushing to complete.

The sun was just coming up, but already she was late. She had a million things to do, including meeting Father Anselm at St. Fran-

cis' Pantry, an outbuilding on monastery grounds that had been converted into a heated storeroom and an impressive larder. Supplies
stored there were made available to anyone in need who asked for
help. Father Anselm, the monastery's chaplain, had consented to
pick up a donation of canned goods from a grocer in the city, and
deliver it to the monastery this morning.

Rolling down the window, she wondered how it could be so hot
already down here in the Rio Grande Valley. Pressing down on the
accelerator, she tried to coax the old car into a little more speed.
Suddenly she heard a metallic thump. The engine sounded louder
but the car seemed to have a little more pep, so she decided not to
stop. Before she'd traveled another mile, however, she heard a siren
and saw a sheriff's car behind her, lights flashing.

"Dear Lord, why are you testing me? You know I'll flunk," she
muttered.

Sister Agatha pulled over to the side of the road and parked,
hoping the engine wouldn't die. As she glanced in her rearview
mirror, she saw a young deputy emerge and amble casually toward
the station wagon. He seemed rather tall, and reminded her of an
overgrown high school freshman, working on a cool, manly-looking
stride in order to impress the girls. The dark sunglasses, she suspected, were standard equipment in the sheriff's department,
regardless of the time of day.

The officer smiled as he reached her window, then took off his
sunglasses and slipped them into his shirt pocket. His eyes were pale
blue, and bright with mischief despite the early hour. "Hello, Sister.
I'm afraid I have some bad news for you."

"Don't tell me I was speeding, Deputy. As you can probably tell
by looking, this car wouldn't go more than forty miles an hour unless
you drove it off the Rio Grande Gorge."

He gave her a wide, toothy grin. "I believe that, Sister. No, you
weren't violating the speed limit. But your muffler did fall off about
a mile back down the road."

Sister Agatha sighed loudly. "So, does that mean I'm getting a
ticket for littering?"

The young officer laughed. "How about a trade? I'll let you off with a warning, and you light a candle for me back at the chapel."

"Sounds like a deal." She wondered if his leniency was prompted by orders from on high. She didn't mean God, of course. The new county sheriff was a long-time friend of hers. They'd dated back in high school and done more than that afterward during her wilder days. She hadn't seen him except for an occasional glimpse on the street since she'd joined the monastery over his protests. But after twelve years, memories of their long friendship should have overwhelmed any lingering hurt.

Of course, it might have had nothing at all to do with Sheriff Tom Green, and everything to do with the fact that she was wearing a nun's habit and it wasn't Halloween. People tended to assume that her prayers would weigh more heavily in God's sight. Little did they know. If God had been the kind to keep score, she could have rented herself as a lightning rod.

"Seriously, Sister, it's risky driving a car in this condition. You need to get it fixed before you get stopped for a vehicle emissions violation, especially while passing through pueblo land. It smokes like a campfire, and a new muffler is probably just the tip of the iceberg on this relic."

"I'll tell Reverend Mother what you said. But I'm afraid that our relic repair fund is very low at the moment. So how about it, Deputy? A few dollars toward a valve job or new oil pump for the God Squad's station wagon?"

"Sorry, Sister. I'm all tapped out this week."

"I'll be on my way then." She put the car in gear, praying nothing else would fall off, at least within the deputy's sight, and gave him a wave.

Ten minutes later she passed through the monastery's open gate. As she stepped out of the car, she felt a drop of rain, quickly followed by a dozen more. She looked up at the marble statue of Our Lord above the chapel entrance. "Why couldn't you have sent rain a half hour ago when I was sweating like a pig trying to get that car started?" Sister Agatha said, then instantly contrite, she sighed. "Not that I'm trying to tell you what to do, of course."

As a native who'd grown up in the area, she knew that rain in

New Mexico was a rare and welcome respite from the baking, mid-summer heat of the desert, and the icy drops felt wonderful. Our Lady of Hope Monastery, a former farmhouse donated to the Church decades ago, was equipped with no system of cooling other than shade trees and windows that could be opened—providing the nun worked out regularly or had been blessed with the strength of Samson.

There was a small fan in Reverend Mother's office and another in the chapel, of course, but they were no match for the three-digit temperatures that could try the body and soul during July. The Sisters of the Blessed Adoration had modernized their old pre–Vatican II habits a long time ago, bravely raising the hemlines three inches from the floor, but they were still long sleeved, made of heavy serge, and nearly unbearable in hot weather.

Since it was still too early for Sister Bernarda to be in the parlor, Sister Agatha reached for her key. Unlocking the front parlor doors, she entered, locked the door behind her, then hurried across the room toward the next set of doors leading into the inner parlor. That doorway led to the enclosure where she would rejoin her cloistered sisters.

Few had access in and out of the monastery like an extern sister. It was a privilege that made her feel especially blessed. She enjoyed two very different worlds. Here, she shared in the communal, contemplative life of the monastery, where prayer for the needs of the world and faith in God became the very essence of what defined them. When her duties as an extern took her outside, however, she got to be part of a very different world—where individual tastes and desires were paramount and became the basis for action and progress.

Extern nuns were the links between the enclosure and the outside world. Someone had to let in a plumber or the computer tech when needed, do the shopping, take the sisters to the doctor—and, as she was constantly being reminded lately, take the Antichrysler back to the auto mechanic to be resuscitated.

With soft footsteps, she made her way down the hall to the scriptorium. To emphasize a nun's complete dedication to God, the white-stuccoed corridor walls were kept bare except for pictures of the saints and a crucifix here and there. The brick floors were barren. Slipping quietly through the open doorway, she entered the scriptorium.

"You're late," Sister Bernarda snapped, looking up from the computer screen. She'd been converting a library's catalogue into a digital format.

Sister Bernarda's voice always made a person want to stand up and salute. Sister had been a sergeant in the marines, serving for twenty years prior to joining the order. But Sister Agatha had found that despite the bluster, Sister Bernarda could be counted on—as a friend and as a sister.

"The car broke down again," Sister Agatha explained, "and I'm afraid to take the interstate now."

Sister Bernarda was the monastery's only other extern nun. She and Sister Agatha were the only ones who had access to all the materials their scriptorium worked on. Here, in a modern twist to the monk's age-old pursuit, they did computer work for several libraries, magazines, and newspapers, often working with quite valuable manuscripts that required special handling. Since that work held a tie to the outside world, the cloistered nuns only worked alongside them here when Sister Bernarda and she were running behind.

As the monastery bell filled the air with its rich, deep tones, she heard the sound of soft footsteps, and the opening and closing of doors as the sisters began their procession to the chapel. It was time for Terce.

"Go on to your other duties, Sister Bernarda. I'll take care of things here," Sister Agatha said, exiting the scanning program on the computer for her. Lastly, she put the documents into a fireproof safe, a precaution the insurance company demanded despite the unique security already present in their walled, locked enclosure.

Once the door to the safe was locked, Sister Agatha went to the outer parlor to take up her duty as portress. As an extern nun she wouldn't be joining the others in chapel—she would stay here to greet visitors and answer the telephone. Extern nuns weren't required to go to chapel for Divine Office.

As the sisters' chant rose from the chapel, a stillness unlike anything she'd ever experienced outside the monastery settled over the entire building and the grounds. It was as if nature itself held its breath, waiting on the word of God. Someone had once said that the angels walked in that silence.

Working as she prayed, Sister Agatha checked the front parlor's turn, a revolving barrel-shaped shelf fitted into the outside wall. The device was used to bring small packages and mail into the cloister without the need to unlock the parlor doors. Children in the parish often referred to it as the nun's drive-up window. During summer vacation, they loved to play tricks on the nuns, depositing everything from live lizards to get-out-of-jail-free Monopoly cards.

Today the turn only contained a folded piece of typing paper. Opening it, she read the message inside.

"Pray the Lord forgives me. I'm going to hurt one of my friends."

The note sounded like it had come from one of the teens in town who was about to break up with her boyfriend. They got a lot of prayer requests of that nature these days—summer loves didn't seem to last long.

Sister placed the folded note in the small wooden box reserved for prayer requests. Each sister would draw from the box later, and pray on behalf of the petitioner they'd chosen at random.

Sister walked back to the desk and began selecting passages from religious texts for their novice to study, and other, less complicated passages for their new postulant to read. As novice mistress, the responsibility for their instruction fell to her, though it was a job she'd never wanted.

If only she could have explained to the abbess how much she disliked doing things that reminded her of the past—when she'd been Professor Mary Naughton, not Sister Agatha. That kind of nostalgia often led to comparisons, and to a heaviness of spirit that she neither liked nor understood. Not that being novice mistress was anything like being a professor, of course, but, teaching brought memories of her years at the university—a life she'd chosen to leave behind.

Now, at age forty-four, she couldn't help but wonder what her own life might have been like if she'd continued her journalism career. She'd always shown a talent for investigative reporting.

It had been her brother Kevin's long illness that had changed everything for her. She'd gone from being a reporter for an Albuquerque newspaper to teaching, in the hope of having regular work hours so she could be at home with him more. It had been a difficult time for her, but it had also been filled with unexpected blessings. While caring for her dying brother, she'd found new meaning in things she'd never valued before. Toward the end of his life, she'd received her calling from God—that stirring of the heart that drove a person to enter a monastery. And by finding God, she'd found herself.

To this day, she remained as certain of her calling as she had been the day she'd entered the monastery, located just outside the small town where she'd spent her childhood. Not that monastery life was problem free—far from it. But twelve years as a Bride of Christ had given her a firm foundation and immeasurable strength to face whatever came her way.

She checked the time. Father Anselm would be coming by soon. She'd have to be ready to greet him along with her helpers, Sister Mary Lazarus, the monastery's novice, and Celia, the postulant. Neither had taken final vows, and contact with the public was discouraged at this point of their formation, but the only person they'd see would be Father Anselm, so no rules would be violated.

After private prayers were finished in chapel, Sister Agatha stood and went to the hall. Twisting the handle of the clapper, a small, wooden device reminiscent of castanets but much less melodious, she summoned the monastery's postulant and novice. It was an efficient paging method, and very much linked to tradition, but, all things considered, she would have preferred a whistle or a bullhorn, like a high school coach.

Sister Mary Lazarus appeared almost immediately, but their postulant, Celia, failed to appear.

As Sister Bernarda arrived to relieve her of portress duty, Sister Agatha focused on Mary Lazarus. "Follow me to the library, please," Sister Agatha said. "We'll start without Celia."

As they entered the small library, Sister Agatha glanced back. Mary Lazarus was staring at a painting of the foundress of their order.

Seeing Sister Agatha looking at her, she smiled sadly. "I wonder how my friends will react once they learn I'm going to be taking my vows. I wrote them, but I haven't heard back yet. None of them showed up for my investiture, but I guess I shouldn't have been surprised. They all thought I was crazy when I entered the monastery."

Sister Agatha smiled. "You should have seen the reaction of my old friends when I told them I was entering Our Lady of Hope. Even the Catholics among them were convinced that a monastery was a place where monks live, not nuns. They thought I was making a joke about going to corrupt monks."

Mary Lazarus smiled, eyebrows raised. "I have a feeling your life on the outside was a little different from mine."

"It had its moments," Sister Agatha said, deliberately not elaborating. The fact was, in her younger days, she'd sown enough wild oats to qualify for a crop subsidy.

"It's amazing how few Catholics realize that the word monastery simply means a place where religious men or women dwell in seclusion, and live a contemplative, cloistered life." Sister Agatha looked toward the entrance. "Where *is* Postulant Celia?" Patience was not a virtue she possessed this morning in any significant quantity, not after spending a fruitless hour working on the Antichrysler and being pulled over by a deputy sheriff half her age.

Celia was a trial to her. The girl meant well, but she had no conception of time. Admittedly, dealing with Celia, her own goddaughter, was difficult for her. Celia was a constant reminder of what she'd been like before she'd found her calling—and of the many duties she'd taken lightly. She'd agreed to be godmother to Ruth's child, but soon afterward had lost all contact with them despite living less than twenty minutes away all that time. When Celia had come to them asking to be admitted into the monastery, it had come as a total surprise to Sister Agatha. She still wasn't entirely comfortable around the postulant.

"I better go find her," Sister Agatha said. "I have a feeling she's still in chapel. That girl can pray with total concentration."

Leaving Mary Lazarus to her work, she walked to the chapel. The only sound that could be heard was the hum of the giant, automatic baker the sisters used to make altar breads. These would be shipped all over the States and, along with the scriptorium's work, had become a major source of the monastery's livelihood, allowing them to become self-sustaining.

Silence was the normal condition of life at their monastery, and twelve years of practice had taught her to move with scarcely a sound. Walking into the chapel, she was surprised to see Celia was not there. She started back down the hall, then heard a sound in the sacristy. Turning, she entered the small room off the chapel and, to her surprise, saw Celia busy sewing one of the priest's Mass vestments, the alb. The long, white garment with the tailored collar fit under the chasuble, the outer cape.

"What on earth are you doing?" Sister Agatha demanded, surprised.

Celia dropped the needle and looked up, startled. "I . . . I was just trying to help. I noticed a split seam in the alb when I was helping Sister Clothilde with the laundry. I know that you've been having problems with your hands, so I thought I'd sew it for you."

It was bad enough that arthritis could make her joints all but useless at times, but to have a postulant treat her like an invalid was too much. "We have rules. You don't choose your own work assignments. Is that clear?"

Celia stood quickly, her head down. "I'm sorry, Mother Mistress. I was only trying to help."

Hearing the monastery's bell chime out unexpectedly, Sister Agatha put the garment away, despite protests from her swollen joints.

"We have to go. The bell is ringing off schedule. That probably means that the food donations I've been expecting have arrived early. We'd better hustle over to St. Francis' Pantry."

Standing in the hall, Sister Agatha summoned Sister Mary Lazarus using the wooden clapper, then led her two charges outside and across the inner grounds of the monastery.

As they walked, she noticed Celia rubbing her hands against her black postulant's dress. "Is something wrong?" she asked.

"My hands really itch. Maybe I'm allergic to the starch Sister uses to press the alb."

"Hurry on ahead and wash your hands. Maybe that'll help."

"Yes, Mother Mistress."

When they arrived, Sister Mary Lazarus hurried inside the pantry to join Celia while Sister Agatha searched for Father Anselm. The parish pickup was there, parked by the side of the building, its bed filled with containers of canned goods. But where was the priest?

Hearing a noise, she looked beneath the truck and saw him crouched on the other side, checking underneath the engine.

"What happened, Father? Is something wrong with the truck?" She'd take this late-model pickup in a second over the monastery's old station wagon. The thought made her pause. Was vehicle envy a sin?

He stood up and, as she did the same, answered her from across the bed of the vehicle. "I thought I'd poked a hole in the oil pan when I high-centered coming off the highway. But it's okay."

Father Anselm was a pleasant, round-faced man with thinning hair and a sparkle in his eye. He brushed the dust and dirt off his black pants, then adjusted his clerical collar as he walked back around to her side of the truck. "Well, what do you think, Sister? Am I still presentable?"

"You look very nice, Father," Sister Agatha said, then with a tiny smile added, "for the most part." Father was thirty-seven, still young for the post of chaplain of Our Lady of Hope Monastery. He was also headmaster at St. Charles, the small K–12 school in Bernalillo many local Catholic children attended. Though too modern in his thinking by most of the nuns' standards, he clearly doted on them, and always made himself available to support them.

"What do you mean, 'for the most part,' Sister?" He frowned.

"I've really got to look sharp today for a meeting with the archbishop. That's why I'm wearing a Roman collar instead of my usual street clothes."

Sister smiled. "Well, I'm sure His Excellency will appreciate your color coordination. After all, the white Roman collar *does* match your sneakers. But, just in case His Excellency isn't in the mood to shoot a few baskets with you after Mass, you might want to bring out your dress shoes."

He looked down and groaned. "You're right. I better go back to the rectory. I changed while I was talking to a parishioner on the phone, and never even stopped to think about my shoes." He looked up at her, a twinkle in his eyes. "But who looks at their feet besides women, anyway? And extremely humble nuns, I should add." He paused, then grinned. "And, by the way, you fit in with the former, not the latter."

He loved to tease her, but it was impossible not to like Father Anselm. "When's your meeting?"

He glanced at his watch. "In thirty minutes."

"In that case, let me help you carry the cases of food inside while my helpers do inventory and stock the shelves."

"Sister, I don't think you should do any heavy lifting with your arthritis. Let your helpers take care of that," Father Anselm said, calling out to them. "Sisters?"

Both women came out. Understanding what was needed, Celia quickly picked up the closest box from the bed of the truck and hurried toward the pantry. As she passed by the priest, Father Anselm touched her on the arm. "Annie?"

Startled, Celia gasped and lost control of the grocery box. It slipped to the ground, and cans rolled in every direction. The young postulant dropped to her knees, scrambling to pick up everything.

Father Anselm crouched in front of Celia. "Annie, it *is* you, isn't it?"

"No, Father. My name is Celia. Perhaps I remind you of someone else." She turned away, hurrying to refill the box, her face red as a beet.

"I'm sure we've met before," Father Anselm said gently, then grabbed the last two errant cans and placed them in the box.

"I just have one of those faces," Celia mumbled, bringing the box up to her waist.

Father Anselm turned away and, avoiding Sister Agatha's gaze, carried a box inside.

Sister Agatha stood where she was for a moment, gathering her thoughts. Something important had just happened but she couldn't quite get a handle on it. The postulant's full name was Celia Anne. She'd been at her christening, and as her godmother, she knew that for a fact. Had this denial been Celia's way of separating herself from her former life, or was she trying to hide something?

Sister Agatha saw the priest looking at the postulant as she came back to retrieve the last box. "Father, is something wrong?"

"No, not at all." Turning and seeing the skepticism on Sister Agatha's face, he smiled, and promptly switched the subject. "Thanks for noticing my shoes and saving my . . . day, Sister. I owe you one."

He stepped back outside and, seeing the back of the pickup empty and the tailgate closed, reached into his pocket for the truck keys. "Well, that takes care of the food. I'll leave you and the sisters to finish stowing everything away."

"Do you have time for a small glass of iced tea before you leave? It'll help you relax before your meeting." And, with luck, she'd get a hint about what had just happened.

He looked at his watch. "The nuns special blend?" Seeing her nod, he smiled. "I'll make time. The monastery's blend is wonderful."

As they walked back inside the pantry, Sister Agatha touched Celia on the arm, getting her attention. "Could you get some of our herbal tea for Father?"

After the postulant left, Sister Agatha turned to Father Anselm. "Make sure you don't wear white socks with your dress shoes. And that's my last fashion tip for the day," she added with a wry smile.

He chuckled. "I'll take it, even if it comes from someone who knows what she'll be wearing the rest of her life."

Celia joined them just then with the iced tea, which she presented nervously to the priest.

As Father took the opportunity to study Celia's face again, Sister Agatha studied him. There was definitely something going on. She'd started to ask him a question, when he stood up, glancing at his watch. "I better get going," he said taking several quick swallows of the tea. "I've got to hurry to the rectory and change these shoes, or I'll be late for sure."

She suppressed a disappointed sigh. She'd have to get to the bottom of things later.

After Father left, Sister Agatha and her helpers got to work putting things away and taking inventory. As she began arranging the shelves, Sister Agatha noticed her own hands had begun to itch. Walking over to the sink, she washed them with plenty of soap. They felt better after that, but she couldn't help but wonder if Celia was right and the culprit *was* the new starch she'd purchased for the monastery.

Time slipped by quickly as they worked. When the job was near completion, she checked her watch and gasped. The morning was nearly gone. Remembering that the priest's vestments still needed to be mended before Mass, she reluctantly sent Celia back to the sacristy to finish the repairs. There was no time for her to do it herself now.

When the bells rang twenty minutes later, Sister Agatha directed the novice to join the nuns, and then hurried to the sacristy for one final look around to make sure everything was ready for Father Anselm.

Noting that Celia had already joined the sisters in chapel, she gave the vestments a quick once-over. She had to admit, Celia had done a good job. Sister Agatha placed the alb in the two-way drawer, which could be opened from the priest's side of the room or the cloistered side, and positioned it so the garments were in full view. She was ready to leave when Father Anselm rushed into the room, wearing tennis shorts and a T-shirt.

"Hello, Sister!" He beamed her a wide smile from the other side of the partition. "I have a tennis match right after mass with one of our parish's biggest benefactors," he explained. "Do me a favor? Don't tell Reverend Mother I'm wearing tennis clothes beneath my vestments. Last time, she told His Excellency, and I came within an inch of having my mail forwarded to Kingdom Come." He placed his tennis racket against the wall.

"How did the meeting with the archbishop go?"

"I postponed it because I had to make an unscheduled visit to a parishioner." He grimaced. "That won't impress the archbishop much, particularly since he hasn't been feeling well. But I'll try to fix things later and, with luck, save the day with a Hail Mary pass."

She forced herself not to laugh. "I'd like to talk to you about Celia after Mass, if possible."

"Can't do it today. Maybe tomorrow. Okay?"

Hearing the nuns in the chapel chanting the Divine Office, she hurried to the door. "Until later then, Father," she whispered.

Sister Agatha took a seat in the first pew near the side door to the chapel and before long Father Anselm came out ready to celebrate Mass. She noted with a smile that he'd remembered not to wear sneakers.

The chapel, like most of the other rooms in the former farmhouse, had been converted to fit the needs of their cloistered order. The nuns who'd taken a vow of enclosure were separated from the priest and the faithful who came from the community by a grille that took up one side of the church. During communion, the nuns walked single file to an opening in the grille and, there, received the host.

As extern nuns, Sister Bernarda and Sister Agatha came to Mass but remained outside the enclosure. Afterward, they'd stay and visit with the parishioners, though usually only a few came to daily Mass, like today.

After several minutes had gone by, she realized that Father Anselm seemed to be having a problem. His face was pale and he was swallowing repeatedly, as if sick to his stomach and fighting to keep from vomiting. Sister Agatha glanced over at Sister Bernarda, who also seemed worried.

Mass continued, but as Father began to consecrate the bread

and wine, he staggered back. He swayed slowly for a moment and fell to his knees, retching violently. Then, clutching his chest, he began to gasp for air.

Sister Agatha rose and hurried to the end of the pew to go help him. Father Anselm was trying to stand up by leaning against the altar, but the effort was too much for him. He collapsed, dragging the cloth and the vessels on it down to the floor with a crash.

When Sister Agatha reached him a second later, her heart sank. Father lay on the red brick floor, his body racked by convulsions. His face was contorted in pain, and his hands grabbed at his chest. He was shivering in the eighty-degree room as if freezing to death, yet his brow was wet with perspiration.

"Everything hurts," he whispered in a broken voice. "But the bells are . . . comforting. They're ringing nearby. Can you hear them? It's a beautiful sound."

As she knelt by the fallen priest, Sister Bernarda joined her. "I ran to the parlor and called nine-one-one."

Sister Agatha nodded. Father's face was rigid, as if all his facial muscles had stopped working. Then he lay perfectly still.

"He doesn't have a pulse. Is he breathing?" she asked Sister Bernarda, who was crouched low, her ear against his chest.

"No. We need to start CPR now." Sister Bernarda loosened Father's collar, then wiped the saliva away from his mouth with a handkerchief and checked that his throat was clear. "I'll give him some air, Sister, you start with the heart massage."

Sister Agatha nodded grimly, remembering their drills with the practice dummy months ago.

They began to work, but deep down Sister Agatha knew it was too late. Father Anselm's eyes were open, staring blankly at the ceiling, looking only at the face of God.

2

B Y THE TIME THE PRIMARY RESPONSE TEAM ARRIVED, THE priest had no vital signs. They worked quickly, trying to restore a heartbeat with the drugs their protocols called for, but the priest failed to respond. After thirty minutes, the physician monitoring their work via radio link told them to call the code—signifying they were to stop their efforts. The district medical investigator, also a physician, would be sent to certify the death. Father Anselm's body now lay shrouded with a blanket awaiting the arrival of county authorities.

Sister Agatha stood near the altar, her throat constricted with grief, her face wet with tears. She believed in the afterlife with every fiber of her being, but to see death come so quickly, up close, like this . . . Father Anselm had been like a breath of fresh air at the monastery. His irreverent humor had always been tempered by his deep and abiding devotion to God. He'd served the Church with his whole heart, and brightened his ministry with a touch of laughter. She couldn't think of a more fitting homage for the young priest.

Hearing heavy footsteps at the back of the chapel, she looked up and saw the sheriff approach. She'd thought she'd never be able to feel anything through the mind-numbing grief that engulfed her, but she'd been wrong. Seeing him up close for the first time in years sent a jolt of emotion through her. Tom Green's dark brown hair had turned gray around the temples, and his face had acquired some hard lines, but the kid she'd known in school was still there—the ten-year-old boy who'd driven Sister Charitas crazy by making a list of the creatures Noah should have left off the Ark, such as flies, centipedes, and schoolteachers. Then the college senior who'd filled their apartment with balloons and roses on her birthday—only to find out he'd gotten the date wrong.

He strode up to her, a scowl on his face. "Are you in charge here now?"

She nearly choked. "No, not hardly." Her gaze fell on the men from the office of the medical examiner as they crouched by Father Anselm's body.

"Who's the head nun? Mother Superior?"

"Reverend Mother Margaret Mary is our abbess," she answered.

"I need to interview her right now, and everyone else who was present at Mass."

"The parishioners who attended Mass have already gone home. Father Anselm's abrupt death frightened them and they left as soon as possible. I didn't try to stop them because they were witnesses to a tragedy, not a crime."

"Get Reverend Mother."

She took a deep breath and tried to get her temper in check. "This is a *monastery*, Sheriff, and we are a *cloistered* order. Most of the nuns here don't have contact with the outside world. You can't just barge in here, order Reverend Mother about, and disrupt every-thing—"

"The priest's death is responsible for the disruption, not me. I'm here to help put things back to normal. Now either bring the abbess here or take me to see her."

As a nun, Sister Agatha should have been used to following orders, but it had always been one of her shortcomings. Right now she was feeling protective. This monastery was her home, the nuns her family. Reverend Mother, in particular, carried the weight of all temporal and spiritual matters that concerned the monastery. She didn't need any additional burdens. She would do everything in her power to protect their abbess.

"You can't enter the enclosure," she said firmly. "You'll have to go to the outer parlor, and she'll come to the grille. You can speak to her there."

"Like a jail, huh?"

She shot him a hard look, and he shrugged. As she started to leave the chapel, she saw Sister Mary Lazarus and Sister Bernarda come out of the hallway that led to the cloister, bucket and scrubbing brushes in hand. They were obviously intending to clean up the chapel—their usual task after Mass.

"Stop right there, Sisters," Sheriff Green's voice cracked through the air like a whip. "No one touches anything until I say so. Is that clear?"

"Tom," Sister Agatha reached out and touched his arm lightly.

He glanced back at her and moved his arm away. "You're Sister Agatha now, and I'm Sheriff Green. Don't try to use our former friendship to manipulate me. I'm here on official business, and I have a job to do. Now go tell your superior I'll need to speak to her in ten minutes. Then come back here. I have to get your statement, too."

"All right. But get this through your thick head. If you intend to get any cooperation from this monastery, you'll treat Reverend Mother with the respect she deserves."

After Sister Agatha and the other extern nun, Sister Bernarda, described the events and their observations and actions leading up to the arrival of the primary response team, Sheriff Green went to speak to Reverend Mother.

The outer parlor was divided from the enclosure by a grid of vertical and horizontal metal rods that physically separated the two areas, though visibility was only slightly impaired. Sheriff Green stood before the grille and stared at the bars with distaste. "Mother

Abbess, I'm here as a law enforcement official. I'd rather speak to you face-to-face."

"We *are* face-to-face," Reverend Mother answered softly, "and we can see each other well enough. You may ask me any questions you have, but our rules of enclosure dictate that it has to be done this way. I hope you'll understand."

"All right. If that's the way it has to be." Green took a breath and regarded her pensively. "The priest, Father Anselm, probably died from a heart attack, at least based on the information I've received so far. But until the medical investigator confirms that, I've got procedures to follow and I need to get some background information. Did you speak to the father today before Mass?"

"No. Sister Bernarda and Sister Agatha met him earlier this morning, when he came to deliver some donated supplies for our St. Francis' Pantry. Our novice and postulant probably helped put food away too, and may have spoken to him. But you'll have to get the details from Sister Agatha. As sacristan, she may also have seen him when he came to celebrate Mass for us."

He glanced at Sister Agatha coldly. She was seated nearby as her duties as portress demanded. "You could have saved me some time and told me this before."

"You didn't ask," she answered simply.

Reverend Mother spoke. "You may find it helpful to remember that, as a general rule, our cloistered sisters do not leave the enclosure except in grave emergencies. Father was allowed inside, of course. He made himself available to us for confession and counseling whenever we needed him."

"Were there any confession or counseling sessions today?"

"No," Reverend Mother responded. "And no one but Sister Agatha or Sister Bernarda could have spoken to him when he came to say Mass. The others were seated with me, within the enclosure, before he arrived." She glanced at Sister Agatha, then back at the sheriff. "Please don't hesitate to ask Sister Bernarda or Sister Agatha any further questions you may have. They'll be glad to help you."

"I can even reconstruct some of what Father did immediately

prior to his heart attack, if you'd like. He spoke to me about his day," Sister Agatha said.

"When I need your help, I'll let you know," Sheriff Green said abruptly.

His rudeness took her aback, but she didn't say anything. Out of the corner of her eye, she noted Reverend Mother's disapproving expression. Had she still been Mary Naughton, Sister Agatha would have cheerfully told him he had the manners of a pig, and showed him the door. As it was, however, she knew she should find a more charitable response. Perhaps she'd pray that Tom Green found a personality donor soon.

"For now, I'm going back to the scene. I'm expecting the district medical investigator, Jim Brown, to arrive shortly. I'll know more once I talk to him."

"Then what you need is medical confirmation that Father had a heart attack?" Reverend Mother asked.

"If that's what it was. If his death wasn't from natural causes, that'll pose a whole new set of problems, and I'll need a list of everyone who was here today."

"Sister Bernarda can supply that for you. She was portress and would have been outside the chapel doors greeting those who came to Mass today," Sister Agatha said. "She's probably in the chapel now, standing by in case she's needed as your people do their work."

That was the most diplomatic way of putting it, Sister Agatha mused. Their chapel was open to the public, so the main reason Sister Bernarda would remain there until they were gone was to make sure no one broached their enclosure.

"How long will it take you to get the answers you need?" Reverend Mother asked.

"I don't know yet. I'll have to let you know."

Muttering a quick thank-you, Sheriff Green strode to the door, apparently heading back to the chapel to meet with his men. Sister Agatha glanced back at Reverend Mother and saw she was standing.

"Come see me in my office."

Sister Agatha nodded, and locked the parlor doors since no other portress was available now, and hurried to Mother's office.

Taking a deep breath and bracing herself, Sister Agatha opened the door to Reverend Mother's office. "Praised be Jesus Christ," she said, as was customary.

"Now and forever," came Reverend Mother's reply.

The sparsely finished room had an austere feel. There were two straight-backed wooden chairs before an oak desk that one of the businesses in town had donated to the monastery. A tall storage cabinet stood against one wall and a statue of the Blessed Virgin had been placed on a stand in the far corner. The only adornment on the white stucco walls was a large wooden cross.

"Sit down, child."

Reverend Mother called everyone child as was their monastic custom. Even elderly Sister Clothilde, who was reputedly in her eighties—no one knew for sure—was "child" to Mother, who was in her late fifties.

"I couldn't help but notice the sheriff's attitude toward you. He came across as a man with little regard for our monastery. If that's due to some history between you, I need to know. Father Anselm's passing was a tragedy, but I have no intention of letting the police turn this monastery upside down. Our Lady of Hope is dedicated to prayer and I won't allow anything to interfere with our duty to God."

"Sheriff Green and I knew each other a lifetime ago, Mother. We've been friends since we were kids and our relationship grew even closer after high school. We lived together our last two years in college. But after graduation, we both knew it was time to call it quits. Our outlooks on just about everything were totally different. We had a huge fight one day and Tom packed up and left."

"So your relationship ended after college?"

"Not quite. We never lived together again, but during the years my brother was sick, Tom would visit us often. I think he always hoped that we'd get back together someday. But our lives had already gone in two separate directions. When I told him I was entering the monastery, he was furious with me. He accused me of everything from being crazy to leading him on." She paused, then shook her head. "That was twelve years ago, but he still seems to bear a grudge."

"He probably thinks we took you away from him."

"But that's not the way it was. The truth of it is that by the time Kevin died, my entire life had changed. During Kevin's illness, I learned to rely on God. He was there and He filled my heart in a way nothing ever had before. Joining the order was the only step that made sense to me after that."

"Did the sheriff know all that?"

"I explained it to him, Mother, but he was too angry to listen. Yet none of this should matter now. He's married. I saw the ring on his hand."

"Do you think Sister Bernarda should be the one to deal with him until this is over?"

"I doubt that'll make any difference. Sheriff Green apparently sees me as part of the monastery and the monastery as a part of me," she said. "And, in that respect, he's right."

Reverend Mother leaned back in her chair. "I want this matter settled, and the police gone. We can't use our chapel for prayer or to chant the liturgy of the hours with those men in there. We've already missed Sext. That has never happened before."

"I'll do my best to see that they're out of here as soon as possible, Mother."

"Come to me immediately if you encounter any problems."

"Yes, Mother."

As Sister Agatha left Reverend Mother's office and walked down the corridor, she could hear men's voices coming from chapel. The sound was jarring.

The devil had brought chaos into the midst of them, but she intended to fight him. Taking a deep breath, she strode out into the chapel, and saw Sheriff Green going into the sacristy where Father Anselm had vested.

"One moment please," she snapped, using her college professor tone.

He turned his head, but continued walking.

"I don't care what you think about me personally, Sheriff, but there are *rules* in this monastery. Half of that sacristy is considered cloister, and you may not enter that half. You also need to be escorted into any area outside the chapel. Unless you and your men respect that, I'm prepared to file a complaint and go all the way to the governor's office if I have to. And he's Catholic."

The smile he gave her was cold. "Rules didn't used to worry you so much. But not everything about you has changed. I see you've still got that temper. And you know what? It still doesn't impress me." He entered the priest's side of the sacristy and began to study the two-way drawers.

She explained the system to him without waiting to be asked.

"I'll need to collect and examine the clothing the priest wore when he came in, and whatever else he left in here."

She'd been a reporter long enough to have that request send a warning signal to her brain. "What's going on? Did you discover something new concerning Father's death?"

"I spoke to the medical investigator. The symptoms apparently don't match a heart attack—at least not exactly. The MI's preliminary ruling is death by an unknown cause—but I think he suspects foul play. The body is being transported to Albuquerque for an autopsy."

Tom Green turned and walked out of the sacristy.

Sister Agatha felt as if his words had suddenly sucked all the oxygen from the room. Murder, here, under their roof? She remembered following police cases as a reporter, then later with her journalism students. If there was one thing she remembered it was that an investigation of this nature left no one untouched. The delicate, orderly ebb and flow of their life at the monastery would be under siege now.

She saw Sister Bernarda in the doorway. "We're in trouble, aren't we, Sister?"

Sister Bernarda's military bark was strangely absent now, and she could understand why. The death of their chaplain had left all of them in shock. But neither of them could indulge their feelings now.

She and Sister Bernarda were the monastery's first line of defense.

"We're about to face an invading army, Sister, and I see no way to stop it."

"I overheard someone say murder . . . is that true? Was Father murdered?" Sister Bernarda's tone grew stronger, but she was still pale.

"They don't know yet, but apparently there's enough evidence to make the law suspect something other than an accident or natural causes."

Sister Agatha saw Sheriff Green walking in their direction with a man in civilian clothes and a blue jacket. He had an ID badge clipped to his pocket.

"Sister Agatha, Sister Bernarda, this is Jim Brown, the medical investigator. He has a few questions for Sister Bernarda." Not giving either woman a chance to reply, the sheriff motioned to Brown, who led Sister Bernarda away to a nearby pew.

Questioning people separately was standard procedure, she knew that from her journalism days, but having these protocols enforced here filled her with dread for what lay ahead. To the police, they were all suspects now—no matter how far-fetched that seemed to her. She and Sister Bernarda were accustomed to interacting with the world outside the monastery. That was part of their duties. But the cloistered sisters would find contact with the police dismaying, to say the least.

"Okay, Sister Agatha, let's get back on track over here. Who else besides you saw Father this morning?" Green brought out a pen and small black notebook.

"He spoke to Sister Bernarda, who was portress at the time. She rang the bell notifying us that he was here. Then there was our postulant, Celia, and our novice, Sister Mary Lazarus."

"No one else? You're sure? Think about it a moment before you answer."

"It's not impossible that he might have seen someone else, because he was already out of the pickup by the time we came to greet him. But as far as I know, it was just us. The cloistered sisters don't come out to the front of our grounds." She met his gaze. "I think you already know that none of us here would have harmed Father. Do you have to treat us like criminals?"

"I'm not treating anyone like a criminal yet. If I were, the lot of you would be trooping down to the station house. I'm treating everyone like a witness to a suspicious death, possibly murder."

"You're showing very little respect for the nuns here, and not an ounce for me. Do you really hate me so much?"

"I don't hate you. Not at all. I'm married, and have my own life. And you've got yours—such as it is."

"Your sweet disposition is well hidden today, then."

"I'm doing my job."

"So am I. What other information do you need?" she added coldly. "I have other responsibilities."

"Look, Mary . . . Sister Agatha. I'm not the enemy."

"Then stop acting like one." Seeing two deputies taking the altar cloth and placing it in a large paper bag, Sister Agatha immediately shifted her attention to them. "What do you think *you're* doing?"

They looked at her, then at the sheriff, who stood behind her, then resumed sealing and labeling the sack.

"Evidence has to be examined and interpreted. I'm trying to cut you some slack, so chill out," Sheriff Green said, shifting until he stood between her and the deputies. "You're going to need to use the chapel, right? Nuns have church *all* the time. The moment this place is cleaned up, any evidence that's here will be compromised. I don't want to risk that until I know for sure how and why Father Anselm died. If you'd rather, I can tape off the chapel for the next few days to preserve what may be a crime scene, and bar anyone from coming in at all. All things considered, I figured you'd prefer to have us take what we may need as evidence and free the scene for ordinary use as soon as possible."

"All right. Remove what you need to examine, but I really don't think you're going to find anything."

"We'll just have to wait and see. Now think back again. Did the father eat or drink anything while he was here, either right before Mass or earlier today? Did he get an injection or take a pill in the infirmary, or anything like that at all?"

"All I know is that he drank a glass of iced tea this morning when we were working in the food pantry—the monastery's special blend."

"Okay. Now, what about the sacramental wine and the communion wafer?"

"He was about to consecrate them when he became ill. So the answer is no, he never got to that part of the Mass."

"All right. If you haven't washed the tea glass he used, I'd like to take that into evidence. If there's still a little bit of tea in it, so much the better. I'll also need a sample of the tea from the source you used."

"Normally that glass would have been washed and dried right away, but today we were so rushed, Celia probably didn't have time. I'll go see."

"I'll come with you."

"That's fine." She suddenly stopped and looked him in the eye. "You think he was poisoned, don't you? But that's nonsense."

"You're a nun. I'm a cop. I won't tell you how to pray, and you don't tell me how to conduct my investigation."

She considered arguing with him but, from what she remembered about Tom, she knew it would be futile. At that precise moment, one of the deputies knocked over a cruet of sacramental wine. Red liquid spilled onto the brick floor. She started to move toward the utility room next to the sacristy so she could get a towel to wipe up the spill, but he held her arm.

"The deputy will clean it up." He glowered at the deputy. "No more accidents. That's inexcusable."

"Yes, sir," the young deputy said, and looked around a few seconds before hurrying out of the chapel.

Sister Agatha stared at the ever-widening pool of crimson wine. It flowed down the cracks between the bricks, staining everything in its path. Like the blood of the lamb that had been spilled for sinners, it ran freely, leaving its mark on everything it touched.

Sadness settled over her spirit. She stepped back as the trail of unconsecrated wine reached the tip of the alpargates she wore—the flat, hemp-soled shoes that were part of the habit. Father's life, like that crimson liquid, was just another promise left unfulfilled.

"Who mixed the herbs for the tea Father Anselm drank?" Sheriff Green asked, interrupting her thoughts.

"I did—it's just a few herbs from Sister Clothilde's garden. I keep a jar of it in St. Francis' Pantry to offer the people who bring donations."

The deputy rushed back into the chapel with a handful of folded paper towels like those found in the chapel's public rest room.

"Let's go see," the sheriff said, ignoring the deputy and gesturing to the door.

As she led Tom Green toward the pantry, one of the monastery bells began to ring. The deep, resonant sound came from the largest bell.

She stopped in her tracks to offer a prayer.

"What's going on?" he grumbled when she looked up again.

"That bell was announcing Father's death," she explained, then continued walking. Reverend Mother would be meeting with the other nuns now. There were nine of them here in their small monastery. Prayers for Father Anselm's soul would be said, and tonight would be a time of mourning. She knew that even Sister Ignatius, who'd never really approved of Father Anselm's youthful levity, would be heartbroken. Death had claimed a member of their family.

They found the glass, still unwashed, on the counter in the pantry. Sheriff Green bagged and labeled it as evidence, after putting on latex gloves. The trace of liquid at the bottom was poured into a labeled plastic medicine-type bottle and sealed. He also took a sample of the dry herbal tea mixture and sealed it in a labeled paper bag.

When they returned to the chapel a short time later, Jim Brown was putting his equipment away, and Father's body, now inside a black zippered bag, was being wheeled out on a gurney.

"Sister, I'd like to talk to you," Brown said, coming over to meet her as the sheriff placed the evidence he'd collected into a cardboard box.

"At your service," she answered, hoping this wouldn't take long. Sister Mary Lazarus was on her knees near the altar with scrub brush and bucket, starting, at last, to clean things up. Sister Bernarda was probably acting as portress right now.

"Let's sit down on one of the benches," Jim suggested.

She did as he asked.

"I have a few simple questions that I need you to answer, since you were trying to help the priest when he died."

"Go ahead."

"What exactly did he say? Did he complain of any pain?"

Sister Agatha related all she could recall, though the details were heartbreaking and her voice shook at times despite her efforts to remain calm. "He suffered—this I know."

"You said that he was having auditory hallucinations. Is that correct?"

"No, I never said that. Father told me he heard bells, but I took that at face value. For all I knew, it could have meant that his ears were ringing, or maybe it was God's way of telling him not to be afraid. When people are about to pass on, they sometimes see and hear things that others don't. I never concluded that he was hallucinating."

"You also mentioned the paralysis of his facial muscles."

"His expression became rigid, yes."

Medical Investigator Brown stared at the floor. Minutes ticked by and Sister Agatha wondered if he'd forgotten she was there.

"Is that all, or do you still need me?" Sister Agatha asked softly.

The man looked up suddenly, as if he'd just remembered where he was. "I heard you tell the sheriff that Father had consumed some herbal tea earlier today. What kind of herbs are in that tea, Sister?"

"Some mint, some chamomile—all ordinary things that grow in our garden. Sister Clothilde has a special section for culinary herbs. The sheriff took a sample of the mixture we used."

"I'd like to talk to Sister Clothilde, and then see her garden."

"I can take you to see the garden, but Sister Clothilde won't be able to speak to you, even through the grille. She's taken a vow of silence."

"How does she communicate with the rest of the order?"

"Through a special form of sign language we've developed to communicate with each other during times of silence. It's very limited. But she can listen, and she can write down answers. She's allowed to do that."

"All right. Show me the herb garden, then we'll see if we need to trouble Sister Clothilde about the rest."

"All right," she said, and stood up. "But Mr. Brown, the herbs Sister Clothilde grows are quite common and completely harmless."

"Accidental poisonings are common in rural areas of New Mexico, Sister. The fact of the matter is that the symptoms you and Sister Bernarda described to me reminded me of another case I worked on when I first became a medical investigator. An elderly Hispanic man died as a result of an overdose of an herbal medicine he took for pain. Which brings me to my next question. Does Sister Clothilde also grow medicinal plants?"

"A few, yes. I've heard her using chamomile to settle the stomach, and something called alegria, which is said to be good for the heart. The Spanish word means 'happiness,' so it worried us at first. We certainly don't need stimulants. But it's harmless. There are also herbs to treat high blood pressure and other ailments."

"Take me to see the garden, then. Herbal medicine isn't always as safe as people think. The elderly man I told you about experimented with the anesthetic properties of monkshood and died because that plant also contains highly toxic alkaloids."

"Let me get Reverend Mother's permission, then I'll take you."

Leaving the medical investigator in the chapel, Sister Agatha went through the corridors of the monastery quickly, and found Reverend Mother praying in her office before a statue of the Blessed Virgin.

Sister Agatha remained by the door, hating to interrupt the abbess at prayer but knowing she had no other choice.

"Praised be Jesus Christ," Sister Agatha said quietly.

"Now and forever," Reverend Mother answered, and turned around. "Have the police finished what they need to do?"

Sister Agatha filled Reverend Mother in quickly, and saw shock and then sorrow in her eyes.

"You were a reporter, and later a journalism professor, child. You understand investigative methods and thought processes more than any of us. I need you to remain with these people at all times while they're here at the monastery. And please make sure poor Sister Clothilde isn't harassed in any way."

"I've told the medical investigator, Mr. Brown, about Sister's vow of silence. He understands that he can't speak to her—at least not directly—and has agreed to that. But he insists on examining our garden to make sure the herb tea didn't contain anything harmful."

"Then show it to him. He'll see for himself that we don't grow anything dangerous here."

"Right away, Mother."

Agatha walked back quickly to the chapel. She had to find a way to convince the police that their answers lay outside the monastery. Maybe once the medical investigator saw their small garden, he'd understand how simple their lives were and that whatever had happened to Father Anselm was in no way connected to the monastery or the sisters.

"Mr. Brown," Sister Agatha said as she came up to him, "I'm ready to show you the garden. It's in the back of the building, and though not behind cloister, it is a restricted area. Please keep your voice low so we don't disturb any of the sisters who might be praying. And should you see one of our sisters, don't attempt to speak to her without checking with me first. Will you agree to this?"

"All right. You've got yourself a deal." Brown nodded.

She walked with the man to the back of the monastery, all of which was enclosed behind a high wall. As they reached the garden—a large field sectioned off into rows of corn, tomatoes, squash, carrots, pinto beans, and chile—she spread out her arms. "This is it. Most of what graces our table is grown here, with the exception of staples like flour, salt, sugar, and such. We're all vegetarians. The herbs are in the last row," she said, leading him to the north side of the garden.

He stepped from row to row, examining the plants and studying the ground between them, then finally reached the row containing the herbs.

"Most of these plants are gifts that the monastery has received from our neighbors in the community."

He spoke aloud as he identified chamomile, mint, sage, rosemary, and various other common culinary herbs. He also snipped off samples of the medicinal plants Sister Agatha pointed out as ones used to treat high blood pressure, fevers, colds, and other common problems. After searching the entire area carefully, he stood up straight and shook his head. "There's nothing out of the ordinary here. Heck, I couldn't even find a weed," he said with amazement. "Is this the only place where you grow herbs?"

"This is it. The only other plants we cultivate and grow here are roses. Everything else, including the trees, is part of the desert landscaping and requires no tending."

She escorted him around the grounds so he could see for himself. "Nothing in our gardens is capable of injuring anyone—unless you count the rose thorns," she said.

"I admire your loyalty to the monastery, Sister Agatha," he said as they reached the chapel.

His words surprised her. This wasn't a matter of being loyal. It was common sense. To think that any of the sisters pledged to a religious life could intentionally harm another living being was completely crazy. They even freely shared the fruits of their labor with the cottontail rabbits who, from time to time, ravaged the vegetables they grew.

As they stood on the front steps of the chapel, she watched the deputies loading the boxes of evidence into their vehicles.

"It's time for me to get going, too," Brown said, then shook hands with her. "With luck, none of us will have to come back."

"God doesn't depend on luck, He gives us prayer and faith instead."

He smiled, then with a wave, walked away from her.

"Don't count on this being the end of it," Tom said as he approached, apparently having overheard at least the end of their conversation. "I've heard about Sister Clothilde's vow of silence, but if the investigation continues, it may be necessary for her to speak to us."

"Communicate, maybe—speak, no."

"Whatever. This isn't over. Mark my words."

"Have you learned something new, Sheriff?"

"Only the names of the people from the community who were here at Mass. Sister Bernarda gave me a list. I'll have to track them down now. But, you know, I've got a gut feeling that this one was an inside job."

"You're wrong." She gave him a long, thoughtful look. "You don't sense any of it, do you? The peace that's here, the quiet purpose—everything that defines this place and makes it special."

He met her gaze and shrugged. "All I see is women living together behind walls. It's no more or less a prison than the one near Los Lunas or Santa Fe."

"We're here in this monastery so we can work for the world. Through our prayers, we make a difference. But like doctors who have to keep a professional distance from their patients, we can do our job better by remaining separate."

"Well, I wouldn't count on staying too 'separate.' If I don't get the answers I need, I'll have to come back. And, if that happens, I won't cut you or the monastery any slack. I'll do whatever it takes to find out what happened to Father Anselm, including getting the paperwork I need to enter your cloister. And if you get in my way, I'll throw the book at you."

She smiled. "For the record, my book's a lot heavier than yours."

As Sheriff Green strode off without another word, she understood that a warning had been given. Sorrow and apprehension weighed down her spirit as she turned around and walked back inside.

3

AFTER LAUDS THE FOLLOWING MORNING, SISTER AGATHA went out with Sister Bernarda to the parking lot. The Antichrysler was in a sad state.

"I had to go out late last night to get some heart medication for Sister Gertrude from the all-night pharmacy, and I barely got back," Sister Bernarda explained. "The car was missing so badly it nearly died three times. I just don't think this vehicle will be able to take Sister to the doctor if she needs to go. There's no way this junk heap will make it all the way to Albuquerque and back again."

The doctor who took care of the nuns was a thirty-minute drive away, at the northwest side of Albuquerque. Although he made special allowances for the sisters, like giving them a reduced rate and never making them wait in the reception area, he could only make house calls if there was a dire emergency.

Sister Agatha rolled up her sleeves, and reluctantly opened the hood. Since the car couldn't be replaced, it had to be fixed, that was all there was to it. She checked the oil, and the sparkplug wiring, and the plugs themselves. They were all correctly gapped and hooked up, which wasn't obvious from the degree Sister had said that the engine was missing.

"Okay, tell me exactly what the car's symptoms were."

"It wouldn't go over twenty miles an hour except downhill, it kept stalling, and it roared like a bulldozer. I tried coaxing, I tried prayer, I even cursed it a time or two, but nothing worked. I consider it a minor miracle that it made the round trip at all."

Sister Agatha started the engine, which rattled and misfired. She continued checking what she could under the hood. Once finished, she slammed the hood closed. "It needs a rebuilt engine to handle the big problems. The valves are knocking like a woodpecker, the carburetor is shot, and the distributor is a joke."

She glanced over at Sister Bernarda. "I'll drive the car over to Mr. Gonzales's repair shop. This is beyond my abilities. We don't have the parts, and special tools are needed as well. Maybe he can do something and keep it going a little longer."

"What we really need is for someone to donate a car to the monastery."

"I know, Sister Bernarda, but these are hard times. By the time anyone around here parts with a car, it's ready for the wrecking yard."

"I'll ask Reverend Mother to have all the sisters pray that the Lord will provide us with some reliable transportation."

"That's an excellent idea."

"Are you going now—before breakfast?" Sister Bernarda asked. "If you are, let me at least get you a couple of tortillas from the kitchen. Sister Clothilde and Sister Maria Victoria must have made stacks and stacks of them from the small sacks of flour Mr. Kelly, the grocer, brought for our monastery."

Sister Agatha smiled, remembering the delivery. Many of the grocers donated staples to their monastery, which helped the nuns stretch their already tight budget. But these sacks had been found to have mealworms, and Sister Clothilde hadn't wanted to store them in the pantry and risk contaminating the other food. She'd also refused to freeze the flour, convinced that the worms would hatch out later. So, all the flour had been carefully sifted and then tortillas had been made and cooked until every last trace of usable flour had been used. Their vows of poverty made it unacceptable that any food would be wasted.

The tortillas now towered in the refrigerator and their large freezer. With the pinto beans they'd grown last year, there'd be plenty of food for everyone. But tortillas would be part of breakfast, lunch, and dinner for the foreseeable future.

Sister Agatha had the Antichrysler turned around and the gate open by the time Sister Bernarda returned from the kitchen. "Here. I took two, and smeared them with peanut butter from those huge cans the grocer gave us, and jelly that Sister Clothilde made with a donation of overripe peaches. Think of it as a New Mexican breakfast sandwich."

The drive to town took even longer than Sister Agatha had expected, and she'd worried that someone might complain as she crossed pueblo land. The old station wagon sputtered and coughed, never going over twenty miles an hour. But at least it kept going. She stayed close to the shoulder in case faster traffic wanted to pass her, but the roads in the early morning hours were blessedly empty except for an occasional piece of farm machinery.

As she approached Paul Gonzales's garage, a wood-framed building with an old West–style false front and a hand-lettered sign that had probably been there thirty years, she saw the mechanic standing out by the side of the road, cup of coffee in hand. Paul was in his late fifties and was built like a fire hydrant—short and stocky. He was wearing a pair of gray-and-white-striped overalls and a red headband fashioned from a handkerchief to keep his hair out of his eyes.

He waved and motioned for her to pull up in front of one of the garage bays.

In addition to all the troubles the ailing vehicle's engine had, there was also still no muffler. It was little wonder that Mr. Gonzales had heard her coming.

Sister Agatha pulled up, braked to a stop, then turned off the engine. Even turned off, it ran a few more seconds, shaking like a leaf, then died. "*Deo Gratias,*" she murmured as she climbed out to greet the long-suffering mechanic, who had donated so much of his time to reviving the monastery's vehicle.

"Mr. Gonzales, our car desperately needs your help again. The muffler is gone, and now, on top of everything else, when it runs at all, it won't go over twenty miles an hour."

He nodded. "I was beginning to think I'd have to go looking for you. Sister Bernarda called an hour ago and said you were on your way. You barely made it, obviously. Let's take a look."

Sister Agatha insisted on helping him push the heavy car into the garage. Then, rolling up her sleeves, she set to work, handing him whatever tool he requested. In spite of his skill, the mechanic couldn't get the engine to run again for more than a few seconds.

"What do you think, Mr. Gonzales? You know we have very little money, but we'll be glad to offer prayers for you and your family for the rest of the summer months, and at Mass. And we can make payments—small payments."

The bonds between the monastery and the community were very strong. Praying for special intentions had become an acceptable method of at least partial payment for many of their supporters. God had been kind to their religious community, and news of favors attributed to the nuns' special prayer vigils had even spread among the less religious townspeople.

"Sister, this car obviously needs far more than a tune-up this time. In addition to a new muffler, I'm going to have to order engine parts—*if* I can get them—and do a major overhaul, maybe even a complete rebuild. If you want reliable transportation, I'm going to need a month or more—and that's providing I can find the parts."

"But we can't wait that long. This monster is our only transportation. Without it, how can we get supplies for the monastery or take sisters to the doctor, or do any of the other things we have to do to keep our house going? Depending on cabs for a month or more will drive us into ruin."

"I don't know what to tell you, Sister. If you need a miracle worker, you're going to have to go directly to the source," he said, pointing up.

Sister Agatha held his gaze, undaunted. "Surely there's *something* you can do for us."

"I have an idea." Edith Gonzales, Paul's wife, came into the garage bay. She was a robust, middle-aged woman with graying hair, and she was smiling at Sister Agatha. "It'll help the monastery, and, at the same time you'd be helping us."

"What did you have in mind?" Sister Agatha asked.

"Our son, Bobby, was given a fancy motorcycle by his uncle. We won't let him ride it yet because he's only sixteen and I've seen the way he drives. If we donate it to the monastery, it won't be around here to tempt him, and the monastery would have some form of transportation. Even Bobby's uncle would approve of that. And we'll also get a nice charitable donation to put on our income tax."

Mr. Gonzales smiled at his wife. "What a wonderful idea!" He went to the back of the shop, turned on the light over a work bench, and pulled a canvas tarp off a large object standing in the corner.

Sister Agatha gasped and a slow grin spread across her face. "She's a real beauty." Any doubts Sister Agatha had vanished the second the tarp came off the 1986 Heritage Classic Harley-Davidson with its matching sidecar. The only difference between this one and the one her brother, Kevin, had owned was the color. Kevin's had been steel blue, and this one was apple red, a custom paint job.

"This is a very generous donation. But are you aware of how special this bike is?" Sister Agatha knew it was a collector's item among cycling enthusiasts.

"All we care about is that it poses a danger to our son. You take it. We'll write it off on our taxes and keep our son in one piece," Edith said.

"I'll have to ask Reverend Mother before I can officially accept this donation," she said, her heart hammering at a crazy tempo.

"Take it today anyway. It's the only way you'll get home. You can drive it, can't you?" the mechanic asked, reaching into his pocket and handing her the key.

"Oh, sure! My brother had one that was very similar." Sister Agatha hiked up her habit slightly, straddled the bike, and eased onto the leather saddle. She inserted the key into the ignition, and touched the electric starter button as she gave it a little gas.

The engine started up immediately with that distinctive engine sound that elicited a wide grin from anyone who'd ever owned a Harley.

"I can see you know what you're doing, Sister. That's your ride back to the monastery, then." Paul smiled. "And here's your helmet," he said, passing her one with a gleaming red devil painting on the side, complete with pitchfork and shooting flames.

"El Diablo? That won't do, Mr. Gonzales," she said sternly.

"It was my son's idea of a joke, Sister. He's not in a gang, or a Satan worshiper, or anything," he added quickly.

She stared at the otherwise perfect helmet for a moment. "Do you have some paint remover or a piece of steel wool?"

Edith responded at once. "I'm an artist, Sister, just give me ten minutes. I think I can do something for you. Meanwhile, Paul can give you the registration, and get a receipt for the donation, pending Reverend Mother's approval, of course."

While Paul Gonzales wrote out the paperwork to transfer title to the monastery, his wife took the helmet into her small studio, which was behind the garage. When she came out again, the paint she'd used was nearly dry.

The red devil had vanished without a trace, and in its place was a white outline sketch of a nun on a motorcycle, with the words Heaven's Angels above it.

Sister Agatha laughed. "Thank you. That's brilliant."

"So you're all set, then?" Paul said. "I'll try to get the car working again for you in three weeks, but I'm not promising anything, even with all you sisters praying for me."

Sister Agatha quickly assured him that they could manage as long as they needed to now that they had this wonderful gift. She smiled as she looked at the motorcycle and ran her hand over the bright red fuel tank. "Lord, I've been praying for a change in my routine duties, and You've outdone Yourself. *Deo Gratias*," she whispered, slipping on the helmet over her veil, then hiking up her skirt so she could straddle the bike and keep the fabric well away from the wheel and other moving parts.

"I'll be on my way then, Paul. But remember, Reverend Mother will have the final say on whether or not we can accept your gift." She switched on the ignition, gave the throttle a little gas with a twist of her wrist, then eased slowly out of the garage into the parking lot. Flipping down the visor on the helmet, she waved at the Gonzales couple, then got back on the road.

It was just like riding a bike. One never forgot how to operate a motorcycle, she thought, testing the feel of the steering through the handlebars. The sidecar was attached, American style, to the right side of the motorcycle, exactly the way it had been on Kevin's Harley. With a sidecar more steering was required when cornering because you couldn't do it by leaning or shifting your weight the way you could on a cycle alone.

All this wonderful and nostalgic information came flooding back to her naturally as Sister Agatha headed back to the monastery. For the first time in years, she found herself thinking of her brother without the danger of tears flowing. With the visor down, only she and God knew that she never stopped smiling all the way home.

As the motorcycle roared through the gate and into the monastery parking area, she saw Sister Bernarda draw back the curtains in the parlor and look outside.

Sister Agatha waved, parked beside the entrance, and quickly removed her helmet. She saw the surprise, then the slow smile of recognition that spread across Sister Bernarda's face.

"I don't believe my eyes," she said, opening the parlor door and stepping outside to look at the red-and-chrome beauty that was ticking quietly as its eighty-cubic-inch engine cooled.

"The Antichrysler is now in intensive care at Mr. Gonzales's garage, and due to remain there for the next three weeks, minimum. Mr. Gonzales donated the motorcycle to the monastery so we would be able to get around without the car." She reached into her pocket and brought out the papers.

"I had a friend in the Marine Corps who loved bikes. I can see that's a Harley. What year?"

"It's an eighty-six, and a dream to drive. I can give you lessons if you've never driven one. And, best of all, I can fix anything this machine needs myself. I worked on my brother's Harley all the time, and he had an eighty-six Classic a lot like this one. We used to take it apart and put it together again in a day just for kicks."

"You're going to have to be the one to sell the idea to Reverend Mother. Do you think you can do it?"

"It's absolutely perfect for the monastery now that we don't have the Antichrysler. It's great on gas and the engine is in perfect condition. The sidecar can easily handle supplies or a passenger!"

"Whoa!" Sister Bernarda laughed. "It's Reverend Mother you have to sell, not me."

Sister Agatha gave her companion a conspiratorial smile. "It *would* help if I could tell her that our other extern sister is also comfortable using this vehicle as transportation. . . ." She looked at Sister hopefully.

"Oh, of course. Tell her that I'm happy to drive whatever the Lord provides," Sister Bernarda said with a broad grin.

"Thanks. And I promise you're going to love it."

Taking a deep breath, Sister Agatha went inside and walked down to Reverend Mother's office.

She found Mother reading a booklet on the sisters' health insurance benefits. Fortunately, the monastery's income from the scriptorium and altar bread sales provided for necessities like these.

Reverend Mother looked up and the usual greeting was exchanged.

Studying her expression, Reverend Mother sighed. "I recognize the look on your face, child. Something has happened," she said, and leaned forward in her chair.

"It's good news, Mother. But the fact that it's a blessing may not be readily apparent." Sister Agatha stopped speaking, and gathered her wits. She was babbling. Starting out by hinting at the negative was a bad idea. "Mother, the Antichrysler is in a coma. It stopped working this morning as I pulled into Mr. Gonzales's garage, and we couldn't get it running again. The poor man said it could take a month or more before he had all the parts he needed to fix it."

Reverend Mother sat up quickly. "Then how did you make your way back here? You didn't hitchhike? I thought I heard a truck a few minutes ago."

"No, Mother. Mr. Gonzales, understanding how much we need

reliable transportation, made a very generous donation. I accepted it—pending your approval, of course."

"He donated a truck? Praised be the Lord!"

"Not quite, Mother. But although it's not what we might have chosen, it's just perfect for us."

"Not a sports car! It would be so . . . pretentious."

"No, Mother, it's a motorcycle," she said in a whisper. "You heard a motorcycle."

Reverend Mother just stared at her.

"It's in great condition, Mother, and I can take care of any repairs it may need in the future myself. I'm very familiar with motorcycles."

"But how will we take our elderly sisters to the doctors? Surely you can't expect Sister Clothilde or Sister Gertrude to straddle a motorcycle, holding on for dear life!"

"No, Mother, but I haven't told you the best part! The motorcycle has a sidecar! Come to the window, you can see it from here," she said, pulling the curtains aside.

Sister Agatha continued extolling the virtues of a motorcycle's gas conservation and every other advantage she could think of.

Reverend Mother stared at it. "The sidecar looks like a canoe on wheels."

"But it's large enough inside to carry the supplies we need to bring from town, and I'm sure the sisters will be very comfortable with the wind screen. The seat is padded and everything." She paused, then added softly, "And, most important of all, we really have no other choice, Mother. We will eventually have our station wagon back, but in the meantime, the motorcycle will save us a lot on taxi fares."

"I suppose it could work," Reverend Mother said slowly.

"Even after the Antichrysler is back, using the bike for small errands will save us a substantial amount on gas, and wear and tear on our car."

"But it's such dangerous transportation."

"Not if we're careful. Sister Bernarda is willing to learn, and I can teach her the basics in a few days. I'll also make sure she gets plenty of practice before going out onto the open road. This motor-cycle would be a real blessing to all of us, Mother."

She unfolded the papers Mr. Gonzales had prepared, signing over the ownership to the Sisters of the Blessed Adoration.

"All right, then," Reverend Mother said with a nod, taking the papers. "We'll accept the donation." She took a deep breath before continuing. "I spoke to the archbishop this morning. He told me that the police now believe Father was murdered," she said, whispering the last word in horror.

"They can't know that for sure, Mother. It must be just one of the many possibilities. If he ingested something poisonous, it still could have been accidental."

"If it *does* turn out to have been murder, the chapel will have to be shut down temporarily, Sister. We'll also need to get in touch with His Excellency the archbishop, because our beautiful chapel will have to be reconsecrated and rededicated."

"And in the meantime?" The possibility that the nuns might be barred from using their own chapel seemed unthinkable.

"I've been giving that some thought. We can move the bare necessities so we can have Mass—" She stopped as her voice broke. "But we'll still need a new chaplain."

"Mother, let me go to the station, talk to Sheriff Green face-to-face, and find out what they've learned first. Father's death may yet turn out to be the result of an accident. Then I'll stop by the rectory and see if there's anything we can do to help Mrs. Williams, Father's housekeeper. She'd been with him for years and must be devastated. While I'm there I can find out if the diocese has found a new parish priest, one who will also serve as our chaplain."

"I'm also concerned about your additional contact with the sheriff. Do you think his seeing you again might make the situation even worse?"

"I wish I could say no with certainty, Mother, but I can't. But I do know that Tom Green is a good human being, and will ultimately treat us fairly. Now that he's had the opportunity to express some long-pent-up feelings, we should be on safe ground again."

"I trust your judgment, child. Go, but come and see me when you return."

When Sister Agatha returned to the parlor, she found Sister Bernarda at her desk reading the Liturgy of the Hours from her breviary. She gave Sister Bernarda a silent nod, allowing her to continue without interruption. As the silence stretched out for a moment, Sister Agatha considered the many ways her life had changed since she'd become a nun. As a kid, "amen" had often been the only part of most prayers she'd been wholly certain about. These days, prayer was the very fabric of her existence. It ordered her day, and gave meaning to everything she did.

"Did Reverend Mother approve?" Sister Bernarda asked at last, closing her breviary.

"Yes. She wasn't thrilled, but knows we have to get around somehow."

She nodded slowly. "I don't know how we could have managed without any transportation at all." She looked up at Sister Agatha. "Are you ready to take over for me here now?"

"No, I'm afraid not. I need you to handle portress duty for a while longer. I have to go back into town to talk to the sheriff in person. I have a better chance of getting the answers Reverend Mother needs that way than over the phone. Will you cover for me?"

"Of course. I can handle things here."

Sister Agatha couldn't envision any situation her companion wouldn't be able to handle. She'd always figured that even in the midst of the Apocalypse, Sister Bernarda would find a way to get things organized and working efficiently.

She headed toward the door, then suddenly stopped and turned around. "And Sister?"

Sister Bernarda looked up at her.

"Pray that Father's death is the result of natural causes or an accident. Otherwise, it's going to be a long time before this monastery knows any peace again."

4

SISTER AGATHA'S HOPE OF GETTING INFORMATION FROM Sheriff Green was dashed the second she arrived at the station. The young deputy behind the desk told her Sheriff Green wouldn't be available for some time. They'd just received new evidence on Father Anselm's death. Although the deputy refused to elaborate, the news sent a cold chill up her spine and instinct told her this wasn't good.

Her first inclination was to go back to the monastery as quickly as possible and talk to Reverend Mother, but Sister Agatha knew there was still work for her to do in town.

She drove straight to the small rectory that stood beside the tall adobe-and-brick church near the center of old Bernalillo, along Camino del Pueblo. This street had once been the main highway, before the interstate was constructed well east of town. Helmet in hand, she walked to the side door and knocked softly.

Frances Williams, who'd been the rectory's housekeeper for as far back as anyone remembered, answered right away. Seeing Sister Agatha, she smiled. "I'm so glad it's not the police again, Sister. I don't think I've got the stamina to answer one more question."

"This must be so hard on you, Frances. Is there anything I can do to help?" Sister Agatha asked her softly.

"Just keep me in your prayers along with Father Anselm, Sister."

"Of course."

Tying back a strand of brown hair that had worked itself loose from the bun at the nape of her neck, the housekeeper led Sister to the kitchen and offered her a glass of iced tea.

Frances sat down wearily, her massive bulk filling the chair completely. "I think you should know that the diocese called a little while ago to tell me that Father Mahoney is being sent to us from a parish in Santa Fe until a permanent assignment is made."

"When is Father Mahoney supposed to arrive?"

"Sometime tonight. I thought I'd wait until he got here so he'll feel welcomed. I just hope he decides to keep me as a housekeeper. Father Anselm liked the way I did things, but everyone's different. Maybe Father Mahoney won't like my cooking or the way I keep house."

"Hey, if he doesn't like the way you cook, send him over to the monastery. Once he tastes our meals, he's bound to think that you're a gift from heaven. And as for your housekeeping, you're the best housekeeper I've ever met. A person could eat off the floor here." She sipped her tea, glad for an excuse to linger.

"If you get lonely and want to see me, call and I'll come by," Sister Agatha offered.

"I will. Right now, it's good to have someone here, if only for a while."

"The rectory sure seems empty without Father Anselm, doesn't it?"

Frances nodded. "It was chaotic earlier, with the sheriff's people looking around. I overheard some of the deputies talking, and it seems the police believe he was murdered. But who would have done such a thing?" she said.

"Do they have a suspect yet?" Sister Agatha asked.

"No, not according to what I heard. Anyone who saw him that morning, including the monastery sisters, is probably a suspect. And apparently the mayor is bearing down on the sheriff, insisting that he solve this before the Sheriff's Posse Rodeo, a big charity event three weeks from now." She paused and shook her head. "Talk about strange priorities!"

"I suppose . . ."

"I heard other gossip, too, that worries me. Some of the Protestant clerics are worried that the killer might be someone with a grudge against religious leaders."

"I hope not," Sister Agatha said, exhaling softly, "but we'll have to wait and see what the police uncover. The sheriff spoke to us at the monastery right after Father Anselm died, but I don't think we were of much help to him. Now that it seems Father's death was not accidental, I'm sure he'll be back with more questions. Can you think of anyone who might have wanted to harm Father?"

"No, and I've been giving that some serious thought. Father made people angry sometimes, because he'd forget his appointments, but that's surely not motive enough for murder."

"It's hard to say what motivates a killer." Sister Agatha stood and rinsed her glass in the sink. "Just don't worry about Father Mahoney. I'm sure he'll love your work."

As she drove back to the monastery, questions circled her mind like hungry wolves. Nothing made sense. Poor Father Anselm had undoubtedly annoyed some people from time to time, but then again, so did she—and on a regular basis. If the ability to be irritating was sufficient motive for murder, a lot of people would have been as dead as doornails.

As she reached the empty, open stretch of road between Bernalillo and the turnoff to the monastery, Sister turned the grip on the right handlebar toward her, increasing the speed. Her arthritic wrist protested, but driving the bike was such a treat she decided it was a small price to pay. Engine roaring, she raced down the road, the bottom of her veil flying in the wind and memories of her brother's laughter ringing in her mind. The alfalfa fields absorbed some of the sound of the bike's passage, and she could tell without looking whenever she passed a telephone pole because the pitch of the engine sound changed for an instant each time.

It was heaven. Nothing could have been more perfect. She could almost feel Kevin beside her. Suddenly the wail of a police siren rose in the air behind her. Sister's blood ran cold. If she ended up getting a speeding ticket, Reverend Mother would pin her hide to the wall.

She slowed down and pulled over, then removed her helmet as the white sheriff's department vehicle parked behind her.

Sheriff Tom Green got out of his unit and walked toward her. She couldn't help but notice that he wasn't holding anything in his hands, so maybe he didn't plan on writing her a ticket. But as he drew near and she saw the look on his face, she felt her mouth go dry.

"Sheriff," she said, and wasn't surprised to hear the unsteadiness in her voice.

"I'm glad I saw you, Sister. Rather than having me call the monastery and leave a message for Reverend Mother with the portress, it would save time if you would convey a message to her," he said somberly. "Preliminary toxicology tests have confirmed the medical investigator's theory that Father Anselm was poisoned. His death is now being considered a homicide."

"What kind of poison was used? And how much time would it have needed to work?" She hoped with all her heart to hear news that would make it impossible for any of the nuns to be considered suspects.

"It was a powerful extract of monkshood, which is a relatively common plant. It has a blue or white, cap-shaped flower and the root is often mistaken for a radish. Death can occur anywhere between ten minutes to a few hours after exposure, and symptoms show up right away."

"Could it have been an accident? Something in a salad he might have eaten earlier? Sometimes he had an early lunch. Anyone know what he ate?"

"He had a grilled cheese sandwich and an orange. No salad or greens."

"Oh." She thought of how carefully Sister Clothilde tended their garden and shook her head. "The medical investigator looked at all of our plants. There wasn't anything like that there or he would have spotted it." She paused thoughtfully. She didn't want to ask the next question, but there was no way around it. "Did you analyze the tea he drank?"

"Yes, but it contained only the herbs you'd mentioned."

The relief that swept through her was so intense her legs nearly buckled.

"I brought the list of the parishioners who attended Mass that morning. Were any omitted?" He held out a page of his pocket notebook so she could read the carefully recorded names.

She read the list twice. "It looks accurate to me. There are usually only a few on weekdays, as you can see. I remember seeing elderly Mrs. Gutierrez, Joan Sanchez, whose husband died a few months ago, and Anne Gellar, for certain. Also Frank Walters, who helps us with our computers. He doesn't come every day, but he was there that morning."

He nodded slowly. "All right. I'll interview each of them now that I know what killed the father. Maybe somebody saw or heard something useful."

"I better get going," Sister Agatha said, reaching for the helmet she'd hooked on the handlebars as they talked.

"I can't believe you're riding that thing wearing a habit."

"We need transportation and this was all that was available. I can't exactly wear jeans and a leather jacket anymore. I'm just thankful that the helmet fits."

Tom stared at his feet for a moment, then cleared his throat. "What you've become seems so strange now after knowing you all these years. Don't you miss your freedom?" Tom asked.

"I'm as free as I want to be. Can you say the same? Freedom is the ability to make the choices you know are right for you. I know I'm doing precisely what I was put here on Earth to do. The sense of purpose my vocation gives me is incredible."

Tom shook his head. "I'll never understand what drove you to become a nun."

"A religious vocation is an invitation from God, not a punishment or an escape route. We're free to turn it down, but when we answer it we're rewarded with an incredible sense of peace." She paused, seeing the skepticism on his face. "It's hard to explain, but let me put it this way. You're a sheriff. That's what you do, and even on bad days you know you're exactly where you should be. You wouldn't be as happy, say, as a real estate broker, would you?" Seeing him shake his head, she continued. "That's the way I feel about being a nun."

"If you say so." He nodded, turned, and walked back to his car without another word.

Tom's expression had told her clearly that his mind had remained closed. It saddened her. She would have welcomed his friendship, but some things were not meant to be.

The bell for Vespers, the evening prayer, was ringing as she arrived at the monastery's outer parlor ten minutes later. "Go to chapel, Your Charity," Sister Agatha said to Sister Bernarda, choosing the monastic term their order used in lieu of a name at times, or instead of simply saying "you." It was a sign of love for another who had also chosen to be a Bride of Christ.

"Mother's asked us all to meet outside by the statue of the Blessed Virgin for Divine Office, though she wouldn't say why."

"Then go join them. You deserve it. You've put in long hours as portress today. I can lock up here after Vespers."

"You've been working as long as I have, and Reverend Mother wants to see you as soon as possible," Sister Bernarda responded.

Since Reverend Mother had already moved the Liturgy of the Hours outside, it was clear that she already suspected what Sister Agatha would have to say. "I'll catch up to her after Divine Office."

As Sister Bernarda left, Sister Agatha said her prayers in Pater Nosters. The musical sounds of the nuns' chanting flowed through the monastery windows like an old violin in the hands of a master. Afterward, Sister Agatha closed and locked the front doors. The monastery wouldn't be open to visitors again until the following morning.

As she walked to the refectory for collation, the term for a simple dinner, she wondered if she'd be able to protect any of them from what lay ahead. If, as the sheriff had told her earlier, Father Anselm had been deliberately poisoned, then the killer's trail might lead directly to them. He'd said that symptoms from poisoning with that particular herb began almost immediately, which suggested he could have ingested the monkshood extract just before or during Mass. One possible explanation was that an intruder had gained access to the monastery, and while there, slipped Father Anselm the poison somehow. Knowing what she did about the sisters at Our Lady, that was the only theory that made sense.

She didn't meet with Reverend Mother until after collation. As she left the refectory, she saw Reverend Mother waiting for her by the side door leading to the garden. "Join me for my walk, child." Once they were away from the building, she added, "Tell me what you've learned today."

After she filled Reverend Mother in, silence stretched between them. Following the prioress's lead, Sister Agatha sat down on one of the benches near the statue of the Blessed Virgin and watched a piñon jay dart among the trees, screeching loudly. The vivid blue birds were the prettiest—and the loudest—of all the creatures that visited their garden.

"I need you to do something for our monastery, child," Reverend Mother said at long last. "Help Sheriff Green find the answers he needs as quickly as possible—whether or not he wants your help. Sister Bernarda can take over your duties as portress and, if necessary, she can also get our novice and postulant to help with whatever scriptorium duties you think they can handle. We need you now to use those skills you developed as a reporter to find the truth and restore our peace."

"Whatever I can do, I will, Reverend Mother."

"I knew I could count on you. Begin your work with the blessing of God." Reverend Mother stood up slowly as if she were shouldering the weight of the world, and continued her walk alone.

Sister Agatha watched her go, lost in thought.

"I'm very worried about Reverend Mother," Sister Eugenia said, joining Sister Agatha at the bench. The loyalty and love that every single nun in the monastery felt for Mother made it hard for them to see her so worried now. "As infirmarian, it's my job to make sure everyone stays healthy, but Reverend Mother barely touched her food today. I offered to bring her something to eat later, but she refused."

"She's worried about our future here. Father Anselm's death and its ramifications have hit her very hard."

"While you were gone this afternoon, she warned us that we might have the police underfoot again. The archbishop's office called to say that they may be forced to grant us permission to allow the sheriff to enter our enclosure."

"Then you know why she's worried."

"I'm certain that Sheriff Green is a reasonable man. He'll see we're not responsible for what happened, and will soon be looking elsewhere."

Sister Agatha didn't answer. She really wished she could share Sister Eugenia's optimism, but in truth, she was afraid of what lay ahead for all of them.

Before Compline, Reverend Mother gathered them together in the parlor to break the news that they wouldn't be able to offer prayers in their chapel for the time being. The chapel would have to remain closed until it could be rededicated and reconsecrated by either the bishop or someone he delegated. No prayer could be said to God in a place that had been tainted by a murder. And although there was no proof the priest had been given the poison in the chapel, he'd certainly died there, and there were enough unanswered questions surrounding his death to cause the rule to go into effect.

The older sisters, like Sister Clothilde and Sister Ignatius, took it as hard as Sister Agatha had expected. A change in their lives had come about suddenly, and in a place where things always remained constant—where the years never left a mark except on the faces of those who dwelled in the enclosure—it marked the beginning of the many trials that were yet to come.

The Great Silence that had begun after Compline now held the monastery in perfect stillness except for the random creaking of the building itself and the song of the crickets outside the walls. The nuns had gone to their cells, the name given to their simple sleeping quarters. As extern sisters, Sister Bernarda and Sister Agatha had cells toward the front of the monastery, near the parlor doors. In case of a crisis, they were immediately available to reach the telephone in the parlor to summon help and to open the doors to a doctor or emergency personnel.

In some monasteries externs had sleeping quarters outside the cloister, but she was glad that wasn't the rule here. Many were the tasks that separated the extern sisters from the choir nuns—a term synonymous with cloistered nuns and used as far back as anyone could remember. It, more than likely, had been taken from the name given to the cloistered and grated sections of a monastery chapel, called choir. Yet despite the differences in duties, unity of purpose defined and bonded all the sisters. They spent their whole lives living together, and what bound their souls together was a common purpose and love as unbreakable as steel.

Sister Agatha looked up at the simple wooden cross above her bed, said a quick prayer, then crawled into bed. She soon drifted into a peaceful sleep.

Sometime in the middle of the night, Sister Agatha suddenly awakened, certain that she had heard the muted creak of a door opening or closing.

Nuns were required to sleep in their habits. Only their belts were taken off and their veils replaced by shorter ones. It was monastic rule, but it was also eminently practical in emergencies.

Without reaching for either her belt or other veil, she stepped out into the hall. A figure wearing the short white veil of a novice was going around the corner.

She sighed. Sister Mary Lazarus was sleepwalking again. As novice mistress, she understood that it was a tense time for Mary Lazarus, even without the strains of being entangled in a murder investigation. In a few months she'd be taking her first vows, should she choose to remain at the monastery. Her two years as a novice were nearly up.

Yet Sister Agatha had a feeling based on the ones who had come and gone from the monastery in the past, that Mary Lazarus wouldn't remain. She'd come to them a few years after the death of her husband, at age thirty-six. Now, after three years with them, the idealistic views about religious life that most postulants and novices clung to were far behind her. In the last six months, Sister Agatha had sensed that Mary Lazarus had begun to question her vocation, and was finding the demands of their life here increasingly burdensome.

Her uneasiness and restlessness were evidenced by her recent and frequent sleepwalking episodes. The doctor had assured them that there was nothing inherently dangerous about them, especially since Mary Lazarus always seemed to follow the same path—one with few hazards. She'd go directly to the kitchen—no matter how much she'd eaten at collation the evening before.

Sometimes the novice had walked in her sleep and neither Sister Agatha nor Sister Bernarda had woken up. Those mornings Sister Clothilde would find tortillas missing, and then Mary Lazarus would confess to having "found" them in her cell. They'd all smiled about it, and had tried not to embarrass Mary Lazarus.

Of course when one of the externs did wake up in time, they'd try to gently direct Mary Lazarus back to her room. Tonight that duty fell to Sister Agatha.

She caught up with Mary Lazarus in the pantry. The novice simply stood there, holding a tortilla in her hand. Without breaking silence, or trying to take the tortilla away from her, Sister Agatha led the wandering novice back to her cell and put her back into bed.

The sisters' cell doors had no locks, so there was no practical way to keep Mary Lazarus in her room. Putting obstacles in front of a door that opened by swinging to the inside was practically a guarantee that a tumble would follow.

Sister Agatha waited in the hall, watching the novice for a

minute. Mary Lazarus seemed to be sleeping peacefully.

Finally assured that all was well, Sister Agatha returned to her cell, and seconds after her head hit the pillow, she fell fast asleep.

Sister Agatha woke up to the sound of the morning bell at four-thirty. She opened her eyes slowly, and as she started to stretch her legs, discovered something was weighing down the covers at the foot of the bed.

The room was still dark and her first thought was that Mary Lazarus had found her way here after a second episode of sleepwalking. As her eyes adjusted, however, Sister Agatha realized that the large shape at the end of the bed bore no resemblance to the novice.

She scarcely breathed. She'd heard of visitations—what nun hadn't? But she'd always assured the Lord and all his saints that none of them had to go to the trouble of visiting her personally. The possibility terrified her.

With a burst of courage, she sat up and reached out toward the dark bundle.

A wet tongue licked her hand. With a tiny shriek, she jumped out of bed and turned on the light.

A solid white German shepherd who looked nearly the size of a Volkswagen lay at the foot of the bed, staring at her, his tongue lolling out the side of his mouth in a contented doggy grin.

Sister Agatha stared at him in shock. What was this animal doing in her room? Where had it come from? Her door was partially open. She always left it like that during the summer to take advantage of the cross-ventilation from the hall window and the one in her cell.

For several long moments, neither she nor the dog moved. He showed no signs of aggression so finally she went over and searched around his neck for a collar, but there wasn't one. "You look too well fed and cared for to be a stray, so I know you've got an owner, boy," she said, realizing how clean the dog's coat was and noting that his nails had been trimmed recently. "Come on. I've got to go now, and you've got to get out of here."

She tried pulling him off the bed, and then cajoling him, but neither worked. The dog lay there, oblivious to her efforts.

Hearing the sisters going outside for Matins, she realized it was time to get going.

"One last chance, dog. You either come with me now or spend the next few hours cooped up in this stuffy room."

The dog stood, climbed off the bed, and joined her at the door.

"That's much better." The dog followed her, and she left him in the enclosed patio area just outside the kitchen doors before hurrying to join the other nuns for Matins.

After Lauds, Sister Agatha hurried back to check on the dog, but some of the other sisters had already discovered him. Sister Clothilde was petting the animal and scratching it behind the ears. Sister Ignatius was feeding it some of the nuns' oatmeal, and Sister Gertrude was trying to brush it.

No one said anything, unwilling to break the Great Silence that would stretch out until after Morning Prayer, but it was clear they were happy to find the dog, and the animal certainly loved the attention he was getting.

Sister Bernarda took one look at the animal, then soundlessly mouthed a message to Sister Agatha. "We've got to talk later."

Leaving the dog on the patio with a large bowl of water, they went into the refectory for breakfast, eating in silence while Sister Mary Lazarus read from the Bible. The table at the front of the room was reserved for Reverend Mother, who never seemed to look up or become distracted during meals. On the front wall, directly to Sister Agatha's right, was a large cross, and beneath it was a table that held a human skull—a reminder that mortal life, with its joys and sorrows, was fleeting.

As always, Sister Agatha did her best to avoid looking at the skull. It made her uncomfortable, but over the years, her wry humor had helped her accept the monastic custom. These days when she looked at it, she always had to fight the temptation to offer the thing a spoonful of their stick-to-your-ribs oatmeal.

After Morning Prayers, Sister Agatha paid the friendly animal a visit. The dog was so sweet natured she was really tempted to take him to the parlor with her. Unfortunately, she was pretty sure what Reverend Mother's ruling on *that* request would be.

As she crouched before him, petting and talking to him, Sister Bernarda appeared. "We used to have service dogs like that in the Marine Corps," she said, a touch of wistfulness in her voice. "Does he know any commands?"

"Like what?"

"Sit!"

Sister Agatha sat on the ground and noticed the dog had done the same.

"Your Charity, I was talking to the dog," Sister Bernarda said with a tiny smile. "But I guess both of you know the command."

Sister Agatha laughed. "It's your tone. A tree would march for you."

Sister Bernarda went through several more commands, then stopped and praised the dog. "You've been trained well." She also automatically checked for dog license tags but, finding none, suggested they call the newspaper, the animal shelters, and the local veterinarians.

Sister Bernarda then went to the scriptorium to work while Sister Agatha took her duty post as portress and made the calls. The monastery had only two phones, this one and one in Reverend Mother's office. Only externs handled incoming phone calls, and these were carefully logged by the portress, who would then make sure the messages were delivered as needed.

An hour later, she sat in the parlor, frustrated. She still hadn't found the owner of the dog. But as she'd worked, one other very disturbing thought had occurred to her and it was something she couldn't push out of her mind.

Sister Bernarda came into the parlor just then. "Reverend Mother asked about the dog. I've told her we're trying to find his owner."

"But not successfully," she muttered.

"Your Charity, I've been thinking about the dog and there's a very important question we need to answer," she said.

"How did he get in?" Sister Agatha said with a nod.

"Exactly. The monastery's doors are locked at night, and the wall around the monastery grounds is too high for him to jump. If he's found a way in—maybe it's a way that's open to a two-legged intruder as well."

"I thought of that, too. Our gate is kept closed at night and padlocked. No one could get through there, or under. The area is graveled with limestone, and that's hard to dig through," Sister Agatha said thoughtfully.

"It's a puzzle, but one we need to answer quickly. He couldn't have come out of nowhere," Sister Bernarda said.

Slowly a smile spread across Sister Agatha's features. "This whole thing reminds me of Father Don Bosco's guardian angel dog, Gerigio. Remember the story? The animal always appeared in times of trouble and guarded Father as he went about his work in the slums in Turin. Maybe this dog's appearance now is a sign that we're being watched over."

"Now you're starting to sound like Sister Ignatius. She's always seeing signs in everything. Of course, in all fairness, she never fails to get them when she prays for one." Sister Bernarda glanced at her watch. "I better get back to the scriptorium."

Sister Agatha spent another unsuccessful half hour trying to locate the dog's owner. By then, Sister Bernarda had reappeared, ready to take over as portress. "I'm going to teach morning classes for Celia and Sister Mary Lazarus. Will you keep making phone calls?" Sister Agatha asked her.

"Of course, and—" She suddenly stopped speaking and met Sister Agatha's gaze. "I don't know why I didn't think of this before, but did you check the dog for a tattoo?"

"You mean one that says Mom?" Sister Agatha teased.

"No, I mean a tattoo with numbers or some code. The military used to tattoo its dogs, and so I wondered . . ."

"I'll go take a look right now."

Sister Agatha walked through the quiet cloistered halls, absently noting that Sister Eugenia, methodical and patient, was counting pills in the infirmary. Sister Clothilde and Sister Ignatius were in the bakery making altar breads. The automatic device could be heard all throughout the monastery making its whirring, rhythmic, mechanical noise.

As Sister Agatha passed the sewing room, she couldn't resist peeking in to take a look at the quilted wall hanging. It was nearly finished and magnificent. Made in a dozen shades of blue and white, it depicted the kneeling Virgin with a dove that represented the Holy Spirit descending over her.

She made a circle with her thumb and forefinger, letting Sister Maria Victoria and Sister Gertrude know that she thought it was spectacular. Both nuns nodded and smiled, pleased, then offered her a closer look.

She ran her fingers over the material. Her hands ached a bit today, but not as much as they had a week ago.

As she examined the very tiny stitches of the quilting, she sighed with envy. She could have worked on this too, had her joints not been so troublesome these past few weeks.

As quickly as the thought came she pushed it back. Envy was a sin—and green had never done much for her anyway.

Bowing to them, she left the nuns to their work and went to find the dog, who was resting in the shade of the building now.

She checked the dog's underside, something the animal was perfectly happy to let her do, providing she scratched his belly while she was at it. She found nothing there. She then checked his ears, and near the top of the right ear, on the inside, she found a number. She wrote it down on a piece of paper and hurried back to the parlor.

"You were right. What we've got here is a working dog," Sister Agatha said. "I know the sheriff's department has a canine unit, since their officers often patrol alone," Sister Agatha said, "but this dog doesn't seem to have the right temperament for a guard dog."

"You can never tell," Sister Bernarda said. "Those dogs, from what I recall of the ones in the military, can be perfectly nice—until the right command is given."

"What's the command?"

"It depends. It can be anything from a foreign word to a simple English 'get him.'"

After two transfers by the switchboard at the sheriff's office, a deputy in the canine unit answered the phone. Sister Agatha described the dog who had found her, and the deputy replied immediately. "We've been looking all over the place for him. I didn't know he was missing until I went out to give him breakfast. He dug a hole beneath his kennel sometime after lights-out and got out. But how did he get into the monastery? I thought your gate was closed and locked at night."

"All I can tell you is that he ended up in my cell—my room—this morning."

"We'll send someone to get him. And don't worry. He's really mellow. One of the reasons we've been thinking of retiring him is because he no longer shows the aggression we need in police dogs. He's too smart, and knows that his training is only a game, so he refuses to attack—even if we give him the right command."

"Is that command a word someone here might mistakenly use?"

"No, Sister. Not unless you speak German."

"Okay." She paused, then added, "What happens to the dogs when they're retired?"

"We usually try to find a home for them, but if that doesn't work out, we euthanize them." The deputy spoke to someone else in the room, then came back to the phone. "I'll pick him up in about an hour. Is that okay?"

"He'll be waiting," Sister Agatha answered, suddenly wishing she didn't have to give the dog back. He'd come to them and it didn't seem right to turn him out. Besides, he was such a nice dog. He deserved a place where he'd be more appreciated. She'd have to pray that he found the perfect home.

After teaching her morning class for the novice and postulant, Sister Agatha went back to relieve Sister Bernarda in the parlor.

"I'll take over for you now so you can get some work done in the scriptorium," Sister Agatha said. "Deadline on those projects isn't far away now."

"This just came in for you," Sister Bernarda said, and handed her a message. "It's from Mrs. Williams at the rectory. She was very eager to talk to you. She said it was urgent."

Sister Agatha called the rectory housekeeper as Sister Bernarda left to go to her next duty post.

"Frances, this is Sister Agatha. What can I do for you?"

"I need to speak to you, Sister—face-to-face, not over the phone. Father Mahoney, our temporary pastor, has been delayed, so I can't discuss this with him, and I don't know what to do. You see, I remembered something concerning Father Anselm that I think may be important. But I don't feel right telling the police about it, at least not yet." She sighed loudly. "It's complicated."

"All right. Wait for me. I'll be there shortly."

5

S ISTER AGATHA WENT TO THE SCRIPTORIUM TO FIND SISTER Bernarda, and was surprised to find Frank Walters there, too, though the local businessman had been granted a dispensation by the archbishop to enter the enclosure and help them maintain the scriptorium hardware. Mr. Walters was tall and in his early forties, with thinning brown hair that was liberally streaked with gray. He'd probably been a bit of a ladies' man in his twenties, and had aged well. But he had never shown any disrespect by flirting with any of the sisters, and was always quite pleasant.

"Hello, Sister Agatha." Frank stood when he saw her enter. "My condolences for the loss of Father Anselm. It was such a shock for all of us who were here when he . . . died. He'll be missed."

"Father is in heaven, Mr. Walters. We'll all miss him, but he's in a better place now." Sister Agatha went quiet for a few moments thinking about Father Anselm as she watched Frank Walters work. "What's the problem with our computers today?"

"Nothing that a cooler work space wouldn't solve." He shrugged. "Actually, I'd come by to offer a prayer and show my respect for Father Anselm, and thought I'd do some routine maintenance on the computers while I was here. I figured the recent crisis might have slowed down your work, and now you'll be needing the computers to work at peak efficiency. As soon as I defrag the files and do a diagnostics check, I'll be on my way."

Sister Agatha smiled. "We appreciate all you do for our monastery."

"I'm glad to help." Frank turned back to the computer monitor, which had beeped a prompt.

Sister Agatha turned to Sister Bernarda, who had been busy at one of the other computers. "Your Charity, I have to go into town. I'm needed at the rectory. Mrs. Williams has a problem."

"That's all right," Sister Bernarda said. "But you and I will have to put in extra hours later to catch up in here. I'm really behind now. Mr. Walter's guess was right on target."

"We'll manage. Reverend Mother has said we can recruit Celia and Sister Mary Lazarus to help us whenever we need, though you and I will have to choose appropriate projects for them to work on."

"That's fine, but I still wouldn't want to leave them in here completely unsupervised."

"Let's work that out one step at a time," Sister Agatha said, taking a deep breath. "My first priority now is finding a way to clear everyone here of complicity in Father Anselm's death. This monastery needs to have its peace restored."

Sister Bernarda resumed portress duties from the scriptorium, something that was possible thanks to the scriptorium windows and the fact their phone had a loud ringer, and Sister Agatha headed to the rectory in town. She followed the required route that took her a short drive east to Highway 313, part of the historic trade route known as the Camino Real, or Royal Road, then south to Bernalillo. With the motorcycle in such excellent condition, the trip took much less time than it would have limping along in the station wagon.

Sister Agatha loved the scent of the freshly mowed hay she passed, and the roar of the Harley and the feel of the wind whistling past her helmet. " 'Make a joyful noise unto the Lord,' " she said under her breath with a happy smile. The motorcycle was surely a gift from God, and such gifts were meant to be enjoyed.

By the time she arrived at the rectory, she felt in much better spirits. As she shut off the engine, Frances came outside to meet her. "Sister, I'm so glad you're here."

The cool air-conditioned rectory, in contrast to the hundred-degree heat outside, seemed like a blessing all its own. They sat in the living room, where Frances offered Sister Agatha a glass of lemonade. "Thank you for coming, Sister. My loyalty is to this parish, and I want to avoid a scandal, but with the sheriff involved I don't know how much I should say."

"About what?" Sister Agatha asked, curiosity piqued.

"Do you know Joan Sanchez, one of our parishioners?"

Sister Agatha nodded. "She's a friend of Anne Gellar's, isn't she? I think she's the one who drives Anne to Mass every day."

"Yes, that's her. Mrs. Sanchez's husband died a few months ago, and she hasn't been quite right since. She used to come around here a lot to talk to Father. And I do mean *a lot*. For a while there, she became almost like a stalker. Wherever Father was, she was, and if she wasn't here, she'd be busy calling the rectory. It was constant."

"Did Father ever say anything to you about that?"

"Oh, of course not! He wasn't one to complain. But Mrs. Sanchez called so frequently that Father started asking me to take messages so he wouldn't have to speak to her so often. He'd *never* done that before."

"And you haven't told the police that yet?"

"I was planning to ask Father Mahoney if I should—I mean, I don't think Mrs. Sanchez had anything to do with Father's death. But now Father Mahoney's been delayed and I don't know what to do. It may be several days before he gets here, I'm told."

She thought of the nuns at the monastery. To some, going without daily mass was nearly unthinkable. "I think the archbishop's office needs to be reminded how much the sisters need their chaplain," she said softly.

"I'll take care of that for you, Sister. I need to call them anyway on a matter concerning this month's bills. But what should I do about Mrs. Sanchez? I don't want to suggest anything about Father Anselm that may give rise to some nasty gossip."

"My advice is to tell the sheriff, but stick only to the facts you know. For example, don't offer any conclusions or speculations, such as a stalking. Just explain about the calls and visits, and that after a while Father started avoiding Mrs. Sanchez's calls. Tell them about the specific instances when you saw her appear at functions where Father was present. No one could fault you for that."

"But that's still going to make her a suspect. What if she's totally innocent? A woman who's gone through the death of her husband might be fragile mentally. If the sheriff and his people start making harsh accusations, it just might push that poor woman over the edge."

"Then explain that to them, just the way you did to me. But you can't keep this from them. You'd be withholding information, and they'll take a very dim view of that once they find out—and they *will* find out. You know how gossip travels back and forth in this community."

"I suppose you're right. I'll call Sheriff Green."

"Good. And if you need me again, just call."

As Sister Agatha drove back up the valley to the monastery, she found her mind racing with questions and possibilities. Maybe Joan had felt Father had rejected her by not giving her more of his time. Or maybe she'd fallen in love with Father and, by keeping her at a distance, Father had turned her into a dangerous enemy. Of course it was all speculation at this point. She'd need to dig deeper.

As she drove through the monastery gates, she saw Sheriff Green walking around the tall adobe and stucco-coated wall that bordered the grounds. The white German shepherd was at his side.

She pulled to a stop, took off her helmet, and walked over to talk to him. "Is everything all right?"

"Something occurred to me when I came to pick up Rex," Tom said.

"Oh, so that's his name!" She bent down to scratch him behind the ears and the dog cocked his head contentedly. "Good boy, Rex." She glanced up at Tom. "So, let me guess. You were thinking that if Rex found a way into the monastery, maybe a human could have done the same thing?"

"Exactly. Someone poisoned the priest, and it most likely happened here. My experts say that symptoms began almost immediately, and no one observed any such symptoms when the priest first arrived. That means it was either one of the nuns or an intruder who set things up and slipped back out unnoticed."

"Have you had any luck finding out how Rex got in?"

He shook his head. "I searched around the outside for paw prints, but I couldn't find anything except for scattered rabbit and bird tracks, plus some from smaller animals, perhaps a prairie dog or two. Then I checked the gate. When it's closed and padlocked, it's impossible for anything larger than a squirrel to squeeze through. So then I started looking for holes under the wall, or in the wall itself. Of course, during the day the gates are open and anyone could have waltzed in here. But I'm thinking that once the nuns are up and about, it would be hard for an intruder to remain undetected."

"You're right. Rex couldn't have hidden for long after all of us were up."

"The wall is over eight feet high and so are the gates, so I'm certain the dog didn't jump over," Sheriff Green said.

"I have an idea. Take the leash off him and see where he goes."

"All right. He's trained to recall on command so it shouldn't be a problem." Tom did as she suggested, but Rex sat beside him at heel.

The sheriff shook his head. "When he's with a cop, he's working, and he knows it. He's been too well trained."

"Well, let me try. Put him back on the leash. I'll lead him away and let's see what he does then."

"All right."

Sister Agatha led Rex to the middle of the garden, took him off the leash, then threw a stick for him to retrieve. The dog enjoyed fetching the stick, and Sister Agatha enjoyed the simple game. But after a few more throws, she crouched down, petted the dog, and walked away a short distance, then turned to observe. The dog sniffed the ground and wandered around, once or twice jumping up trying to catch a butterfly, but he clearly had no particular interest in any specific location.

"This is a waste of time," Sheriff Green said at last, snapping the leash back on the dog. "He's just playing. If he remembers where he came in, he's not about to clue us in, and he certainly doesn't have to leave that way now with the gate open."

She continued walking with him, inspecting the adobe wall as they circled the monastery grounds on the inside. "The gates are securely locked for the night after Vespers, a little before six. Then there's dinner, recreation, and the last office—Compline. After that is the Great Silence, but the nuns still go about freely, in and out of the building, finishing personal chores and the like before bed. I can practically guarantee that Rex wasn't here then."

"I know he wasn't. My deputy said that the dog was in his kennel at ten P.M. when he went by to check on him."

"Where does the deputy live? How did Rex find this place?"

"Our handler, Ralph Ortiz, is from San Felipe Pueblo. He lives down by the highway, not three miles from here."

"So Rex had a pretty good walk, but one that's well within his capabilities. I wonder why he went this way down the road instead of south or east?" Sister Agatha asked.

"Maybe he smelled the river, further west. He's gotten out before, and gone elsewhere."

"I'd give anything to find out how he got into my room," Sister Agatha said.

"Do you have a window?"

"A small one, but there's a bigger one down the hall. We considered the possibility he came in through that window, but that still doesn't explain how he got into the compound in the first place."

"True." A cream-colored sporty-looking sedan pulled up outside the monastery gate, stopped, and a tall, leggy blond woman in tight clothing stepped out. Sheriff Green exhaled softly, then waved, and the woman waved back.

"A friend of yours?" Sister Agatha noted that the sheriff's face had become set and flushed. Something about the woman's appearance had turned his mood sour.

"My wife, Gloria. I was supposed to meet her for lunch. I guess she found out where I was and came to remind me."

"We went to high school with a girl named Gloria Anderson. But her hair was brown. That isn't her, is it?" Sister Agatha smiled, remembering how Gloria had flirted with Tom for months, and had been quite jealous of the relationship he had shared with her their senior year in high school.

"The very same. She's a blonde now. She chased me until I caught her, Gloria likes to say," Tom joked halfheartedly.

"I'll have to visit with her again sometime and catch up on our school years."

"Yes." Tom looked at his wife, and she waved again. He waved back even less enthusiastically this time.

The silence became awkward for a moment, then Sister Agatha finally spoke. "Well, I'm glad you're considering the possibility of an intruder. Hopefully you'll soon rule out the sisters as suspects entirely."

His expression suddenly became cold. "Don't jump to conclusions. You, Sister Mary Lazarus, and that postulant, Celia, are still very much suspects, and so are the parishioners who were here for Mass. And, just so you know, what I personally think doesn't matter. The evidence is the only thing that does."

"I think you're going to be getting some news that will lead you away from our order soon," she said.

His gaze narrowed. "What do you know that you're not telling me?"

She hesitated. This was information she wanted him to get directly from Frances. Then she heard the beep of a car horn and saw Tom turn to glance at his wife, anger flashing in his eyes.

Before she could speak, the bells began to ring for Sext, the midday prayer. She saw that as the perfect opportunity to duck his question. And, from the looks of it, he also needed a chance to square things with his wife. "We'll talk later. I have to go now." With any luck, he wouldn't know that externs were excused from chanting the Divine Office with the choir nuns.

"Where? I thought the chapel was closed."

"Yes, but the grounds aren't. That's where we'll meet to chant the Divine Office."

"You're not getting off the hook that easy. I need to know what you've heard."

"You'll find out soon, I promise."

As she headed back toward the building where the sisters were gathering, Tom walked quickly to his car. Sister Agatha took one look back at her old friend's wife outside the gate. Gloria was leaning against the car now, and even at this distance, Gloria's body language implied that she was upset.

Focusing on her own duties, Sister Agatha hurried to meet the sisters. Divine Office was a time when the monastery's song was said to join that of the angels who, in the presence of God, eternally sang praises to him. Sharing that with her sisters in Christ would strengthen her now that everything they valued was being challenged.

After prayers, the sisters went to the refectory. Their meals were taken without conversation, listening to a reading that would nourish their souls as they fed their bodies. Still determined not to look at the skull and think of many practical jokes her brother, Kevin, would have pulled with it, she kept her eyes glued on the plate before her.

For a second, her mind wandered to Tom, and his wife, Gloria. *I bet his ear is being bent as well,* she thought, uncharitably allowing a small grin to escape. Then she focused back on the reading from Thomas Merton's works.

Afterward, Sister Bernarda hurried to the scriptorium and Sister Agatha left to go to her post in the parlor. As she opened the enclosure doors to step into the parlor, Reverend Mother came up behind her. "One moment, child."

Sister Agatha turned and lowered her head out of respect. "Yes, Mother?"

"I was notified this morning by the archdiocese that Sheriff Green will be given permission to enter the cloister. But I have gained a concession, too. He must be accompanied by one of our externs at all times when he is among us. I would like that extern to be you."

Sister Agatha stared at Mother in surprise. "I just saw the sheriff and he never said a word to me about this."

"He doesn't know yet, but he will soon."

Sister Agatha sighed. "That man is determined to find answers—and I'm afraid he still thinks they're here." She told Reverend Mother about her discussion with Tom Green.

"I don't know what's more unsettling—that we're suspects, or that we may have had an intruder." Reverend Mother paused. "What worries me most is how the pressure of the investigation will affect the older sisters. Our monastery should be a place of peace and security to all of us." She shook her head, her gaze on the rosary fastened to her cincture. "One thing you must do as soon as possible, child, is find out how that dog got in. It's very dangerous to have an access point we don't know about."

"I'll go over every inch of the grounds, inside and out. Maybe I can find something."

"Have you heard anything more about when we can expect our new chaplain to arrive? I understood that he has been delayed."

"They told Frances Williams it could be a few days, Mother," she answered. "I asked her to remind the archdiocese that we desperately need a chaplain. I know that not using the chapel is very upsetting to everyone, and not having Mass is much worse, especially to Sister Clothilde and Sister Ignatius."

Reverend Mother smiled. "Not anymore. It seems Sister Ignatius started one of her special novenas to St. Theresa of Lisieux. She has quite a devotion to the little saint. This time she asked for a sign that we would have a chaplain very soon. And she got the sign she wanted this morning."

"What was it? I remember when she asked for a fresh rose in the middle of winter, and then there was the time that the blue butterfly appeared in chapel."

"Do you have to ask?" Reverend Mother gave her a patient, amused smile.

It took Sister a beat to figure it out. "A white dog!"

"There you have it. Praised be Jesus Christ, child."

"Now and forever," she answered.

Sister Agatha took a detour and stopped by the scriptorium. There she found Sister Bernarda hard at work. Sister Agatha told her about Sister Ignatius's sign. "Can you believe it? Sister Iggy *always* gets answers! I wish my track record was half as good."

"It's no surprise that it isn't. Sister Iggy believes with all her heart that she *will* get an answer. You only half expect results, so that's what you get."

Sister Agatha gave her an owlish blink, stunned. As usual, Sister Bernarda's answer was right on target.

Sister Agatha woke up the next morning to feel a familiar weight resting on her feet. Rex couldn't have gotten out again—let alone into the monastery. Sister Bernarda and she had gone over every entrance and exit, making sure everything was secure. They'd only made one concession to the improved security—leaving the hall window with its broken screen open. The breeze that circulated down the hall and trickled into the rooms beyond offered the only respite from the unrelenting heat.

Sister Agatha tossed the covers back and turned on the light. The dog lay at the foot of her bed again, giving her a panting grin. He had a musty smell today, like he needed a bath.

"You've been sent to test me, haven't you?" Sister Agatha said, then gave him a quick hug. He was a nuisance, but impossible not to like. "I don't suppose you'd care to tell me how you got in?"

The dog laid his head back down on the bed and regarded her with big black eyes.

"Okay. I'll figure it out for myself. Now we have to get going."

She got ready for Matins and Lauds, put the dog outside, and saw Sister Clothilde come out to feed him some of the monastery's oatmeal.

It was déjà vu all over again. After prayers outside, Sister Agatha studied her fellow nuns' faces. By now everyone had seen the dog and they clearly welcomed his presence.

Enlisting Sister Bernarda's help after breakfast, they started to inspect the grounds again. The broken screen at the end of the hall was sitting crosswise in the window, having come loose from one of the top hooks. Not remembering how securely it had been fastened in place, they couldn't rule out a breeze as the culprit rather than a large dog. It was decided to put a screen-door hook at the bottom and fix the screen before the next evening.

Leaving Sister Bernarda for a few moments, Sister Agatha took Rex from Sister Clothilde, who had just given the dog a tortilla spread with peanut butter. Rex was furiously licking the roof of his mouth to get at the peanut butter that had leaked from the tortilla.

"I'm afraid I need to take Rex on a mission of discovery. Pray he shows us how he's getting in," Sister Agatha said.

She met with Sister Bernarda a few minutes later and they set out. They examined the gap between the hinges on the gate and the wooden posts that anchored it to the wall. It was only four inches wide, too narrow for a dog as large as Rex. There was just enough clearance under the closed gate for a fat snake, and the limestone gravel underneath was compacted by traffic and showed no sign of having been disturbed.

Next they walked outside the enclosed grounds, examining the ground there. The earth was hard packed, which meant little or no tracks, so they broadened their search. As Sister Agatha glanced around her, she noted the fenced-in electrical transformer that provided power to their area. Tall tumbleweeds lined the inside and outside of the fence, and a warning sign in English and Spanish cautioned against the shock hazard. The narrow gate was padlocked, and obviously hadn't been used in a while, judging by the weeds growing against it on both sides.

They walked all the way around the area bordering the monastery grounds, leaving no stone unturned, even when crossing the abandoned, concrete-lined irrigation ditch that had been there since the 1920s. They looked for rocks or high spots on the outside of the wall that could have given Rex a jumping platform of sorts, and searched the ground for paw prints that might give them a clue as to the route he'd used, but there was nothing obvious.

Finally they walked over to the cottonwood tree closest to the wall. Sister Agatha looked up at the relatively low branch that extended above the wall.

"Nice try, but dogs don't climb trees," Sister Bernarda said, laughing.

"Let's see if it *could* be done. When I was a child I saw movies where dogs did some amazing things," Sister Agatha reached up and grabbed a limb, pulling herself up slowly until she was standing on a stout branch six feet up, holding herself steady by grabbing the branch above her head.

"I think you're wasting your time—and likely to fall," she said suddenly, concerned by the height Sister Agatha had reached.

"Let's see what happens. Rex, come!" Sister Agatha called to the dog, who'd been watching her curiously.

To their amazement, the dog leaped up to a fork in the tree about five feet off the ground, then walked up the same limb Sister Agatha was standing on. As she moved forward, the branch started to droop toward the wall.

"Look, I could walk all the way over to the wall, and I bet he could too," Sister Agatha said.

"Okay. Now get off there before that branch breaks, and the order has to spend a fortune on duct tape to put both of you back together."

"One more minute."

"Even if he can do it, the fact remains that we don't know if the dog would have thought of doing that on his own. The only way we could consider it proof is if we'd seen him doing it *before* now."

"But this method would explain why he couldn't get back out once he was in," Sister Agatha said slowly.

Sister Bernarda called Rex, who climbed back down easily. For Sister Agatha getting out of the tree was more difficult. Her long, heavy habit kept catching in the branches and tangling about her feet. Finally, she was back on the ground.

"If we rule out the tree, or someone using a ladder to come and go, then rubbing out their tracks, there's only one other possibility,"

Sister Agatha said. "One of the sisters is letting the dog in and keeping it a secret."

"Ridiculous. None of the professed sisters ever walk close to the wall. This part of our grounds isn't an area that's open to them. And even if Sister Mary Lazarus decided to wander, she wouldn't be able to do it—all her time is regimented between instruction, prayers, and chores."

"I know all that," Sister Agatha said, "but that's the only possibility left, and that's the conclusion the sheriff will surely reach. Unfortunately, the implications could bring an enormous scandal to us."

It took Sister Bernarda a moment to follow Sister Agatha's train of thought, but as soon as she understood, she was immediately horrified. "You mean he'll think one of us is letting a man into the enclosure, and the dog followed in on his own?"

"To us, the idea is absurd because we know everyone here and we understand the value of a vocation. But to Sheriff Green . . ."

"You're right." Sister Bernarda sighed. "Well, we know it's an absolutely ridiculous proposition, so we'd better work twice as hard to find out how this dog is actually getting in!"

They went around the property once more, and this time they searched around the buildings as well as the walls looking for paw prints near every single window. Finally they were forced to give up.

"We have other duties waiting for us, Sister Agatha. This is getting us nowhere. Maybe we should rethink this and try again later."

They'd just reached the front doors when they heard a car approaching.

"That's Sheriff Green," Sister Agatha said, and to her credit managed to suppress a groan. "I'll go deal with him."

Sister Bernarda nodded and passed through the parlor doors and back into the enclosure.

As Tom Green got out of his car, Sister Agatha stood by the entrance, and the dog came to stand by her side.

Green gave the dog a frustrated look, then walked toward the animal. "Rex, come!" he said, and attached a leash to the dog's collar as soon as he responded. "Any idea how he got in this time?" He stopped by the steps, and Rex sat at heel.

"We just went around the entire wall, inside and out. The only possible way we could come up with is if he used that tree." She pointed. "I climbed out onto the low branch there, near the wall, and you know what Rex did?" Sister Agatha said smugly.

"He followed you?" Tom rolled his eyes. "He was trained in agility. If you call him, he'll come, but that doesn't mean he'd have done such a stunt on his own." He shook his head. "I don't think that's the answer, and I bet you don't either."

"Maybe not, but we can't rule it out completely. He's obviously a very smart animal."

"That he is, and that's what makes it so tough to handle him." Tom looked back at his car, but then turned and stared at the dog thoughtfully. "I'm not sure I should take him back to the station."

"Where else would you take him? His kennel at San Felipe?"

Tom took a deep breath, then let it out again. "Rex is close to seven and a half now. He's served our department well, but it's time to retire him so we can get a younger dog. We haven't been able to find an approved home for him, so that means we'll soon be putting him to sleep."

Sister Agatha's eyes widened. "You can't do that. He's perfectly healthy."

"He has a touch of arthritis in his back legs from time to time."

"I have a 'touch of arthritis' too, but Reverend Mother's not considering putting me to sleep!" she said indignantly.

He laughed. "It's not the same thing, though I'm glad to hear you feel this way. I have a proposition for all of you, but I expect Reverend Mother needs to be in on this before I say anything more. Can we go to the parlor?"

"Of course."

Sister Agatha left Tom with Rex in the parlor as she went to find Reverend Mother. She found the abbess helping Sister Maria Victoria with the quilted wall hanging. Once again she had to force down a stab of envy wishing she could have been able to work on it too.

On the way back down the hall, Sister Agatha filled Reverend Mother in on what they'd learned in their search, and what they'd found out about Rex. "The sheriff didn't say so," she added as she finished, "but I think he wants to give us the dog."

"It's funny *that* should come up now. I had a long talk with Sister Ignatius. She feels that the presence of the dog is a sign of protection from God and that, should the opportunity arise, we should volunteer to take care of him."

"Sister Ignatius's signs are legendary, Mother. But, then again, there's something to the law of averages. Half the time Sister Ignatius also thinks it's a sign if we get rain, or if she sees a field mouse in the monastery." She paused, then added, "To be perfectly honest, I'd like to think of Rex as the guardian angel in dog form that Father Don Bosco had. But the truth is, I know Rex is just a dog. Having said that, many monasteries *do* keep dogs. . . ."

"That dog came to us twice—whether by divine intercession or coincidence, I can't say," Reverend Mother replied. "To return him to people who are only going to euthanize him so they won't have to pay for his support doesn't seem right to me. But we're getting ahead of ourselves. Let's see what Sheriff Green has to say."

Reverend Mother took her accustomed seat behind the grille that opened to the parlor, and Sister Agatha went to the other side, joining the sheriff.

"Reverend Mother, I want you to know that I've received permission from the archbishop to come into the enclosure if I need to, just like the other repairmen."

"So I've been told."

"But I want you to know that my only interest is determining who killed Father Anselm and why. That's a goal we have in common, so try to focus on that."

Sister Agatha noticed that his tone was far less rude than it had been. Unless she missed her guess, Tom wanted something from them.

"We'll accept the necessity of your presence among us, but we'll insist that Sister Agatha accompany you when you're here if you have to go into our cloistered areas. That's the same rule all workmen follow."

"Agreed." The sheriff looked at Sister Agatha calmly, nodded, then looked back at Reverend Mother. "The other matter I wanted to discuss with you concerns Rex here. He's an exceptionally well-trained police dog, but he's grown mellow over the years and now isn't as aggressive as we need him to be. Although he's not working out for us, he's a fine dog and I think he may be exactly what the monastery needs right now in light of what's going on out there."

"What do you mean?" Reverend Mother asked.

"If this dog can get into the monastery as easily as he seems to be able to do, it's possible that a human intruder is doing likewise. If that's the case, Rex is the best deterrent I can think of. I'm sure the dog will protect you and the sisters."

"Do you think *we're* in danger? Please be very honest, Sheriff. We need to know the truth." Reverend Mother leaned forward, insistent.

"I'm not sure if anyone else is in danger, but none of us can afford to disregard the possibility that Father Anselm's death was caused by an intruder. Under the circumstances, a dog like Rex is a good asset for you all to have on your side."

Reverend Mother considered the sheriff's words for several moments, her eyes closed. "All right," she said at last, looking first at the sheriff, then at Sister Agatha. "Rex is welcome to make his home with us."

"I think you've made the right decision. But there's one more thing. Rex is a police dog and will require training with a new handler. Since he seems fond of Sister Agatha, you might consider letting her be the one who works—" He stopped speaking as bells began ringing.

Reverend Mother waited until the bells had stopped before answering. "Done. Now, if you have no further need for me, the bells are calling me to Terce, the prayers for the third hour."

As she stood and left, they heard the soft swish of Reverend

Mother's habit and the click of her rosary beads, but her footsteps were silent.

"Looks like you've got yourselves a dog," Tom said, handing Sister Agatha the leash.

As she took it, Reverend Mother suddenly reappeared at the grille, startling both of them. "By the way, since we already have one Rex here—Our Lord—we'll have to change the dog's name. I was thinking of Pax."

"That shouldn't be a problem," Sheriff Green said. "The sound is similar. He's smart and will catch on quickly."

"Pax it is, then, Mother," Sister Agatha said, and looked down at the dog who was sitting beside her. "You're now a member of our monastery, Brother Pax, and you'll be the guardian of the gate."

The dog looked first at the sheriff, then back at Sister Agatha, then lay down by her feet.

"So it's done," Tom Green said with a satisfied nod. "I better get going. I have an appointment with the rectory housekeeper."

As he left, Sister Agatha heard Sister Bernarda come up behind her. "Your charges, our novice and postulant, will soon be waiting for you at the scriptorium."

"Thank you for the reminder." Sister Agatha stood. "Come, Pax. As our newly appointed brother and guardian, you're welcome to share the enclosure with us."

6

D URING CLASS, SISTER AGATHA TOOK THE OPPORTUNITY TO talk to Celia alone. "I've been thinking a lot about Father Anselm lately, Celia, and there's a question I've been meaning to ask you. Did you know Father Anselm? If I remember correctly, he seemed to think so," she said, deliberately keeping her tone casual.

"He was our parish priest. I went to confession with him lots of times. But around town I was always known as Celia, Mother. You can ask anyone."

"Then why were you so upset when you saw him?"

She hesitated before answering. "Father was an important part of this monastery. I wanted to make a good impression. But then I dropped the box, remember, Mother Mistress? And since I'd already made you angry with me that morning, the last thing I wanted was to get in trouble again."

It seemed reasonable, and she knew that everything Celia had said was true, but instinct told her that there was more the postulant wasn't telling her. She let the matter drop for now. Pressing her now based only on her own speculations would get her nowhere.

After her scheduled classes with the novice and the postulant,

Sister Agatha took Pax to the patio behind the kitchen and went to see Reverend Mother.

"Mother, with your permission, I'd like to go to Bernalillo and pay Joan Sanchez a visit," she said, and explained what Frances Williams had told her.

"Does she live in a safe neighborhood? I'm told that some sections of town are getting dangerous."

"The neighborhood isn't the finest, but I'll be all right, Mother. I'm positive."

Reverend Mother considered it. "You may go, but not alone. Take the dog with you."

"Mother, we don't have the Antichrysler at the moment."

"But the motorcycle has a sidecar. That was one of your selling points, wasn't it?" Her eyes twinkled. "Don't dogs like hanging their heads out of car windows anymore and letting their ears flap around in the wind?"

Sister Agatha smiled. "You're right, Mother, I'll see how Pax likes the sidecar."

"You're not to go alone if Pax won't cooperate." Seeing Sister Agatha nod, she continued. "Before you leave, I'd like you to stop by your cell. You'll find a pair of long pants we've set aside that should fit you. They're for you to wear under your habit while on the motorcycle."

"Thank you, Mother." Her habit was loose and long, and still covered her legs when she rode. Nothing really showed, so she hadn't bothered to think about it, except to enjoy the wind on her legs. But this was one concession she knew she had to make.

"A word of caution," Reverend Mother added at last. "The sheriff will also want to talk to Mrs. Sanchez, I'm sure. He won't like the idea of you beating him to the punch."

She smiled slowly. "But I'm not going as an investigator. I'm simply going to talk to people who knew Father Anselm and were here when it happened so I can offer comfort and let them know about the funeral services. Of course, I'll need to find out from Frances Williams what arrangements have been made for the funeral—

unless you already know, Mother." She looked at the abbess questioningly.

Reverend Mother nodded. "The service will be the day after tomorrow at ten-thirty A.M. at the parish church. He'll be buried in St. Augustine's cemetery directly afterwards."

"That must mean that the new priest is finally on his way."

"It does. Father Mahoney is said to be eager to leave Santa Fe and come to serve us here in less affluent surroundings."

It never ceased to amaze her how Reverend Mother, who never left the enclosure, knew so much about the community. The direct line to her desk must have been ringing off the hook lately, though only other clergy had that number.

"Does he know the circumstances surrounding Father Anselm's death?"

Reverend Mother nodded once. "From what I was told, he's not in the least bit concerned. He used to be a professional wrestler. His stage name, if you will, was Apocalypse Now. I understand he traveled quite a bit, and was quite well-known to those who appreciate that type of entertainment. Father Mahoney assured His Excellency that if anyone can take care of himself, he can."

Sister Agatha nearly laughed. "If you don't need me anymore then, Mother, I'll be on my way."

Sister Agatha went to her cell, and retrieved what turned out to be a pair of large black slacks with an elastic waistband—undoubtedly part of a clothing donation meant for St. Francis' Pantry and rerouted for repairs to the monastery.

Sister Agatha then went to get Pax and, after a brief search, found him with Sister Ignatius in the library.

"He was outside." Sister Ignatius gave her one of her laser-sharp looks. "This animal was sent to us from God. He should be inside with us, and we should be grateful for his company."

"We are, but he needs to be outside some of the time," Sister Agatha said, bending down to pet him. "If you don't mind, I'm going to take him with me now. Mother wants him to accompany me on an errand to town."

"Then he'll be your protector while you're away from the monastery."

"That's the idea." Sister Agatha thought about putting the leash on the animal, but decided that could wait. With his training as a police dog, she could trust him to stay close. Sticking it in her pocket, she went outside with Pax. Before she could even point to the sidecar, the dog jumped in and made himself comfortable, turning around to look forward, and poking his head around the small curved windscreen. She looked at the dog and toyed with the idea of putting a helmet and goggles on him, then laughed. "Okay, Pax, hang on, and I sure hope you don't mind bugs in your teeth."

As they passed through a section of San Felipe Pueblo, people stopped what they were doing and watched her and Pax. Some laughed, some looked appalled, but there was no way to avoid attention when a nun was traveling on a motorcycle with a dog the size of Pax riding in the sidecar. Trying to surreptitiously follow a suspect would be impossible. All the more reason to leave the dangerous work to Sheriff Green, she realized.

Twenty minutes later, she reached Mrs. Sanchez's home a few blocks west of Camino del Pueblo. At one time, she was sure this house had been beautiful. Now the two-story frame house with a corrugated metal roof needed paint, a new screen door, and some serious landscaping. Tumbleweeds and goatheads competed for ground. The picket fence was full of gaps, and several slats were broken, dangling in place.

As she parked at the curb and switched off the engine, Mrs. Sanchez, a woman in her late thirties, came out onto the wooden porch. Unlike the conservative dark clothes she wore to church, Mrs. Sanchez was wearing tight jeans and a long, faded pink T-shirt that fit her snugly. She had long, dark hair fastened in a ponytail at the base of her neck.

She was beautiful, but there was a hard edge about her that put Sister Agatha on her guard. She took Pax with her on the leash walking up the bindweed-choked sidewalk to the porch.

"Hello, Sister Agatha, isn't it? What brings you here on a flashy motorcycle with a big dog?" she added, laughing.

"The motorcycle is a recent donation, and so is Brother Pax. Do you like dogs?"

Mrs. Sanchez leaned down to pet him. "Bring him inside with you if you want. It's too hot to stay out here boiling in the sun." As they sat down in the air-conditioned room, Joan Sanchez watched Sister Agatha curiously. "Now tell me, Sister. What brings you to my house?"

"I came to let you know about Father Anselm's funeral services."

Mrs. Sanchez bit at her lip nervously. "When is it going to be held?"

"The day after tomorrow," she said and gave Mrs. Sanchez the details.

"I still can't believe he's dead," Joan said, her voice trembling. "But they always say the good die young."

"I understand your name appeared in Father's appointment book at regular intervals. Were you in counseling with Father?"

"My husband died a few months ago," she said with a nod. "It's been a difficult time for me."

"It's never easy to accept the death of someone you love," she said, remembering Kevin's passing. "I'm glad Father was there for you when you needed him. And I'm sure our new priest, Father Mahoney, will do the same for you when he arrives."

"Father Anselm helped me a lot at first, but I guess he eventually got tired of my coming to him. For the past few weeks, I hadn't been able to get hold of him. I had the feeling he was deliberately avoiding me."

"Maybe there was another parishioner with a more pressing need."

"I don't know about that. All I can tell you for sure is that he really let me down," she said, standing up and beginning to pace. "I really thought I could trust him and count on him. He's a *priest*. But I should have known better. You can't count on anyone these days."

Their eyes met, and Sister felt a cold chill up her spine. There was something confused, and dangerous, in this woman's gaze. Joan Sanchez had clearly experienced deep pain, and hadn't quite emerged whole on the other side of that dark tunnel. People like that, in an attempt to ease the pain, often blamed others for what had happened to them, and sometimes the ones who tried to help them paid the highest price.

Sister Agatha was climbing back onto the Harley just as Sheriff Green pulled up and got out of his car. She left the engine off, and waited for him to approach. Anger was clearly etched on his features. If he had been a cartoon character, smoke would have been coming from his ears.

"I haven't even questioned this suspect yet, and here you are. You're interfering with a police investigation. Are you aware of that?"

"I only stopped by to inform Mrs. Sanchez that Father Anselm's funeral is going to be held the day after tomorrow."

"Oh, please. You don't expect me to believe that's all you talked about."

Rather than get into a useless argument, she took a deep breath and filled him in on what she'd learned. She made sure to mention that Mrs. Sanchez had been counseled by Father Anselm, and what Mrs. Sanchez had said about the priest avoiding her recently.

"Thanks for being honest with me, but I guess that's par for the course with a nun—even one on a Harley with a K-9 in the sidecar." He started to smile, but stopped himself and grew somber again. "But understand this—I will *not* tolerate you interfering in my case."

"I'm just helping."

"I don't need your help, but if you insist on meddling, then you better get one thing straight. *Anything* you learn, you turn over to me. Otherwise I'll slap you with a charge of obstruction of justice."

"Of course I'll share whatever I find out with you. We're not competing, Tom." She stopped and smiled. "And you should be glad that we're not, or it would be like it was in high school and college. You wouldn't have a chance."

"Oh, really?" The challenge made a familiar competitive spark light up in his eyes.

"Yes, really. I depend on God now. That gives me an even greater advantage." She smiled. "Mind you, there's no doubt that you're bigger and tougher in some ways than I am, but remember David and Goliath? News flash. The little guy won."

"Just so I'm clear—we *are* on the same side?"

"You bet," she said. "You want answers, and I want you to find them quickly so the monastery will be at peace again."

"All right. Now let me tell *you* something about Joan Sanchez that should encourage you to steer clear of her in the future. It's not exactly confidential. You could find it in the courthouse records if you looked hard enough. But I'd rather you avoid doing that, okay?"

"Sure."

"Her husband died in a shooting incident that the district attorney and the investigating officer concluded was 'accidental.' But I reviewed the evidence recently, and I've got to tell you, I wouldn't have closed the case so quickly. Her story was that Mr. Sanchez was teaching her how to load the weapon and the gun went off. But the report says she was covered with cuts and bruises. Mrs. Sanchez stated that she got the injuries when she fell, running back to their car to get help because they were in the middle of nowhere. But I don't buy it. The cuts weren't the kind one gets from tumbleweeds and rocks, and they were mostly on her face. She insisted she fell, but the profile screams battered wife."

"Why didn't the investigating officer look into it some more?"

"She'd never pressed charges, so there was nothing else he could do. He found no previous record that she was the victim of spousal abuse. A couple of neighbors said that they heard screaming some nights, but she never called the police or mentioned abuse to anyone."

"You think she killed him?"

"I can't prove it. But, in a word, yes. I think she set him up, too, so there'd be no witnesses."

"And you're linking that to Father Anselm's death . . . how?"

"Circumstantial evidence indicates she had a thing for him. Or maybe she said something during confession, then decided to get rid of her confidant."

Sister Agatha shook her head slowly. "There's nothing I'd like more than to know the killer has been found, but now that I think about it, I don't think she did it. I can see her wanting to rid herself of a man who was abusing her, but not one whose help she needed. It doesn't make sense. If she'd stopped calling Father all of a sudden, giving up on either herself or him, that would have been a different story."

"Poison is a weapon that requires premeditation and finesse, if you will, and it's a method often attributed to women. If Joan Sanchez killed her husband, then a second murder would have come easier to her. From what I've learned, I think it's possible she may have had a grievance against the Church. If that's the case, as a nun, you're also an enemy. Keep that in mind and steer clear of her, you hear?"

Sister Agatha knew he wanted her to give him her word, but she couldn't do that. She was in pursuit of answers, just as he was, and there was no telling what she might have to do in the future to get them. Quickly switching on the motorcycle, and patting Pax on the head, she gave the sheriff a thumbs-up. "Be seeing you!"

As she drove away, she caught the look on his face in her rearview mirror. His jaw was set and his expression hard. It didn't take a genius to know what was going through his mind. Although he had accepted the fact that he couldn't stop her from investigating, he would do everything in his power to keep her on a short leash.

7

KNOWING THAT EVERYONE CONNECTED TO THE DEAD PRIEST was a potential suspect, Sister Agatha headed next to the Catholic school where Father Anselm had been headmaster.

On the way, she saw a light-colored vehicle parked by the side of the road. No one was behind the wheel and no one seemed to be about. She glanced around, wondering if someone needed help, but seeing no one, drove past it, never giving it another thought. A second later, glancing back one last time in her rearview mirror, she caught a glimpse of the sedan pulling out behind her onto the road.

Surprised, she watched it for a second. It didn't make sense unless the driver had ducked down to avoid being seen as she'd driven by. The theory made her uneasy, but the fact that he now appeared to be keeping pace with her, staying about three car lengths behind, supported it.

Not knowing if she was being followed by a killer or simply someone curious about the bike, she decided to make a random change in her course. She'd take a side road and see if the vehicle stayed with her.

"Hang on, Pax." She quickly turned up a side road without signaling.

Moving past a large alfalfa field, she looked into the rearview mirror and saw the other vehicle turning in the same direction.

Of course, it didn't mean for certain that the driver was tailing her. He or she could live at, or be visiting, a farm farther down the road. But, just to be sure, she made a left turn at the next intersection, which circled the big field, then roared back down to the highway, leaving a cloud of dust. When she reached the highway, there was no traffic coming and she quickly accelerated toward Bernalillo.

The car failed to catch up, and Sister Agatha breathed a sigh of relief. The whole incident had unnerved her. Pushing the cycle for more speed, she arrived at St. Charles Academy in record time.

Sister Agatha parked, then walked Pax to a shady spot beneath a pine in front of the administration building. Looping his leash loosely around a low branch, she petted the dog. "Stay here. I'll be back soon."

The dog lay down, perfectly content to stay on the cool grass.

As she cut across the yard, she saw that the schoolyard was nearly empty except for the basketball game taking place on a large concrete slab that served as the court. A gym teacher wearing shorts and a St. Charles T-shirt was coaching the kids. Sister Agatha realized that most of the students attending the abbreviated summer session were probably inside in class. Summer sessions were always busy here. Many of the parents weren't comfortable unless the kids were occupied during the summer, so St. Charles always had an active summer session.

As she went into the main office, she saw Mrs. Romero, the assistant principal, inside one of the private offices.

Seeing Sister Agatha, Patsy waved at her to come in. "Hi, Sister! It's good to see you!"

"Do you have time to talk? I needed to ask you a few questions about Father Anselm," Sister said. Patsy was a heavyset woman in her fifties who seemed to struggle perpetually with her weight. Of course, the candy bars that she always seemed to have within easy reach were undoubtedly part of the reason for that.

"What do you need to know?" Patsy got up and shut the door, giving them some privacy.

"Were any children or parents here at St. Charles a thorn in Father Anselm's side?" Sister Agatha noticed a photograph of the priest on the wall. It had been draped in black cloth.

Mrs. Romero sat back down and followed Sister's gaze. "You're looking for an idea of who might have wanted to harm him?"

"We need to find the truth. The nuns are about to have their whole world turned upside down by a police investigation, and things will probably keep getting worse unless the sheriff clears things up or finds a suspect outside the monastery."

"Surely Tom Green doesn't think that the sisters had anything to do with Father's death!" Assistant Principal Romero shook her head, thought about it for a moment, then addressed her question. "Most of our students are really great, but kids are kids. Some, I swear, are only on this earth to serve as a reminder to their parents that sex comes at a price."

Sister Agatha chuckled. "What about the parents?" she asked.

"Those who send their kids to our academy and pay our tuition are usually very aware of what's going on in their kids' lives. That can create friction when they don't feel their kid scored high enough on a test, and that sort of thing. Parents want to know they're getting their money's worth. Parental pressure is less on the scholarship students, but that's probably because those kids are very highly motivated themselves. They know if they don't perform, they'll lose their scholarships."

Hearing the bell ring, she casually glanced out the window. "What in heaven's name—" Patsy rose to her feet quickly. "I'm sorry, Sister, I've got to get out there. The next period will be lunchtime for some and there's a motorcycle parked on the grounds with a huge dog beside it. I don't recognize either and some of our kids are already heading over there."

"Don't worry. It's ours—the dog included," Sister Agatha said, and Patsy turned around in surprise. "Our old car is at Mr. Gonzales's garage again, its second home, apparently. That beautiful red motorcycle and sidecar was a donation. It was originally intended for Bobby Gonzales, but his parents gave it to the monastery so we'd have some transportation while our car is being repaired. It's been a lifesaver."

"The keys aren't in it, are they, Sister?"

"Absolutely not," Sister Agatha said, holding them up by one finger. "And Pax won't hurt anyone. Let me go out there. I've taken up enough of your time. But call me if you think of anyone who might have had a grudge against Father Anselm."

"Sure thing, Sister Agatha."

As she walked across the schoolyard, she saw the kids were hesitant to approach Pax. Although the dog was lying down, perfectly calm, his size alone was enough to make most of them cautious.

Two teenaged girls crouched down and tentatively began to pet him. Pax's tail began wagging furiously.

"Hello, girls," Sister Agatha greeted.

"Sister Agatha, is this *your* dog? He's so beautiful!" the tall black-haired girl with almond eyes said.

"Not mine, the monastery's."

"If you come to substitute teach this summer, will you bring him?"

Substitute teaching was a task Reverend Mother had assigned her as a way to help the parochial school, but she hated doing it. It was too much a link to her past. "I don't know, I really hadn't thought about it."

"Wow, does that Harley belong to the sisters too?" said a heavyset boy wearing black-framed glasses and a purple St. Charles T-shirt. She thought she recognized him from a class she'd taught for the gifted program, and recalled his name as Jason. "It's awesome!"

"It sure is. And, yes, the motorcycle belongs to the monastery as well."

"Wow. A nuncycle. Sister, you need boots and a black leather jacket to ride that thing," Jason said. "With redundant zippers and metal studs."

She laughed. "No, I don't think the Vatican would authorize that radical change in the habit."

As they clustered around, others joining the group, she saw a fragile-looking boy in a baggy gray knit shirt pushed aside roughly. "Hey, newbee, step aside." A tall junior or senior wearing a football jersey growled, then laughed when his victim nearly fell.

"Show some respect for others!" Sister Agatha said firmly, turning and looking the bully right in the eye. Pax stood and came up behind her, staring at the teen as well. He bared his teeth but remained silent.

"Sorry, kid," the bully mumbled. "Sorry, Sister Agatha."

The smaller boy gave her a grateful smile, and she turned her attention back to Jason, who was asking her something about the motorcycle. By the time she turned back around, the boy who'd been shoved was gone. Most of the other students were beginning to wander off as well, heading to their cars or beginning to walk home.

"Who's the boy in the gray shirt? I don't recall seeing him before." Sister Agatha asked the girl closest to her.

"That's Timmy something, Johnson maybe. He's new at St. Charles. I heard that all the medications he takes for asthma have stunted his growth. He doesn't take PE, and a few of the bullies give him a hard time about that, but that's probably because he's smarter than all of them put together. He has a full scholarship, I think."

Sister Agatha's heart filled with sympathy. Kids could be unbelievably cruel without giving it a single thought.

Grabbing her helmet, Sister gave Pax the command to get into the sidecar. As the kids watched, she roared away on the motorcycle.

She found Timmy at the end of the school grounds. He was walking very slowly, and from the movement of his shoulders she suspected he was having problems breathing. "Would you like a ride home, Timothy?"

He breathed heavily and nodded. "Thanks. I'm having some problems right now." He brought out a white inhaler, used it, then climbed up behind her onto the big saddle. Sister handed him her helmet, and made a mental note to find a second one for passengers.

"Put this on, Timothy. You can leave the visor up to make breathing easier. But snap on the chin strap, okay?"

He nodded, then put on the helmet. It was too big, and he

could barely see out because it rode so low on his head, but his mouth and nose weren't blocked.

"Where's home?"

"It's not far, Sister, but on a hot day like today it takes me a while." He gave her directions that she knew led to a poor neighborhood close to the railroad tracks.

Sister Agatha drove slowly, hoping that the ride and fresh air would help the boy.

Following his directions, they quickly arrived at a run-down trailer home. No one seemed around.

"Is someone here in case you have a problem with your asthma?"

He climbed off, then handed her the helmet. "I can take care of myself, Sister. We have a phone, and I can call my mom at work."

Somehow the assurance from this frail boy didn't convince her. "Is there anything I can do?" she asked, noting that his breathing seemed better, but was still labored. She didn't want to leave unless he was out of danger.

"I'll be fine once I take my afternoon pill. I had a chocolate bar, and chocolate doesn't like me very much—particularly with peanuts."

"But sometimes the temptation is too much, huh?"

He smiled broadly. "You got it, Sister." He paused, then looked at her, showing a little red on his cheeks that she knew came from embarrassment. "You did something nice for me, so now I'd like to do something for you. I've seen your motorcycle before. It used to belong to Bobby Gonzales. He said he was going to give it away to a guy he owed money to, then tell his dad about it later. Now Bobby is worried because his dad gave it away, and he can't give the guy the motorcycle like he promised. From what I hear, the guy's really angry, and wants the Harley."

"Who's the man wanting the bike?"

Timothy shook his head. "I can't tell you, Sister. I wasn't supposed to know about it anyway. I just heard it by accident. And Bobby knows I know. If word gets out, he knows where I live. Just be careful riding around after dark." He glanced at Pax. "It's a good

thing you have that dog with you. He's almost as dangerous as I am."
Timothy tried a tough expression, but it wouldn't sell.

Sister glanced back at Pax. He was panting and his fangs gleamed.

"Timothy, you have to tell me the man's name, particularly if he's as bad as you say."

"He *is* bad, Sister, and please don't tell anyone what I said. I can take care of myself at school, but I worry about my mom. And one more thing. Thanks for not calling me Timmy. I hate that stupid name."

Sister Agatha watched the boy go inside, lost in thought. She was glad to hear the click as he locked the door behind himself. She wondered if his story about the motorcycle had just been something made up or misinterpreted by a lonely little boy. She didn't think so, but there was clearly no way for her to substantiate it right now without putting someone else on the spot. If she told Reverend Mother the Harley was a source of danger, she'd be forbidden to use the motorcycle, and that would place an enormous hardship on the sisters who'd be left without any transportation at all. Maybe she could find a way to ask Mr. Gonzales about it when she checked up on the Antichrysler.

As she drove back to the monastery, she kept an eye out for the car that had followed her before, but it never appeared. Thanking God for the peaceful ride home, she wondered if the driver she'd seen had been the man who'd wanted Bobby's motorcycle.

When she pulled through the monastery's gates a short time later, she was surprised to see Sister Bernarda rushing out. "We have an emergency. Sister Gertrude is very sick. I've called an ambulance."

Sister Agatha rushed inside the enclosure, fear biting at her. "What happened?"

"The choir nuns were in the middle of chanting Divine Office when Sister doubled over and fell to her knees. Sister Eugenia helped her back inside, and they're both in the infirmary right now. Though Sister Gertrude insists she's fine now, she'll need to be taken to a hospital for an examination." Sister Bernarda looked at the motorcycle. "But, obviously, not in that. Even in the sidecar, she'll be terrified."

"An ambulance will take forever. They're never quick to respond to people outside the city. Let me call over to St. Charles Academy. Someone might still be there, and be able to give us a ride."

Fifteen minutes later, with Patsy Romero driving, Sister Agatha and Sister Gertrude were on their way in the assistant principal's minivan. Sister Gertrude kept her eyes closed, praying the rosary.

"How's she doing?" Patsy asked, looking in the rearview mirror.

The passing scenery was going by at a blur. Sister Agatha realized that Patsy must have been going eighty miles per hour or more down the interstate. Sister Agatha started to tell her to slow down, but after glancing at Sister Gertrude's face, decided that speed was a good idea.

"She'll be fine," Sister Agatha said calmly. "Our Lady will help her. Sister Gertrude has a great devotion to the Blessed Mother."

Finished with her rosary, Sister Gertrude opened her eyes. "The pain's gone now. I'm all right. We can go back to the monastery."

"We have to get you checked out, Your Charity," Sister Agatha said. "To serve God well, you need your health." She knew from experience that it was the only argument that had even a remote chance with Sister Gertrude. "But, with luck, we'll be back home soon."

As they rode on in silence, Sister Agatha prayed for her. It was very hard for cloistered nuns to leave the enclosure. The trip itself was bound to tax Sister's heart. Sister Gertrude was a stern nun who seldom spoke to anyone except when absolutely necessary. Her motto was that one couldn't listen to God if one's own mouth was operating at the same time.

"Don't worry, Sister. I'll be with you every step of the way," she said. "You'll be fine."

"I'm not afraid of dying. I'm afraid of going to the hospital."

"I don't blame you, Sister. I don't trust any profession where people occasionally wear masks like robbers," Sister Agatha said, teasing her.

Sister Gertrude almost smiled, and as far as Sister Agatha was concerned, that qualified as a miracle.

As silence stretched between them, Sister Agatha considered asking Patsy if she'd given any more thought to what she'd asked her earlier concerning Father's possible enemies. But, as she glanced at Sister Gertrude's drawn face, she quickly discarded the idea. Talking about something like that would only upset Sister Gertrude even more.

When they arrived at the satellite Catholic hospital on Albuquerque's west side, nurses came out to meet them, thanks to Sister Bernarda's call. As they wheeled Sister Gertrude to the examining room, Sister Agatha made sure that she stayed close by. She knew that seeing an extern nearby was one of the most comforting things for a cloistered nun who'd been forced to leave her beloved monastery.

Fortunately, there were other nuns and a priest at this hospital as well, and they would be stopping by to offer comfort and prayers, no doubt.

After the doctor had conducted several tests, he asked Sister Agatha to meet him in his office. Leaving Sister Gertrude to rest, Sister Agatha met Dr. Cassidy, a parishioner who was on staff at the hospital and knew all the nuns. He was tall, with salt-and-pepper hair and eyeglasses that were so thick Sister Agatha often wondered how the bridge of his nose could sustain the weight.

"I just received a very strange call from Sheriff Green in Bernalillo."

So Tom had heard already . . . not that she should have been surprised. "Let me guess. He wanted to know if Sister Gertrude had been poisoned?"

"Correct."

"She wasn't, was she?"

"We've ordered tests that will answer that question. But I suspect that she had a mild heart attack. You heard her tell me that she's been having chest pains for months now."

"She'd never mentioned that before now to anyone that I know of," Sister Agatha said. "But we've all been under a lot of stress lately."

"I'd like to keep Sister here overnight for observation and run a few more tests this evening, but unless she has another episode, you'll be able to take her home tomorrow. For now, I've arranged for her to be placed in a private room and I've notified our chaplain so he can pay her a visit."

"Thank you, Doctor. We appreciate it."

Sister Agatha knew it would be a long night. As long as Sister Gertrude was here, she would remain with her. As she left Dr. Cassidy's office to go tell Sister the news, she saw Sheriff Green striding down the hall toward her.

"How's Sister Gertrude doing?"

"Better, thanks."

"From what I've been able to gather so far, it doesn't look like she was poisoned. But if the tests come back with suspicious results, I'm going to get a search warrant and look through that entire monastery with a fine-tooth comb."

"It's not poisoning, based upon what the doctor just told me." She paused, gathering her thoughts. "I know you've been given permission to enter the cloister, but unless you absolutely have to, I sure wish you wouldn't. The nuns are having a really hard time with all this. To see you coming into the cloister, searching for a killer . . ." She paused, then added, "The nuns really need you to give them a break."

"You should look at it another way. If I went into the enclosure and found the evidence I need, only one person would lose—the murderer."

"You're wrong. All the nuns have already lost. When you or your deputies come to the monastery, it feels like our enclosure— our way of life—is under siege."

"The killer is responsible for disrupting your lives, not the police. We're just part of the cleanup."

She watched Tom walk away, wishing there was something more

she could have said to make him understand. Yet she knew duty had locked him on his course. But she had her own responsibilities—to the nuns and the monastery. She'd help him find the killer, but not at the expense of the innocent.

8

S ISTER AGATHA WOKE UP TO THE SOUND OF THE MORNING-
shift nurse coming in to check on Sister Gertrude. As she
straightened out in her chair, the muscles in her back screamed
in pain.

"I bet you're regretting not sleeping in the bed down the hall
now," the nurse said sympathetically, taking Sister Gertrude's vital
signs with brisk efficiency, and writing down the results on a clip-
board.

"We each have our duties," Sister Agatha said, wishing she had
half a dozen aspirins. She hadn't taken any of her arthritis medication and her joints were all stiff and sore.

The nurse smiled, wished them both a good morning, and
quickly disappeared. Five minutes later a perky brunette in her twenties, whose name tag read Maria Leahy brought a breakfast tray for
Sister Gertrude that included a dish of yogurt. "Now that you're
away from the monastery, you should take advantage and indulge
yourself a bit!" she said cheerfully.

Sister Gertrude looked at the young woman as if she'd suddenly
grown two heads.

Sister Agatha glanced at Sister Gertrude, smiled and shrugged
wordlessly. For some odd reason, people always assumed that leaving

the monastery was like a vacation for a nun. They just didn't understand that the cloister was the world they loved. Everything in there spelled order, stability, and security to the nuns. It was the same yesterday, today, and tomorrow. Out here in mainstream society there were too few people who considered their life's work a source of happiness and satisfaction, and even fewer who'd given their hearts to the professions they'd chosen. They existed from day to day, marking time without a goal that would give their lives meaning and carry them beyond their time of death. And yet they felt sorry for the nuns!

As the doctor came in to further examine Sister Gertrude, Sister Agatha stepped out into the hall, giving Sister Gertrude her privacy. Doctors, like priests, were in positions of trust. Rosary in hand, she waited in the corridor until the doctor finally emerged.

"How is she doing, Doctor? Will she be released today?"

"She seems fine. You can take her home. To be perfectly honest, I think she'll rest easier at the monastery. And there's been a newspaper reporter nosing around. I think she wants to do a story about the cloistered nuns at the monastery and link them to Father Anselm's death."

"There is no link," she said coldly. "But if the reporter insists on pursuing this, she must talk to Reverend Mother first. I won't have anyone bothering a sister who's here because she had a problem with her heart."

"Agreed. I just hope she doesn't try to slip past the desk and find Sister's room."

"Trust me, Doc, even if she got past the desk, she'd still have to go through me, and I'd make that attempt an experience she'd never forget."

He laughed. "I believe that, Sister. You and Sister Bernarda are very protective of the cloistered nuns."

"They're family."

He nodded slowly. "Once she's back in the monastery, make sure she gets lots of rest and that she eats a balanced diet and drink plenty of liquids. No fasting."

"It's Ordinary Time now, not like during Lent. None of us is fasting."

"All right. I'll order the discharge paperwork."

"Before you go, can you tell me if the blood tests came back?"

He nodded. "It wasn't poisoning."

Sister Agatha went to the desk and asked where she could make a private call. She didn't want to use the phone in Sister Gertrude's room in case Sister Bernarda had any news or questions about the investigation that required a response from her. She wouldn't take a chance of upsetting Sister Gertrude right now.

The nurse looked both ways, said something about "not supposed to do this," then handed her a phone and pushed the number nine. Sister Agatha thanked the nurse and dialed. Sister Bernarda answered after the second ring.

"Sister Gertrude can come home this morning, so we'll be ready to head back as soon as we can find transportation. Will you tell Reverend Mother?"

"Of course." There was a pause. "Sister Mary Lazarus was sleep-walking again last night. I found her in the kitchen and led her back to her cell."

"That's usually all it requires," Sister Agatha answered.

"And believe it or not, I left Pax in your cell, but when I led Sister back to her cell I saw the dog was wandering around outside. I didn't call him back inside. I was too tired. Yet he was back in your cell this morning again like it had never happened."

"We never fixed that screen in the hall."

"It wasn't dislodged, but the screen itself is so torn . . . I don't know, maybe that *is* his doggie door." She paused. "By the way, Frank Walters is here again, fixing two of the computers. He says we need to upgrade soon."

Sister Agatha sighed. "Maybe we can get someone to donate what's needed."

"Well, I can certainly put prayer power to work on that."

"Who's in the scriptorium now with Mr. Walters?"

"No one, but Sister Mary Lazarus is sitting in the hall just outside the scriptorium. She's been told she's not to talk to Mr. Walters. If he needs something, or if he's ready to be escorted back out, she'll come get me. If Sister Mary Lazarus *is* seriously considering being an extern nun, she might as well get used to the extra duties."

Sister Agatha paused. "I'm sorry, Your Charity. I haven't been much help to you lately, have I?"

"You're doing what we need you to do—for all of us."

"Agreed." Seeing a nurse stop at the counter and look in her direction, she made a hand gesture telling her she wouldn't be long. "I think they want me to get off this phone. Can you find someone with a car to give us a ride?" Sister Agatha asked. "Patsy won't mind, if she's free."

"I'll take care of it. Don't you give it another thought."

It was over an hour before their ride arrived. It was Sister Bernarda driving—of all things—the Antichrysler. It was still burning oil and sputtering, but it ran.

"Mr. Gonzales heard about Sister Gertrude yesterday, and he stuffed on a muffler and fixed the car as best he could with salvaged parts," Sister Bernarda explained. "It'll still need a complete overhaul, but because of everything that's happened, he's offered to come to the monastery when he can and work on it there. That way we'll have it available in case of a similar emergency."

As they passed through the monastery gate, she saw Sheriff Green's car in the compound. He was walking along the wall beside the gate and feeling the adobe with his hand, as if he were hoping to find a hidden opening.

"Let me out here," she asked, then looked at Sister Gertrude. "Sister Bernarda will help you inside, Your Charity."

"Stop treating me like an invalid. I'm fine."

"Yes, Your Charity." Sister Agatha glanced at Sister Bernarda. "How long has the sheriff been here?"

"Since eight o'clock, but before I left, I warned him that the parlor doors would be locked until I got back. He said he'd wait for you if he needed to go inside, but I think he's really hoping it won't be necessary."

"I'll try to find out what's going on."

"Hopefully he'll be gone soon. Our new chaplain, Father Mahoney, is arriving in about an hour. He'll be doing the rededication and reconsecration ceremony for the chapel. The archbishop had wanted to do this himself and kept hoping that his doctor would say that he was finally well enough to travel, but the doctor's holding firm."

"Is Frank Walters still here?"

"No, he left just before I did. He reminded us to back up our work on floppies every time we finish a file. He's still not sure what's making the computers crash so frequently."

"Will you greet Father Mahoney when he arrives and make sure the vestments he needs are ready? Father Anselm's alb was taken by the police, so we need to get another one out from the storage closet. As sacristan, I should do that, but I have to speak to Sheriff Green, so I can't be sure I'll get to it in time."

Sister Bernarda agreed and Sister Agatha went to join the sheriff. She hoped she'd be able to help him and, at the same time, hurry him along. She really wanted to attend the rededication ceremony, but Reverend Mother had asked her to give this case priority. If she needed to escort the sheriff inside, or if he needed to ask her any questions, she'd have to remain at his disposal. As it had been so often in the past, the vow of obedience was the one she found hardest to honor.

"Hello, Tom. Have you found anything interesting?" Sister Agatha asked, joining him. She noted a bruise on his face below his eye, but didn't mention it, choosing to wait and see if he said anything.

He shook his head. "This place looks to be as secure as Fort Knox."

"Yet Pax goes in and out as if we had a revolving door." She told him what Sister Bernarda had said.

"I don't get it. He not only gets into the grounds but he now has his own doggie door somewhere to let him in and out of the monastery building itself. It's too bad I can't blame the turn," he added half jokingly. "But he'd never be able to open it."

"Or fit in it," Sister Agatha said, laughing.

She took a deep breath, then let it out slowly. "I've been thinking a lot about this, Tom, and I've got a new theory."

"Let's hear it."

"I'm not thrilled about this, but here it is. I think one of the sisters, hoping to make you focus on the possibility of an intruder, is letting the dog in and out. The keys to the front door are left on a hook in the parlor at night." She leaned against the wall, feeling its solidity against her back, and absently fingered her rosary beads, noting again the mark on the sheriff's face. "It may not be right, but I'm sure whoever is doing it is simply trying to protect the others."

"In a warped way, that makes sense," he conceded. He lapsed into a thoughtful silence.

She knew he was weighing the other possibility—that one of the nuns was inviting an intruder in, but he didn't say anything and she was grateful for that. It would have been awkward, to say the least, to discuss that possibility with him.

"Tell me something. How long is the alb stored in that drawer generally? I'm sure it has to be laundered and pressed at times."

Noting the abrupt change in subject, she wondered where this was heading. "I usually take it to Sister Clothilde to wash and press every Sunday after Mass. We have two sets, so another is put in its place in the drawer you saw and they're rotated that way."

"Then, since Father said his last Mass on Monday, the alb he used had only been there overnight?"

"Yes, but what are you getting at?"

"The toxicology reports were faxed to me this morning—which, by the way, should tell you how important this case has become. These things can take weeks, but in this case, it's taken only five days."

"What did you find out?" she asked, her heart hammering inside her chest.

"Father Anselm didn't ingest the poison. He absorbed it through his skin. A test of fibers from the alb's collar show that the garment had been contaminated with a concentrated extract made from monkshood."

"I don't believe it."

"It's true. So unless we can figure out how an intruder could have gotten into the monastery to doctor the alb, then one of the nuns *has* to be responsible. And there's something else you should know. The amount of poison Father Anselm took in would not normally have been fatal to a person his age and size. What caused his death was that the aconite initially stimulated, then paralyzed, his already weakened heart. Father Anselm, according to the medical examiner who did the autopsy, had an undiagnosed heart condition."

Anger over Father's senseless murder nearly choked the breath out of her. She tried to calm down and remember she was a nun, and that she was supposed to love others as herself. Hatred for an enemy, no matter how justified, wasn't an acceptable option.

"I have to admit, it sounds like a malicious trick—a dangerous stunt gone wrong—not premeditated murder. None of our sisters would ever do such a thing. I'd stake my life on it," she said with absolute conviction.

"It sounds more like a high school prank to me, like doctoring cookies with a laxative, but the nuns would have spotted a stranger in here, even a kid." Tom shook his head. "I need a suspect who had the opportunity to handle the alb, contaminate it, then put it away again. It would have had to be someone who knew where such things were kept—a nun, or a relative, or someone who prayed alone in the chapel and got a chance to sneak around. Maybe even an altar boy—or someone who was an altar boy once. Or, if not that, then we've got to find how an intruder could get in here and leave before being seen."

"We seldom have altar boys but our chapel is always open during the day, as well as the gate. Maybe someone did go into the sacristy unnoticed, but our chapel is never left unattended. The Blessed Sacrament is kept out for adoration during the day. One of us is always there—except after we lock up, of course, at night"

"Maybe someone got hold of the key. You said it's kept out on a hook in the public parlor. There's an answer, Sister, and we better find it soon. Unfortunately, the only suspects I have right now are those known to have been around the alb the day of the murder—you and that postulant, Celia."

"Celia didn't harm anyone, and neither did I," she said firmly.

"I'll still have to question Celia again—at the station if necessary."

"If you take her out of the monastery, you'll delay her formation. When she returns to us, that will be considered her first day as a postulant and the almost three months she's already spent with us won't count toward the twelve months her postulancy requires. So before you tamper with her future, Tom, think of the way this is shaping up. In addition to being our chaplain, Father Anselm was also the headmaster of St. Charles Academy. This whole business screams that a kid did it. Your test results agree that this wasn't meant to cause his death—just to make him sick. It appears to be a prank that turned lethal. From the beginning, we've been looking for a huge hole or entry spot—something an adult could use to gain access to the monastery. But if the culprit is a kid, any window might do, and climbing a tree is second nature to them."

"Okay. I'll go check out the kids at St. Charles next. Pray that I find a lead there. Otherwise, I'll come right back here and do what I have to do."

As she walked him back to his car, he glanced over at her. "Think back real carefully. How long was Celia alone with the alb—altogether?"

Memories crowded into her mind—of Celia rubbing her hands against her postulant's dress, of her own hands itching, of Celia's encounter with Father Anselm in St. Francis' Pantry. Then, in her mind's eye she saw the fear that had been on Celia's face as she'd picked up the fallen groceries and rushed away.

"Hello? Earth to Sister Agatha."

"Celia had just tried to help me out," she said, recounting how she'd found Celia repairing the alb the day Father Anselm died, sticking just to the facts and leaving out her speculation concerning Celia's reaction to the name Annie. It didn't seem right to subject Celia to some tough police questioning based only on her interpretation of what she'd seen. Celia's own explanation had been just as plausible. "But what you have to take into account is that when I found her, all she was doing was mending the garment," she added. "I didn't let her finish the first time. We both had other duties. So I sent her back just minutes before Mass."

"So she *could* have poisoned the cloth."

"With what? I'm her novice mistress. I know every inch of her cell, and how she spends every waking minute of her time." She shook her head. "No, it wasn't her, believe me. In fact I think it was already contaminated when she handled it. I remember her trying to wipe her hands and saying that they itched."

"Did you experience the same thing?"

"Yes. At the time, I put it down to an allergic reaction to the new starch I'd bought on sale for the monastery." She paused for several moments. "But you're missing a very important factor. That extract of monkshood had to be prepared. I mean boiled, distilled, evaporated, or whatever to make the concentration it did. Celia wouldn't have had the means to make such an elaborate preparation. If she had access to such equipment, she couldn't have kept it a secret from me."

"Maybe she found a hiding place and did it on her own time."

"There's no hiding anything from the novice mistress," Sister Agatha said with an amused smile, recalling her own days as a postulant and novice.

Tom remained silent for a few moments, then finally spoke. "If we could just find out where the monkshood came from, we'd have a big piece of the puzzle."

"It's not here on the grounds. The medical investigator searched for it himself."

Tom nodded and climbed into his vehicle. "I better get going. While I'm at St. Charles Academy, I'm going to see if any of the school science classes might have played with this type of thing— not monkshood extract exactly—but a distillation or extraction process." He looked up at her. "In the meantime, watch yourself. Trusting the wrong people could get you into a heap of trouble."

Sister Agatha knew that Tom meant the other nuns, but this

time, *he* was the one she didn't trust. He was under community pressure to close the case, and that meant he'd be likely to accept whatever answers presented themselves quickly. But she had a feeling that to find the right answers, they'd have to dig through layers and levels of truths.

Sister Agatha turned and headed to the chapel. The choir nuns were in their stalls, watching the reconsecration ceremony from behind their grille. She went in silently through the side door as their new chaplain began blessing the chapel with holy water.

His words rang clearly as she knelt down. " 'May God who is wonderful in all His works be with you all.' "

She prayed along with Father Mahoney, asking for wisdom and discernment, but fear underlined every syllable she uttered. She still wasn't sure if she should have told Tom about Celia's reaction to Father Anselm. She hadn't because she'd been almost certain he'd jump to the wrong conclusions, and everything she knew about the postulant assured her that Celia was incapable of harming Father. It was instinct, both as a nun and as a former professor, but she trusted it. Playing that kind of prank on Father Anselm would have been completely out of character for Celia. Whatever the postulant's secret was, it didn't include murder.

" 'If any man defile the temple of God, him shall God destroy; for the temple of God is holy,' " Father Mahoney prayed.

Nothing was simple now, but one thing rang continuously in her mind like an endless litany. She had to protect the monastery and her sisters in Christ from two threats—the murderer, and the lawman who was determined to stop at nothing to catch whoever that might be.

9

THE NUNS' VOICES ROSE AS ONE AS THEY CHANTED THE DI-
vine Office called None, which stood for the ninth canonical
hour of prayer—three in the afternoon, the time of day when
Jesus was said to have died.

Tranquility descended over the chapel. Somehow, no matter
what happened, she knew they would persevere. Even now, suspicion
hadn't poisoned the sisters' faith, or their sense of unity. There was
a rightness about their life that no amount of shadow could ever
destroy. Light was always the master of darkness.

The rebirth of their beloved chapel had renewed her hope.
Chaos had touched it, but now peace had been restored. Faith and
prayer were the shields of those here—it was a power few understood, but no one who'd ever seen it in action could discount its
capability.

Sister Agatha left the chapel long after the other nuns but, as
she reached the corridor, she saw that Reverend Mother had waited
for her.

"Now that we have the Antichrysler back, I'd like you to put
the motorcycle away until the next emergency," she said. "I've been
very worried about you driving that thing."

"Mother, the Antichrysler still sounds like an asthmatic trying to run the marathon. If we run our small errands with the motorcycle, we may be able to extend the life of the car longer. And the motorcycle is far cheaper to operate."

Reverend Mother took a deep breath, then let it out slowly. "All right, then. For now we'll continue to use it." After a brief pause, she added. "Are you or the sheriff any closer to finding answers?"

"The key may be in finding the source of the monkshood. I'm trying to come up with a way to do that."

"Follow through on it quickly, Sister. I don't want any more nuns falling ill because of the pressure we're all under."

Sister Agatha drove the Harley back to St. Charles with Pax in the sidecar, hoping to catch Patsy Romero. What she needed now was the name of three or four students—ones who excelled in biology or chemistry—and the name of any person, student or parent, who might have had a problem with Father.

As she arrived, she met Patsy coming out of the building with her purse and briefcase in hand, heading for the parking lot. Sister hurried toward her. "I'm so glad I caught you before you left!"

"Is something wrong?" She gave Pax a worried glance, but the dog sat beside Sister and yawned. "Are you sure that dog is safe? He's so big!"

"He's a teddy bear," Sister replied, placing her hand on the dog's head. "And he can be easily bribed. He even eats monastery oatmeal."

Patsy laughed. "I'll remember that."

"By the way, have you given any more thought to what I asked you?"

"About Father Anselm's enemies?" Seeing her nod, Patsy continued. "I can't think of any serious disputes Father had with anyone. He had disagreements with both parents and kids, but they were routine, not extreme."

"All right, then." Sister Agatha tried not let her disappointment show. "I need your help with something else. Can you recommend two or three kids who are responsible and good at botany who might be willing to help me find a particular species of plant?"

"I can be trusted," a quiet voice said from behind her. "And I've just finished a semester of botany."

She turned and saw Timothy Johnson. His breathing seemed much improved. "Hello, Timothy, what brought you back to school after hours?"

"A computer repair place in Santa Fe went out of business and we got the owner to donate his old computers—ones he'd used for spare parts—to our class. Now we're trying to put the drives, power supplies, and monitors together and get them running. With luck we may end up with three additional working computers. But I'm through for the day, so if you need something . . ."

"What I need will take a lot of walking."

"I do that every day. I walk to school and back. It's supposed to be good for me. I may be excused from PE, but I still need exercise."

"Okay, then," Sister Agatha said, unwilling to turn him down. "But we'll need a little more help."

"The kids coming out of the building now are all in the gifted program with Tim. They're hard workers and very responsible. They might be willing to help," Patsy said.

Jason, the tall, brown-haired boy who'd come to see Pax and the motorcycle was among them. His heavy glasses were always slipping down his nose, and he was constantly pushing them back up into place.

Sister Agatha explained that she needed to know where a particular plant was growing locally, wondering just how good the boy's vision was.

"Don't let the presence of glasses fool ya, Sister," he said, noting her scrutiny. "They call me Radar around here. I can spot anything once I know what I'm supposed to be looking for."

Two other boys and a girl who had come along with him nodded in agreement. The girl was small, nearly Timothy's size, with a pixie face and almond-shaped eyes. She'd also petted Pax the other day and the dog remembered.

After introducing herself as Grace, and offering to help with

Sister's project, she bent down to play with Pax. She was so full of energy that Sister wondered with a burst of nostalgia if she'd ever been *that* young and energetic herself.

"I'm supposedly hyperactive," Grace said quickly, "but I get my work done and everyone just puts up with the rest. If you need something done, Sister, I'm your girl."

"Okay. You're in," Sister Agatha said.

One of the boys was tall and extremely quiet. She'd heard the others call him Monk.

The remaining boy with them was of average height, but he looked as sturdy as a tree trunk. His eyes were dark and his hair almost jet black. He introduced himself and extended his hand. "I'm in too. Call me Chunk."

"I'll leave you, then, Sister," Patsy said.

Sister looked at them and smiled. This might just work out. "I need to find a particular plant," she said, describing monkshood in detail for them. She wished she'd had a picture, but the blue or white cap-shaped flowers were distinctive enough to give them a solid lead. "I'd like you to help me search for it around the community."

"That's a lot of ground to cover, Sister," Grace said. "I mean we can do it, but it'll take time."

"That's what killed Father Anselm, isn't it?" Monk asked.

"We heard he was poisoned," Grace said. "So you want to find out if the killer found the herb around here, or grew it in their backyard?"

They were sharp, she'd give them that. "Yes. I know it will take a lot of searching, but will you help me?"

"When do you want to do it? After school every day until we find it?"

"Yeah. Starting today if it won't get you in trouble with your parents. Just don't miss any classes, or break any of your family's rules, promise?"

The students nodded.

"Okay. We should split up and take sections. Shall we start right here in the school grounds?" Radar asked.

"Yeah, I suppose so. Does anyone have to go home right away?"

They looked at each other, then shook their heads.

"Great. Then let's get started." They paired up and Timothy stayed with her.

They searched the grounds carefully, even between the portable buildings and the caretaker's mobile home.

As the others searched some distance away, she took the chance to talk to Timothy again.

"Timothy, I know you're new to the community, but do you think any of the kids from St. Charles might have wanted to play a prank on Father Anselm and make him ill?"

He considered it before answering. "It's possible. Father didn't allow any of the guys to get away with causing trouble. He had strict rules. But, to be honest, most of the guys I've met here wouldn't know one plant from another, let alone know what to do with monkshood after they found it."

"Who would?"

"Grace. She's sharp. But she cried when she heard about Father Anselm. A lot of the kids did. The only other students here who know plants real well are Monk and me. The three of us all took botany last year, though I took it at a different school."

His words echoed in her mind as they continued to search. Most of the open spaces here on campus were barren except for gravel and silty river-bottom sand. There was a grass-covered soccer field, too, but after an hour of fruitless searching, they branched out and went into the neighborhood surrounding the school.

Time passed, and this time their search met with positive results. Monkshood was found growing in a half dozen places, including flower gardens, a small park in the downtown area, and in a low spot beside the railroad tracks. Unfortunately, none of the locations seemed to point to any individual who'd been at church lately. More important, a close inspection of each site had not uncovered signs that any of the plants had been harvested recently. Soon, everyone was gathered again at the school.

"Do you kids have transportation? Our work has been productive and I thank you all, but I'd like you to help me search one more area—right outside the monastery walls. But if anyone has to leave now, go ahead."

Nobody spoke up, so Radar said, "I've got my car. I can give the others a ride home after we're finished."

"Perfect. Pax and I will lead the way. Oh, and one more thing. Should you all happen to see any of the sisters, don't try to speak to them. Understood?"

They nodded.

Sister Agatha took the teens north down the old highway past Santa Anna Pueblo, then turned west along the gravel road that led to the monastery, and stopped outside the gate. Getting them organized, she assigned each team a specific area.

They scoured the ground within fifty feet of the monastery walls, even searching behind areas thick with native plants. They found several clusters of blazing stars, a wildflower that was common in certain areas of New Mexico. The blooms, before they were completely open, appeared to be cup-shaped, but that was as close as they got to finding the hood-shaped blue or white flower that characterized monkshood.

"I've got to get home soon, Sister," Grace said, glancing at her watch.

"Me, too," Monk added. "Mom and Dad like me home when they get off work."

"Then you guys better all get going."

"We'll continue to keep an eye out around town. If we find any more plants, we'll check to see if there's any sign that they've been harvested or tampered with in any way, and let you know," Grace said.

"I appreciate your help. And thanks for today," Sister Agatha said. As she heard the monastery bells ringing the call to Vespers, she felt glad that Evening Prayer could be said in the chapel again.

She waved as they drove away, lost in thought. If either Timothy or Grace or Monk had been responsible for the attack on Father Anselm, it sure wasn't obvious from their behavior today. Everyone had found monkshood and eagerly pointed the plants out to the others. They all seemed equally unlikely as troublemakers or pranksters. Everyone had searched hard, too, she'd made sure of that. Had she been hoping to find a suspect among the teenagers simply because she couldn't face the alternative—that the murderer was someone inside the monastery? She just didn't know anymore.

She shook free of the thought. The nuns weren't guilty, and the kids she'd just been with were clearly innocent as well. There had to be another answer. At least they hadn't found any monkshood close to the monastery itself.

As Sister Agatha went inside the monastery to join the sisters in prayer, she felt the weight of responsibility that rested on her shoulders. The nuns were all counting on her.

She remembered one of the rules of their order. If difficult or even impossible tasks were laid on a sister, she was to accept them in perfect obedience. The Rule of St. Benedict was as old as the origin of their order, and still stood as a marker of conduct in monasteries worldwide.

After Divine Office, she made her way to Reverend Mother's office, hoping to catch her there before she left for the refectory. The abbess would want to know what progress had been made.

She was halfway down the hall when she heard faint footsteps behind her. Turning her head, she saw Sister Eugenia, who cocked her head, motioning toward the infirmary.

Experience had taught her that to resist one of sister's requests was completely useless. Once they were in the infirmary, they were free to talk. Although the Great Silence wasn't in effect, silence was the natural order of the monastery, except in the infirmary. Here, the monastery's emphasis on silence took a backseat to compassion and charity.

"Sister Agatha, I saw you rubbing your hands during the Divine Office and I know you're in pain. Your arthritis won't go away on its own. Use the prescription you've been given. The pills will help keep the inflammation down—but for them to work, you've got to actually take them."

"They're so expensive, Sister, and make me vulnerable to infections after a while. And right now with Sister Gertrude having been hospitalized . . ."

"We'll get by, but you can't investigate and find answers if you're in so much pain you can't think clearly."

Sister Agatha looked at her hands and noted her swollen joints and the redness that had been developing all day. The vibration of the motorcycle had soothed them for a while, but now the pain had returned. They felt as if she'd dipped them in fire. "It looks worse than it is, Your Charity," she said, hoping to sound convincing.

"I doubt it. Take two now, with plenty of water, and come back tomorrow morning for two more. These have to be taken on a regular schedule, and at meals."

Sister Agatha stood up slowly, swallowed the pills she was handed, and washed them down with a tall glass of water. The medicine would work. It always did. She tried to allow the relief she'd feel once the pain was reduced to outweigh her guilt over the expense. "Thank you."

"I'll watch out for you, Sister Agatha, even if you don't watch out for yourself."

Sister Agatha smiled, then bowed slightly and left. She was on her way to the parlor to lock up for the night when she saw Pax pacing by the open door to the scriptorium. Seeing her, he sat and whined. Curious, Sister Agatha approached him and, as she did, heard the soft sounds of someone inside the room crying.

Whoever it was, maybe she could help. Glancing inside, she found Celia at her carrel on the far side of the room, her face down in her hands.

"Celia, what's wrong?" Sister Agatha asked, immediately going up to her.

"Mother Mistress, *everything* is! I can't seem to do anything right. When Sister Mary Lazarus is in here, the computers practically sing for her. But every time I try to do something, they go into cardiac arrest."

"It's not you. It's these old machines. You just have to reset them once they stop responding. And save your work often, otherwise you'll lose whatever you inputted since the last time you saved, every time it crashes."

"I'm trying, but I've been working on and off all afternoon, and

I've only managed to do three pages of work. Every time I touch this thing, it locks up and I have to turn if off and start all over again."

"Leave it for now, then. You're not supposed to be working after Vespers anyway. Come on, let's talk. I've been wanting some time to speak with you alone for a while now."

Celia stared at her lap and Sister Agatha pulled up a chair. "Celia, has life in this monastery been what you expected? Peace should fill your heart here, yet I sense you've been very troubled. If you came to us from a mistaken reason—like trying to escape something on the outside—you'll never find happiness here."

"I never thought of the monastery as a place to escape," she answered softly. "If I'd wanted a place to escape to, I'd have picked Tahiti, or at least a monastery with air-conditioning." She smiled, wiping away a tear. "But, to me, this monastery has always been like a fortress. I remember looking up the road every time I passed by on the highway when I was a child. Even back then I knew this would be my home someday. Our Lady of Hope called to me." She paused, then shook her head. "I'm not putting this very well."

"Yes, you are. Go on."

"Whenever I'd see nuns from other orders in the city, wearing their short habits and racing here and there like the laypeople, I always felt sorry for them. Their lives couldn't have the peace that came from living in cloister. It's hard to stay focused solely on God in the confusion of everyday life on the outside. But here, He's in everything we do, because our thoughts are centered on Him all day."

"That's a very idealistic outlook. There are problems here, too, remember, and not just those that require funds. I have a tendency to rattle my rosary beads—a habit that drives poor Sister Bernarda nearly crazy. And Sister Maria Victoria is a perfectionist when it comes to her sewing, and has to remind herself to be charitable with the ones who help her. Because we live side by side in such close quarters, little things like that can become a quite a trial, particularly when we haven't had enough sleep, or we're fasting. It's not an easy life. Have you experienced that yet?"

"No place is perfect. But I want to belong here. And that's why I get so upset with the computer. I want to do my share, but I don't seem to have any talents at all. Sister Maria Victoria is a seamstress, Sister Ignatius can comfort all of us with her prayers and her signs, Sister Eugenia tends to the sick, you and Sister Bernarda are externs and keep everything running smoothly. But I don't seem to have even one skill that will make me useful here." She paused. "You probably sensed that all along, and that's why you never wanted me here."

"I didn't want to be novice mistress—that's the reluctance you sensed. It had nothing to do with wanting or not wanting you here," Sister Agatha said softly. "God invited you. I would never try to interfere with that."

"Well, now I'm here and I'm doing my best, but I'm just not much help to the other sisters. My mom always said I was slow and stupid. The one talent I do have doesn't seem of much use here."

"What's your talent?"

"I sometimes see what other people miss. Little things, you know?" When Sister Agatha gave her a puzzled look, she added, "I can tell who's happy, who's afraid, and who's sad, even here among the sisters." She paused for a moment, then continued. "It's the sad ones who worry me most. They're like moths beating their wings against the window glass until they damage themselves."

"Who are you talking about?"

Celia hesitated.

"Go on. Speak freely."

"You're always worried," she said, not answering directly. "You love all the sisters here, but I can tell that you're afraid that you'll fail them. You spend a lot of time searching for answers, but you fail because you keep trying to make the facts fit in the way you'd like, instead of seeing what's really there. You can't make any progress if you're afraid of what you'll find."

Sister Agatha stared at Celia in mute surprise. Uncertain what to say to the postulant, she stood up and tried to regain some of her composure. Celia had struck a very sensitive nerve.

Sister Bernarda walked in with Sister Mary Lazarus before she could say anything. "Oh, good, you're both here already. Reverend Mother has excused us from collation so that we can continue our work. I've had Sister Clothilde prepare sandwiches and we can eat them at our carrels. With all of us working now, we may finally make some headway."

Sister Agatha excused herself for a few minutes and hurried to make a quick call to the sheriff. Tom wasn't there, so she left voice mail for him, asking if he'd learned anything new about Joan Sanchez, or when he'd visited St. Charles, then telling him what she'd learned about the small group of students she'd recruited to search for monkshood.

Returning to the scriptorium minutes later, Pax accompanying her, she began to work. Her hands were still a source of pain, but as the medicine took effect the discomfort dissipated somewhat. Typing was still out of the question for the time being, however, so she took on the job of scanning the pages of an original manuscript by Willa Cather. Pax lay beneath a table, out of the way.

Since the team in the scriptorium had given up their recreation hour, the other nuns each stopped by to offer support in an endless stream of solidarity. Sister Ignatius told them that she'd lit a votive candle for them. Sister Maria Victoria came by with a vase of roses. Sister Eugenia dropped in to take Pax for a walk.

As time passed, Sister Agatha kept an eye on Celia, making sure the young postulant didn't lose her battle with the computer, and encouraging her whenever she could.

At the sound of the bell, Sister Bernarda gathered all of the original documents and within minutes had put them away in the safe and locked them up. Feeling tired and achy, Sister Agatha gladly followed the sisters to chapel. This month Sister Eugenia was Hebdomadaria, the nun whose task was to officiate at the Divine Office.

Sister Eugenia's voice had the clarity of fine crystal as the two sides of the choir began the chant, one in a slightly higher pitch than the other. Their voices raised in prayer and praising God in this, their last canonical hour of the day, reverberated through the chapel. Their devotion was as real as the altar and the cross that hung above it. For that moment, they were one—with God and with each other. This was what gave meaning to every minute of their day.

When Compline ended, the sisters left the chapel, but Sister Agatha lingered, praying for strength and for the wisdom to find the answers the monastery so badly needed. Hearing the soft click of rosary beads behind her, she turned her head and was surprised to see Sister Bernarda in her stall. She nodded once, letting her know that she was there to support Sister Agatha's prayers with her own.

The gesture filled her with gratitude. *Magnificat anima mea Dominum.* My soul doth magnify the Lord.

With the words still echoing in her mind, Sister Agatha glanced at Sister Bernarda and smiled. No words were needed. The weight on Sister Agatha's shoulders no longer seemed unbearable.

She stood and genuflected facing the altar. She was simply a nun with a job to do, with backup more powerful than anyone could ever dream.

10

ON THE WAY TO HER CELL, SISTER AGATHA MET PAX IN the corridor outside the chapel where he usually lay waiting until her prayers were finished. They hadn't gone more than a few feet when Sister Eugenia caught up to her. "Sister, please come to the infirmary," she whispered.

The Great Silence, which began after Compline and ended after Morning Prayer, was broken only during grave emergencies, and her stomach tied into knots as she followed Sister Eugenia down the long hallway to the infirmary.

As she entered the room, she saw Sister Gertrude on one of the beds, her face pale.

Sister Agatha looked quickly at Sister Eugenia. "What happened?"

"The medication they gave her isn't working. I've contacted her doctor and he's prescribed something different but I'll need you to pick it up for us at the all-night drugstore in town."

"At your service, Sister."

"It'll be waiting for you when you arrive."

Sister Eugenia pulled out a holy card from her pocket and handed it to her. "Tell the druggist that our prayers are with him and his family. He does so much for this monastery by providing all our medications at cost," she said quietly.

Leaving Sister Eugenia to take care of Sister Gertrude, she hurried outside with Pax, who had remained at her side. Sister Agatha straddled the motorcycle, but as she flexed her hand to insert the key in the ignition, she winced. The pain in her joints had diminished, but it wasn't gone. With luck, the swelling would go down completely before morning. But, right now, she had a duty to attend to.

Pax jumped into the sidecar, and they were under way as soon as she closed the monastery gates behind her. The stretch of graveled road leading to the highway was completely empty. Sister felt a nagging sense of uneasiness she couldn't shake despite the bright headlight and the presence of Pax in the sidecar. She glanced around often. There was a full moon out tonight and it was easy to see the entire width of the road. No one was close, but the vegetation of the bosque, the forest of cottonwoods, willows, and flood-plain plants lining the ancient banks of the river hid everything more than a few feet away.

Slowing for a sharp curve, she discovered a large clump of leafy willows blocking the center of the road. As she moved to the shoulder to avoid the hazard, a large pothole jarred her. Nearly losing her grip on the handlebars from the pain in her swollen hands, she braked to a stop, turned off the engine, then checked Pax. Thankfully, the dog was fine.

Sister Agatha climbed off the bike and checked the tires and the sidecar for damage. "Well, looks like everything's all right, so let's get going again."

Pax growled and, before Sister Agatha could take a breath, she heard the snapping sound of twigs breaking and footsteps coming from somewhere to her right. Someone or something was hiding in the nearby stand of Russian Olives.

"Who's there?" she demanded.

Pax's growling intensified, but no one answered.

Uneasiness turned into fear. Mounting the bike, Sister Agatha ordered Pax into the sidecar, started the engine, and left the area quickly. Timothy's warning still echoed in her mind. Maybe someone had been watching the monastery, hoping for an opportunity to steal the motorcycle. Then, when they'd heard Pax's growl, they changed their minds.

She arrived at the drugstore ten minutes later. Leaving Pax to guard the motorcycle, she hurried inside. The prescription still hadn't been filled. She paced the store, impatience gnawing at her. Still worried that someone might have followed her, she looked outside often to check on Pax.

Finally Mr. Templeton called her name. She rushed up to the counter, and waited as he explained the medication's side effects and accepted the holy card. "Thank you, Sister. We'll send the statement at the end of the month."

With the pill bottle in her pocket, Sister Agatha hurried outside. Suddenly a young man stepped away from the building and stood in her way. "Nice bike, Sister, though I could do without the sidecar."

He was in his late teens and dressed like many of the toughs that hung around night spots along the main road. He had on a denim vest, no shirt, and a gang tattoo covered his left arm. "I'd love to take it for a ride."

Pax, who'd jumped out of the sidecar to wander on the small stretch of grass between the sidewalk and the store, saw him and came running up.

The dog made no overtly threatening moves. He simply sat at attention beside Sister Agatha, his gaze fixed on the man.

The young man stepped back. "Nice dog, too."

"He's very protective of me and the Harley," she said firmly.

"Ride safe." The man shrugged, then turned and sauntered down the sidewalk toward the One Shot Bar.

"Pax, I don't know how I'll wrangle it for you since we don't eat meat at the monastery, but I owe you a giant soup bone on top of your regular dog chow."

The dog licked his lips as if he'd understood.

Soon they were heading back to the monastery. She'd have to find a safe way to talk with the kids from St. Charles next time she saw them, and try to find out more about the person Timothy had warned her about without compromising the boy's safety. If the man Bobby Gonzales had promised the bike to posed a serious threat, she had to know.

She thought about telling Reverend Mother, then decided against it. The abbess had enough on her mind, and she wasn't certain yet that there really was a danger to anyone. She'd poke around and see what she could uncover first.

Lord, if you didn't want me to meddle, you should have added another commandment.

The following day, Sister Gertrude was well enough to join the other nuns for Matins and the monastery community greeted her warmly. After Morning Prayer, before Sister Agatha could report to the parlor for portress duty, Reverend Mother intercepted her in the hall.

"We need to talk, child."

Sister Agatha followed Reverend Mother outside and sat with her on one of the benches near the statue of St. Joseph. Pax, who'd been outside since Matins, came over to join them.

"Sister Bernarda came to see me this morning. She tells me that scriptorium work is still behind schedule and the scanners and computers are breaking down nearly every day."

"We try to fix things, or work around them, Mother, but it's not easy. Frank Walters is the only parishioner willing to share his specialized knowledge. He's been more than generous with his time, but even he recommends we get new equipment."

"Is there any way we could learn to fix the computers?"

"I've learned some by watching, and do pretty well with the software, but when the equipment breaks down, it's another matter. I'm far from an expert. But I'll keep trying, Mother."

"Good. Child, I'm going to tell you something in confidence. With Sister Gertrude having been so sick, I've taken her usual duties as cellarer—keeping track of the monastery's finances." She paused. "We're in serious trouble. Two large donations we had been expecting recently from regular supporters didn't come in. Sister Bernarda has tried to contact those benefactors on the phone, but hasn't been able to reach them." She paused. "I don't think they want to be reached."

Reverend Mother took a deep breath. "I suspect that Father Anselm's death has cast a long shadow over Our Lady of Hope. Nobody remembers the last time anyone was murdered at a monastery, and I've been told that the story is in the news across the Southwest. People don't want to donate to a monastery that is shrouded in scandal, but without donations and support from the community, we're going to be very hard-pressed to make ends meet."

"Mother, I'm still working to find the answers we need, but I'll talk to Sister Bernarda, too. Maybe, if we pull together, we can finish at least one of the scriptorium projects, despite the problems with the computers. That should bring some money in."

"Thank you, child."

Sister Agatha retreated to the scriptorium with Pax at her heels and found Postulant Celia and Sister Mary Lazarus helping Sister Bernarda, who was trying to fix Celia's computer. They had moved the computer and the attached scanner to a table beneath the window to make better use of the outdoor light while Sister Bernarda checked all the wires and connections.

"Is anything loose?" Sister Agatha asked.

"Not on this one, but the other computer, the one I normally use, also crashed and doesn't want to start back up. Our two remaining computers are having their usual problems crashing too, but at least they still work."

"Let me take a look at the one you've been using," Sister Agatha said.

Sister Mary Lazarus signaled Celia and they moved a wheeled cart near the window, then carried the monitor and tower over there.

Sister Maria Victoria, who was passing down the hall on the way to the sewing room, glanced into the room. Seeing them moving heavy equipment, she came in. "Sisters, if you could use an extra pair of hands . . ."

"We'd appreciate it," Sister Agatha said quickly.

Working together, they repositioned two more carts near the east window. The scanners and one monitor were placed there along with the keyboards and mice.

"Let's have a look inside the tower," Sister Agatha said.

Sister Bernarda gave her a worried look. "What if we damage something?"

"They won't work now, so leaving them alone isn't going to help us either. Mr. Walters hasn't been able to figure this out, and it's not fair to keep calling him in. He has his own business to run."

"He said to call, day or night. He likes knowing that all the sisters pray for him," Sister Mary Lazarus said.

"Sisters, we all have to do our best to cut down expenses right now. Reverend Mother needs our help."

"Is it the hospital bill?" Maria Victoria said with a long sigh. "Sister Gertrude really feels badly about that. I tried to tell her that the sisters need her, and the money couldn't have been better spent." She paused and her normally serene face grew troubled. "But I don't think I helped. In fact, I may have made things worse. It's too bad I'm not as good at giving comfort to the sick as I am with a needle and thread."

Sister Agatha smiled. "We all have our strengths—and our weaknesses. If I were made cook, for example, we'd need a tireless infirmarian."

Sister Bernarda exhaled loudly. "Celia's computer seems to be working now, but the on-screen message says it can't find the scanner."

"What if the software has gone south? Can we reinstall it?" Sister Mary Lazarus asked. "I had that happen to me once before with one of the computers."

"First, I think we'd have to uninstall the software that's in here now," Sister Agatha answered, "and when we reinstall it, make sure we have the same settings as before."

"That might be better than taking off the back of it and fiddling with things," Sister Bernarda said. "To me, that sounds a bit like raising the hood on the car and wiggling things until it works."

"But it won't do any good to fiddle with the software if the problem is a loose connection between the computer and the scanner. Actually, it's not unlike working on an old car. Sometimes all the heating and cooling of parts in an old computer causes loose connections and all kinds of problems. I've been reading up on this."

Sister Agatha loosened the screws and, together with Sister Mary Lazarus, moved the cover forward, up, and off. Inside were circuit boards, hard drives, and floppy drives, and several cards plugged into long sockets with gold bands that matched up with the gold stripes on the cards.

Sister Maria Victoria bowed slightly to the others, signaling her departure. She'd renewed her silence now, since it wasn't urgent, or a matter of charity, that she speak.

Sister Agatha checked the computer she was working with, then glanced over to Celia's computer. "See if the bottom card is loose, Sister Bernarda. That controls the scanner."

"It is loose at one end," she said, and Sister Mary Lazarus leaned over to tighten it.

"So maybe we fixed at least one of these," Sister Mary Lazarus said.

Sister Agatha tested the drive connections on Sister Bernarda's computer and found some that had worked loose. She wondered why Frank Walters hadn't checked more thoroughly. Then again, he only charged them half price, and was always switching used components to save them money. Being critical wouldn't help anyone now.

"Okay, let's put the covers back on, hook up the connections again, and see what happens," Sister Agatha announced.

After this was done, Sister Bernarda restarted Celia's computer while Sister Agatha finished checking the other. The one with the loose scanner card now worked, but the other still gave an error message they couldn't understand.

There was a collective sigh among the sisters. "You don't suppose lighting a votive candle would help, do you?" Sister Mary Lazarus asked.

"I was thinking of a swift kick, actually," Sister Agatha muttered.

"Let me go call Frank Walters. With luck, he'll donate the service call and not charge us at all once I explain how short of funds we are now."

"With only two working computers, we'll never make deadline. We need to scan and input data, and that has to be done on separate computers. We could work in shifts, but I don't know if the computers that are left can stand round-the-clock use for several weeks in this heat," Sister Mary Lazarus said. "And if we get a reputation for being unreliable, our clients will find someone else to do the work next time. We can't afford a loss like that."

Mary Lazarus had always been precise—both in her work and her prayers. To date, she had been the only postulant Sister Agatha had ever seen who had never gotten lost chanting the Divine Office. Her observation now about deadlines was accurate but irritating.

"We'll work overtime, and in shifts if we have to, but without the proper equipment, there's nothing more that can be done," Sister Agatha said.

"Maybe you can pressure Mr. Walters to come right away so we can get going?" Mary Lazarus suggested.

"That was my intention," she said, doing her best to curb her temper. The novice was just trying to help. It wasn't her fault that she had no idea how annoying she was at times. Love thy neighbor, she thought, trying to convince herself.

Sister Agatha glanced at Sister Bernarda who seemed to read her mind. "Go make the phone call, Sister. We'll handle things here."

Sister Agatha went directly to the parlor and called Frank Walters. It was hard not to feel like they were taking advantage of him. But these were tough times.

"Hey, Sister!" Frank greeted her after she introduced herself. "I've missed you around the scriptorium lately. It's been a while since we've had a chance to talk. Lately the only extern I see is Sister Bernarda. How are things going?"

"Mr. Walters—"

"Frank, please. When you call me Mr. Walters, I think of my dad, God rest his soul."

"Frank, then," she said quickly, feeling even guiltier. Not only was she going to ask him to donate his service call, but now she'd made him feel bad.

"We have a problem with the computer equipment," she said, and explained everything they'd done. "I know you're a very busy man, but we're right up against a deadline for one of the libraries, and unless all of our computers are up and working I'm really afraid we'll miss it."

"I'm surprised you're that close to on schedule with all the breakdowns you've been having."

"Frank, I hate to push, but we need you right away, and we also need you to donate the cost of this service call. Our finances are very tight at the moment. Will you do it? The kindness you show us God will reward a hundredfold."

There was a pause. "All right, Sister. I realize it's been difficult at the monastery since Father died, especially with the bad publicity and it being called a murder. I imagine some of your benefactors are thinking twice about being linked to the monastery right now. Businesses have to protect their images."

"And will that include you, too?" Sister Agatha asked.

There was a lengthy silence. "I'm not going to turn my back on Our Lady of Hope. I know the sisters wouldn't have harmed anyone—regardless of what the news reports suggest."

There it was—a qualification ribboned around the reassurance. "Thank you so very much. If you could come today and help us repair our computers, we'd be very grateful. In fact, I'll personally start a novena for your intentions right away."

"You've got yourself a deal, Sister," he said. "I'll be over soon. Oh, and I'll be bringing my son, Joey, with me. He's still learning the business."

Joey was Frank's twenty-four-year-old son. He had no personality as far as she could tell. That young man could get lost in a crowd of two.

Reminding herself to be more charitable, she quickly thanked Mr. Walters then placed the phone down. Both Frank and Joey had been cleared to enter the scriptorium whenever they were needed, but Reverend Mother would need to be notified.

Hurrying down the hall, she found Reverend Mother in the scriptorium talking to Sister Bernarda.

"I have good news," she said after greeting them. "Frank Walters has agreed to donate the service call in exchange for the sisters prayers and a special novena I'll be starting right away for his intentions. He and his son should arrive shortly. They don't live far from here."

"Well done, child. Will we make our deadlines if the Walters can get the machines working?" Reverend Mother asked.

"We'll do our best, Mother," Sister Agatha answered.

Out of the corner of her eye, she caught the look on Sister Mary Lazarus's face and knew that, had it been permissible, she would have answered Reverend Mother herself. But novices and postulants weren't allowed to speak to the choir nuns, unless absolutely necessary. From what she knew about Mary Lazarus, Sister Agatha was certain that she would have been willing to stay up all night for a week if that's what it took to make the deadline. It was really too bad that her feelings for the monastery and her vocation weren't as absolute as her dedication to deadlines.

"Walk with me, child," Reverend Mother asked Sister Agatha.

"Yes, Mother." Sister Agatha followed Reverend Mother outside to the small enclosure that faced the recreation room. Sister Eugenia had planted some cosmos seeds her niece had sent her and the flowers were now in full bloom. "We will cut some of these for the altar. They're so beautiful, don't you think?"

"Yes, Mother." She knew Reverend Mother hadn't bothered to bring her out here for the flowers. Something else was going on.

"I need to speak with you about Sister Gertrude." She paused, then continued. "Some of the tests they ran while she was at the hospital have now been seen by a second physician. Her heart is very weak and her condition more serious than we thought. It's imperative that she not be upset, so I'm not permitting her to resume her duties as cellarer. There's something else I'd like you to know, but you can't share what I'm about to tell you with the others here in the monastery."

"Whatever you tell me, Mother, will stay between us."

She nodded, then proceeded slowly. "Canon law dictates that each monastery has to provide for its own needs. We've done well, but, right now, we've been hit with some very large bills we need to pay, and our financial situation is not good. The regular income we have from the baking is not sufficient to make up the current shortfall. We're behind on our renovation loan as well as on recent medical bills. That's the reason I need to know that the scriptorium work—and our expected fee from it—will be in on time. If you need help, depending on the kind of work that needs to be done, I may be able to assign other sisters to work with you, perhaps Sister Maria Victoria and even Sister Gertrude."

"That might become necessary, Mother. But, for now, we have enough workers. We just need to get the machines up and running so we have the tools to do the job. That's where the slowdown is taking place."

"I'm also going to ask the sisters to be more frugal in their use of lights, and conserve our utilities even more than usual. We have enough to eat for a long time, between the vegetables in the garden, the beans, and the tortillas in the freezer, so food is one thing we won't have to worry about."

"But no one here is extravagant, Mother. I honestly don't see how we can cut back much more. We already hand water each plant, and there's almost no waste in the kitchen."

"I don't know either, to tell you the truth," she said with a long sigh. "But if donations don't resume, particularly the ones from our primary benefactors, this monastery may have to shut down."

"Mother, surely it won't come to that."

"I hope not, Sister. But pray for us. If there ever was a time for that, it's now."

Sister Agatha watched Reverend Mother walk away as the bells for Terce rang. Her head was bowed as she went to the chapel, ready to fulfill her prayerful duty as a Bride of Christ.

The contemplative life was not an easy one. There was no way to keep the world at bay. They were forever part of it, though they'd chosen not to belong to it. Yet their very isolation made them vulnerable.

Unfortunately for all of them, humanity was seldom kind to the vulnerable things in this world.

11

SISTER AGATHA MET FRANK AND JOEY WALTERS AT THE door. Joey, who stood nearly as tall as his dad, was slender and had dark brown hair. Unlike his conservatively dressed father, Joey wore baggy black slacks and a sports jersey with some athlete's last name on the back. He had a perpetually sullen and vacant expression.

Sister invited them into the parlor and offered them something cold to drink. Frank declined, but then added, "Sister, what I'd really like to find out is whether Sister Clothilde will be baking her special oatmeal-pecan cookies this year for our Fourth of July Town Fair."

She smiled. Sister Clothilde's cookies were famous around town. She only made them twice a year—for sale at the Fourth of July fund-raiser, then on Christmas as a special treat for the sisters. Yet, despite the rarity of her baking sessions, word had spread, and she'd received special requests from VIPs like the archbishop and the New Mexico state governor.

"You can count on it," she said. "She loves making her own contribution to the things the monastery sells at the fair."

"Good. Save me a dozen. Deal?"

"Deal."

As soon as they arrived in the scriptorium, Frank began to work, sending his son back out to their van for tools and supplies. "What I'm going to do is upgrade some of your existing equipment, but not your hard drives. That would cause more problems for you than it would solve. Upgrading will be expensive, but less than the cost of all new computers. Consider it part of my donation. Of course, in addition to the cookies, I'll expect a month's worth of novenas from you," he said, then added with a smile, "and the prayers of the other sisters as well."

"Is there a particular intention you'd like us to ask for?"

"Just pray that my company gets out of the slump it's in right now."

"You've got it." She smiled. "We've all got a stake in you."

Checking the time, Sister Agatha stood up. "I need to go to check the sacristy, Frank. Father Mahoney may come in early, but I'll be back soon." She looked at Sister Mary Lazarus and Celia. "Go to chapel for private prayer, Sisters."

"With your permission, Mother Mistress, Sister Ignatius asked that I help in the bakery. She needs to get a shipment of altar bread out today and really needs an extra pair of hands," Mary Lazarus said.

"You may go to her."

Leaving Sister Bernarda with Frank and Joey, she hurried to the sacristy, checked the mass vestments carefully, then placed them in the two-way drawer, ready for Father Mahoney. As she did, she was reminded of Father Anselm's last Mass, and a pang of sorrow stabbed through her. "We'll find out the truth, Father," she whispered to the empty room, knowing the priest's spirit would never be far from them. "I promise."

She returned to the scriptorium immediately afterward and looked around. Joey was there alone, working in his usual slow motion way. "Where's Frank?" she asked Sister Bernarda.

"He said that he needed some fresh air, that the heat in here was making him edgy," Sister Bernarda said quietly.

"He's always recommended a cooler room for the computers, but there's nothing that can be done about that," Sister Agatha said. The room wasn't too bad so early in the day. Eighty degrees was pleasant by comparison to the heat in some other parts of the monastery. There were rooms like the bakery that went well over ninety despite the coolness of the monastery's adobe construction. Working there in the summer was a true penance.

Joey, who'd moved the computer chassis he was working on next to the open window to take advantage of the light and the breeze, continued what he was doing. "You really should listen to him, Sisters. Computers don't work very efficiently in high temperatures."

"I'll go to ask him what can be done," Sister Agatha told Sister Bernarda.

She went outside, suspecting that she'd have to soothe ruffled feathers. Working on a computer that was certain to malfunction in the middle of summer was bound to affect anyone's good nature.

Sister walked out to the parking lot and looked around for Frank, but he was nowhere to be seen. She circled around into the garden, but stopped when she heard angry voices just beyond the pyracantha hedge.

Curious, she moved silently down the tall hedge toward the path. Through the gaps, she could see Sister Mary Lazarus and Frank Walters standing face-to-face. They appeared to be arguing.

"Frank, you're going to have to take some action. You already know Joey is undependable. You've got to cut him loose."

The anger she heard coming from Sister Mary Lazarus surprised her almost as much as the fact that the novice was lecturing a benefactor on his personal business.

"The kid just needs some time to get his life figured out. Sure, he goofs off and gets into trouble. At his age, I did the same thing."

"Stop making excuses for him. He's an adult now, and has to learn to stand on his own two feet."

"I really wouldn't go there if I were you. You haven't been doing that for years."

Stepping back, uncertain if she should make her presence known, Sister Agatha snapped a twig under her shoe. Frank looked her direction.

"Excuse me. Am I intruding?" she said, approaching.

Sister Mary Lazarus's face went as white as her novice veil. "The heat got to Sister Ignatius and she left the bakery to take a break, so I came out here to get some fresh air before going back," she managed weakly.

"And then I ran into her, and we started talking," Frank said. "I was the one who persuaded her to show me the grounds. I needed to cool off before going inside and tackling that computer again. I hope you understand."

"It sounded like you two were having an argument," Sister Agatha said.

Frank laughed. "Oh, Sister, that's not arguing. She was expressing her opinion and I was doing the same. But now I better get back to work."

Sister Agatha looked at Sister Mary Lazarus, but waited until Frank was out of earshot to speak. "We do have rules, Sister," she said. "You may be preparing to be an extern, but until you are no longer a novice you don't go walking around and speaking with a monastery guest. Next time you need fresh air, you might try volunteering for something constructive, like helping Sister Maria Victoria prune the roses around the statue of the Blessed Mother. Sister is there right now, as a matter of fact."

She walked with Mary Lazarus to where Sister Maria Victoria was working. "Our novice would benefit from giving you a hand with the roses," Sister Agatha said.

"I'd welcome some help," she said, handing Mary Lazarus some pruning shears and cotton gloves.

They watched the novice for a moment as she began to work, then Sister Maria Victoria took Sister Agatha aside. "Our novice has come a long way, don't you think?" she said with a chuckle. "I still remember a few months ago when she offered to help us as we worked in the garden during recreation."

Sister Agatha nodded somberly. "She had a terrible allergic reaction to something while she was weeding. Her poor hands were so swollen she could barely hold her breviary for days. I don't think Sister Eugenia ever figured out what caused it."

"No, but look how accomplished she is now," Sister Maria Victoria said. "We just have to make sure that she always wears a pair of work gloves."

"Sister, let our novice help you a while longer, then please ask her to return to the scriptorium." She paused, then added, "How's the quilted wall hanging coming along?"

"We've been working very hard, but the small decorative stitches take a long time and are the hardest to do. That's why I'm out here. I find I need a break every once in a while."

"Enjoy your break, Your Charity." Leaving them to prune the roses, Sister Agatha hurried back to the scriptorium. She found Joey and Frank hard at work, or at least Frank was working hard, and Sister Bernarda was helping wherever she could, holding a part or finding the correct cable.

Though Joey always seemed to follow Frank's directions, he worked slowly, doing only as much as he was required to do. It was almost as if he were trying to prove to his dad that he wasn't cut out for this type of work. She had long sensed tension between father and son, but unlike her outspoken novice she had never commented on it.

Sister Mary Lazarus returned to the scriptorium about twenty minutes later. Celia followed shortly afterward. While they all worked under Frank's direction, Sister Agatha kept a subtle watch on Mary Lazarus and Frank. Their computer guru was making a point of not looking at the novice, but Mary Lazarus cast furtive glances at him frequently. Their behavior only served to raise more questions in her mind.

Sister Agatha positioned herself close to one of the small front windows. If she sat just right, she could see the driveway from here and the phone was loud so she knew she could hear it from the scriptorium. Doing double duty as portress while working in the scriptorium was almost routine on some days.

As the bells for Mass rang, Sister Bernarda gave Sister Agatha a worried look. Someone had to stay with Frank. To ask him to leave was unthinkable, particularly when they needed the machines so badly, and the upgrade work wasn't yet finished. But Mass was difficult for any of them to miss. It balanced their day and focused their thoughts.

"I'll stay with Frank and his son, Your Charity. You and Mary Lazarus and Celia better get going," Sister Agatha said.

Sister Bernarda started to protest, but Sister Agatha signaled her to stop. Her offer hadn't been altogether altruistic. She had a few questions she wanted to ask Frank when there were fewer people around.

Bowing their heads, the three left for Mass.

Sending Joey to the van for a part, Frank continued to work. "Tell me something, Sister," he said, his eyes still focused on the power supply he was installing. "Do you favor the intruder theory?"

"Yes," she answered. "It's the only thing that makes sense. Everyone who's part of this monastery is completely trustworthy."

"Does the sheriff go along with that too?" he asked, finally turning to look at her.

"I'm not really sure." She held his gaze. "Now I'd like you to answer something for me. How well do you know Sister Mary Lazarus?"

He smiled. "Great way to phrase it—not 'do you know' but 'how well.' "

"I assumed from the unguarded way she spoke to you that you and she were old friends."

"I knew her before she became a nun," he answered obliquely.

There were a lot of questions she wanted to hammer him with, but she held back. It wouldn't exactly be smart to antagonize their scriptorium's sole and much-needed benefactor right now.

Joey walked in just then, and Frank resumed working. Accepting that her opportunity for questions had passed, at least for now, she opened her breviary and prayed as he worked.

After about an hour, he looked up, and motioned for his son to start packing up their tools. "Okay. I think these should work now. But remember there may still be a few bugs in the system. I haven't used new parts."

"Can we give them a test run now before you leave?"

"Sure."

Sister Agatha scanned a page from her breviary, and waited. A perfect copy came up on the monitor, the file was saved, and they printed out the page. She repeated the test on the second computer. "They look perfect. In fact, I can see they work even faster than before."

"That's the idea. I know you only use the other two for word processing, but I think you'll find those will run smoother as well," he said, then added, "Now that you're all set up, Joey and I better go to the office. Let me know how things go, Sister, and if any glitches turn up."

She walked the men outside, then closed the parlor doors behind them. She was about to return to the scriptorium when she heard another vehicle driving up. A police unit was coming through the gate. Seconds later, she saw Tom Green emerge.

As his gaze took in the grounds, his face was set and hard. She knew him well enough to know the sheriff was here on a mission, and he was bracing himself for an unpleasant task. Instinct told her to brace herself as well. None of them would like the news he was bringing today.

12

SISTER AGATHA OPENED THE PARLOR DOOR. "WHAT CAN WE do for you, Sheriff?"

"I'm taking Postulant Celia with me to the police station for questioning," he said flatly.

For a moment she stared at him in muted shock. "But I explained what that would mean to her. You can't."

"I can as long as I'm wearing this badge," he said tapping his chest. "Now bring the young woman here and call Reverend Mother and anyone else you want in on this."

"Are you charging her?"

"Not yet. I just want her in for questioning."

"But why?"

"I've followed every single lead I had, even those out in left field, such as students pulling a practical joke. But now, Celia, for several reasons, has jumped to the top of my list. I want her at the station where I can guarantee no one will interfere with her questioning. You can call an attorney and have him present during questioning if you want."

"If you haul Celia down to the police station, you're going to choke the life out of this monastery. Word will spread, and even if she's eventually cleared of suspicion, no one—including our bene-factors—will ever trust any of us again."

"It can't be helped."

"Since I handled the alb that day, too, I assume you'll want me to go to the station as well?"

"No. Celia's the one I want. She fits the profile better. I've looked into her background. Her mother's a fruitcake. There's no telling what Celia's really like inside."

"Celia's mother is a very nice woman, *not* a fruitcake."

"She's a religious zealot. We both went to high school with her, remember, when her last name was Chandler. She's changed a lot since then. How long has it been since you visited Ruth Moore?"

Sister Agatha didn't answer because she didn't want to admit it had been more than a decade. Ruth had dropped out of high school her senior year to have the baby, and, after that, their lives had gone in different directions.

"That's what I thought. I bet it has been years. Believe me, she's changed. Really changed."

"Please don't take Celia out of the monastery. If you do, you'll undermine everything she's worked for these last few months. Let's make a deal."

"What do you mean, a deal?" The sheriff's eyes narrowed.

Sister Agatha knew Celia had a chance now. She'd better not blow it for her. "Interview her here, now, but through the grille. Except for the setting, would it be any different from questioning her at the station? You weren't going to lock her in a cell first, were you?"

"Not yet."

"Then we can do it here. What other requirements do you have?"

"*If* I agree to interview her here instead, I want a guarantee that I can talk to her one to one—with her attorney present, of course, should she decide she needs a lawyer."

"That's irregular, but I think it can be arranged. Have a seat, and let me talk to Reverend Mother. I'll be back in a few minutes."

She walked down the corridor and found Sister Bernarda in the scriptorium. She asked the extern to keep an eye outside in case anyone else came up to the parlor.

"Something's happened, hasn't it?" Sister Bernarda asked, quickly putting the manuscripts she was working on into the safe.

"It's not good," she answered quietly. Seeing Sister Mary Lazarus and Celia had also returned and were working at the far end of the room, she lowered her voice until it became a barely discernible whisper. "What are they working on?"

"A recipe archive for a magazine."

"That's not terribly valuable. Instead of locking up their work as well as yours if you have to go to the parlor, do you think we could let them continue working? I know we'll be violating the insurance rules if neither of us is present while they work, but we're so far behind."

"All right. If I have to go, I'll leave what they need out, and lock up the rest, particularly the valuable manuscripts, in the safe."

Leaving Sister Bernarda to her work, Sister Agatha approached the novice and the postulant. "We'd like you to keep working if Sister Bernarda has to step out to the parlor. We'll leave what you'll need to continue on your desks. The rest will be locked up as usual."

"If you leave the safe open, Mother Mistress, I can start on something else if Sister is delayed," Sister Mary Lazarus suggested.

"We can't do that. Should you finish your current project, start working on the readings you've been assigned as part of your instruction," Sister Agatha said.

She saw frustration flash in Sister Mary Lazarus's eyes but, without being reminded of her vow of obedience, the novice nodded. Sister Agatha went to the door, then stopped and looked back.

If they only knew what lay ahead nothing else, including their deadlines, would seem quite so important. The clarity of mind all nuns needed, especially those in formation, was about to be shattered.

⚜

Reverend Mother turned her back on Sister Agatha and faced the crucifix on the wall. "I don't want any of our sisters taken out of the monastery. Not when we still have a legal leg to stand on. If they don't have a court order authorizing them to remove her, Celia can be questioned right here."

"We really need to call an attorney, Mother. It'll be for Celia's protection, and ours too."

"I'll make the necessary phone call myself. Tell Sheriff Green that if he'll talk to Celia here in our monastery, we'll do our best to meet his other conditions and not interfere."

Sister Agatha could hear the fear in Reverend Mother's voice. The abbess had given her life to this monastery. She hadn't chosen the office of prioress, she'd been elected to it, and would continue to hold it as long as she was needed in that role. But the weight of shouldering all the worries of running the monastery, particularly lately, could be seen clearly in the lines of fatigue on Reverend Mother's face. The dark circles under her eyes suggested she wasn't sleeping well.

As Sister Agatha returned to the parlor, her thoughts turned to the other members of her order. If the monastery was forced to close down, she wasn't sure the elderly nuns like Sister Clothilde or even Sister Gertie would survive the upheaval. The realization that the innocent would pay as much as the victim, or the guilty, made her heart ache.

Somehow, she had to find the truth and then, together, they'd find the strength to deal with the aftermath.

One hour later, John Bruno, an attorney provided by the archdiocese, sat with Sister Agatha and Celia in the inner parlor.

Bruno, preparing Celia, firmly advised her to answer the questions simply and to avoid volunteering any information. Celia had tried to reassure him that she was in no danger because she was innocent of any crimes, but he'd held firm and Celia had agreed.

Once he felt Celia was ready, John Bruno went out to the outer parlor and met with the sheriff. Celia remained on the other side of the grille and waited for the men to come to her.

Sister Agatha stood farther down the hall. She'd been ordered not to interfere, but she was afraid for the postulant. Yet, despite the circumstances, Celia seemed calm and remarkably self-possessed.

Minutes ticked by with agonizing slowness as Sister Agatha forced herself to retreat into the scriptorium and try to do some work while giving Tom the privacy he'd demanded. Everything about this seemed wrong. A postulant shouldn't have been talking to outsiders, but the police business took precedence now.

Trying to think of something that would help point the sheriff's investigation back toward an intruder—the direction she firmly believed would lead to the killer—she mentally went over everything she remembered about the days leading up to, and including, the day Father Anselm died.

She recalled that morning, before he arrived with the food donations, visualizing everything she'd seen or heard. Then she'd met with Sister Bernarda in the outer parlor.

As she went over her routine, she suddenly recalled the enigmatic note she'd found in the turn. At the time she'd assumed it was simply a teenager facing a breakup, but now, knowing what had happened afterward, she wondered if perhaps the author of the note had given them an important warning—one much more ominous than she'd ever dreamed. The first time she got the chance, she'd have to tell the sheriff about that possibility.

Finally, almost ninety minutes later, Celia came to get her and she put her thoughts about the note aside for the moment.

"How did it go?" Sister Agatha asked quickly. Celia looked tired, but was still composed.

"It was difficult. Sheriff Green wanted to know things I couldn't answer, like where monkshood grows, what my relationship to Father was . . . that kind of thing." The postulant kept her head down while speaking.

"And what did you answer?"

"I don't know where monkshood grows, but I can probably find out in any library. And Father was the parish priest in our community, so he heard my confession from time to time, but I don't think you can call that a relationship."

"Was that all? Surely those few questions didn't take such a long time," she pressed.

"The sheriff would focus on some aspect of my answer, then question me even harder. When I told him about confession, for example, he then asked me if I was afraid Father knew me too well." She shook her head and sighed.

"What did you say to that?" Sister Agatha studied her expression carefully, but Celia remained calm.

"I told him the truth. Some of the things I said to Father were very embarrassing, but everything was under the seal of the confessional, and I knew he'd never say anything."

"So you insisted that Father never made you nervous at all?" Sister Agatha challenged.

"No, I couldn't say that," she answered. "The truth is that I *was* afraid that if he recognized me, he wouldn't think I was worthy of being a member of this monastery. He wouldn't have said anything, I know, but what worried me was that he might not be able to hide his feelings. The other nuns would eventually begin to wonder why he didn't like me, and maybe start to question if I should be here at all. Since the entire monastery has to agree that my monastic vocation fits in with our order and with this community before I become a permanent member of this monastery, I was afraid that he would inadvertently make things difficult for me." Celia met her gaze directly. "But I would *never* have harmed Father in any way."

Sister Agatha watched the postulant. Instinct told her that Celia was still holding something back.

"Oh—I nearly forgot. Mr. Bruno asked that you join him in the parlor," Celia said at last.

"Go to the chapel, Celia. You need peace and prayer to refocus your thoughts. Ask the Lord to help us all."

As Celia left for the chapel, Sister hurried back to the parlor. John Bruno was waiting for her just inside the inner parlor. Although Mr. Bruno had been given permission to enter their enclosure, she knew it wasn't something he did lightly. In this case, she suspected he wanted to say something to her before she saw the sheriff.

As she approached him, his somber expression warned her that there was more bad news to come. "The sheriff has nothing conclusive on the postulant, but had enough probable cause to get a warrant to search the monastery itself, and not just the grounds." Hearing the sound of vehicles coming down the drive, he went to the window. "Apparently he's now ready to execute it. Go tell your abbess."

Sister Agatha hurried to get Reverend Mother. With every step, she tried to gather her courage. Failing, she stopped a few feet from Mother's office and leaned against the wall, fighting the tears that threatened to fall. Despite her training, despite her efforts, she'd failed Reverend Mother and the sisters thus far.

Suddenly she felt a hand on her shoulder. Sister Agatha turned her head and saw Sister Ignatius smiling gently at her. Following the dictate that held that charity was to be valued above the rule of silence, the same dictum that allowed the infirmarian and her patients to speak freely, she leaned closer to Sister Agatha's ear.

"Your Charity, remember the story of Elisha. He was hopelessly outnumbered, and to mortal eyes his situation looked grim. But he knew he was safe with God and confidently assured his frightened servant, 'Fear not; for there are more with us than with them.' At that moment, his servant's eyes were opened and he saw that chariots of fire were all around Elisha. So remember, my dear, no matter how it seems, with God on our side, we can't be defeated. As a teacher of mine used to say, 'One with God is always a majority.' "

Before Sister Agatha could draw in a steadying breath to reply, Sister Ignatius continued down the hall.

Sister Agatha stood up straight and took a deep breath. With Sister Ignatius's words ringing in her mind, she knocked lightly on Reverend Mother's door.

Sister Agatha told Reverend Mother what had happened.

"Let them come, child. The rest of us will go to our stalls in chapel. There, secure in our own seats in choir, we'll pray while they search to their hearts' content. We'll take our troubles to Him. Adoration of the Blessed Sacrament always brings us many graces. Can you and Sister Bernarda look after our visitors while they're here?"

"Mother, we'll do everything in our power to stay with them each step of the way."

The search team descended like a plague of locusts—or cockroaches, depending on how charitable one felt. As they scattered, each going in separate directions, Sister Bernarda and she hurried to talk to John Bruno.

"We'd like to go with them. Is that legal?"

"You can't interfere, but you can go with them, watch, and even take notes if you want."

Sister Agatha went with the teams that were searching the cells while Sister Bernarda accompanied the deputies looking in the scriptorium, the kitchen, and storage areas.

Each nun's assigned cell was searched thoroughly, including hers and Sister Bernarda's. The deputies found nothing, but it wasn't for lack of trying.

Outrage filled Sister Agatha as Sheriff Green searched Mother's cell. Forced not to interfere, she watched him look beneath the abbess's mattress, then study her writing pad. Finally he upturned the Bible on her table, scattering holy cards all over the surface.

She stood aside, furious at what he'd done, yet unable to stop him. Prayers wouldn't come until her anger subsided.

Finally she followed him and the deputies to the postulant's sleeping quarters. Sheriff Green led the search. He looked through the few possessions Celia had brought with her and found nothing of interest. Then, as he lifted the mattress, a small notebook fell to the floor.

He read a few pages, then leafed through it some more.

"Are you planning to keep that?" Sister Agatha asked coldly. Many postulants and novices kept journals, and Celia, from the looks of it, had been no exception.

"I have a right to seize any books, papers, and records that may establish the identity of the killer. It's in the warrant. In addition, I can confiscate any monkshood in herb or drug form or derivative thereof or paraphernalia that may point us to the killer."

He read a few more pages, then skipped to the last few entries. This time his expression changed and his concentration became focused on the page before him.

"Celia was afraid of Father Anselm—it wasn't as simple as she let on. Listen to this," he said, and began to read.

" 'Father could take away my dream. I belong in this monastery. God brought me here. I'm going to pray really hard until God tells me what I need to do.' "

Sister Agatha scoffed. "Come on, Tom, that scarcely screams premeditated murder. She was taking her problem to God. We all do that here."

"What if she thought God told her to punish the priest? A lot of confessed killers have testified that God spoke to them through little voices in their heads. Maybe Celia looked at it as a modern twist to the story of Abraham and Isaac. Remember that it's unlikely the person who put the monkshood on the alb meant to kill anyone."

"Celia's not crazy. She's very devout and wouldn't harm a soul."

"Get her and bring her to the parlor again. I have a few more questions."

Her heart hammering a mile a minute, Sister Agatha rushed to the chapel and went directly to Reverend Mother's stall. Seeing her, the abbess rose and hurried out of the chapel with Sister Agatha.

Once she'd been given permission, Sister Agatha took Celia to the parlor where they met Bruno and the sheriff.

"I'd like Mother Mistress to stay," the young postulant said quietly, looking at the sheriff.

Sister Agatha looked at him. "I won't interfere. You have my word."

"You've already spoken to me alone, Sheriff. I have nothing more to tell you now than I did then. Surely having Sister Agatha present won't cause you to become distracted."

Sister Agatha had to bite her lip to keep from smiling. By appealing to his pride, the postulant had won the round.

"Stay if you want, Sister—but I'll handle the questioning," he said, taking out a small tape recorder.

"Of course," Sister Agatha said.

Tom placed the journal on the table so Celia could see it clearly. Then he brought out his handcuffs and placed them beside it. Sister Agatha had to bite her lip to keep from protesting the obvious attempt at intimidation. Bruno frowned, and shook his head, but Tom ignored him.

Celia stared at the handcuffs and her journal, her jaw dropping slightly.

"Did you get your answer from God when you prayed about your problem with Father Anselm? Were you told to punish him?"

"No, of course not! I had planned to talk to Father, that's all."

"But you were alone with the alb. Did you place the poison on the collar?"

"I was sewing it. *That's all.* If I'd put something so dangerous on the alb, I wouldn't have gone anywhere near it. Why would I risk getting that stuff on my hands?"

"As a smoke screen, or to misdirect the police?"

A tear ran down Celia's cheek, but she wiped it away quickly. "You're so determined to believe I'm guilty that you're not really listening to anything I say."

"You're still playing games, Celia. Just like your mother always said you did." He stood and leaned forward, resting his palms on the table. "How about the truth this time? For once in your life?"

Celia began to shake. "My mother doesn't know a thing about me. She never did," she whispered. "I've told you the truth."

John Bruno stood. "And that's the end of this interview, Sheriff. I'm not letting you badger my client, or intimidate her with that cheap handcuff trick. If you want to bring charges against my client, do so. I'll have her out on bail by the time you finish booking her. And then we'll talk to the district attorney, and maybe even the state attorney general about your tactics."

"I don't have all the evidence I need to make an arrest yet," Tom said, his voice low, hard, and cold. "But I will get it. And when

I do, I'll be back." His eyes focused on Celia. "Being a nun won't keep you out of prison if you killed Father Anselm."

Sister Agatha went to Celia's side and led the postulant out into the corridor. She could feel the young woman shivering, though it was close to eighty degrees in this part of the monastery right now. "Go back to chapel. I'll be there shortly."

As Celia walked away, John Bruno came up to the grille. "The sheriff wants to talk to you now. I think I should stick around."

"Fine, but it's the sheriff who'll need protecting, not me," she said, then took a deep breath, bringing her temper under control. "Let's go."

As she reentered the parlor, Sheriff Green's eyes focused on her. "I have only one question for you, Sister. Did you know about Celia's problem with Father Anselm?"

"I knew nothing for sure," she said, heeding Bruno's advice and keeping it simple.

"But you had your suspicions. Why didn't you tell me before now?"

"Don't answer that until we talk, Sister."

She glanced at Bruno and shook her head. "I'll go ahead and answer." Sister Agatha looked back at the sheriff. "Tom, I'm going to be perfectly honest with you. I wasn't withholding evidence. There was nothing to discuss except an incident I'd witnessed between Father and Celia—and that happened *after* I found Celia sewing the alb. Until that moment, Celia and Father Anselm had never actually met face-to-face." She gave him the details about the encounter with the food delivery.

"That couldn't have been their first meeting. They must have seen each other prior to that. Doesn't she go to communion every day?"

"I don't think he ever noticed her. It's one thing to see someone on the outside, and another to see a postulant in her veils as you're giving communion to a line of nuns who come up to an opening in the enclosure grille. And during confession, there's a screen between the priest and the penitent." She took a deep breath, then continued. "Think about this, Tom. It doesn't add up. Why would Celia have tried to make Father Anselm sick? It would have served no purpose. Father wouldn't have broken the seal of the confessional no matter what Celia had told him in the past."

"But we only have her word that everything that passed between them was under the seal of the confessional. Father Anselm isn't in a position to contradict anything."

John Bruno held up one hand. "All you've got is speculation. The monastery has done all you asked. That's enough for one day."

"There is one more thing I need to tell you," Sister Agatha added before the lawyer could usher Tom out of the building. "I didn't think it was important at the time it happened. But now, under the circumstances, I believe it may be. I remembered it while you were questioning Celia," Sister Agatha said. "I think you should hear this, too, Mr. Bruno."

The lawyer shrugged. "All right. One more thing."

"With everything that happened since Father Anselm died, this had slipped my mind. But I realize now that it could have been connected directly to the person who harmed Father." She proceeded to tell Sheriff Green about the note in the turn, the one that had suggested someone was about to be hurt.

"Where's that note now?"

"It was thrown away after the requested prayers were offered the night of the murder. But it came through the turn, which means that someone on the outside left it there. This may be linked to the intruder we suspect caused Father's death."

"Tell me what you remember about the note, and give me the wording exactly as you remember it." Green brought out his notebook, and she complied as well as she could.

"This may or may not help the case against the postulant. Unless we can track the note back to the author, and find a new motive for the crime, nothing has changed," he warned.

"Except it raises doubts about the direction your investigation is going in," Sister Agatha answered. "The postulant isn't permitted in the outer parlor."

Sheriff Green shrugged, reaching for the doorknob. "Don't get your hopes up."

John Bruno waited until the sheriff left. "You handled him well, Sister, and that piece of new information about the note may help muddy his trail of evidence, too. But be careful. He's got the reputation for being like a pit bull when he's on a case. He'll play with your head."

"Maybe, but it's hard to confuse someone who's telling the truth. That's our best defense."

He smiled. "And it's a good one." He paused. "But your postulant does have some secrets she's not telling, Sister. I've been practicing law for too many years not to know when someone is holding things back."

"I'm certain that it's nothing that will implicate our postulant in Father Anselm's murder. But I'll find out what's going on. Or, if I can't, Reverend Mother will. You can count on it."

Sister Agatha let John Bruno out, then went directly to Reverend Mother. After telling her what had happened, including the information about the note in the turn, the abbess went with Sister Agatha to join Sister Bernarda, who was waiting in the hall outside the chapel.

"The cells need to be straightened up," Sister Agatha reported.

"The same holds for the kitchen and the infirmary. The provisory," Sister Bernarda said, using the nuns' term for the pantry, "is in the worst shape of all. Food is everywhere. Sister Clothilde will have a fit when she sees it."

She was about to suggest that they gather Celia and Sister Mary Lazarus and try to make things better before the nuns returned from chapel, but a soft murmur beginning to rise from the corridor told her it was already too late.

Here, that murmur was the equivalent of a roar. Silence soon settled over them again as Reverend Mother signaled they could leave chapel. Without saying another word, the nuns formed teams and began to work quickly to restore order to their house.

With the exception of stopping for the Liturgy of the Hours, they worked tirelessly. By the time the period for Manual Labor was over the monastery showed no evidence of the sheriff's visit.

Knowing that all of them needed to connect with the One they served now, both Sister Bernarda and Sister Agatha locked the parlor doors and attended Vespers. This time would be set aside for the sisters, their monastery, and God.

Afterward, strengthened, the nuns took up their routine tasks, trying to set the earlier confusion aside once and for all. Sister Agatha looked around for Reverend Mother and found her outside, rosary in hand, Pax by her side.

The dog had adopted all of them now, and he seemed to be acquiring the ability to find those who needed his company the most.

"Praised be Jesus Christ, Mother," Sister Agatha said as she approached.

"Now and forever."

"Mother, I'd like your permission to visit Ruth Moore, Celia's mother. It's clear that Celia is holding something back that concerns her past life, something that is deeply disturbing to her. I don't think that it's anything to do with Father's death, but I'd still like to know what it is. And Mr. Bruno feels it's important as well. I think the time's come for me to go and speak to Ruth directly."

"Godspeed, then. But take Pax, child. Celia's home, I was told by Celia herself, is in an unsavory part of town."

"I'll do that, Reverend Mother."

Without waiting for Sister Agatha to call him, Pax stood and went over to her. He then followed her, staying close beside her, as she walked down the path that led to where the Harley was parked.

13

I T WAS AFTER SIX WHEN SISTER AGATHA SET OUT WITH PAX IN the sidecar. She hadn't seen Ruth since high school. Back then, the world had seemed filled with infinite possibilities for both of them.

As Sister Agatha rounded a bend in the highway, heading south toward town, she caught a glimpse of a large black pickup approaching at high speed from behind her. An uneasy feeling began to creep up her spine. She slowed slightly, and the big Ford truck roared around, cutting close in front of her. Dropping her speed to avoid a collision, she tried to get a look to the driver of the truck, but all she saw was the headrest. The license plate was missing.

Thinking it was most likely a youngster who'd been drinking, she kept a careful watch as she continued into town.

About two miles farther along, she noticed a black truck, probably the same one as before, coming in her direction. Fear touched the edges of her mind, and she automatically slowed down, looking for a possible turnoff and wondering what would happen next.

A few seconds later, the truck moved to the center of the road, taking half of her lane. It was coming right at her. "Hang on, Pax!" Sister Agatha braked hard, pulling over as far as she dared onto the shoulder and scanning the terrain in case she had to leave the road completely.

The truck roared toward her. At the last second, the driver leaned on the horn and swerved back into the proper lane. There was no chance this time for her to even try to get a look at the driver.

"We're getting out of here," she yelled to Pax, and eased the Harley back onto the highway. The bike and sidecar seemed all right, despite the jolts of their ride on the unpaved shoulder, so she twisted the throttle and brought the speed up to sixty, sneaking glance after glance in the rearview mirror. Soon the truck was just a black dot in the distance.

Had she just faced a drunk kid out to harass a motorcyclist, the unnamed man who had hoped to get the Harley in payment of a debt, or Father's killer? If it had been an attempt to unnerve her by the person who'd been promised the motorcycle, it had worked.

"Pax, you're sticking with me like glue from now on whenever I leave the monastery. I don't like what's happening out here." Her hands were shaking and her body felt cold, though it was still very hot outside.

Switching directions at the last minute, she headed into the center of town, deciding to stop by the sheriff's office next. He needed to know what had just happened. With luck, she'd be able to convince him not to tell Reverend Mother and worry her. As she pulled into the parking lot, she saw him and his wife standing near the giant Dumpsters at the back. From their expressions it was easy to see they were having a fight.

She hesitated, wondering if she should make her report now, or wait. As she watched, Gloria raised her fist, but he intercepted her hand quickly and forced it back down. The side door opened then, and as a deputy came out, Gloria stalked off through the hedge that separated the station from the neighboring residential area.

Tom glanced around, a scowl on his face, and suddenly saw her.

She had no choice now. As he approached, she set out to meet him halfway. "We have to talk. Do you have a moment?" she asked.

As he led her to his office, he remained silent. Stealing furtive glances at him, she weighed the implications of what she'd seen, and began to suspect that the bruise on his face had been one Gloria had given him. The purplish mark was still there, though fainter now.

"Is everything all right between you?" she asked softly.

He shrugged. "Gloria's got a temper, that's all."

"Did she hit you?"

He glanced at her coldly. "You mean this?" he asked, pointing to the bruised area below his eye. "Nah. We were horsing around that day, that's all. But let's not get into that. I've taken enough ribbing from the men here."

He never looked her in the eye, and she suspected he was lying. The bruise hadn't been the result of an accident. But she had to respect his privacy.

He waved her to the chair across from his desk. "What's up?"

She told him about the black truck and saw his expression grow hard and guarded. "Did you see the driver, or the license plate?"

"No, but I thought I'd better tell you about it. I wondered if it could be the man that Bobby Gonzales owed money to," she said, then filled him in. "I wish I had a name to give you. I sure don't like the idea of someone preying on kids around here."

"You did the right thing telling me. I'll look into it."

"Be careful how you go about it. Timothy is a good kid. He doesn't need the backlash."

He smiled. "Looking out for the underdog? That was always your style."

"He needs it. He's a good kid."

She stood and he walked her to the door. "I suppose Joan San-chez is in the clear?"

"Not in the clear, no, but my chief suspect is Celia."

She nodded once. "Well, I better get going."

"Be careful. And if you see that black pickup again, call me as soon as possible. And try to see if it's got any distinguishing marks."

"I'll give it my best shot." Leaving him to his business, she went back to the Harley with Pax.

As she set out, she took a deep breath and forced herself to focus on her meeting with Ruth. She remembered her as a girl whose main career goal had been to marry the high school football star and have a bunch of kids. But from what she'd heard from the town gossips over the years, that dream had gone awry.

As she drew near to the house, Sister Agatha realized that the neighborhood was even rougher than she'd remembered. A car full of young men was parked beside the curb, and two of them, in identical color headbands, were leaning out the street-side car windows, drinking beer and yelling back and forth at two girls on a porch. She hadn't heard language that rough in years.

Graffiti covered the neighborhood walls, and an abandoned brick building on the corner, cordoned off by yellow crime-scene tape, had all its windows broken out or covered by pieces of warped plywood. In the alley, just beyond the police tape, an old man in a heavy coat was pushing a grocery cart that apparently contained all his worldly possessions. This section of town now held the unmistakable stamp of poverty and despair.

Sister Agatha drove slowly up a narrow residential street, maneuvering carefully to avoid running over pieces of broken beer bottles on the pavement. There, at the end of the cul-de-sac, was a shabby one-story, flat-roofed adobe house. Several individual adobe bricks visible on one wall told her the building needed work, but in that respect it was no different from any other house on that block.

Ruth's home bore little resemblance to the same house she'd remembered visiting at the time of Celia's birth. The dwelling had been well maintained and landscaped back then, with flower boxes filled with geraniums, and wildflowers bordering the brick walkway from the gate to the door.

Now the archway that held the gate was gone, as well as most of the low adobe wall around the property. What was left was crumbling and blanketed with graffiti. Near the side of the house she could see a vegetable garden, and that was the only section of the grounds that appeared well tended.

"Come on, Pax. Stick with me." The truth was, she needed courage. It had been a shock to see how much things here had deteriorated, and she had a feeling that she'd have more unpleasant surprises before this visit was over.

Sister Agatha knocked on the door, and soon a woman came to answer. She was wearing a loose blue cotton knit top, a long, baggy, shapeless red skirt, and worn house slippers. It was a colorful outfit, but even less flattering than a nun's habit.

"Mary . . . Sister Agatha, is that you?"

Sister Agatha took a closer look at the woman's face then. It took her a few seconds before she realized that this was her old friend. Age had hardened Ruth's features beyond her true years, and her eyes were haunted as if she'd seen too much. She wore no makeup. Her face was pale, and the dark hair that framed it had been dyed a ghastly red-brown. She looked as lifeless as a store mannequin, but not as well dressed.

"Hello, Ruth," she greeted her, trying to sound upbeat.

"What brings you here? Don't tell me my kid is giving *you* a problem now!" she said, gesturing for Sister to come inside. There had once been a screen door, apparently, but all that remained was the bare wood and scars where the hinges had been removed. Noticing Pax for the first time, Ruth suddenly froze. "Whoa. That's a big dog."

"He's a teddy bear, really. His name is Pax, and he's the monastery's new unofficial guardian."

Ruth smiled, stepping aside to let Sister and Pax enter, then closing the door behind them. "Well, if you vouch for him, he's welcome inside and out of this heat, too." She led the way into the living room. A large fan stood on an end table, moving back and forth to stir the hot, stale air.

Sister Agatha followed Ruth into the kitchen. The interior of the house was encased in a gray gloom, but the house was neat and orderly. The only light besides that filtering around the edges of the dark, faded curtains came from dozens of votive candles that flickered atop a metal TV tray behind a two-foot-tall statue of the Blessed Virgin that dominated one corner of the living room. Ruth had never been particularly religious, so seeing that statue and the candles took Sister Agatha by surprise.

"Do you have a special intention you're praying for?" she asked, then instantly chided herself. *Smooth, Sister.*

"It's for protection. A woman and her daughter living alone in this neighborhood need all the help they can get."

"Whatever happened to Jerry? Does he ever come around anymore?" she asked, referring to Celia Clines' dad. Celia seldom, if ever, spoke about her parents. Now she was starting to realize why.

"He left me when Celia turned eight. He just went out for cigarettes one day and never came back. That wasn't an easy time for any of us."

She remembered Jerry Clines, the high school star quarterback. He and Ruth had been madly in love. She remembered their wedding and the high hopes they'd shared for their future. But, from what she'd heard, they'd never left town to follow their dreams.

"So how's Celia doing? That girl was such a wild one when she was at home. But maybe now that she's changed her ways and joined the monastery, the Lord will save her from eternal damnation."

"Celia is very devout," Sister Agatha said cautiously.

Hearing a rock station playing softly from another room, Ruth bolted to her feet. "Wait a sec." She hurried down the hall, then threw open one of the doors on her right. "You turn that noise off right now, Betsy. I don't allow the devil's music in this house and you know it. If you want to keep that radio, you'll listen to the stations I select. Is that clear?"

"Mom, I was just changing—"

"I'm not interested in excuses. And why haven't you cleaned this room yet? Laziness is the first symptom of wickedness, young lady. Now get to work."

"Mom, I already cleaned my room!"

"There's dust on the windowsill. I can see it from here. After you're finished, I want you to memorize Psalm Fifty. The psalm of contrition will do you a world of good. When you're ready, come out of your room and recite it for me."

"Mom, I can't! Not now. I have to meet Michelle at the library."

"You're not going anywhere. I know what you're up to. You'll tell me you're going to the library and end up in the backseat of some boy's car. You might as well forget it. It's not going to happen, Betsy."

Ruth returned to the kitchen a moment later. "Sorry about that. Betsy is at an age where I've got to watch her every second. She's fourteen and already boys are calling her here at home. I put a stop to it, of course, but I can tell she's going to be a slut, just like . . ." Her voice trailed off and she looked away.

"It's normal for her to have friends, Ruth. We did." She'd heard Ruth's conversation with her daughter, and the entire exchange had left her stunned. The Ruth she'd known once had never been like that. "You and I were famous schoolwide for not letting rules get in the way of fun, remember?" she added with a tiny smile.

For a moment she saw a flicker of life in Ruth's eyes and the woman nearly smiled. But then, in a heartbeat, her somber expression returned.

"Life can be very hard, Sister. You work, you dream, then you get your heart broken. Neither one of my daughters is going to go down the same path I did. I want them both to be God-fearing, moral children. God only protects those who turn to Him wholeheartedly."

"I agree, Ruth," she said softly. "But the key is balance. Kids need time to be kids, too."

"You're in that monastery now. You have no idea what temptations kids face these days. I won't have Betsy become an abomination unto the Lord."

Sister Agatha stared at Ruth, trying hard to understand what had happened to the young carefree girl she'd known once. "It must have been very hard on you to raise your girls alone."

"The hardest time of my life came when Jerry left me. He was the one great love of my life," she said softly, then continued. "At first I didn't know what had happened, if he was hurt or dead. But no one fitting his description showed up in crime reports or at the hospitals, and I found out when the bills came in that he'd cashed a check for exactly half the money we had in the bank."

"I'm so sorry. That must have been a shock."

"It was. Eventually, I figured out why he'd left me. When there's never enough money to make the bills month after month, it wears a soul down. And, truth be told, no matter how hard we worked, we never had enough money to make ends meet. Things fell apart a little at a time, but we didn't even realize it until it was too late." She paused, her voice strained. "A year later, I was contacted by the police. He'd been in a convenience store when it got robbed. He got shot. He died before he could even say good-bye to his kid."

"I'm sorry to hear that. But you did a wonderful job raising Celia. She's going to be a real asset to the order."

Ruth smiled wearily. "It was sure an uphill battle, believe me. Did you know that when she was just twelve—two years younger than Betsy—she tried to commit suicide by taking an overdose of herbs I kept in my pantry?"

"Herbs?" Sister Agatha repeated, a sick feeling in the pit of her stomach.

"I was married to Mike Moore back then, and although he had a good job, the company he worked for was small and didn't offer benefits. We had no medical insurance, so I learned to depend on herbal medicine like a lot of the folks in the Spanish community."

Ruth gazed at an indeterminate spot across the room, a faraway look on her face. "I remember making hyssop tea for my girls, to keep them pure, you know? I'd read a psalm that said, 'Purge me with hyssop and I shall be clean.' I also found out that the herb had been used to cleanse the temples during biblical times, so I started keeping crushed leaves and flower tops in little containers all through the house. It made things smell nicer."

"You were saying something about Celia trying to commit suicide?"

"Oh—yes. She was such a moody child back then—clinical depression is what the doctors called it. They blamed her problems on the fact I'd married Mike and Celia didn't accept him, but I don't know. I think Celia was at that age—becoming a teenager."

"What happened?" Sister Agatha pressed. Obviously, Ruth was hoping to sidestep the whole matter, but Sister Agatha had no intention of letting it go.

"I'd kept pennyroyal on hand back then—some of the herb and a small amount of the oil. The herb can be used as a decongestant and a cough remedy. The oil, though, is trickier—two tablespoons can cause death. The only reason I'd kept it around was because it was a great insect repellent. You could add just a little to regular skin cream and not have a mosquito or a fly bother you all day. I'd cautioned Celia never to touch it. If she wanted to use it, she was to come to me. But one day while I was out, she went into one of her dark moods and tried to kill herself by drinking some of the oil."

"Were you the one who found her?"

Ruth nodded. "I took her to the university hospital in Albuquerque the second I found her. They saved her life, but they told me she needed psychiatric help or she'd try again. With the help of some people from the welfare office, they arranged to have Celia spend time at Nazareth Hospital in Albuquerque." Ruth rubbed her temples as if pained by the memory of that trying time.

Taking a deep breath, she looked up and continued in a more positive tone of voice. "But those days are behind her now. She got the help she needed and that's all that matters. Of course, I never told anyone around here *where* she was. I just let them think that Celia had gone to spend some time with my sister in California."

"I'm so sorry you had to go through all that. I wish you'd have written me. I was living in Albuquerque then, but that's still close. I might have been able to do something to help you."

She shook her head. "There was nothing you could have done. Even Mike gave up on all of us after that," she said sadly. "But I prayed about it day and night, and now my Celia is going to become a cloistered nun in a monastery where she'll always be protected from the evils of the world."

Sister Agatha wasn't sure what to say about that. Obviously evil touched everything—including their monastery. But rather than arguing the point, she decided to stay on her investigative course. "Tell me, which herbs do you keep these days?"

"A little of everything. Is there something you need?"

"What can you tell me about monkshood?"

"Not much, except that the local gossips say it was used to kill

Father Anselm. Personally, I've never used it, or heard of anyone who does. I'm told it can be used for reducing fever, and as a topical anesthetic, but it's highly dangerous."

"The plant is supposed to have beautiful, distinctive blue or white flowers, and people often mistake the root for a radish."

"There's no danger of that in this family. I hate radishes, and I always have."

A long silence stretched out between them. Then there was a soft sound, like muted footsteps in the living room. Pax, who had curled up by Sister Agatha's feet, lifted his head.

Suddenly Ruth bolted out of her chair so fast that Sister Agatha followed, worried that something terrible must have happened.

They found Betsy by the front door. She was wearing tight jeans and a tube top that exposed her middle. Her lipstick was dark red, almost black, and her eyelids thick with poorly applied makeup.

For a moment Ruth just stared, her face crimson. "You harlot! Get into the bathroom and clean off that paint. How dare you try to sneak past me, especially dressed like that!" She grabbed Betsy by the arm, pulled her into the bathroom, and shoved her inside.

Sister Agatha held Pax firmly by the collar. She could tell he was nervous at Ruth's rough handling of the girl, and she wasn't sure what he might do. Taking him outside, she ordered him to stay on the porch, then went back inside.

As she did, she heard Ruth's voice coming from down the hall. "Wash your face, then put on some decent clothes. Then I want you on your knees while you memorize that psalm I gave you. You are *not* to leave this room until you've done that." She shut and locked the door from the outside.

Sister Agatha heard Betsy sobbing, and felt a cold chill go up her spine.

"Don't look at me like that," Ruth snarled. "Do you want her pregnant like I was, not even out of high school? I won't let her ruin her life like I did. She *will* glorify God, not dishonor him."

"She shouldn't have tried to sneak out, I agree, especially dressed like that. But if you want her to turn to God, don't use Him as a weapon to punish her," she said, trying to reason with her.

"You're not a mother, and you don't have a child to raise. You can't possibly know what I go through. Stick to what you do, Sister, and I'll do the same. If you really want to help, pray for Betsy's soul. She's going down the road to perdition as surely as there's a sunset at the end of each day."

When Sister Agatha left Ruth's home, she felt more troubled than ever. Celia had undoubtedly wanted to keep her suicide attempt a secret. But Sister still didn't know for sure if that was the secret Celia and Father Anselm had shared—the one Celia seemed determined to hide. She thought of the herb Celia had used . . . pennyroyal. The very mention of that herb had disturbed her, but she couldn't figure out why.

Stroking Pax's massive head, she stood next to the motorcycle, trying to decide what to do next. The bookmobile wouldn't be much help, even if she were lucky enough to catch it in town. That's when she remembered the extensive library in the rectory. Father Anselm had made it a point to collect books on almost every subject, usually getting them at low cost at garage sales or estate sales.

She'd pay Father Mahoney an unscheduled visit. Maybe he'd let her take a look through the books there and see if she could find out more about pennyroyal.

When she and Pax arrived at the rectory a short time later, Frances answered the door and invited them in. "I've been hearing about you two all over town!" she said, leaning down to pet Pax. "He's a beauty, isn't he, and so big."

The dog wagged his tail happily.

"Pax, vanity is a sin," Sister Agatha said in mock reproach. She laughed when the dog gave her one of his happy panting grins.

Hearing their conversation, Father Mahoney came out of a nearby room. "The famous Sister Agatha and Brother Pax!" he said. "It's a pleasure to see you here. I hope that all is well with the sisters."

"Father Mahoney," she greeted, and shook hands with him.

"Father Rick, please. It's less formal, and I prefer it."

"Father Rick, then. We're all fine, thank you, and relieved to have a chaplain again."

Father Rick was wearing shorts and a T-shirt and looked as if he'd been in the middle of a workout. The priest had more muscles than any other human being she'd ever seen. She thought he could probably bench-press a Buick without raising a sweat.

"You'll have to forgive me, Sister. Had I known you were coming by I would have postponed my weight training. I may not be a wrestler anymore, but I've found that staying fit makes it easier to keep up with the demands of God's work. Now tell me, Sister, what can I do for you?"

"I hoped to look something up in the library here. Would you mind?"

"Not at all. Come in." He led her to the book-lined study.

Sister Agatha looked quickly through the well-organized collection and soon located a large volume on folk medicine.

"Are you looking for information about the herb that killed Father Anselm?"

Sister Agatha paused. "No, right now I'm investigating what may be a related matter. Since it may not be connected, I'd rather not discuss it yet, but Reverend Mother asked me to follow all the leads that presented themselves. The sheriff, you see, believes one of the sisters is somehow involved in Father's death, and that's making things very difficult for all of us. He even wanted to haul our postulant to the station for questioning."

Father shook his head. "I really wish there was more I could do for you all."

"You're our chaplain. Your support and prayers are more than enough." She lifted down two smaller books on herbs and carried them to the sofa. "I'll get out of your way as soon as I can."

"Take your time. I'll go back to my workout. Let me know if there's anything else I can do for you."

Alone, Sister searched through the books. Since so many rural communities in New Mexico used herbal remedies, Father Anselm had collected several books on the subject. He'd told her once that he considered it his business to learn the practices and customs of his parishioners.

There was no mention of pennyroyal in the smaller books, but as she opened the large one and checked the index, she found it. Four pages described the herb and detailed its uses. Suddenly she knew why she'd felt so disturbed by Ruth's mention of the herb.

Throughout history, pennyroyal oil had been used with disastrous results by young women who'd wanted abortions. She remembered an incident many years back when she'd been a professor. One of her freshman students had bought the oil extract at a shop in the city and used it to terminate her pregnancy. The very toxic preparation had resulted in her death as well as that of the child she'd carried.

Had Celia's suicide attempt been something more than the result of depression? If what she now suspected was true, she could understand why the postulant had been so afraid that she'd be asked to leave the monastery.

Frances came in with a glass of iced tea. "Here. I thought you could use this. I've got Pax in the kitchen eating dog biscuits. Well, old cookies I was going to throw out."

Sister Agatha smiled and thanked her on behalf of both of them.

As Frances glanced down at the book, she added, "Are you trying to find out more about Celia?"

"Just seeing this page made you think of her?" Sister asked.

Frances sighed. "You know, I've lived here all my life, and in a town this size, it's darned near impossible to keep a secret. I remember hearing all about her so-called suicide attempt years and years ago. Then Celia was sent away. There was a lot of talk going around then. Celia didn't return for almost a year and a half, but while she was still away, Ruth showed up in town with an infant girl—her adopted daughter, Betsy."

"I bet that caused a stir."

"There was a lot of talk. At first some thought that maybe she'd finally flipped and kidnapped a child because she was lonely. Mike Moore had left her by then and she had no one. Others thought that maybe it was Celia's baby and Ruth had adopted it. In those days it wasn't at all uncommon for unmarried, pregnant teens to leave town to have their babies. It saved embarrassing their families."

"And I suppose Ruth never tried to clear things up?"

"She hardly spoke to anyone. But Sheriff Salazar checked things out, and the baby's adoption papers were in order. Later, Ruth told people that her sister had been overwhelmed by the birth of her sixth child, and had asked her to adopt Betsy. That kind of private arrangement was the only way anyone figured Ruth could have qualified as an adoptive parent." She shrugged, then added, "But I don't think Betsy knows that Ruth isn't her natural mother, so keep it to yourself."

"Sheriff Salazar moved away years ago, didn't he?"

"Yes. A lot of people miss his old-fashioned style of law enforcement. He kept the town clean."

"He was one tough cookie. I remember him from when I was growing up here."

She smiled. "People used to say that if a rattlesnake ever bit him, the rattlesnake would die. He was mean, all right, but only to those who broke the law." Hearing the phone ring, the housekeeper left to answer it.

A few minutes later, Pax padded into the room. "You must have ESP, Pax. It's time for us to go," she said, replacing the books she'd used back on the shelf. "I've got more information than I ever expected to get—and no idea what to do with all of it."

If Betsy was fourteen now and Celia had only just turned twenty-seven, Sister Agatha knew that the chances were good that Betsy was Celia's child. The theory fit on many levels, but she still had no solid evidence, and conjecture alone wasn't enough to warrant turning Celia's and Betsy's lives upside down.

After saying good-bye, Sister Agatha headed back to the monastery. The gravel road ahead of her was deserted, but she could see headlights behind her. A shudder ran up her spine. Even thinking of the big black pickup that had forced her off the road made her heart begin to race.

Soon the road around her became dark as pitch. She went

slowly, realizing that on a moonless night she'd never be able to see the ruts in the gravel road well enough to steer clear of them.

She saw the flicker of lights in her rearview mirror, but if someone was tailing her, they weren't making any effort to close in on her this time. On the other hand, if they were coming this way on purpose, she'd soon learn who it was, because the road led to few other places besides the monastery.

Checking back again a few moments later, she saw only red taillights. The vehicle had turned around. The next time she looked, they had disappeared.

By the time she returned home, Compline had been chanted, and the monastery was shrouded in silence. Sister Agatha went to the scriptorium and worked for a long while beside Sister Bernarda. Though neither of them broke the Great Silence, the look exchanged between them told Sister Agatha that Sister Bernarda knew that something was troubling her. It was often that way between the Sisters. They knew each other too well to hide what they were feeling. When one sister was having a problem, all tried to share her heaviness of spirit so the burden would be easier to shoulder.

She remembered the ancient formula said on the day a nun made her vows. To the bishop's query, "What do you ask?" a nun would reply, "The Mercy of God, the poverty of the order, and the company of the sisters." That defined the family they became, and the bond that strengthened them.

Celia came into the room then and sat down by one of the computers. Sister Bernarda silently gave her materials to work with, then returned to her own computer.

Sister Agatha continued working, trying not to look at Celia. Few postulants made it past the first six months. It was the way of things. Yet, despite everything she'd learned today, in her heart, she still felt that Celia's vocation was real and that she hadn't killed Father Anselm. But that still left two very important questions— who was the real killer, and why had the priest been a target?

As Sister Mary Lazarus came into the scriptorium, Sister Agatha stood up. Signaling the others to continue the work they'd begun, she left everything in the capable hands of Sister Bernarda, and went to the infirmary. Her hip and her hands were hurting too much to ignore any longer today. She'd take her pills now, and with luck, the pain would ease by morning.

But there was another pain, one deep within her, that pills would never reach. That would remain with her until the day she found the truth . . . and maybe long after that.

Sister Agatha took the first shift of portress duty the following morning. It was roughly nine-thirty when Sister Bernarda appeared at the inner door leading to and from the enclosure. "Reverend Mother wants to see you."

Sister Agatha bowed her head and, leaving Sister Bernarda in the parlor, hurried to find Reverend Mother. The abbess was just down the hall, near the patio.

Reverend Mother smiled at her, then led her out into the garden. "Tell me what you've learned, child."

Sister Agatha detailed everything she'd found out the day before. "Mother, all I have are suspicions. I'm not even sure Celia was trying to commit suicide—I think it might have been an abortion attempt. But I'm basing that solely on the properties of the herb pennyroyal."

Reverend Mother sat down heavily on one of the benches shaded by the tall cottonwood near the statue of St. Francis. "It just gets worse and worse, doesn't it?"

Sister Agatha didn't answer, knowing Mother really didn't expect it.

"We can't ask Celia to leave the monastery for sins she may have committed as a child. No one has ever entered our order free of sin and our Lord's commandment on forgiveness is clear. Who are we to do something other than follow the example He set for us? Of course I'll have to have a long talk with her, but before I do, I'd like to know the whole story."

"I'll try to find out more today, Mother." With a small bow, she left Reverend Mother and hurried inside.

Sister Agatha knew she couldn't involve Sheriff Green in this.

He'd see the possibility that Father Anselm might have known about Celia's alleged abortion attempt as a motive for his murder. But one way or another, before the day was through, she would learn what they needed to either clear Celia or condemn her.

Although the prospect of damning her own godchild filled Sister Agatha with dread, she knew the time for truth had come. She had to be fearless and see through what she'd started, before it destroyed everyone and everything she loved.

14

SISTER AGATHA SET OUT FOR THE SCHOOL WITH PAX, A PLAN firmly in mind. She was certain Betsy Moore was a student there. With her mother's strong feelings about religion, she couldn't see Ruth sending her to public school. Twice, she thought someone was following her at a set distance. The vehicle was a light-colored sedan, not the pickup this time. And on both occasions it disappeared just as she turned around to go check things out.

She was certain it was being done deliberately to intimidate her, but she'd never cared much for bullies, and always made a point of standing up to them. The only thing this person harassing her had done was make her even more determined to find out who he was as soon as possible.

She arrived at the school thirty minutes later and headed for Patsy Romero's office, Pax by her side. She found the woman sorting through stacks and stacks of files.

"Hi, Sister," she said, looking up and pushing her glasses farther up her nose. "I see you brought Pax inside with you. That's a good thing. It's hot, and shady spots outside are few and far between to-day."

"I'm glad you're okay with it," she said. Looking directly at her,

Sister Agatha continued. "I'm here to ask a favor. I'd like to take a look at Betsy Moore's student records."

"Betsy? She's a good kid and bright too, one of our scholarship kids. But her mom's a loon. Why are you interested?"

"I'd rather not say, but Patsy, you know I wouldn't ask if it wasn't really important."

"Okay, I'll leave the matter between you and your conscience. The records are private, and open only to authorized school personnel. You're on our substitute teacher list, so I'll authorize your access. Remember, though, you can make notes, but we don't allow copies to be made unless the parent requests that records be sent to another school."

Patsy went to one of the cabinets in the adjacent office and, after a brief search, found the requested file and pulled it out. "You can use the conference room down the hall for as long you need. After you're finished, just return the file to me. I'll put it back."

Sister Agatha walked to the other end of the administrative offices, Pax at her side. Making herself comfortable in the conference room, she began to study the records. The file was filled with information, but not the kind she needed. Betsy's birth date was right, about six months after Celia had been sent away to Nazareth Hospital. There was also a date of issue on the birth certificate. New Mexico birth certificates normally didn't include that. This indicated that a second birth certificate had been issued to the adoptive parent. But that still didn't tell her who Betsy's birth mother was. All the records here simply listed Ruth as the girl's mother and Michael Moore as the father.

Disappointed, she leafed through the rest and found some notes on a recent student-parent-teacher conference. Ruth had refused to cooperate with Betsy's teacher, accusing the woman of being lax in discipline and irresponsible. At one point, the report stated, Betsy had run out of the room crying.

Sister Agatha leaned back. How could anyone have changed so much? At the public high school they'd all attended in Bernalillo, Ruth had been voted the most likely to change the world. Now she was an embittered middle-aged woman who used God as a weapon.

"You look like your thoughts are miles away," Lenora Martinez, the office secretary, said, coming into the room to place some files inside the cabinet in the corner.

"I was just thinking of an old friend, Ruth Moore. She's changed so much! When we were growing up she was always upbeat and idealistic. She had so many plans for herself, but I think life twisted her dreams until they became nightmares and she's become very disillusioned."

"With what I know about Mrs. Moore now, it's hard for me to sympathize with her. She's made her daughter Betsy's life as miserable as her own. Of course, since people confide in me all the time, I've learned that happens more often that we like to think," Lenora said somberly. "Fortunately, things can turn around sometimes. You've got a good example of that right in your own monastery."

"Excuse me?"

"Anita Linney . . . I mean Sister Mary Lazarus. Her marriage was a disaster, though she stuck to it for over ten or fifteen years, in perfect faith. After her husband passed away, she was finally free to follow her heart but, by then, it was too late for her and her first love to get together again. Lucky for her she found her calling. Otherwise, she might have ended up like Ruth, bitter and lonely."

"I never knew about all that."

"Well, I guess it was after your time. I mean they were at least four years behind you in high school. But it's no great secret. Anita and Frank Walters were close in high school, but Frank didn't want the responsibility of marriage, so she settled for second best. Unfortunately, things didn't work out very well. After her husband died, she tried to rekindle the flame with Frank, I heard. But Frank's still not the marrying sort. He never even married Joey's mom."

"Do you think Sister Mary Lazarus entered the monastery because she gave up on Frank?" If that was the case, Sister Agatha could finally understand why their novice had not found happiness at Our Lady of Hope. The monastery wasn't for people running away from something. It only filled the hearts of those turning toward God.

"Honestly? I don't know. There was a lot of gossip at the time, some of it just wild speculation that I didn't want to listen to, but Sister Mary Lazarus and God are the only ones who know the truth for sure."

After Lenora left, Sister Agatha stood up and went to the computer set up on a small cart against the wall. Using the monastery's password, she checked diocesan records for Betsy's birth, and then for her baptismal records, but both recorded only Ruth as Betsy's mother.

She turned off the computer and leaned back in her seat. Something wasn't right. But there was only one way to find out more, and that was to visit Nazareth Hospital in Albuquerque, less than forty minutes away. She knew a former nun who worked there now. Maybe Suzi would be able to help her.

Sister Agatha stood up, ready to return the file to Patsy, when Timothy Johnson came in with a note addressed to the school secretary.

"Hey, Sister Agatha. Whatcha working on?"

"Just looking for a few pieces of information," she said vaguely, keeping Betsy's file close to her so he couldn't see the name on it.

"Is Pax with you?" he asked.

She gestured to the corner. Pax was lying underneath the air conditioner vent enjoying the cool breeze.

"Smart dog. It's pretty hot out there today."

"How's the search for monkshood going?" she asked. Right now she needed to get him thinking like a team player. It would help her get him into the proper mind frame before she asked her next question.

"We haven't found any more plants, Sister. But we haven't given up."

"If you do find a good stand of monkshood plants, especially if it looks like some have been cut back or pulled up, make sure you let me know right away. You can either call the monastery, or if it's after parlor hours and you're in the neighborhood, you can always leave a note in the turn."

"The nun's drive-up window?" Seeing her nod, he continued. "I've heard the kids use it to leave prayer requests."

As she thought about it, she realized that they hadn't received any requests lately. Like Mass attendance, requests had dropped considerably.

"Timothy, I really need your help. Will you give me the name of the man who thought he was going to get Bobby Gonzales's Harley—the one the monastery owns now?"

He looked around nervously. "Sister, you shouldn't talk about that here. What if somebody comes in?"

"I give you my word that no one will ever know you told me. Look at it this way—if you can't trust a nun, who can you trust?"

He hesitated. "Sister, I've heard this guy's really bad news."

"I'll be careful, but I'll be safer if I know who he is. Won't you help me?"

He considered it for a long moment, looked around again, then selected a small piece of scrap paper and wrote something down on it. "All right. It's one of the names on this paper, but I need to be able to swear I didn't tell you, so you'll have to figure out which one it is for yourself. After you finish, destroy the paper. Don't leave it here."

She looked down at the paper. The first name on it was George Washington, the second St. Jude, and the third was Don Malcolm. She nodded, and wadded up the paper before placing it in her pocket.

He dropped his voice to a whisper. "He owns a pawnshop here in Bernalillo, and I heard somebody say once that he owns an adult book place, too."

Sister Agatha had heard of Malcolm as well. He sometimes let farmers pawn items during drought years, when times were hard, then charged them excessive fees when they came to get their valuables back. Father Anselm had mentioned Don Malcolm to her a few times. One of his elderly parishioners had paid for her husband's funeral with her diamond engagement ring, and Father had tried to get it back for her, but hadn't been able to do so because of the high interest tacked on to the redemption fee.

"Thanks, Timothy."

"I better get to class. You might want to burn that paper at the monastery with a candle, just to be on the safe side."

On her way out, Sister Agatha stopped by Patsy Romero's office and returned the file. After saying good-bye, she left the building with Pax by her side, and drove over to the rectory. She hoped Father Rick would be willing to give her some sort of authorization to go through the records at Nazareth Hospital so she wouldn't have to ask her friend Suzi to bend the rules for her. And it wouldn't hurt to get a little more information on the place before she actually approached anyone there. At the moment, all she knew was that it was a psychiatric facility.

As Pax left with Frances to the kitchen, she joined Father Rick who was in his office working on Sunday's homily. "I'm afraid I don't know anything about Nazareth," he explained in response to her request, "and I have no authority to permit you to access their records. But Father Thomas Mullins, the chaplain there, is a friend of mine. He may be able to tell you whatever you need. But I warn you—Father Thomas is a stickler for rules, so don't expect him to cut corners for you."

Unfortunately, that was exactly what she needed. "Thanks, Father Rick."

Just as she was ready to leave, someone knocked on the front door. She glanced around and, not seeing Frances, decided to answer it herself.

"Sister Agatha! What are you doing here?"

Sister Agatha suddenly found herself face-to-face with Joan Sanchez, who was dressed much more conservatively than the last time they'd met. It was easy to see from Joan's face that she hadn't slept much lately. Sister Agatha thought of Reverend Mother, who had shown signs of the same affliction. Father Anselm's death was sparing no one.

"Is Father Rick around?"

"Yes. Come in," she invited, then showed her to the couch. "Joan, are you all right?" she asked softly.

Tears immediately filled the woman's eyes, and she clutched her small purse so tightly her knuckles turned white. "No. I'm in a mess, Sister. People are saying that I killed Father Anselm. Father was the only person who was ever kind to me in this petty little town. Why would anyone think I would hurt him?"

"One of the things that small towns excel at is gossip. It'll die down. Don't worry."

"But Sheriff Green thinks I'm guilty, too. He keeps coming around, asking questions about Father Anselm and me."

"Don't take it personally. We're all getting questions from him these days. He's just doing his job—trying to piece everything together so he can figure out what really happened." Charity demanded that she keep her thoughts to herself, but it was a tremendous relief for her to find out that Tom was still looking outside the monastery for answers.

Joan looked at Sister Agatha. "The thing is that I want to move and start out fresh someplace, but the sheriff's told me not to leave town. As long as I'm a suspect, it could look bad for me. Can you talk to him? I'm not guilty of anything. I shouldn't be treated like a criminal."

"All he wants is to find whoever killed Father Anselm. My talking to him on your behalf won't help you. He'll just see it as interference. If you feel you're not being treated fairly, talk to him about it face-to-face. Asking someone to speak on your behalf is likely to make him more suspicious. I know Sheriff Green. When he's working, he can come across as very cold and impersonal, but his heart is in the right place."

Father came in just then, and Joan repeated her request, asking him to help her.

"I can't. That's a police matter, not Church business," Father Rick said gently. "Perhaps you need to consult an attorney, who would know more about these matters than I do."

She stood up abruptly. "I should have known this was a waste of time. Both of you think I killed Father Anselm, too. Well, fine. Be that way."

Joan stormed out, leaving the door wide open before either Father or Sister could say a word.

"That went well," Father said, his wry smile softening his sarcasm as a car roared down the drive.

"She'll calm down," Sister said, closing the door. "And if she asks anyone else who knows Sheriff Green, they'll tell her the same thing I did."

"If she'd asked me for anything else, I would have done my best to help her, but I can't tell the sheriff how to do his job. As it is, I'm going to be on shaky ground when I meet with him tomorrow. The question I need answered may be privileged information, but I'd really like to know if he thinks Father Anselm's murder was a crime committed against him specifically, or if it was motivated by what he stood for. I can take care of myself, mind you, but there are a lot of people that I come in contact with, such as the housekeeper, altar boys, the choir, and all the parishioners. I wouldn't want to see anyone else end up as a victim if there's an attack on me."

"I know you must be worried because you're replacing someone who was murdered," she said softly, her heart going out to him. "But all the sisters will be keeping you in their prayers."

"I appreciate that."

She left the rectory a moment later feeling troubled. From the evidence, she doubted that whoever had killed Father Anselm had a grudge against priests in general, but the truth of the matter was that she just didn't know enough yet to rule anything out, and she suspected Tom Green didn't either.

She and the dog were walking over to the motorcycle at the curb when suddenly Pax stopped and looked off into an alley to the north, growling.

She looked in the direction he was staring, caught a brief glint of chrome, then heard a car drive off in the opposite direction.

She took a deep breath. Someone was following her. Visiting Nazareth Hospital could wait a little longer while she sorted things out here. Now that she thought about it, it would be better to call Suzi first and find out when she'd be available. Meanwhile, it was noon and in the light of day she felt decidedly brave. If Don Malcolm was haunting her because of the motorcycle, it was time she got that matter settled once and for all. He could have the valuable collector's motorcycle—if he was willing to donate good, reliable transportation to the monastery—a new car, for example. Reverend

Mother was sure to approve of that, and as much as she loved the Harley, the monastery's needs came first.

"Let's go, Pax." The big white German shepherd jumped effortlessly into the sidecar.

Sister drove to the south end of Bernalillo and approached Malcolm's Pawnshop, located in an area with numerous trucking firms and industrial operations. The graveled parking lot contained three late-model sports utility vehicles and a van. Apparently either Mr. Malcolm's business was booming, or else he attracted prosperous customers.

Parking the motorcycle near the entrance, she went inside with Pax at heel. The store, to her surprise, had very little inventory, and most of that seemed to be gathering dust. But there were sounds of activity from a back room.

A large, dark-haired man in a colorful tropical print shirt stared at her and Pax openly. "You're in the wrong place, Sister. This isn't a veterinarians's office, you're not blind, and I'm not Catholic. Hell, I'm not even a Christian most of the time. So you're out of luck if you're looking for a rabies shot for Snowball, or a handout."

"I know exactly where I am, and I want to speak to Mr. Malcolm."

His eyes narrowed. "You're talking to him now."

"Mr. Malcolm, I've heard that you think the Harley-Davidson motorcycle and sidecar that was donated to the monastery should have gone to you."

"You know about that, do you? Well, the Gonzales kid owed me some serious money. That's why he offered his wheels in exchange for canceling out his debt. But hey, no problem. Since I didn't get the bike, he'll just have to either raise the cash or work off his debt some other way."

"Since he's a minor, perhaps you should speak to his parents about it."

"Sister, I don't need a nun telling me my business. Now, unless you're here to turn over the bike to save Bobby's butt, it's probably best if you leave."

She took a deep breath. Don Malcolm had the kind of personality that grated on her nerves as much as screeching chalk on a blackboard, but she wouldn't let him get to her. "I actually came to make you an offer. If you're really that interested in the Harley, the monastery might be willing to sell it to you, or exchange it for suitable transportation—like a new car. Maybe a van or truck like one of those outside now."

He burst out laughing. "I'm supposed to buy you a new car for the chance to get a bike that, by all rights, should have been mine in the first place? Do I look like I just fell off the pumpkin truck, Sister?"

She was thinking that he looked like he'd just been run over by the pumpkin truck, but she couldn't say it. Instead, she gave him that special stare that nuns had perfected over the years to squelch any disrespect.

Malcolm never even flinched.

"You could think of it as doing a good deed for the monastery, and you'd still get something very valuable out of it. That Harley is a collector's item, you must know that already."

"Good deeds get you nowhere, Sister. I learned that a long time ago. Take the bike—for now."

"What about Bobby Gonzales's debt?"

Malcolm shrugged. "He's working it off."

At that moment a teenaged boy in baggy clothes, with a baseball cap on backward, came out of the back room. "We have some new merchandise that just came in."

Sister Agatha only caught a glimpse when the boy opened the door, but the back room was filled with video games, VCRs, stereo components, and even some computers.

Malcolm saw her trying to get a better look and motioned to the teen, who ducked back inside, quickly closing the door.

"Sister, don't you have a soul to save someplace? I'm already going to hell."

"Perhaps not. We need to talk, Mr. Malcolm. I don't like the idea of a boy as young as Bobby owing you so much money."

"Sister, life's a . . . rough. Get used to it. Now you better take off. I have work to do." He took a step around the counter toward her, but Pax stood up quickly and bared his teeth.

"My dog gets very nervous when people exhibit behavior that he considers threatening, sir," she said.

He stepped back. "Just go away, Sister. We're both wasting time."

She turned to leave, keeping the man in sight as she walked toward the door with Pax at her side. Suddenly three sheriff's cars and two state police cars raced into the parking lot, two heading around toward the back.

Malcolm ran for the side door, but before he could reach it, four uniformed and heavily armed officers rushed the door, weapons raised. "Hands up where we can see them," one shouted. "This is a raid."

Pax growled, and one of the officers yelled, "Rex, guard!" Pax recognized his former keeper and stood alert beside Sister Agatha, watching a state policeman in his charcoal gray uniform. All the sheriff's deputies wore khaki.

A moment later, Sheriff Green came into the front room from the back, holding a shotgun. "We're secure, sir," a deputy said.

Tom quickly took in the room. "What in the name of—" Moving quickly, he took Sister Agatha's arm and started to lead her out, but Pax growled and bared his teeth.

"It's okay, Pax, easy," Sister Agatha said quickly. "He's still a friend—I think."

Tom released her, but cocked his head toward the door. "Let's go."

Sister Agatha, Pax, and the sheriff hurried outside while the other officers searched the store.

"What the heck are you doing here?" he demanded. "Did the monastery send you to pawn something to raise money?"

"No. I came to find out if Don Malcolm was the one who has been following me." She gave him a quick recap, describing the light-colored sedan, which had never gotten close enough for her to identify, and reminding him about the black pickup she'd already told him about.

"Malcolm owns a black pickup, so I think he's probably the one who went after you. I'll try to find out for sure when I question him. I have no idea about the sedan, but I'll look into it."

"Is that why you're here—following up on the black pickup?"

He shook his head. "After you told me about Bobby's problem, I went to speak to him and his parents. Malcolm had been leaning on Bobby pretty hard, and had the kid scared spitless. I convinced him that we would protect him if he'd testify, so he agreed to co-operate with us. I knew Malcolm had a huge fencing operation but, until now, I hadn't been able to prove it."

"I saw a kid or two inside."

"More than a few were involved, believe me. Malcolm's been doing business with some of the high school seniors. He'd find one needing money, maybe trying to raise enough for textbooks at the university next semester, or for fixing a broken-down car they needed for an after-school job. With Bobby Gonzales, it was for money he'd already borrowed but couldn't pay back. His parents didn't know about it. Malcolm would loan them the money—but it came with an exorbitant interest rate, like a loan shark. When they couldn't square the debt fast enough, he'd offer them a deal—in lieu of break-ing their fingers. The kids were forced to break into homes or cars until they stole enough merchandise to clear the debt—except, with the interest he kept charging, it never would have been cleared."

"I'm glad you were able to shut him down."

"So am I, but don't ever try to deal with people like this man on your own again. You have no idea how much trouble you could have gotten into without some backup."

"I had Pax with me."

"If Malcolm had decided that you were a threat to him, he would have shot the dog first, then you, then dumped both your bodies out on the west mesa somewhere. There was a shotgun behind the counter in there."

He was so matter-of-fact about it that it chilled her to the bone.

Just then two deputies led Malcolm outside, past Sister Agatha. Malcolm turned and snarled at her. "You're no nun—you're a cop, right? What you got under that outfit, a tape recorder?"

For a moment, Sister Agatha thought he was going to spit at her, but in a heartbeat Tom stepped in front of her.

"Try it and you'll be sucking your supper through a straw for the next month," Green said, his voice low. "She's a nun—the real thing. Show some respect." Green glanced at the deputy. "Get him out of here."

Malcolm sneered. "Hey, make sure your boys lock up the place after they leave. There have been a lot of thefts in this area lately."

As two more teens were led out of the pawnshop, Sister Agatha noticed that a television station's van had arrived, and a camera-woman and a young reporter were moving in their direction.

"What are you doing here, Sister? Are you part of the sting, or an undercover officer?" the reporter asked, then held up the microphone.

"Don't say a word," Green told her quickly, then got into the reporter's face. "This is a crime scene. You'll have to step back until we cordon off the area. Then we can arrange for a briefing."

"I have an afternoon deadline. Just give me the bare bones. I saw the officers being briefed at the station, then followed them here. But I never expected to see a nun at the scene of a police raid. Is she a cop, or is she under arrest? And is she from the monastery? They sure seem to generate a lot of headlines lately."

"The sister has no relationship whatsoever to this case, so be careful what you print. I don't think your station can afford to take on the Church in a lawsuit," he warned.

Turning his back on the reporter, Tom walked with her toward his car, which was parked beside the Harley. "You and Pax are coming back to the station with me. I need to get a statement from you, and then we're going to talk about this stalker you've picked up."

"But I really have to get back to the monastery. Poor Sister Bernarda has been doing double duty lately—"

"Save it. This isn't open for negotiations."

She stared at him thoughtfully for a moment. "Sheriff, you haven't changed. The hardest thing for you to give—is in. I'll meet you at the station." Sister Agatha swung onto the Harley, signaled Pax into the sidecar, and roared off.

Once at the station, while Pax visited the deputies, most of them old friends, Sister Agatha spent the better part of an hour describing what had occurred each time she'd thought she'd seen someone tailing her. Of course, there wasn't much she could tell him, and that didn't improve the sheriff's mood.

"I thought it was Malcolm trying to intimidate me so I'd give him the Harley. But after talking to him, I'm not so sure about that anymore," Sister Agatha said.

"You didn't expect him to confess, did you? He doesn't admit to anything—even when you've nailed him. But this sort of thing is precisely why I didn't want you to get involved in this investigation in the first place. It's public knowledge now that you're on the trail of the killer. The person following you in that sedan could be anyone—a reporter, a motorcycle nut after the bike, or even the killer himself."

"If it is the killer, why hasn't he tried to harm me? I've been alone every time—except for Pax, of course."

"He may want to find out what you know first. Then, if he sees you as a threat, he'll try to take you out next. The perp's already killed once, so there's very little to stop him from doing it again."

"I won't back off—not until the monastery is totally in the clear." On his desk was a photo of Tom, his wife, and two boys. Gloria had been a pretty, young, dark-haired woman. She was still pretty, but now she was apparently blond. She and Tom had two mischievous-looking boys. They looked happy. She felt a momentary twinge of nostalgia for what might have been hers.

Tom leaned back in his chair. "Pax can only protect you to a point. When you two are out on the road in the Harley, his strength and speed are no help to you. And if the killer is armed . . ."

"I'm not relying strictly on the dog. I'm also trusting God to help me so I can do what's right."

"God helps those who help themselves."

"That's not in the Bible."

"It's in the Sheriff Green New Translation—coming soon on CD."

"Tom, I have to follow through on this. The monastery needs it to be settled. They're counting on me and I can't let them down."

He leaned forward and studied her expression. "You're on the trail of something, aren't you?"

She started to deny it, but then stopped. She wouldn't resort to lying to him or anyone else.

"I knew it," he said when she didn't answer right away. "What have you found out?"

"I have some suspicions, nothing more. If I learn anything you might find useful, I'll let you know right away."

He nodded once. "All right. One more thing. If you see that sedan following you again, call me as soon as you can get to a phone. Don't try to handle it alone like you did today."

"All right. Can I go back to the monastery now? I really have to talk to Reverend Mother as soon as possible. If the newspaper runs those photos of me at the raid, she's bound to get some calls and I'd like to prepare her for that."

"Go ahead. But stay in touch, you hear?"

"Loud and clear, Sheriff." With a wave, she walked out of the station with Pax by her side and headed home.

Today had sure turned out differently from what she'd planned. On the other hand, she knew more now than she had before. Tonight she'd call Suzi and arrange to meet her. Tomorrow, she'd visit Nazareth Hospital. With a little bit of luck, by the time she left there, she'd have more of the answers that had eluded her so far.

15

THE BELLS RANG SHORTLY AFTER DAYBREAK SIGNALING THE start of Lauds. Sister Agatha, who'd already been up more than an hour, joined the others in chapel. Chanting the Divine Office during the predawn hours, then at daybreak, was something she looked forward to each day. With her daily excursions outside the monastery, she needed the strength and focus it gave her more than ever now.

Seeing Tom Green so often these days was confusing. Apparently not all the feelings she'd had for him once had died. She'd thought they had—if they'd ever really existed at all. But now things just weren't as clear, and it wasn't just the stress they were all going through.

Sister Agatha worked in the scriptorium until after Terce trying to catch up on the work that needed to be done. As the bells rang, Sister Agatha stood and went to their weekly chapter of faults. The birth of St. John the Baptist would be celebrated soon, and the sisters were asked to pray for his blessing on them and for his help. Bowing until their foreheads touched the floor, each nun accused herself of her failings before Reverend Mother and the others.

When Sister Agatha's turn came, she knelt before the abbess and followed the example the others had set. "At times, I get so angry, Mother! I want the ones on the outside to understand what we do here—and, more, to *value* it. But they seldom do and then I find myself resenting them."

"You must try to be more patient, child," Reverend Mother answered. "You and Sister Bernarda carry a great burden because you're the face and the voice of this monastery to the community. Anger plays no part in your service to God. This week I want your prayers to focus on those who have lost their way, who may need a patient word or a kind gesture to remind them that their souls are precious to God."

"Yes, Mother." Sister Agatha retreated. The chapter of faults could be difficult, but it always left the sisters feeling renewed. It was like receiving a much-needed compass heading that never failed to get them back on the right course.

After the other nuns left to fulfill their duties, she met with Reverend Mother. Thankfully, her duties as novice mistress had been reassigned to Sister Eugenia, who was doing a wonderful job.

"Mother, I have to go to Albuquerque," Sister Agatha said, and explained everything she'd learned about Celia so far and about the arrangement she'd made to meet her friend at Nazareth Hospital.

"You may go, of course, if it's necessary. But please take the car. I won't worry nearly as much. I'd like you to stay low profile after yesterday's incident. And I'm extremely concerned about you being followed."

"Mother, I wasn't being threatened. Whoever they were *always* kept their distance—well, except for that time with the black pickup. But the sheriff told me Mr. Malcolm owns a truck of that color and strongly suspects it was him. Now that he's in jail, he poses no danger to anyone. The person in the sedan, on the other hand, is probably just a reporter. That's Sheriff Green's theory and I agree." She decided not to mention the other alternatives the sheriff had suggested.

"I want you to take the station wagon, drive where there are plenty of other vehicles around, and be extremely careful in Albuquerque today, child. Also, take Pax with you."

"All right, Mother."

"You'll come straight back as soon as you're finished at Nazareth?"

"I'd like to leave that open-ended, Mother. Depending on what leads I uncover, I may want to follow them up right away."

"All right, but report back to me as soon as possible. I'm going to delay speaking to Celia until after I've heard from you. And, child, be *very* careful."

Sister stopped by the scriptorium and saw Sister Bernarda working along with Celia and Mary Lazarus.

"Sister Bernarda, I'll need you to cover portress duty for me again today," she said.

Sister nodded. "Sister Gertrude will be keeping regular hours in the scriptorium so I don't need to do double duty there and in the parlor. Sister Eugenia is now doing a wonderful job with the postulant's and the novice's instruction. And Sister Maria Victoria tells us that the work on the quilt is nearly done. Somehow, it's all working out."

"Praised be Jesus Christ!"

"Now and forever." Sister Bernarda took her away from the others, then in a hushed voice asked, "Are you any closer to finding out who killed Father Anselm?"

"I'm making progress, but for every answer I uncover, I get three new questions. Once the answers catch up to all the questions, I'll have the solution."

"May the Lord bless your work this morning, Sister."

"God reward you, Your Charity, for all you've done for us," Sister Agatha said, meaning every word.

As she walked out with Pax to the station wagon, she glanced back. Despite the high walls, the monastery itself was just a building. It was the strength of the sisters who lived there that made it a fortress.

The Nazareth Hospital psychiatric facility in Albuquerque was less than an hour's drive away. Driving the Antichrysler in the heat, without air-conditioning, and at the slow speed that was all the vehicle was capable of, was an exercise in patience. The car chugged along at forty-five miles per hour, making enough engine noise to wake the dead. But at least the muffler was no longer trumpeting like Joshua.

Pax was standing beside her, his head hanging out the window, enjoying the wind on his face. She probably should have told him to sit but she just couldn't bring herself to do it. If she could have, she would have stuck her own head out the window—anything for some air!

Before she'd even reached the city limits, she saw flashing lights behind her, and she pulled over. Sheriff Green came out of his unit and walked toward her.

"What's this? Skipping town?" he said, half jokingly.

"I've got to go to Albuquerque on behalf of the monastery," she answered, not ready to tip her hand just yet. "Have you managed to turn up anything new on Father's murder?" Even saying the word "murder" left a bad taste in her mouth, but she looked at him steadily and waited for an answer.

"My background check on Ruth Moore revealed that she has an extensive knowledge of herbs. Celia probably picked up a lot of information from her. Was that the lead you're not ready to talk to me about?"

"There are many people in the area who make use of herbal remedies," Sister Agatha answered, avoiding the question. "I really wish I could convince you that Celia's not the killer. Every instinct I have tells me that we should keep looking."

"That's loyalty—an admirable trait, but it can really get you hung up during an investigation. Also, at the risk of sounding like a macho jerk, I have to say again that poison *is* a woman's weapon."

"You're right. That makes you sound like a macho jerk," she said with a wry grin. "But come to think of it—"

"Only you can get away with saying something like that. Just so you know."

"We're on the same side, Tom, believe me." As she glanced over his shoulder, she noticed a light-colored sedan parked off the side of the road about two hundred yards back.

"We have the same goal, but we're working from opposite sides of the fence because your own bias blinds you." He frowned, noticing she was distracted.

"The one thing you have to understand is this," she said, looking directly at him. "I would no more shield a killer than I would stop being a nun." As she looked away from him, she saw the vehicle was still there, a driver at the wheel.

He turned his head to follow the direction of her gaze. "What are you looking at?"

"The sedan sitting by the road. It reminds me of the one that was following Pax and me yesterday. Did you notice it behind you earlier?"

"No, I was trying to catch up to you. But I'll go back and see who it is."

"Too late. It's already turning around and heading back toward Bernalillo." She could see it had New Mexico license plates, but could not make out the code.

"I'm gone. Later." He ran back to his unit. His tires squealed as he swung the vehicle around and, sirens on, roared off in pursuit.

Sister Agatha returned to the Antichrysler. Don Malcolm was in jail, so that ruled him out. As she thought about what had just happened, she wondered if perhaps this time, the person had been following the sheriff, not her. She was almost sure she would have noticed the sedan earlier if it had been tailing her.

She tried to figure things out. If the sedan had followed the sheriff and her on separate occasions, then it seemed likely that the person in the sedan was a reporter, as Tom had suggested.

Satisfied with that explanation for now, she continued on her way. She stayed on the slowest route to Albuquerque, taking Highway 313, passing through Alameda rather than using the interstate. She wasn't stalling—the Antichrysler was. Whenever it went above forty-five miles an hour it screamed as if in pain. She tried to push it to fifty, wondering if the screamlike noise would go away on its own. But then Pax began to howl, so Sister Agatha had to resign herself to traveling at a snail's pace.

When they arrived at the hospital, Sister Agatha parked in the back of the large facility. Leaving Pax in the shade of a large cluster of pines outside the main entrance, she patted him on the head. "You behave and relax. I'll be back as soon as I can," she said, leaving the leash tied loosely around the rear door handle.

As arranged, Sister Agatha walked to the lobby, and asked for Suzi at the desk. Minutes later, she was directed to Suzi's office in a rear section of the facility.

Suzi, a middle-aged black woman with salt-and-pepper hair sat at her desk filling out some forms. Hearing footsteps, she looked up and smiled broadly. "Well, hi, stranger! It's good to see you again."

Sister Agatha's gaze fixed on the far wall. There in beautiful calligraphy was a quote from Ephesians. Live a Life Worthy of the Calling to Which You Have Been Called. She smiled. "That's one of my favorite quotes, too."

"It helps keep me focused, particularly on days when things aren't going well." She leaned back and regarded Sister Agatha thoughtfully. "So what brings you here?"

"I'm trying to track down some information on a former patient."

Suzi's expression turned somber. "That's going to be next to impossible. We have to respect confidentiality, for the patients and their relatives."

"What I want is less official—not necessarily something found in patient files." She paused, took a deep breath, and continued. "It involves our newest postulant—Celia Clines. It's absolutely crucial that we learn more about her. She's going through a crisis now, and we just need to understand her a little better so we can help. We've learned she was here about thirteen, maybe fourteen years ago. She would have been about that same age, too, at the time."

"I was here back then, but that name just doesn't ring a bell. Can you tell me a little more about her?"

"She came here after she apparently tried to commit suicide using a dangerous herb. She may have been pregnant at the time, too."

Suzi's expression gentled as memories crowded into her mind. "I remember a young teenager who was here in that situation around then. But her name wasn't Celia. . . ." She focused on an indeterminate object across the room, lost in thought.

Sister Agatha remembered the name Father Anselm had called Celia. Playing a hunch, she asked, "Was it Annie?"

Looking surprised, Suzi nodded. "That was it," she said.

"Did Father Anselm work here at that time too?"

"Oh, sure. He was our chaplain back then. He came in three times a week. He was really good with the kids, too. He tried to become a friend to the ones who seemed to have no family to depend on. If memory serves, I think he had a special rapport with that girl Annie. But, I should tell you, Annie never admitted she'd been trying to kill herself. In fact, she emphatically denied it, which surprised Father and me. People who attempt suicide generally don't bother to deny it, either because they're crying out for help or they really do want to be dead."

"Then you think it was just an accident?"

"No, not at all. Father and I asked her that same question repeatedly, but we never got a straight answer from her, which made us even more suspicious. I, personally, had the feeling that Annie's mother had given her something to make her abort the child, miscalculated the dosage, and nearly killed her daughter by mistake. Her mother was one of those quacks—a self-trained herbalist with a remedy for everything."

"Do you happen to remember Annie's last name?"

"I never knew it—and neither did Father. Our policy is to safeguard the identities of all our underage patients. We know them only by their first names, or sometimes just a nickname. Last names aren't even listed on their charts—just code designations. Even if I were to access our computer records, I still couldn't get information on a specific patient based on name alone. Everything is encrypted."

"How long did Father work with Annie?"

"Most of the time she was here—close to a year, if memory serves. I think he was the one who arranged for Annie to come to Nazareth and made sure her bills were covered through different state aid programs. The girl's mother had no medical insurance and she made it clear she couldn't afford the prices we charged and that she had no intention of going into debt to pay for the sins of her daughter. She was a real nightmare."

"What happened to Annie's baby?" Sister Agatha asked.

"The baby was born here. She was premature, but in perfect health, and was adopted almost immediately."

"By whom?"

"I don't know. Catholic Charities handled it and those records are sealed tighter than the files at the CIA. But there was talk and, well, Annie's mom had a baby with her when she came to take her daughter home months later. I always suspected that Annie's mom had adopted the baby herself. But I prayed I was wrong."

"Because of the way she treated Annie?"

"Exactly. A slave would have gotten more respect than that poor kid did. That woman was constantly berating Annie. It was no wonder that the kid had a perpetually defeated look about her."

Suzi paused and met Sister's gaze with her own. "But how does this fit with your new postulant? You think Annie and Celia are the same person?" Her eyes suddenly grew wide. "Oh, please don't tell me that you're going to use the information I just gave you against the postulant. I have no way of proving if we're even talking about the same person and—"

"Relax. It's nothing like that."

"So what's this all about, then?" When Sister Agatha hesitated, Suzi added, "Hey, I trusted *you*."

"You're right. You deserve an answer," she said with a nod. "It's been a very difficult time for all of us at the monastery. You must have heard about the death of Father Anselm."

Suzi nodded. "We had a special remembrance service in our chapel."

"You've probably also heard by now that he was poisoned?" Seeing Suzi nod, she continued. "Well, the sheriff believes Father was murdered, and our postulant has become his prime suspect. None of us believe that she's guilty, so I'm here trying to find evidence that will clear her. In looking into the matter, I came across information that led me to believe there was a connection between Celia and Father Anselm and that they might have met here. I'm still trying to put the pieces together, and what you've told me has been a great help."

"Annie *adored* Father Anselm, and would have done anything for him. I think he was the first adult who ever showed her any kindness." She paused. "And, more than that, Annie was a gentle child, never dangerous to anyone except herself. If she'd been prone to violence, we would have seen signs of it here in her dealings with others. She was emotionally starved, but she was *not* violent."

"Thanks, Suzi. I appreciate you talking so candidly to me."

"Bear in mind that we have no way of proving if Celia and Annie are the same person or not, and it would take all kinds of court orders and permissions to verify that."

"I know. But *we're* not out to prove anything in a court of law. We just want to find the truth. For confirmation of that, we'll talk to Celia herself. But what you've told me is very reassuring." She hugged her friend. "Thanks for everything."

After saying good-bye, Sister took Pax for a short walk, then loaded him up. She still had nothing conclusive and Celia's future demanded more from her than hearsay. She'd have to go to the county clerk's office and, if she could pull off what she had in mind, she'd have the information she needed. If not, she'd be in a world of trouble.

Determined to take the risk, she kept Pax with her on the leash at heel when she arrived and walked into the records area.

Sister Agatha knew that here bravado would spell the difference between success and failure. She had to come across as someone who had authority and knew what she was doing.

She introduced herself to the clerk, then added, "I need to confirm some information from a Catholic Charities adoption that occurred in March of 1987. The birth mother's name was Celia Clines, and the adoptive mother, Ruth Moore. I just need to confirm the date of birth we have for the baby—March seventeen—with the one listed on the *original* birth certificate."

The young woman didn't even blink. Had it been a private

adoption, she wouldn't have had a chance, but her nun's habit coupled with the fact that she was asking about Catholic Charities gave her the edge she needed.

"We have those records computerized now—it makes our job easier. Let me see what I can find."

Sister Agatha was sure that the clerk had gone to Catholic school. Questioning a nun never came easy to a former student.

"The date you have is correct," she said turning the monitor so Sister Agatha could see for herself. "The same date is listed on both the adoption birth certificate and the original."

She nodded somberly at the clerk. "Thank you. That's all I needed."

Sister Agatha walked back to the car with Pax at heel, slowly mulling over everything she'd learned today. She knew now that Celia had given birth to Betsy. The birth certificate the clerk had shown her proved it. She could now fully understand why Celia would have felt a certain kinship with Father Anselm, who had befriended her during what was probably the worst time of her life. She didn't believe Celia would have betrayed that memory with murder. Yet she knew Tom would argue that Celia's fear of discovery might have turned her violent.

As she drove back to the monastery, she was glad for once that the Antichrysler wouldn't go much over forty. It gave her a chance to think. She'd have to tell Reverend Mother what she'd learned, and Tom, too. But right now she was dreading both conversations. Yet, despite everything, her instincts were telling her that Celia wasn't guilty, but the fact *was* she couldn't prove it.

After arriving at the monastery, Sister stopped to speak to Sister Bernarda who was at her post in the parlor. "I've left Sister Mary Lazarus, Sister Gertrude, and our postulant working in the scriptorium," Bernarda said. "They're really making progress today. I believe we'll make deadline on the magazine's recipe archive, and we'll also have that new branch library's collection digitally catalogued on time so they can go on-line the day they'd planned."

"So only the antique manuscript that we have to scan by hand is still behind schedule?"

She nodded. "That's not too bad, considering."

"You're right. I'll see if I can pick up some speed with the scanning."

"It's a shame that it's a job you and I have to do personally," Sister Bernarda said. "But it's our responsibility to make sure nothing happens to those pages. It's a valuable document."

"And how does Sister Eugenia say our postulant and novice are doing with their instruction?"

Sister Bernarda hesitated. "She said that Celia's studies are going well, but Eugenia is having a harder time with Mary Lazarus, apparently."

"What's going on?"

"Eugenia confided to me that she thinks Mary Lazarus's heart isn't in her studies. She has serious doubts about Mary Lazarus's vocation."

Sister Agatha nodded slowly. In all honesty, she'd felt the same way about the novice. "I'll try to make time to talk to Mary Lazarus later tonight. If it's a crisis of faith, maybe I can help her through it." She glanced at her watch. "But right now I have to speak with Reverend Mother."

"I saw her not too long ago weeding the planter in front of the statue of the Blessed Virgin."

Sister Agatha went outside, Pax still at her side. Seeing Reverend Mother, Pax greeted her warmly, then went running off after a butterfly, clearly aware he was now off duty.

Reverend Mother stood up. "Walk with me, child."

Sister Agatha briefed her on everything she'd learned about Celia as they strolled through the garden.

"How I envy that dog right now," Reverend Mother said quietly, after considering what Sister Agatha had told her. "To him, the world is one giant playground. He glorifies God by being exactly who and what he is and never turning down an opportunity to enjoy His creation."

They sat down on one of the *bancos*, beneath the shade of a large pine. "Mother, I don't know what to do. I probably should tell the sheriff what I've learned, but if I do, it'll create more problems.

Even though, to me, this proves Celia isn't guilty of harming Father, Sheriff Green is not going to see it in the same light."

"I'm not sure what should be done about that either. Let's pray about it first, and then decide."

As they approached the monastery's cemetery, they saw Sister Ignatius by Sister Regina's grave. The sisters who had passed were still considered to be part of their community—they'd simply gone home to God. Occasionally, in times of trouble, the sisters would pray to their departed friends, asking for help and special graces.

Sister Ignatius, who'd just placed a small sunflower on the grave, heard them approach and turned around.

Reverend Mother placed a hand on Sister Ignatius's arm. "Are you all right, child?"

"Yes, Mother. I came to ask Sister Regina to ask Our Lord to help us. Every time we turn around lately, something else goes wrong. Now our automated baker is burning the altar breads into a crisp. Sister Maria Victoria helped me adjust the settings, but the oven is old and tired. Maybe after Sister Maria Victoria is finished with the quilt, which should be any day now, I can get her help with the altar breads on a regular schedule. Sister Clothilde helps me as much as she can, but she's laundress and cook and her schedule is full. Although it's been difficult tending to it mostly on my own, I have to say that I'm glad Sister Gertrude's new duties take her out of the heat of the baking room."

As Sister Ignatius went toward the main building, Sister Agatha looked at Reverend Mother. "She meets every crisis with unshakable faith. Sometimes I wish I was more like her."

Reverend Mother resumed their walk. "We've all placed a great weight on your shoulders, Sister Agatha. Don't ever forget to ask God to help you. In a lot of ways, it's easier for the choir nuns to focus solely on Him because He's the center of everything we do in the enclosure. But He's wherever you go, too. God is everywhere— He's omnipresent. If you base everything that you do on the sure knowledge that you're in the presence of God no matter where you go, then your work on behalf of this monastery will become an offering of love to Him."

She knelt down before Mother. "Will you give me your blessing, too, Mother?"

Reverend Mother brought out a small vial of holy water and touched a drop to her forehead, making a small sign of the cross. "Continue your work with the blessing of God."

Sister Agatha thanked her and stood. In Mother's eyes, she could see wisdom that far exceeded her own, and beyond that, her love and dedication to the life they'd chosen. "I won't let you or this monastery down, Mother."

"I know you won't. Now go find Celia and let's both talk to her."

Sister Agatha searched the monastery and found Celia helping Sister Ignatius with the automated baker. Making altar breads was an important source of income for their monastery, but the machine had a mind of its own lately. It would work fine one moment and ruin the next batch completely.

She found Celia scraping a burnt section off a tray while Sister Maria Victoria readjusted the oven settings.

"Celia, I need to speak with you," Sister Agatha said quietly, "when you're finished with that tray."

Celia quickly washed the baking sheet, then followed Sister Agatha down the hall. By the time they arrived at Reverend Mother's office, the abbess was already there, waiting.

"Sit down, child," Reverend Mother asked Celia.

Celia did so, then waited, her head bowed in humility.

"We need to ask you some questions," Reverend Mother said.

Celia nodded but, in keeping with the practice of maintaining "custody of the eyes," continued to stare only at her lap.

"Are you familiar with herbs?" Mother asked.

Celia looked up at Reverend Mother, then over at Sister Agatha. "I know about medicinal herbs. I learned a lot from my mother." She glanced back at Reverend Mother and met her gaze steadily. "But, Mother, I give you my word of honor that I never harmed Father Anselm."

"We know he helped you a great deal when you were at Nazareth," Sister Agatha said gently.

Celia looked at her in surprise, then, with a sigh, nodded slowly. "He helped me when no one else would. I owed him for that." She paused, and took a deep breath. "My mom made my life miserable and, although people knew, no one ever spoke up or tried to help me." She clutched her rosary in her hand, then continued. "She never let up. She'd make me memorize passages from the Bible and, if I made a mistake, she'd make me stand outside in the sun with my arms outstretched until I'd fall down from the heat," she said in a matter-of-fact voice that made the revelation all the more chilling.

Mother gasped softly, but Celia seemed unaware of her audience.

"She'd tell me that I was a mortal sinner and that she had to wash the sins off me—then she'd make me wash in hot water. I'd have to wear long sleeves the next day so people wouldn't see how red my arms were. But, even if they had noticed, I don't think anyone would have cared. They would have just thought it was my own fault, I'm sure. That's what Mom always said."

Sister Agatha stared at Reverend Mother, tears forming in her eyes. "I didn't know."

"I don't blame *you*," Celia said quickly. "You had your own life to live."

"We know about your suicide attempt, and about the baby," Sister Agatha said in a gentle voice, looking at Celia once more.

Celia said nothing for a long moment, but tears formed in her eyes. "Yes, I was pregnant, but I never tried to kill myself. I would have never done that."

"But you took pennyroyal oil. Were you trying to abort the baby?" Sister Agatha pressed. No matter how much she sympathized with Celia, they had to learn the truth.

Celia shook her head and gave them a bewildered look. "I would have never done something like that. But one night when I couldn't sleep, I asked Mom if she knew of something that might help, and she gave me—" She stopped abruptly, and lowered her head, staring at her lap again.

"Your mother gave you an herbal tea with pennyroyal oil in it?" Sister Agatha asked, outrage in her voice.

"It was *my* fault," Celia said quickly, shaking her head. "She'd left some tinctures and herbs I could mix to make a tea at the front of our cupboard, but somehow I must have picked up the wrong ones. It was my fault. I made a stupid mistake. She wasn't to blame."

Sister Agatha couldn't breathe. A new picture was emerging in her mind. A woman with limited resources, afraid of what the town would say when they learned her daughter was pregnant, and desperate to find a solution, any solution.

"Why didn't you tell me about this when you first came to us?" Reverend Mother asked. "What bothers me most is that you tried to hide this."

"I didn't try to hide it, Mother. The reason I didn't tell you more about my past was because I saw it as part of the life I was leaving behind. From the moment I stepped through the monastery's doors, I knew that to serve God, I would have to relinquish everything I'd known, and everything I'd been. Nothing less would be acceptable to Him. For months, I'd been memorizing the Prayer of St. Ignatius that says, 'All that I have, all that I am, Thou has given me, and I give it all back to Thee, to be governed according to Thy will.' " Her words rang with utter conviction.

"You should have told us everything, Celia," Sister Agatha said softly. "We wouldn't have had any reason to distrust you then."

Celia's gaze rested on Reverend Mother—pain, sorrow, and regret mirrored there. "Mother, I don't care how the world judges me. But I care what *you* think. Can you accept me knowing I've made some terrible mistakes? And believe me when I swear I never did anything to harm Father Anselm."

Reverend Mother opened her arms and hugged Celia. "Dear child, we've all made mistakes and God always forgives us. Who are we to do any less?" She released the postulant a moment later. "We believe you, child. Go to the chapel now. Then return to your duties."

Celia bowed her head. "Yes, Mother."

After they were alone once again, Reverend Mother leaned back in her chair, her gaze fixed on Sister Agatha. "How well did you know Celia's mother?"

Sister Agatha exhaled softly. "When we were kids we always got along fine, but as it often is once you leave high school behind you, life took us in separate directions. These days, she's nothing like the girl I knew. Ruth's had a very hard life. That's bound to take a toll on a person. That doesn't excuse her, but it's all I can say in her defense." She gazed up at the crucifix on the wall, and added, "I never knew what she was doing to Celia, my own godchild, and that failure is something I'll have to live with for the rest of my days."

"The One who called Celia here knew what He was doing. We have to protect her now," Reverend Mother said. "She's not guilty. I truly believe that. But now you have to find the truth—no matter what it takes."

When Sister Agatha left Reverend Mother's office, her heart felt as heavy as a block of concrete. She couldn't even imagine what Celia's life had been like. Suddenly another thought made her blood turn to ice. Betsy . . .

Sister Agatha couldn't allow that child to endure the same treatment Celia had received. She remembered the scene she'd witnessed between Betsy and Ruth just the other day and a cold chill went up her spine. She'd call Patsy Romero and talk to her about this. Together, they'd figure out what to do.

She was on her way to the parlor to relieve Sister Bernarda when Sister Clothilde caught up to her. Motioning for Sister Agatha to follow, she led her to the refectory and pointed to a bean-filled tortilla.

Though she'd missed the midday meal, Sister Agatha wasn't in the least bit hungry. But Sister Clothilde wouldn't take no for an answer. Knowing that collation, their dinner meal, wouldn't be for hours yet, and was generally very light, Sister Agatha began eating. Once finished, she washed her plate, and looked around for Sister Clothilde to thank her, but the elderly nun was gone. As the bells rang for the canonical hour called None, she knew where Sister had gone.

Sister Agatha was halfway down the hall to the scriptorium when Sister Bernarda came rushing up. "Your Charity, Sister Gertrude just came to get me before going to Divine Office. Some of the photo files we're archiving for the newspaper are gone. Thankfully, the manuscripts are safe, but those photo files are very important to the newspaper."

For a moment Sister Agatha couldn't respond. "What do you mean 'gone'? They can't be," she managed at last.

The possibility of an intruder once again took center stage in her mind, but she pushed it back. The simplest answer was probably closer to the truth in this case. "We'll find them," she said flatly. "They've got to be in the scriptorium someplace. None of the material ever leaves that room."

As the two externs stepped into the scriptorium, their gazes fell on Sister Mary Lazarus, who was there alone, crouched down in front of the safe, trying to open it. By her feet were several file folders.

"What do you think you're doing?" Sister Bernarda demanded.

Sister Mary Lazarus jumped to her feet.

Sister Agatha gazed at the novice. At that moment, Sister Mary Lazarus looked like the very portrait of guilt.

16

SISTER BERNARDA STRODE PAST SISTER AGATHA AND CHECK-
ed the safe, making sure it was still locked. "How do you know
the combination?"

"I don't. If I did, I would have opened it," Sister Mary Lazarus
said, her voice hushed.

"Why? What were you doing?" Sister Agatha looked at the novice in confusion.

"It's all my fault, Mother Mistress," she said, then looked at
Sister Bernarda. "The photos from the archive aren't missing as Sister Gertrude thought. I worked on that project yesterday, then accidentally put a folder of interim printouts on top of it. When it was
time to quit, I didn't see the photo archive folders underneath, so I
forgot to put them back. When Sister Gertrude opened the safe and
found them missing, I suddenly remembered."

"And you weren't planning to say anything?" Sister Bernarda
asked.

"Not right away. I knew you'd be angry when you found out
what I'd done, so I was hoping to put the files back first. Then, once
you were assured everything was okay, I'd tell you. The safe usually
isn't locked during the day now that we're working on such a tight

deadline so I was trying to jiggle the handle to see if it would pop open when you walked in."

"You should have told us the second you realized what had happened, Sister. You almost gave *me* a heart attack and Sister Gertrude's heart isn't as strong as mine. If this monastery was run like the marines, I'd have you running laps right now," Sister Bernarda barked.

Sister Agatha had to bite her lip to keep from laughing. For one brief moment, Christian charity had given way to the habits of Sister Bernarda's earlier life.

"Sister Bernarda, could you inventory all the materials that are supposed to be in the safe and make sure everything is as it should be while I speak to our novice?" Sister Agatha glanced at Sister Mary Lazarus. "Let's go for a walk."

As Pax ran ahead of them in the garden, Sister Agatha allowed the silence to stretch out between them.

"I know you think I'm a horrible person," Sister Mary Lazarus said finally.

"No, I don't think that at all," Sister Agatha said calmly.

"Everyone says Celia belongs here—no matter how much trouble she's brought to the monastery. But nobody thinks I do. And I've really worked hard to try and fit in."

"Is it really what others think that's bothering you, Mary Lazarus? Or are you just having second thoughts about staying with us?"

"Maybe you're right," she said with a sigh. "I've been trying to work things out in my mind, and I'm not sure anymore that I've got a real vocation. But I've given up everything for the chance to become a nun, and the possibility of walking away now after almost three years leaves me feeling empty inside—and a little scared, too."

"You have to follow your heart, but think things through carefully. There is a place for you here, Mary Lazarus. You were destined to become an extern nun, something our monastery needs very badly."

"Nothing is simple anymore," Mary Lazarus answered. "If I stay, I want to make sure it's for the right reasons—not just because I'm afraid of going back out into the world. And, to be honest, that thought does scare me. You see, I had to sell everything to pay my husband's medical bills. There's nothing out there for me anymore."

"Pray and ask to be guided, then make your decision. There's still plenty of time. You don't have to rush. You may simply be facing a crisis of faith. We're all tested at times."

Sister Agatha led Sister Mary Lazarus to the chapel. There was no sign of Celia. The postulant must have finished her prayers and returned to work as Reverend Mother had directed. After saying a brief prayer with the novice, Sister Agatha rose, leaving Mary Lazarus to continue privately. It was time for her to find Celia. There was something she had to know and she couldn't postpone their conversation any longer.

Sister Agatha went to the scriptorium and there, as expected, found the postulant with Sister Bernarda. "I need to speak to you, Celia. Please step out into the hall with me for a moment."

Celia went with her and waited silently.

"I need you to answer one question for me, and it's absolutely imperative that you be completely honest."

"Of course, Mother Mistress. What would you like to know?"

"Are you worried about what's going to happen to Betsy?"

Pain clouded Celia's eyes, and she didn't answer right away. "I learned a long time ago that there are certain things I can't change," she said at last. "What I can do—and what I do every single day without fail—is pray for her."

"Do you think Betsy is being abused as you were?"

"No, in fact I know she's not. I've kept in touch with Betsy. To her, I'm her big sister and she trusts me. She and I are close, but we're also very different from each other. She stands up to Mom whenever she has to, and won't allow Mom to hurt her. Mom beat her once, and Betsy told a counselor at school. Mom had a lot of trouble with Children's Services after that and hasn't struck Betsy since."

"All right. Thank you, Celia."

As the postulant went back to her carrel and resumed her work, Sister Agatha considered what she'd learned. Celia had already dealt with a great deal for someone her age. There was no doubt in her mind that Celia's relationship with Ruth was filled with emotions that constantly warred against each other—love against hate, anger against fear.

Yet despite Celia's assurances that Betsy was all right, Sister Agatha couldn't quite let the matter go, not after the verbal and emotional abuse that she'd seen the other day. She'd have to talk to Patsy Romero, Betsy's assistant principal, today. Betsy's fate was too important for her to just let the matter drop.

After Vespers, Sister called Patsy at home, then drove into town to meet with her. It felt good to ride the motorcycle again. She'd told Reverend Mother about the Antichrysler's problems staying in the flow of traffic, and they'd agreed to use the car only for emergencies.

Pax sat up in the sidecar, enjoying the air. Following his example, she stilled her worries and enjoyed the scent of rain in the air and the coolness the approaching storm was bringing. It wasn't until she drew near to Patsy's home that she brought her thoughts back to the business at hand.

Patsy was on her porch, waiting, as Sister Agatha pulled up. Her small adobe home was not fancy, but it was well maintained. Wildflowers had been planted along the small wooden fence that bordered the property. There were no sidewalks here, as it was in much of semirural New Mexico. There was the street—sometimes paved, more often, not—and the beginning of someone's property marked only by the appearance of a patch of grass or a barking dog.

"What brings you here?" Patsy asked as she approached. "It sounded urgent on the phone." She led Sister Agatha and Pax inside to a cool, whitewashed home with simple but elegant Southwest furnishings and a kiva fireplace.

Sister Agatha told Patsy about Celia's revelations, but if Patsy was shocked or surprised, she didn't show it. When Sister Agatha finished, Patsy leaned back in the leather sofa and stared at Pax, who'd settled down on the brick floor, enjoying the coolness it provided.

"I've known about Ruth for years. I overheard Betsy talking

about her mother to one of her friends one time outside a classroom. After that, I kept my eyes open, and asked the counselor to do the same. Then one day Betsy came in with bruises on her face and wearing long sleeves, even though it was over eighty degrees outside. I called Betsy into my office and I got to the bottom of it after a few minutes."

"Did you report Ruth to the authorities?"

"I did, but before I even mailed the paperwork, I got Tom Green—he was deputy sheriff then—to come with me and we paid Ruth a visit. We came down on her like a ton of bricks. Tom made it clear that if Betsy was ever injured, no matter what the reason—if she got struck by lightning, or fell crossing the street—we would bring in social services to take Betsy from her and place her in foster care. Just to cinch it, Tom guaranteed her jail time, and I promised her that everyone in this town would know what she'd done to her daughter. She'd never be able to hold her head up anywhere again."

"I hate to tell you this, but you're still going to have to keep an eye on Ruth." Sister told her what she'd witnessed the day she'd visited Ruth. "The danger of emotional abuse is very real, and still there, though the marks from it don't always show up right away."

"Unfortunately, as Betsy's Mom, Ruth's entitled to discipline her child. But don't worry. I'm still watching Betsy with an eagle eye. If anything happens to that kid, I promise Betsy will go straight into foster care."

"Now I'll be able to sleep at night. Thanks, Patsy."

"Hey, tomorrow's our Fourth of July Town Fair. Is Sister Clothilde going to bake her special cookies?"

"Oh, sure! I expect we'll have over five hundred cookies for sale, like we did last year," Sister Agatha said.

"They'll go in a flash. You really should give them a name and trademark, then market them. You'd all be famous and live in a mahogany-paneled monastery with a wading pool!"

Sister Agatha laughed. "I can see it now. Sister Clothilde's Cloister Clusters!"

"Hey, put that up on a sign in your booth. It'll catch on! You'll see."

Sister Agatha drove back to the monastery in much better spirits. As soon as she returned, she went to find Reverend Mother. It was time for recreation and she found the abbess walking on the grounds, as was her custom.

Sister told Reverend Mother about her visit with Patsy Romero while they watched Celia planting a packet of seeds by the cemetery entrance. "Ruth sent her those," Reverend Mother said softly. "Celia was really surprised."

Sister Agatha shook her head. "I don't understand Ruth, Mother. She used to be such a loving, idealistic woman. The fact that she sent her daughter that small gift shows she still has feelings for her. Yet she abused her terribly."

Before Reverend Mother could answer, Celia stood up, brushed the soil from the front of her postulant's dress, then bent down to pet Pax who'd come over. "You're such a good dog!" She smiled at Reverend Mother and Sister Agatha as they walked by. "Mother Mistress, isn't he terrific? I'm sure he can be really mean sometimes—he was a police dog—but if you treat him right, all he wants to do is love you," she said, laughing as Pax licked her on the face.

"Amen to that," Reverend Mother said softly.

Hearing the bells ring for Compline, Sister Agatha bowed her head, and followed Reverend Mother inside.

The next morning came too soon for Sister Agatha. She hadn't managed to get a lot of sleep the night before. On her way to the bathroom, she'd found Sister Mary Lazarus sleepwalking and had brought her back to her assigned cell. She'd then stayed with the novice until she was sure she wouldn't wander around again.

When the morning bells rang, her eyes would scarcely open. But there was no time for sluggishness today. There was too much to do.

After Morning Prayer ended, Sister Maria Victoria and Sister Gertrude brought the quilted wall hanging to Reverend Mother's office. It was the custom of their monastery to present all finished work to Reverend Mother for her approval.

Reverend Mother inspected the delicate, tiny stitches and the workmanship carefully as the nuns held their breath. Finally she looked up and smiled. "Well done!"

Next several small jars of jam were presented and admired in turn.

Then Sister Clothilde offered Reverend Mother two of her special cookies. Mother savored one for what seemed an eternity, then smiled. "This is your best batch yet, child!" She looked at all of them, then with a smile added, "Dear ones, may God grant you a good day. Go with the blessing of God."

Sister Agatha felt the excitement of the others shift as they turned to look at her and Sister Bernarda expectantly. It was their job to bring their monastery's work to the buyers in the community, and hopefully return with a good price for their labors. Heaven knew they needed the income right now.

Sister Agatha bowed down before Reverend Mother. "Reverend Mother Abbess and holy community, may God grant you all a good day."

With Sister Bernarda and Mary Lazarus helping Sister Agatha they began gathering all the trays and plates of cookies, each wrapped in colored plastic wrap donated by food stores in the community. A half hour later, the back of the Antichrysler was loaded to bursting with cookies and jars of jam. Last of all, they brought the wall hanging. Mary Lazarus was given the job of holding it on her lap.

Today there would be no portress. But it was that way on community and religious holidays.

As they got ready to leave, Pax came up, his tail wagging. Not waiting for an invitation, he jumped into the front seat of the car. Sister Bernarda dove to intercept him before he reached the cookies, which he'd detected immediately. "You have to stay here, boy."

"Pax!" Reverend Mother called. "Come."

The dog, now a full member of the monastery, obeyed Reverend Mother on the first call. Of course at least two of the sisters, hearing only the last word, automatically started coming toward Mother as well. There was something about Reverend Mother's voice that compelled you to obey whenever she issued an order.

They arrived in town a short time later and quickly got to work setting up their tables. Their booth would be at the far end of a long line of attractions and near the exhibition hall where the wall hanging would be auctioned. Sister Bernarda marched down the row of booths to the gallery to attend to the display of the wall hanging.

While Sister Bernarda was gone, Sister Agatha and Sister Mary Lazarus hurried to set up the monastery's booth—a simple wooden frame decorated in red, white, and blue crepe paper.

The tables soon held a treasure of cookies and jams the sisters had prepared to sell to fair visitors. As they were placing the last container of cookies on a table, Patsy Romero hurried up and handed them a small cloth banner. It read, Sister Clothilde's Heavenly Cloister Clusters.

Sister Agatha read the matching price sheet Patsy had made for them to affix to the back of the booth and gasped. "Patsy, no one will pay that much!"

"You wait. You'll make a fortune today. Try it."

Sister Agatha hesitated.

"Go for it, Sister!" Chunk yelled from the St. Charles booth, which was opposite their own.

Laughing, they affixed the banner and got ready for business. The fair was hectic, but the public response to the sisters' efforts was wonderful. Despite the high price and the incredible number of cookies that had been baked, the trays emptied quickly, while Sister Bernarda stood guard over the proceeds in the metal box beside her. It was soon clear that the day was off to a successful start.

"Didn't we promise Frank Walters a plate of cookies?" Sister Mary Lazarus asked. Sister Agatha looked up and noticed Frank making his way down the line of booths leading to the exhibition hall.

"We did." Sister Agatha took a plate from the bottom shelf. "Here. Take it to him now before we forget and sell it to someone else. And tell him the sisters are praying for his intention, as promised."

Sister Agatha had "forgotten" the cookies on purpose to give Mary Lazarus a chance to see Frank away from the monastery. She wanted Mary Lazarus to make her decision on whether to stay a nun or return into society freely. To do that, Mary Lazarus had to know precisely what she'd be gaining and what she'd be leaving behind forever.

She had planned to watch Frank and Mary Lazarus, but then more customers arrived and she and Sister Bernarda got too busy to do anything but attend to the business at hand. The novice was slightly flushed when she returned a few minutes later, but soon regained her composure and began working quickly and efficiently.

Hours later, they'd sold everything except for one jar of jam. Sister Agatha, Sister Mary Lazarus, and Sister Bernarda walked to the exhibit hall for the auction. The quick look exchanged among them as they entered the building assured Sister Agatha that they were all praying hard that the quilt would be sold for a good price.

Frank handled the auction superbly, and Sister Agatha scarcely breathed as the bids on the wall hanging climbed steadily higher. The final price on the quilt took them all by surprise, and the crowd gathered there applauded loudly. A dealer from an out-of-state art gallery had liked the idea of a work done solely by the nuns, and he'd bought the wall hanging for triple the price they'd expected.

Sister Bernarda beamed as she joined Sister Agatha after turning over the quilt to the buyer and receiving the promised price. "Now we can go home. The sisters will be overjoyed."

"I wish we could be here for the fireworks," Sister Mary Lazarus said with a sigh.

"That won't be for several hours, and we can't stay," Sister Bernarda said. "Go take that last jar of jam to the man who bought the quilt as a special thank-you, Sister. We'll meet you back at the car."

Sister Agatha and Sister Bernarda took down the banner from the booth and got a rough count on the proceeds in their cash box.

Leaving Sister Bernarda to finish packing up, she began carrying the decorations back to their car. As she reached the parking area, she saw Tom and his wife, Gloria, standing by a cream-colored sedan.

Sister Agatha shifted the packages she was carrying and waved. Gloria didn't even acknowledge the greeting as she stalked off, but Tom, left standing alone, waved at her, then came over. "Let me give you a hand," he said, helping her set things in the back.

She suspected they'd just had another fight, but decided not to comment on it. "Thanks! I'm glad I saw you. Did you ever find out who was following me?"

He avoided her gaze. "I handled the matter. If it happens again, just let me know."

"Who was it?"

He shook his head. "I'd rather not comment on that. But you were in no danger. You have my word on that."

She started to ask him more, but Tom held up his hand. "I'm asking you to trust me on this one. Can you do it?"

She took a deep breath, then nodded. "Of course."

"I better get going. I have to keep a close eye on things today," Sister Agatha said.

As he walked away, she went back to the booth to help Sister Bernarda finish up. "We've had such a good day!" Sister Agatha said, glancing around the crowd for Mary Lazarus.

"The novice has gotten sidetracked," Sister Bernarda said, searching the crowd. "You better go get her, Sister. I'll look after the proceeds and meet you two at the car."

Sister Agatha, still in an undeniably good mood, went back into the exhibition hall, where the quilt's new owner was still showing his purchase to onlookers. Along the way, she had to pass through an aisle of booths, where a small crowd had gathered, buying snacks. Sheriff Green and his wife were there, talking to a group of women. As she made her way through the crowd, she lost sight of them. Then, suddenly, she felt a tug on her habit.

Turning around quickly, she looked at the faces around her, but nobody seemed to be paying any particular attention to her. If it had been a pickpocket, he would be sorely disappointed. She had nothing worth stealing.

Reaching into her pocket absently, she discovered a wadded-up piece of paper there. Sister Agatha moved quickly to the side of the room. Then, standing near the wall, she unfolded it. Written on the paper with a bold red pen were the words "Remember your vows!"

She stood there, puzzled, trying to connect the message to something she'd done. Perhaps it was from some crank who thought she'd had something to do with the murder, or had seen her at the pawnshop the other day. Or could it be her stalker?

She scanned the crowd looking for someone she recognized. That's when she saw the novice standing outside, with Frank Walters. Although she couldn't hear what they were saying, their expressions left no doubt that they were having a serious discussion.

She hurried toward them but as she approached they both controlled their expressions.

"Is there a problem?" she asked them.

"No, not at all. But let me walk you to your car, Sister Agatha. Even though the bulk of your proceeds for today is in the form of a check, you really shouldn't leave Sister Bernarda alone. She's carrying all the cash you made from your booth sales and that could tempt the wrong person. Make sure you deposit all the cash and the check in an ATM as soon as possible." He gestured for the sisters to precede him down the aisle to the parking area.

"We will. But please don't be concerned for our safety. We're not far from home," Sister Agatha replied, seeing Sister Bernarda waving from the car, not far away.

"You trust too much, Sister," he said with a sigh. "The world isn't as kind as you'd like it to be. I'll follow you to the monastery just to make sure."

They set out a short time later. Today Frank was driving his car instead of the van. As he kept pace with them, Sister Agatha remembered the sedan that had followed her. It had stayed behind, maintaining its distance evenly, just as Frank was doing now. She forced the thought quickly out of her mind. If she started to suspect everyone who owned a particular-colored sedan, the suspect list would be miles long.

"We should say a special prayer of thanks, Sisters," Sister Agatha said. "The money we raised will be put to very good use soon."

"But the problem that put us in a position where we need funds so badly still remains," Sister Bernarda said softly.

"The truth is there. We'll find it." But even as she spoke the words, she wondered if she really would be able to do it. Every time she closed in on a lead, the path twisted, sending her away from the answers and toward more questions.

17

THE NEXT DAY AFTER MORNING PRAYER, SISTER AGATHA sat in Reverend Mother's office. Today, regular routines had been suspended and the nuns had all been given a free day to celebrate yesterday's success. There would be no labor today, though the canonical hours would still be observed.

Reverend Mother stared at the simple wooden crucifix on the wall for an eternity before finally speaking.

"I called you here, child, because I wanted to tell you about a new problem facing this monastery. The company that insures our property and the materials we work on in the scriptorium has threatened to suspend our coverage until the matter of Father Anselm's murder has been resolved."

"But why? And can they legally do that?"

"A story that ran on the Internet and in the local newspapers has claimed that one of our nuns is the prime suspect in Father Anselm's murder. This was confirmed by the police. The insurance company, simply put, doesn't want to be associated with us, and they're using the fact that our insurance premium was a bit late as grounds to consider suspending our coverage."

"Don't we have a grace period on payments?"

"We exceeded that, I'm afraid, so we're at their mercy now.

Sister Gertrude usually totaled up the donations we'd received during the month and then took only as much as was necessary from our interest-bearing account to pay our bills. But the date for mailing the bills passed while she was in the hospital. I didn't realize that the checks hadn't been mailed until I took over her duty as cellarer while she recuperated. I've turned the matter over to our attorney now, but if we lose our insurance coverage we won't be able to accept scriptorium work any longer. Unfortunately, without that income, we may not be able to keep our doors open." She paused, then added, "If this matter about Father's death could be settled, I know our benefactors would come forward and the insurance company would drop the issue."

"Mother, I'm doing everything I can—"

She held up a hand. "I know. I just wanted you to know that time is of the essence now, child."

Bowing her head, Sister Agatha left the abbess and went to the parlor to relieve Sister Bernarda.

As the other extern began to rise from her chair, Sister Agatha gestured for her to remain seated. "Do you have a few moments, Your Charity? I need to brainstorm with someone about this case."

"I'm at your service, Sister."

Sister Agatha paced back and forth rubbing her aching hands as she spoke. "Right now, Celia still is the sheriff's most likely suspect, but I'm convinced that she's being framed by circumstantial evidence. Celia's hands bothered her after she worked on the alb, and so did mine. To me, that indicates that when she and I handled it, it was already contaminated with monkshood."

"She may have put it on the alb *before* you found her." Sister Bernarda steepled her fingers, lost in thought. "We have to look at things clearly—not see only what we want to, but what is."

Hearing the soft padding of a nun's shoes on the other side of the grate, Sister Agatha turned her head.

Celia was standing there quietly. "Mother Mistress, I *want* to help. What can I do to prove I'm not guilty? The real murderer is out there getting away with it while everyone's wasting time focusing on me."

"Think back, Celia," Sister Agatha said. "Did you see *anyone* or *anything* out of the ordinary the day you went to the sacristy to repair the alb?"

"No, I didn't. And I've gone over and over it in my mind. But I think we're looking at things from the wrong perspective, and that's why we're not finding answers."

"What do you mean?" Sister Agatha asked.

"We've been looking at what actually happened that day—instead of what *should* have happened. Think back with me. I broke the routine, because no one expected *me* to fix the alb. That was your job—and something that you would have done long before Mass if we hadn't received a shipment for St. Francis' Pantry that day. Had you repaired the alb, of course, you would have taken even longer than I did because of your arthritis, so your contact with the poison would have been more prolonged."

Sister Agatha's heart began to pound fiercely and fear left a bitter taste in her mouth. The observation Celia was making led to only one conclusion. "Father Anselm wasn't the target. *I* was. But to what end? The amount on the alb wasn't enough to kill, under normal circumstances, according to the lab reports. The only reason Father died was because he also had a heart ailment that made him particularly vulnerable to the effects of monkshood."

"It wasn't meant to kill you, but someone clearly wanted you to get sick," Sister Bernarda said with her usual bluntness.

"But who'd do such a thing, and why? What would anyone have to gain from it?" Sister Agatha said a quick prayer, then pushed back her fear, tossing ideas around in her head as she frantically searched for answers.

"It makes no sense at all . . . unless it was meant as a diversion, or a way to delay or incapacitate you for a day or two," Sister Bernarda said. "Did you have a special meeting scheduled or any appointments in town?"

Sister Agatha thought about it for a moment, then shook her head, and said, "Only the usual errands for the sisters. This makes no sense. If anyone here had wanted to get me out of the way for a while, that would have been simple enough to do. Asking for my help with something complicated was all it would have taken. Seeing it as a diversionary tactic makes no sense either. Divert me from what? Parlor duties? If I'm not here, you are, and so it's not as if my presence is crucial. And there's no reason to divert me from Divine Office, or my classes with the novice and postulant, which are now in Sister Eugenia's hands."

"Yet someone wanted you sick," Bernarda repeated.

"*If* we're right about this theory—and I admit that it does sound plausible." Sister Agatha suddenly remembered the note she'd found in the turn the morning of Father's death, apologizing in advance for harming someone. She'd never considered the possibility that the note had been meant specifically for her.

"Whoever did this is not one of us," Celia said firmly. "Remember the last line of the Prayer of St. Ignatius? It's what we all live by. It says, 'All I ask is Thy grace and Thy love. With these I am rich enough and I do not ask for anything else.' That's the spirit of our monastery. Whoever did this may be in the monastery—though I'm not convinced of that—but while she may be among us, she's certainly not a part of us."

Hearing the clapper calling her to instruction, Celia left them and went to find Sister Eugenia, who was in charge of her instruction now.

"*In* the monastery but not *of* it—Celia just described herself, Your Charity," Sister Bernarda said, "and our novice as well."

"I know."

Sister Agatha didn't go out that morning. Today her joints were worse than ever in spite of the medicine she'd been taking, and too many questions were still raging in her head. Half of the time she wanted to believe that the answer lay with someone outside the monastery, but she wasn't sure that wasn't just a case of wishful thinking. Yet she *had* been followed outside the monastery—though one instance was explained, another remained a mystery to her. And there was the matter of the note left in the turn. Instinct told her that the time had come for her to concentrate on the monastery itself.

Pax, sensing her troubled mood, had remained with her all day as she shifted from parlor duties, to scriptorium work, then back again. Today was the feast day of St. Anthony Zaccaria. It was strange how it had become easier for her to mark time by feast days than by the calendar.

She took Pax for a short walk outside to reward him for his loyalty, then returned to the desk. Today she felt inadequate—and worse, old. The pain in her joints was unrelenting. She'd taken the pills that Sister Eugenia had left for her near her plate in the refectory, but they hadn't taken effect yet.

Hearing a visitor approaching, she stood up and went to answer the door.

"May I come in, Sister?" Joan Sanchez asked, standing before her.

"Of course," Sister Agatha responded.

"You look surprised to see me," she said.

"I am, but you're always welcome," Sister said with a smile.

Joan was wearing a denim skirt and a short-sleeved blouse—a cool-looking summer outfit Sister Agatha found herself envying. When the temperature was in the high nineties the sisters' long habit could be torture.

Setting aside her envy, Sister Agatha took time to notice that Mrs. Sanchez looked calmer and more in command of herself than she had the last time they'd met.

"I came to see you because I was hoping you could tell me the best way to approach Sheriff Green. I held something back from him when he first questioned me—something he needs to know."

"If you have police business, Joan, you shouldn't be talking to me about it."

"You don't understand. This involves Father Anselm."

Sister Agatha took a deep breath. She had a feeling that Joan had found a way to prove she wasn't guilty of poisoning Father. There was something about her tone of voice and her manner that indicated a confidence she hadn't shown before.

"I have an alibi for the morning Father was killed, and the night before that, too, if it comes to that. I couldn't say anything about it until now, because the person I'd been with didn't want to be involved. But now he's changed his mind."

"I'm still not understanding you."

"I spent that night and most of that morning with Don Malcolm, at his home. I know Don has a bad side, but he's always been kind and generous with me. Father Anselm told me Don was a criminal, and strongly advised me not to see him, but I'd seen a side of Don most people never have and I loved him." She swallowed. "Then Father got killed. Since I'd seen so much of Father, and many people had heard us arguing, I knew people would sooner or later start thinking that I'd had something to do with his death. But I wasn't worried about it until Don refused to tell the sheriff that I'd been with him. He told me he didn't want to get involved in a police investigation, so I had no way of clearing myself—that is, until now."

"What changed?"

"Don's already in jail, so he has nothing more to lose. And, of course, it would also prove that Don had nothing to do with Father Anselm's death either."

"I'm not sure how much good that man's word will do for you with the sheriff," Sister Agatha said slowly.

"It's not just Don's word, others saw us together that night, and then the following morning. But they're Don's friends, and some of them are under investigation now too, I believe. The thing is, how do I get the sheriff to accept my alibi?"

"Go tell him the whole story as soon as you can. Let him look into it himself. If you have more than one eyewitness, I think he'll respect that—but settling this has to be between you and him."

"He's got to believe me. It's the truth."

"Then tell him that. You might offer to take a lie detector test, too. I don't know if that'll help, but it may convince him you're not hiding anything anymore."

"Thanks, Sister. I appreciate it."

Sister Agatha let the woman out, then returned to her desk, her heart heavy. As the bells for Mass began to ring, Sister Agatha let a restless Pax go outside again, locked the parlor door, then hurried to chapel. She had no doubt that the vestments had been put away properly and everything was ready. Sister Clothilde had taken over that responsibility recently and she could always be counted on.

Instead of offering comfort, the thought filled Sister Agatha with guilt. As a novice, she'd been taught that any lapse in duty, from a torn veil to a badly mopped floor, was a fault—a failing in the duties a nun performed for God. These days, she was not only failing to perform her regular duties, which had been assigned to others, she was failing at the primary duty Mother Abbess had given her to perform—to find the truth.

She had to do better. *Lord, this monastery can only survive with Your help. We're not conventional housewives, but we still need Your help to open a jar every once in a while.*

Sister Agatha took her place in the chapel and stayed there long after Mass and Sext, the Divine Office that was chanted right after Mass, knowing that Sister Bernarda was scheduled for portress duty following Mass.

Minutes passed slowly, but she needed this time in prayer and reflection to capture her focus and peace. After a long while, Sister Clothilde came into the chapel and tapped on the grille that separate the choir section from the public chapel.

Sister went up to her. Honoring her vow of silence, the elderly nun pointed to her mouth, signaling to Sister Agatha that it was time for their meal.

Sister Agatha smiled and shook her head. "Thank you, Your Charity, but I think I'll stay here for a while longer."

Time passed as she tried to sort out her thoughts. Yet, no matter how hard she prayed, no answers came to her. Finally, feeling tired and in pain, she went to the parlor to relieve Sister Bernarda. Today, Celia was there, too, sitting behind the grille, so Sister Bernarda could supervise her studies.

"Where's Sister Eugenia?" Sister Agatha asked.

"She's with Mary Lazarus and just about everyone else in the bakery. They're fighting the automated baker again." Sister Bernarda stood, then offered Sister Agatha the now vacant chair. "Sister Clothilde left a sandwich for you," Sister Bernarda said. "There it is," she added, pointing to the other side of the desk. "She slipped a holy card beneath the plate, too. I tried to take a look at it, but she nearly slapped my hand when I tried," she said with a smile.

Sister Agatha chuckled. "She really worries about all of us."

"The pills next to the sandwich came from Sister Eugenia. She told me I was to stay with you until I actually saw you take them. And she insisted that you should do no manual work for the rest of the day, including assisting in the scriptorium."

"She wants me in good working order." Sister Agatha sighed.

"So do the rest of us. We're counting on you, Sister. Your background in investigative reporting is the best hope we have now."

"I wish my skills were sharper," Sister Agatha said, swallowing the pills with a bit of water. "I don't even know if it's that I'm not asking the right questions or if I'm just in over my head."

Celia who had, until now, been reading quietly beyond the screen, looked up at them. "When we try too hard, Mother Mistress, we tend to make a mess of things. Remember how I was when I first came? I couldn't even find my way around the monastery. Then Sister Ignatius helped me one day by pointing out that with all the fretting I was doing, God couldn't possibly get a word in edgewise. Sometimes we need to let go of a problem in order to solve it."

Sister Agatha looked at Celia and smiled. "Thank you, Celia. I'll keep that in mind." She dearly wanted to forget the problem, but it kept right on coming. And it was beginning to look like solving it would take a minor miracle.

Hearing the clapper, Sister Bernarda glanced at Celia. "That means that Sister Eugenia is ready for you again. You may go."

Once Sister Bernarda left for the scriptorium, Sister Agatha ate her sandwich. The holy card Sister Clothilde had left showed the Blessed Virgin with the Baby Jesus. It was clearly a special keepsake, hand painted on parchment and was quite old—no doubt something the elderly nun had treasured for many years. The gesture—and the love behind it—touched her deeply.

Prohibited from further work in the scriptorium today, Sister

Agatha took all the shifts in the parlor, freeing Sister Bernarda to work with the computers.

Frank Walters arrived in the middle of the afternoon, having been summoned to take care of an ailing computer. Though the recent upgrade had gotten them nearly back on schedule, some further adjustment and repairs had proven necessary. He was so frequent a guest these days that his presence in the monastery had almost become routine.

The day passed slowly. She checked in with Tom, but there were no new developments on the case. Shortly after the bell had rung for Vespers, Sister Agatha turned around and saw Pax lying down just beyond the grille. She opened the door between the parlor and the enclosure and let him in. "Where have you been all afternoon and who let you back into the enclosure? I let you out myself this morning."

The question preyed on her mind as she locked up the parlor a bit early and made her way to chapel.

Pax stopped in the hallway, about four feet from the chapel door, and lay down in his favorite spot as she went inside and joined the sisters already there chanting the Divine Office.

All through Evening Prayer, the question of how Pax got in and out of the enclosure nagged at her. Minutes ticked by, but she found it impossible to put the matter completely out of her thoughts. Finally, after Vespers was concluded, she came up with a plan.

Tonight she'd leave Pax outside and then sneak out and watch him. Her joints still hurt too much to let her get any sleep anyway.

Her dark habit would be perfect for a clandestine operation, too. With a little bit of luck, she'd finally have a definitive answer to at least one small mystery.

18

L ONG AFTER COMPLINE, SISTER AGATHA WALKED DOWN THE hallway toward the refectory with Pax. As she opened the side door, Pax rushed out into the cool night air. Sister Agatha closed the door, then went around to the front and stepped outside, locking the doors behind her.

She'd intended to remain out of Pax's sight, but the dog had circled around the grounds and spotted her almost immediately. Unwilling to give up, she sat down on the bench near the statue of the Blessed Virgin. Pax remained with her, lying at her feet, not moving.

It was going to be a long night if the dog decided to remain with her the entire time. As the temperature dropped, she breathed in the cool air, grateful for the respite from the blistering July heat. Eventually Pax began to relax and wander about the garden, but he never went far. Her eyes had adjusted to the darkness long ago, and she could see quite well under the moon and bright summer stars of the Milky Way.

She was about to give up on him when she saw the kitchen door open just a crack. A heartbeat later someone came out, then the door was shut once more. In the darkness, she couldn't make out the person's face, but it was a nun. Then she recognized the pattern of the habit, which left no doubt that it was Sister Mary Lazarus.

Sister Agatha approached slowly, coming out of the shadows that concealed her from casual view, more curious than anything else. Then, as the moon came out from behind the clouds, a muted light illuminated the garden.

Sister Mary Lazarus was walking toward the adobe wall that bordered the monastery. Seeing her, Pax went toward her, tail wagging. When he got close, she held out her hand as if to pet him, but missed and, oblivious to it, kept going.

"Sleepwalking," Sister Agatha muttered with a sigh. But maybe she'd still found the answer to the puzzle. Perhaps Pax had been inadvertently let in and out of the enclosure by the sleepwalking novice, who was evidently aware of her environment just enough to get around.

Sister Agatha caught up to Mary Lazarus and gently led her back inside. By the time they reached the door, Sister Bernarda was there and nodded to Sister Agatha as she entered with the novice and Pax. Silence would not be broken now, but it was clear from her expression and the fact that she was there that Sister Bernarda had heard the novice's movements and had followed her to prevent the sleepwalker from injuring herself.

As far as Sister Agatha knew, this was the first time they'd ever found Mary Lazarus outside the monastery. It was clear now that the novice knew no boundaries when she wandered about at night.

By the time Sister Agatha reached her own bed she was exhausted. She slipped off her shoes and veil, then lay down. Within seconds, she was fast asleep.

After breakfast, Sister Agatha met with Reverend Mother and recounted the events of the evening before.

"So you think that Sister Mary Lazarus was the one responsible for letting the dog in and out of the enclosure?" Reverend Mother asked.

"Our doors can be unlocked by hand from the inside without keys. Of course that doesn't prove anything—it carries no more weight than my theory for how Pax got onto the grounds, but it seems a reasonable guess."

"We'll have to find a way to curtail Mary Lazarus's nighttime walks. It's just too dangerous now, especially if there's a chance she's inadvertently allowing an intruder into our enclosure."

"Mother, I don't know how to keep her in her cell at night without actually posting a guard at the door. None of the cell doors have locks, and if we put anything in her path, she could end up injuring herself in the dark."

"Maybe we can persuade one of the merchants in town to donate a dead-bolt lock for our kitchen door that requires an inside key. We'd not only have added security but we'd guarantee the novice can't let herself out of the building. But, come to think of it, that might be too dangerous in an emergency."

"You're right. Unless the key is kept close by and available, the lock could also trap the rest of us in the building during a crisis. Maybe we can get some kind of simple alarm that will wake just Sister Bernarda and myself if Mary Lazarus leaves her cell. I'll see what I can do, Mother." She bowed slightly, then left for the parlor.

She found Sister Bernarda at the desk. "I need to talk to you. Can you spare me a few moments?"

She nodded. "You're worried about Mary Lazarus, aren't you? I happened to hear her wandering about last night. But by the time I could follow her, she was out of sight. Up to now, she simply went to the refectory or the kitchen, but this time, she was gone. I was so relieved when I spotted you bringing her back inside."

"I couldn't believe she'd actually gone outside! If that's what she's been doing on occasion, she's a danger to herself and to all of us as well."

"Her sleepwalking is the symptom of a bigger issue. I don't think she's happy here," Sister Bernarda said.

Sister Eugenia came up to the grille. "Forgive me for listening, Sisters, but I agree with both of you that Sister Mary Lazarus has had a change of heart. And it's not just her sleepwalking that's a sign of it. I treated her for hives a few weeks ago. Her arms were red and swollen. She blamed it on gardening and allergies—the same type of thing she had months ago, when she first started gardening—but I don't think that was it this time. I remember my niece getting the same kind of welts on her arms every time she had an exam, or there was some big event at school. What Mary Lazarus had most likely was a case of nerves, pure and simple."

"In all fairness, she does have allergies, and she had been gardening a lot lately to spare Sister Maria Victoria, and Sister Gertrude," Sister Bernarda pointed out.

"I'll talk to the sisters, then," Sister Agatha said. "Maybe one of them can shed some more light on this."

"Try to hurry. Frank Walters is coming. Once he gets here, one of us will take over portress duty while the other stays with him in the scriptorium. Sister Gertrude won't feel comfortable being there with him."

"All right." Sister Agatha found Sister Maria Victoria outside pruning roses. "I hate to interrupt your work, Sister, but I need to talk to you about Sister Mary Lazarus."

Sister Maria Victoria nodded, but continued working. "She's such a hard worker. She wasn't always enthusiastic about gardening, but she's recently had a change of heart. I think she began to understand what I'd been telling her—that flowers are our gift from God—one we, in turn, share with Him when we place a fresh bouquet of flowers in the chapel. Since the end of April, she's taken on gardening jobs without even being asked. And she now does the work with a great deal of skill."

Sister Agatha stared at the ground, lost in thought. Maybe Sister Mary Lazarus was working out some of her restlessness by gardening. That was common enough.

"Look at how she prunes the roses," Sister Maria Victoria said, showing her the way the branches had been cut back to sections with four or more leaves. "She used to just cut off the spent blooms."

"You're an excellent teacher."

"No, it's not me. She actually made it a point to read the books we have in the library about desert gardening. She's become quite informed—both on plants and horticulture. The very job she hated now gives her a great deal of pleasure. I'd say that's nothing short of a miracle."

"Thank you, Sister."

As the bells for Terce rang out, Sister Agatha hurried into the parlor. Maybe she could relieve Sister Bernarda a little early. Extern sisters didn't always get to chant the Divine Office with the choir nuns, and this was one small gift she could give Sister Bernarda for all the extra work she'd had to take on lately.

As Sister Bernarda went to the chapel, Sister Agatha sat at the desk in the parlor. She'd recently learned that Celia was well versed in herbs because of her mother's expertise, which was one of the reasons the sheriff considered her a prime suspect. But now, Agatha reasoned, with Mary Lazarus's interest in gardening, her own knowledge could have grown and could have been considerable as well.

Hearing a knock at the door, Sister Agatha went to answer it.

Frank Walters stood there in the early morning light. "Good morning, Sister. I figured I'd come early so I wouldn't interfere with Mass."

"Come in. I'll walk you to the scriptorium."

She stayed with him there until Sister Bernarda, Sister Mary Lazarus, and Celia came in a few minutes later. By then, Frank had completely dismantled the computer that kept locking up. "I don't think this is a software problem. I think what you're facing is a bad mix between new software and old operating systems. But I'll see what I can do."

Sister Bernarda signaled Sister Agatha and met her out in the hall. "Have you made any progress on the case?"

"Nothing substantial," Sister Agatha replied vaguely. "But I won't be going into town quite as often anymore. I have a feeling many of the answers I need are right here. Pray that the truth I find sets us free instead of burying us."

"It's a shame that truth makes no allowances for people's feelings," Sister Bernarda said with a wry smile.

"I need you to do something for all our sakes," Sister Agatha said. "If I'm not around, will you keep an eye on Mary Lazarus—without letting her know what you're doing?"

"Mary Lazarus? I thought for sure you'd be asking me about Celia."

"Don't read too much into my request. I'm groping in the dark right now. My next stop is our library. If you'd listen from the scriptorium for the door and the telephone, I'd appreciate it."

She hurried to the library before Sister Bernarda could ask her any more questions. Investigating had seemed simpler, and less heartbreaking, when she'd been convinced that the answer lay with the townspeople, not within the monastery.

The library was simply a large room with one window that faced the back garden. One single briar rose on a trellis made its way up the outside wall beside the window, climbing steadily toward the sun.

Sister Agatha looked around, passing shelves filled with liturgical tomes and volumes on the lives of the saints. She knew the monastery had a few gardening books somewhere.

Looking through the smaller shelf, Sister Agatha found what she'd been searching for. Taking the gardening books to the table, she looked them over carefully, but none of the books included information about monkshood.

Discouraged, she went to return them to the shelf, but as she pushed some books aside to make room for the ones she'd taken out, she spotted a heavy-looking book on medicinal plants lying flat behind the others, hidden from view.

Sister Agatha picked it up and checked out the index. It listed monkshood. She then checked the back for signatures. Theirs was the old checkout method. There were no computers here in their small library.

No names appeared on the back card. That indicated that it hadn't been officially checked out.

She studied the information on monkshood. The book went into great detail about the buttercup family, which included monkshood. It explained the chemistry of the Aconitum genus of plants, told how to form a tincture in alcohol for anesthetic purposes, and warned that the quantities had to be kept very small and that it was never to be taken internally.

The danger the root posed was clearly stated, but so was the method to distill it. Sister Agatha sat down on a wooden bench near the window, the book open in her lap. Sunshine streaming through the pane fell on a small piece of crochet thread near the binding. It was a cream color and would have been almost impossible to make out under artificial light.

She picked it up between her thumb and forefinger and studied it. The color and texture made it clear that it hadn't come from a habit. But the real question was how it had come to be on that particular page.

She took the piece of thread and placed it inside her breviary, then placed the book in the pocket of her habit. She then hurried back to the scriptorium to relieve Sister Bernarda.

"I'm back now, Sister Bernarda. If you like, I'll take over for you here," Sister Agatha said. "After the marathon hours you've been keeping in the scriptorium, portress duty should be like a vacation."

"Are your hands less sore today?"

"Much."

"Well, don't overdo. Let Sister Mary Lazarus do the scanning and Celia input data. She's a much faster typist."

"All right. Thanks for the tip."

Glancing across the room, Sister Agatha watched Celia working. Her fingers moved at lightning speed. The postulant's concentration was total, and she seemed unaware of anyone else in the room.

"She works just the way she thinks," Sister Bernarda said softly as she turned her carrel and the valuable manuscript she'd been scanning over to Sister Agatha. "Nothing sidetracks her from a goal. She focuses on what she has to do so thoroughly that it's nothing short of amazing."

As Sister Bernarda left for the parlor, Sister Agatha watched Mary Lazarus, who had walked over to hand Frank a tool. The furtive looks the novice and Frank gave one another when they each thought the other wasn't looking unsettled her. She acted on that quickly.

She cleared her throat to get the novice's attention. "Please go to the sacristy to help Sister Clothilde get things ready for Father Rick."

"But Frank needs help. He doesn't have Joey with him today and the machine—"

"Sister, please go to the sacristy now," she said a little more firmly.

There was a flash of anger in the novice's eyes, but she nodded and stopped arguing immediately. "Yes, Mother Mistress."

As Mary Lazarus left, Sister Agatha glanced at Frank. "If you need my help, please let me know. Otherwise, I'll be working."

"To tell you the truth, Sister, I'm going to have to quit for a while. I'll need to load in new versions of software that I just don't have with me." He paused, then added, "You really have to speak to Reverend Mother about getting at least one new computer, particularly now that the quilt brought in such a good price."

"That money is already slated for other things, like fixing our car, but I'll tell Reverend Mother what you said. Do you know anyone in town who might be persuaded to donate a computer?"

"Not offhand, but I'll ask around." He gathered up his tools. "I'll be back later."

After placing the rare edition she had planned to work on back in the safe and locking it, she walked their visitor to the parlor, then Sister Bernarda showed him to the door.

Saying a quick good-bye, Sister Agatha returned to the scriptorium, lost in thought. For the first time since she'd become part of the monastery, she was afraid of what the future would hold for them. They seemed to be facing one financial disaster after another.

Sister Agatha crouched by the safe and began unlocking it when she heard a soft rustle of cloth and realized that Mary Lazarus was behind her.

"What can I do for you?" Sister Agatha asked the novice curtly.

"The sacristy and the vestments are ready. Should I pull something from the safe and begin working?"

"No, it's time for your studies. You, too, Celia. That has to take precedence."

"Shall we find Sister Eugenia?"

"No, I'll take care of it today. What have you been reading?"

Celia showed her the book she had with her. It was St. Theresa's *Way of Perfection*. Sister Mary Lazarus had been reading a book on the Rule of St. Benedict. She instructed both of them to continue their readings. "After a half hour, we'll discuss what you've learned."

"Mother Mistress, it's good to be working with you again," Celia said.

"Thank you, Celia. Now work. Meditating on these works will help prepare you for the gift of contemplation."

As Sister Mary Lazarus opened her book, the pages parted, revealing a cream-colored crocheted bookmark. It seemed a close match to the crochet thread she'd found in the library book.

Sister Agatha took a deep breath. This was no time for snap judgments. And there was no telling how long the thread had been in the book. It was entirely possible that Mary Lazarus had looked up monkshood after learning what had happened to Father Anselm. Yet a disturbing suspicion remained at the back of her mind.

What she needed was a tiny thread from that bookmark so she could compare it more closely to the one she'd found.

Leaving them alone for a moment, she went to Sister Bernarda and asked her to take Mary Lazarus away on an errand and keep her busy for a few minutes. Sister Bernarda's eyes lit up with questions, but she agreed to do as she was asked.

Moments later, Sister Mary Lazarus left the scriptorium to help Sister Bernarda move the parlor desk so she could clean beneath it.

Sister Agatha glanced at Celia, but the postulant was completely absorbed in her reading. Pretending to be straightening up the room, Sister Agatha wandered past the place where Mary Lazarus had been seated and took the bookmark from the book in one deft move. Using a small pair of scissors, she worked a little piece of crochet thread loose from the center stitch and snipped it off. Then she surreptitiously returned the bookmark to its place.

Every instinct she possessed told her that this would end up pointing the way to the answers she'd been searching for, but she felt no sense of triumph, only a lingering sadness.

An hour and a half later, as the bells for Mass began to ring, Sister Agatha watched Celia put her work away and set it inside the safe as she'd been taught, then leave for chapel. Mary Lazarus did the same and she and the postulant went to join Sister Bernarda and the choir nuns.

Sister Agatha carefully locked the safe and set out across the long hallways. She had one more duty to perform before going to chapel.

Moments later, she entered the empty infirmary, whispering a silent prayer of thanks that all the nuns were in good health. She thought of Sister Gertrude's recovery, and said an extra Hail Mary in gratitude.

Weaving past the infirmarian's desk, she made her way into the dispensary. On the desk there was what she'd come in search of—a microscope. The aged device had belonged to Sister Praeterita, a nurse who had joined their monastery long before Sister Agatha's time. Sister Praeterita was buried in the cemetery outside now along with others, but the microscope remained—along with a silent hope that someday someone else with Sister Praeterita's training would join them.

It had been a long, long time since Sister Agatha had used a microscope, but it didn't take her long to place the two pieces of thread on a clean slide, side by side, and get the lens focused.

They appeared to be identical. Of course she was no forensic expert, so this was all very circumstantial—but it was still a lead. She considered telling Sheriff Green, but it didn't seem right to do that yet. On the scanty evidence she had, it could almost be termed bearing false witness.

She took two small plastic bags from the drawer, and marking and labeling each, placed the threads securely inside them. She then placed both bags in her pocket. Walking quickly and trying not to think about this new burden of responsibility that now rested on her shoulders, she hurried to the chapel for Mass.

After Mass, she walked to the refectory for dinner. Today she'd eat with the nuns, sharing their silence as the lecturer read from the life of one of the martyrs.

Throughout the meal she stared at the skull on the table before the cross. She felt as dry spiritually today as that remnant of what had once been a human being.

Sister Agatha hid her thoughts deep within her. She felt like Judas, knowing she was intending to betray one of her own. But she had a duty to see through.

The first thing she had to do was find out if there was any way at all Mary Lazarus could have gotten hold of some monkshood. Sister Agatha considered the possibilities. If Mary Lazarus had found monkshood by accident, then her wanderings might reveal a vital clue. She didn't expect to find any monkshood around now—the grounds and the building had been searched—but, with luck, she'd spot traces of where it had been.

She'd start by following Sister Mary Lazarus whenever she was outside. But following the novice during recreation without being seen would be nearly impossible. Trailing her after the fact . . . that was possible—with a little ingenuity, of course.

19

THE KEY TO HER PLAN WOULD REQUIRE SOME DELICATE MA-
neuvering. All the nuns wore identical shoes, except for minor
variations in size. Tracking the novice would be impossible
unless she could mark the rope soles of Sister Mary Lazarus's alpargates, so that the tracks would be distinctive.

Seeing the novice mopping the hall floor, an idea formed in her
mind. Sister Agatha pretended to slip on the wet floor and knocked
against the water bucket in the process. As water sloshed over Sister
Mary Lazarus's sandals, the novice yelped softly.

Sister Agatha did her best to look mortified. "Let me help you,
Sister. I'll bring you the extra shoes from the closet down the hall.
They're kept there for emergencies such as this. If you'll give me the
shoes you're wearing, I'll place them outside to dry. In this heat, it
won't take long."

Sister Mary Lazarus removed her soggy shoes. "It's all right,
Mother Mistress. I'll take care of it."

"No, it's best if you finish your work quickly, Sister. We don't
want the hall to be slippery when Reverend Mother or one of the
older sisters comes through when it's time for None."

"God reward you, Mother Mistress," Mary Lazarus said, handing
over her wet shoes.

"At your service, Sister."

Sister Agatha wrapped the shoes in a small towel kept in the cleaning cart, then went to get Sister Mary Lazarus the dry pair. The spare shoes in the closet turned out to be at least three sizes too big for Mary Lazarus's small feet.

Feeling a little guilty at the problems this would create for the novice, and at the deception, Sister Agatha quickly made her way outside. Alone on the small patio at the end of the long hallway, she reached into her pocket, took out the keys to the Antichrysler, and used them to dig into the soft sole of Mary Lazarus's shoes, cutting a line down each of the heels. She then placed the shoes in the sun to dry.

As she looked up, she saw Pax was outside lying on a small patch of grass in the shade of one of the cottonwoods. She envied him. At least lying on the cool grass was one way to beat the infernal heat.

Sister Agatha spent the next hour in the scriptorium. Though the medication was helping, her joints were still stiff and a little swollen, so she concentrated only on scanning work.

Celia, who'd come in to help after finishing her assigned manual labor, looked up from the typing and gave Sister Agatha a worried glance.

"Mother Mistress, if it's painful for you to work, let me do the scanning as well," she said softly, coming up to her. "I really don't mind."

"No, there's no need for you to do that. But God reward you for your concern."

Sister Bernarda came in with Frank Walters a moment later.

"I think I'm finally going to be able to fix this one," Frank announced, pointing to the machine he'd been working on earlier that day. "I hope so, anyway."

"Deadline is only two weeks away," Sister Bernarda said in a no-nonsense tone. "We'd sure appreciate that."

"This computer's down again, too," Celia said softly, then pointed to the blue screen with an error message. "It locked up."

"Did you save what you'd been working on?" Sister Agatha asked her.

"Yes, but not recently," she answered. "I'm sorry, Mother Mistress."

"How much did you lose, do you think?" Sister Agatha asked.

"Maybe an hour's work, but if you'll allow it, I can make up for it later tonight after Compline."

"You've given me a really good idea, Celia," Sister Bernarda said. "Let's all work after hours today. What do you say, Sister Agatha? I'm sure Mary Lazarus would jump at the chance."

"It's fine with me," Sister Agatha replied.

"This computer's working now, Sisters," Frank said, as the start-up screen came on. "That means you've got three up and running. But the fourth won't be ready until later today. It's going to take me a while to back up your files and install new software."

Sister Agatha sighed. "I think I'll pull out the big guns—let me enlist Sister Ignatius, and have her start praying nonstop that we can meet our deadlines without any more mishaps."

"You better have her start praying right now. With the hard drives in bad shape, files can get corrupted, and there's no telling what you'll find when you check your backup disks."

Sister Bernarda took Sister Agatha aside. "After you speak to Sister Ignatius, why don't you take over parlor duties instead of coming back here to the scriptorium? Your hands look swollen, and I imagine they hurt."

"All right," she said, unable to refute the physical evidence.

Sister Agatha left the scriptorium. On her way to find Sister Ignatius, she passed by the doorway to the patio and checked on Sister Mary Lazarus's shoes. They'd dried in today's hundred-degree heat in record time.

Tucking the shoes under her arm, she quickly went to the bakery. Sister Ignatius would be there packing their altar breads and getting them ready to be mailed out, along with Sister Maria Victoria.

Not disrupting the monastic silence of the others as they

worked, Sister Agatha took Sister Ignatius aside, and softly asked her to pray, explaining the situation in the scriptorium.

"Your timing is perfect, Sister. We always pray for special intentions as we package the hosts that will feed the faithful. We'd been praying for Mr. Walter's intention also, so we can easily add in our own scriptorium needs."

Hurrying back down the hall, Sister Agatha found that Sister Mary Lazarus had finished waxing the floor. "Here you go, Sister. These shoes will fit you better than those you're wearing now," she said, handing them to the novice. "When you're finished here, will you please report to the scriptorium? All other activities are suspended for you this afternoon. You're needed there. Celia will tell you what the new schedule is."

By the time Sister Agatha arrived at the parlor, someone was knocking on the outer doors. She answered it and found Sheriff Green waiting.

As he stepped into the room, Tom wiped the perspiration from his brow with a handkerchief. "It's hot enough to melt rocks out there today. But it's pretty warm in here too. You really should get an air conditioner. I don't know how you all stand it during summer."

"It can be a trial," she admitted. It had to be close to ninety inside the building. "What brings you here today?"

"I needed to talk to you," Tom said slowly. "I've been checking Father Anselm's routines, reconstructing everything he did the week he died. As far as I can tell, there was nothing unusual—except for one thing. On the day he was killed, he postponed a meeting with the archbishop. Now, you and I know he wouldn't have done *that* unless something extremely urgent had come up. I followed up on that and learned that he met with Ruth Moore, Celia's mother."

She took a deep, heavy breath. She understood now what had happened. Father had realized Celia was Annie Clines, and had decided to go talk to her mother.

"There's more," Tom continued. "Betsy, Celia's sister, told me that Ruth called the monastery the morning Father Anselm died. Betsy said that they'd planned to come to Mass here, but Ruth had changed her mind at the last minute."

"Did Ruth corroborate that?"

"She says she doesn't remember. I'm working on getting a court order to check her phone records. Meanwhile, I wanted to ask you if the monastery keeps a log of incoming calls."

"Yes, we do."

"Can you check it and see if Ruth tried to contact Celia that morning?"

Sister pulled out a small black notebook from the bottom drawer, flipped to the right date, and then went through the entries. "Here it is. Sister Bernarda took the message. It wasn't an emergency, so she didn't notify Celia about the call until later that night at recreation. That's the way we routinely handle things like that."

"Relatives aren't allowed to call and speak to the nuns?"

"Of course they can, but there are restrictions here just as there are in many workplaces on the outside. For instance, I'm sure there are a lot of times your wife can't reach you on the phone, right?"

Tom looked at her strangely, and she hesitated for a moment, wondering about his reason for that reaction. Then she continued. "Well, it's like that here, too. In Celia's case, in particular, calls are very restricted. The months of postulancy are a formation period and can be especially hard, so we discourage contact with the outside."

"One question. How do you know that Celia didn't just sneak off to a phone sometime that morning and call home—like after she saw Father."

"It's not impossible, but a postulant has very little unsupervised time. Also, keep in mind we only have two phones—one in the parlor—and an extern is usually here—and the one in Reverend Mother's office, and she's usually there."

"I think you know what my next question's going to be, don't you?"

"You want to talk to Celia again?"

"Yeah. I may also have to get permission to look at the monastery telephone records. Or subpoena them."

"So we should get John Bruno?"

"I would, if I were you. It makes sense under the circumstances," Tom said.

"Then make yourself at home, 'cause it'll be a while."

John Bruno came a half hour later, much sooner than Sister had expected. He had a practice in Albuquerque and was generally booked solid for weeks. But, as it turned out, today he'd taken the day off and had stayed in town.

John Bruno spoke to Celia alone for several moments in the inner parlor. Finally they invited Sheriff Green, who had dispensation to enter the enclosure.

"May I stay when you speak to Celia this time?" Sister Agatha asked Tom.

"Yes, if she doesn't mind. But you can't interfere."

"I'd like her to stay," Celia said simply.

Sheriff Green looked at Celia. "I want you to know that I'm giving you special consideration. I can escort you to the station for questioning. You *are* a suspect in a murder case."

"But I'm not guilty."

He didn't comment, just switched on a small tape recorder. "I need you to tell me again exactly what you did on the day Father died. And don't leave *anything* out."

Celia complied, looking at Sister Agatha every few minutes as if for confirmation.

"Stop looking at Sister Agatha," Sheriff Green snapped. "She can't help you. Now, when did you tell me you spoke to your mother?"

"To Mother?"

"No, to *your* mother."

"Reverend Mother *is* my mother."

"I mean your maternal mother," he said, biting off the words. "Ruth Moore. She called you that day."

Celia stared at him. "She did?"

He gave her an incredulous look.

"Sheriff, I honestly don't remember. Things were very confusing that day."

"Let me rephrase the question. Did you speak to Ruth, your mother, sometime after Father dropped off the canned goods and before Mass?"

"No. I don't have access to a telephone."

"Did you talk to her later that night? Keep in mind that I can subpoena all the phone records, so I'll know if you're lying."

"I didn't call her. I'm sure of that, but I honestly can't remember if she called me that day or not. The only thing I know is that I haven't spoken to her in a long time."

"Exactly when was the last time you spoke to your mother?"

"I don't know, but our portress can check for you and give you more information."

"Have you ever left this monastery after hours?"

She stared at him. "Left?"

"Yeah. Have you ever sneaked out for any reason."

Celia stared at him in confusion. "Why would I?"

"You don't have to answer that," Bruno cautioned.

"But I have nothing to hide," Celia said. "The sheriff's question is just crazy." She looked directly at Tom. "If you only knew how badly I wanted to come to this monastery, and how many years I've spent dreaming of becoming a nun, you'd never ask such a silly question. This is my home. Why on earth would I ever leave?"

"Just how far were you willing to go to protect your life here? If someone tried to force you to leave, wouldn't you have done whatever it took to stop them?"

"Like resorting to violence? No, I wouldn't have. Physical confrontations don't come naturally to me or, I imagine, to anyone who becomes a nun. It goes against the grain. What I can do—probably better than you realize—is endure."

Sister Agatha watched Tom carefully. He couldn't break Celia. But he knew that there was something more going on behind Celia's stoic face—something she wasn't telling him. The next thing he would do was dig even more deeply into Celia's background. He'd learn everything there was to know about her, then he'd close in for the kill. The prospect filled her with such intense dread she shuddered involuntarily.

"What else are you keeping from me, Celia?" he asked menacingly, leaning over the table. "You're holding something back. Don't bother to deny it."

"You're harassing my client," Bruno said abruptly. "If you're charging her with something, then go right ahead. Otherwise, that's it for today."

"No charges, Counselor," Tom said. Then he looked at Celia and held her gaze. "For now."

John Bruno stood up. "Then have a good afternoon, Sheriff."

As the sheriff stalked out, John Bruno remained thoughtful. "From now on, Sister Agatha, don't let him talk to Celia or anyone else here unless I'm present. Is that clear?"

"Very. I'll tell Reverend Mother."

"What's going to happen?" Celia asked quietly.

"I've known Tom Green for a while," Bruno said. "He's sniffed out a trail and it has led him here. That could mean major trouble for this monastery."

"But I'm the one he wants, right?" Celia asked.

He nodded. "My guess is that he's convinced himself you're guilty. That means he'll tear this monastery apart, one adobe brick at a time, until he has enough evidence to convict you."

"Then let him arrest me," Celia said quickly. "I can't allow any harm to come to the sisters or the monastery—not because of me."

"Celia, no, that's not the answer. The sheriff is wrong. He'll see that soon enough. Your sentiments are noble, but the monastery doesn't need a martyr. Now go to the chapel and pray . . . for all of us," Sister Agatha said.

"Yes, Mother."

An instant before the postulant glanced down at the floor, Sister Agatha saw a flash of an emotion she couldn't readily identify in Celia's eyes. It worried her, but there was no time to dwell on it. Sister Agatha let John Bruno out, then walked him to his car.

"Thank you for getting here so quickly," she said.

"Sister, this case has taken a very serious turn. I'm going to try and find out what's really going on in Tom Green's head. I know you and Tom were childhood friends, but make no mistake about it, he's on the trail of a killer—and he'll use whatever tricks he's got in his bag to accomplish what he has to. You can't trust him—not if you want to protect the monastery."

"Understood. In the meantime, with God's help, maybe I'll find some answers on my own before this investigation ends up destroying an innocent."

"If you uncover anything I can use, tell me right away, Sister Agatha. Remember, I'm on your side."

As the attorney drove away, Sister Agatha walked back inside. Remembering the flash in Celia's eyes, she suddenly realized what the emotion had been—defiance.

There was no denying the zeal of a postulant, and in this case, it could spell major trouble. Worried, she went to look for Celia and found her exactly where she should have been—in the chapel praying. All was well. Still, uneasiness stirred inside her.

She stayed with Celia in the chapel, praying in silence for a few minutes, then returned to the parlor. Her job as portress had never been more demanding, because of all the confusion that surrounded the monastery these days.

Sister Agatha checked the turn, wondering if the kids had left a note. Finding nothing, she returned to her desk and opened the book on the Rule of Life, the order's monastic guidelines, and tried to concentrate on that. Maybe the structure and discipline it contained would help focus her thinking.

Sister Bernarda appeared at the inner door of the parlor shortly before Vespers escorting Frank Walters, who was finished for the day. After he left, she glanced over at Sister Agatha. "We're going to have to supervise Celia's scriptorium work more closely from now on, Your Charity."

"She made a mistake? She's usually so precise."

"She was distracted today and I suppose I should have expected that but . . ."

"Was it something major?"

"She was working on the recipe archive for *New Mexico Cooking Magazine*. But instead of listing one four-ounce can of hot green chile, she typed it in as a fourteen-ounce can of hot green chile. Those chicken enchiladas would have had flames shooting out of people's mouths."

Sister Agatha laughed, surprised by how refreshing it felt. It had been a long time since she'd had occasion to laugh.

"Did the sheriff give her a very hard time today?" Sister Bernarda asked.

"Yes, he did," she admitted, growing somber again. "That's why I sent her to chapel rather than straight back to the scriptorium," Sister Agatha said.

"Do you think Celia's ready, mentally, to put in extra hours tonight? Sister Gertrude offered, but I don't think we should accept. I'm afraid she'll get overly tired. And with her weak heart . . ."

"I agree. On the other hand, work will be good for Celia right now—even if we have to proofread her entries. I may be able to help, too. Let me see how things go. My hands don't feel too bad right now, and proofreading won't tax them the way data entry would."

"I'll leave that up to you, Your Charity. You know where to find us after Compline."

When the bells announcing Vespers rang, Sister Agatha locked the parlor doors early and hurried to chapel. She liked the Evening Prayer and, tonight, she needed the serenity that came with the Magnificat, the prayer commemorating the Virgin Mary's response to the angel of the Annunciation, taken from the Gospel of Luke.

During collation, Sister Agatha watched the postulant as she ate her helping of bean-filled tortillas. The reading tonight from the martyrology was particularly graphic, detailing the death of St. Maria Goretti. Some of the passages describing the brutal attack on her were particularly difficult to take on a full stomach, yet a new calm appeared to have settled over Celia.

Sister Agatha tried to figure the young woman out. Postulants were undeniably devout, but often totally unpredictable. She made a mental note to talk to Celia later and make sure she didn't do anything spectacularly crazy in hopes of protecting the monastery.

When it came time for recreation, Sister Agatha kept a furtive eye on Mary Lazarus, but tonight she seemed content to sit on one of the benches, playing with Pax, who always saw this special time of the day as his opportunity to teach the nuns to play. Sister Mary Lazarus first threw a stick for him, then played tug-of-war, using a piece of rope that had seen better days as a portion of clothesline.

"I've been keeping an eye on her as you asked," Sister Bernarda said, coming up to join Sister Agatha, "but she hasn't been acting any different from any other novice getting ready to take her vows."

"Except for the sleepwalking. I wish I could be as sure. . . ."

"There's one thing that bothers me." Sister Bernarda hesitated. "It's just a feeling I get when she's around Frank. I used to think that they couldn't stand each other, but I'm not so sure anymore."

"What makes you say that?" More than anything, Sister Agatha wished she hadn't had to ask the question. But there was no room for hesitancy now. Her duty was to God and their monastery.

"It's not that she's acted inappropriately," Sister Bernarda said. "It's the way she looks at him when she thinks he's not looking." She shook her head. "I know it sounds flimsy, and it's extraordinarily subjective, but there it is."

Sister Agatha knew that Sister Bernarda preferred hard facts— there she was on solid ground, and her confidence was unshakable. The ex-marine hated the intangibility of speculation. To have shared this bit of information with Sister Agatha was something she would have found distasteful, and that proved how important Sister Bernarda felt the observation was.

"Continue watching them whenever he comes around—but don't make it obvious."

Despite Sister Agatha's hope that Mary Lazarus would take her usual long evening walk, the novice spent all her time with Pax. By the time the bells for Compline sounded, Sister Agatha felt completely frustrated.

Tonight she had no desire to pray. She was angry—with herself and with God. All nuns, sooner or later, faced a time when they felt abandoned or lost—a crisis of faith. That time was now upon her, and it was as dark as any moonless night.

After Compline, the Great Silence began. The only sound in the scriptorium was the clickety cadence of the keyboards and the internal hums of the computers.

While Celia was completing the recipe archives and Sister Mary Lazarus concentrated on the library's collection, Sister Bernarda and Sister Agatha took the jobs that demanded the most attention and responsibility.

The pages of the original manuscripts they were scanning for the Special Collections Library had become brittle in the dry desert heat. They had to be handled with extreme care. The original, hand-written manuscripts by J. Robert Oppenheimer and Willa Cather were quite valuable and the nuns were now required to wear cloth gloves so that the acid and perspiration on their skin wouldn't taint the pages.

Sister Agatha worked methodically, scanning each page, then verifying that it had transferred properly. It was monotonous work, but the importance of it kept her alert. Once she got tired, she'd take a break by proofreading Celia's work.

It was close to midnight when Sister Bernarda flicked the light switch, signaling everyone to stop. Silence would not be broken in the monastery now, but an almost audible sigh went around the room.

After they turned off the equipment and put away their work, they all went to their cells. As they parted, something about Celia's guarded expression piqued Sister Agatha's curiosity. Celia should have been exhausted like the rest of them but, instead, there was purpose in her steps, and a new, almost nervous energy. The observation made a chill run up Sister Agatha's spine.

Trouble was brewing. She felt it as clearly as the beat of her own heart.

Once inside her cell, Sister Agatha loosened her cincture, the rope belt that was part of her habit, then removed her veil. When she'd first come to the monastery, sleeping clothed seemed like a daily penance, but once she'd learned about rising at four-thirty in the morning, or having to get up in the middle of the night during Lent, she'd come to really appreciate that part of their monastic customs. The nuns seldom needed more than a few minutes to get ready for chapel. Proverbial Brides of Christ, they were ready at a moment's notice to meet their groom.

Repeating the same prayer they'd all said during Compline, asking that God's angels dwell in their house and bring them peace, she closed her eyes and drifted off to sleep.

Normally, on a pain-free night, she would have slept soundly until morning, but something stirred her awake. Wondering if Mary Lazarus was sleepwalking again, she reached for her veil and the rope belt, and stepped out into the hall. It was as quiet as a graveyard in the hall. Peering inside Sister Mary Lazarus's cell, she found the novice asleep.

Sister Agatha stood in the middle of the hall and listened. Something had awakened her. As she stood there, Pax came up beside her, whining softly. She looked at the dog, wondering if he was hurt, but when she crouched down to check him, the dog backed away from her. She stared at him, puzzled.

Pax walked to Celia's cell and sat in the doorway staring at Sister Agatha.

Curious, she went to where he stood and glanced inside. The bed was made and a cross lay on her pillow as was their custom before leaving their rooms each day. But the postulant was gone, and it was the middle of the night.

Celia was her responsibility—a grave one. Each new postulant represented the future of their monastic order. But now . . .

Sister Agatha hurried down the corridor and let herself out the door, Pax at her side. Dreading what she'd find, she went directly to the front gates, but they were shut and still locked.

Perplexed, she stood there for a moment. That's when she noticed a torn piece of cloth caught on the rough wrought iron at the top of the gate. Unless she missed her guess, it was from the brown dress the postulant wore. There was no question in her mind now about how Celia had gotten out. She'd climbed the fence.

Sister Agatha unlocked the gates, then hurried to get the motorcycle. Unwilling to wake Reverend Mother and the other nuns with the roar of the engine, she rolled the Harley past the gates, though it was a struggle because of the sidecar. The second she straddled the motorcycle, Pax jumped into the sidecar.

As Sister Agatha drove away from the monastery, she scanned the sides of the road in the darkness, hoping for a glimpse of the missing postulant. Disturbing thoughts crowded her mind. It was clear that Celia had left to protect the others. Her devotion to the sisters and to God was unquestionable. But a desperate girl alone at night on a desolate road . . .

A chill touched her spine. There was no time to lose.

20

A MILE OR SO DOWN THE ROAD, A SLOW, DRIZZLING RAIN began to fall, but to Sister Agatha, those gentle drops felt like spikes against her tired face and swollen hands. Pax, on the other hand, seemed to be enjoying the water.

Sister Agatha focused on Celia, trying to think like the postulant. Not knowing exactly how long Celia had been gone made it difficult to gauge how far she'd gotten. Sister Agatha guessed that the postulant would head into town, but the rain would slow her down. Even upset and depressed, as she undoubtedly was, Celia would have looked for shelter. Remembering the biker bar she always passed on her way to town—The Hog—she headed for the establishment.

She glanced regularly in the rearview mirror, always careful to watch these days to see if she was being followed, but no one was there. Remembering the note she'd found in her pocket after the fair, she wondered if it had been written by someone upset with her involvement in the investigation, or merely someone distressed by other recent changes in her life, like riding the Harley.

As she approached The Hog, a touch of fear crept up her spine. The regular clientele was rumored to be a pretty rough group, and at this time of night those still out and about were likely to be the dregs. Still, instances of trouble there were supposedly few. Praying that didn't change now, she pulled into the parking lot.

Sister Agatha left Pax to guard the motorcycle, then, saying a quick prayer, went inside. As she'd expected, her entrance drew attention from the moment she stepped through the doors. A small crowd of men and women of nearly all ages, dressed in strange-looking caps, leather jackets, and jeans, most carrying wallets with chains attached, nudged each other, then stared openly at her as she made her way across the room, searching for Celia. A rumble of curiosity went around the room, interrupted by occasional bouts of laughter and the hoisting of a few bottles of beer in her direction.

She'd only gone halfway when she spotted Celia at a table in the corner, having an animated conversation with an apparently angry waitress. Celia was dressed in the simple brown dress all postulants wore, but she'd taken off her short veil. As she approached, Sister Agatha tried to focus on what they were saying.

"What do you mean you haven't got any money?" the waitress demanded.

Celia stared at her and shrugged. "I can wash dishes or clean up to pay it off."

"That's not the way it works. This ain't a charitable institution. Pay up or get arrested."

A rough-looking biker sauntered up to them. "I'll pay your tab, sweetheart," he told Celia, "providing you come to my place afterwards and do a little straightening up in my bedroom. How about it?"

"Back off." Sister Agatha's voice cracked through the air like a whip. "Time to go, Celia."

Celia stared at her wide-eyed. "I—"

"Let's go," Sister Agatha repeated more firmly.

"Wait a minute, Sister. She hasn't paid her bill. Are you going to cover her tab?" the waitress asked.

"I don't have any money with me," Sister Agatha said, then looked directly at the lean-looking biker, who had long black hair fastened in a ponytail that trailed down his back. "But you do. Will you pay her bill in exchange for the prayers of all the nuns?"

He laughed. "Prayers? I don't think so. I had some other kind of offering in mind, Sister."

"Is this how you show respect for two nuns away from their home on a cold night?" she snapped, and looked around. The people in The Hog were more interested in how she was going to handle things than in helping her and Celia. They were on their own.

Spotting a pool table next to the wall, she gestured toward it. "Let's play a game of eight ball. If I win, you pay for her meal."

"And if I win?" the man asked, a broad smile on his face.

"I've got a 1986 Heritage Classic Harley outside with a matching sidecar. The bike roars like a cougar. You could take it out for a spin—just as long as you bring it back here within the hour so we can still get home before dawn."

He met her gaze and laughed. "How do you know I'll bring it back?"

"It would make no sense for you to steal it and leave your own bike behind for me to use to identify you. And even if you walked here, or hitched a ride with someone, you wouldn't get off. Everyone in this room would know you're the thief, and the sheriff would be after you almost immediately."

He met her gaze, then produced a crooked grin before grabbing a cigarette from behind his ear and lighting it with a silver lighter. "Okay. You've got yourself a deal, Sister. I'm always up for a game, and I've been looking for some real competition tonight."

When the man walked over to rack up the balls, the waitress leaned close to Sister Agatha's ear and whispered, "Back out of this now, Sister. He's a hustler. I've never seen him lose unless he's setting someone up for an even bigger-stakes game."

"I don't have a choice. No one else has offered to pay for her meal."

"Don't look at me. I barely make enough to feed myself and pay my rent."

"Then my course is set." Sister Agatha looked at the man who'd accepted the challenge as he handed her a cue stick. She placed it down on the table and saw that it had a slight curve about halfway down.

"I'll pick my own cue, thanks." She walked over to the wall rack, looked at two, then picked a third that looked straight and had good balance. Now if she could just remember her days playing with her grad students and the other professors in the student union building.

"Lag for break?" he asked.

"No. Just go ahead. Even if you put a few balls in, I'll catch up soon enough." She smiled, trying to appear confident. No way she was going to let him know that she couldn't even remember the rules of eight ball at the moment. But, with him going first, she could watch and maybe pick up enough to fake it without giving herself away.

The biker walked back and opened a slender hard-sided case, picking out a two-piece cue that he screwed together casually. It looked expensive, and that was a bad sign.

As he took his position, she glanced over at Celia. The postulant waved just as the biker hit the cue ball. He didn't even notice, which meant his concentration on the game was total, another bad indication.

That's when Sister Agatha started praying. There was no saint who specialized in games of pool as far as she knew, so it would have to be St. Jude, patron saint of the impossible.

As one of the solid balls, a four, dropped into the side pocket, the biker looked up and smiled. "Shooting solids."

He looked at the table, walked around to her side, and eyed a blue ball close to the end pocket. "Two at the end," he called, and proceeded to knock it in. The cue ball followed, but bounced off a side cushion, setting up his next shot.

Sister Agatha glanced over at Celia, who looked pale all of a sudden. Obviously, Celia already believed she'd lose the game. Desperation and determination made Sister Agatha pray harder.

The biker proceeded to mix a combination of shots, putting away the ball he called every time. It was going to be her shortest game ever, at this rate.

Then, as he lined up his next shot, there was a resounding crash from the bar. Several glasses and an empty bottle had toppled to the floor off a serving tray. "Hey, Bubba, sorry about that," the bartender yelled.

But the damage had been done. The ball had bounced off the side pocket instead of going in. The biker shot the bartender a look that made the temperature in the room drop by thirty degrees. "Your turn, Sister," the biker growled.

Sister Agatha lined up her first shot, which looked pretty easy. With luck it would be like riding a motorcycle—a skill that was never lost. As she bent over, she realized that in the excitement of the moment, her joints didn't even hurt, despite the high humidity at the moment. Confidence surged through her. "Nine ball in the corner pocket."

She lined it up, took a deep breath, and struck the cue ball a little below center. It struck the nine squarely, which shot right into the pocket. The cue ball had enough back spin to stop short, but just barely.

"Luck." The biker chuckled.

"Talent." Sister Agatha turned and smiled at the man, then looked for her next shot. This would be harder, all the way across the table to sink the three ball, just outside the opposite corner pocket.

"Take your time," the biker heckled, crossing in front of her as she was lining up the shot.

"Put a sock in it, dude," Celia yelled from across the room. Several onlookers laughed, and Sister Agatha stopped and waited for the noise to subside.

"Three ball in the corner." Sister Agatha barely tapped the cue ball, then her stomach sank as it suddenly occurred to her that she'd hit it *too* gently. The white ball rolled across the table almost leisurely, and all she could do was watch and pray. With a click, it struck the three, which slowly eased to the corner and dropped with a thunk.

"Nice going, Sister," the bartender said. Celia applauded, but when she noticed she was the only one clapping, she stopped. Everyone else laughed except Sister Agatha.

Sister Agatha concentrated and hung on, barely making the

next shots, each time silently praising God for His backup. By now, everyone in the room was watching, and she was feeling the pressure. Finally all she had to do was put the eight ball away.

"You've gotten lucky with a couple of slop shots, Sister, but now you're going to need some skill. Do you really think you can put the game away?" the man asked with a laugh. "Even *I* would have trouble at that angle without scratching. Of course, once you move it just a little, I'll sink it easily."

"Did you ever hear the story about David and Goliath? The giant with the leather armor, custom-made sword, and loud boasting was very impressive—but the little guy won."

The man just sneered.

"Go for it, Sister," the bartender urged.

Sister Agatha lined up the shot. "Opposite end off the far cushion." She hit the ball squarely and it flew down the table, bounced off the end cushion, then traveled back nearly the entire length of the table, barely missing the cue ball on the way. The eight ball rolled slowly over to the pocket, then teetered on the edge, coming to a stop.

At that instant, the door was thrown open and several bikers strode in, laughing and shoving each other as they entered. The gust of wind that caught the door wound around the bar, rattling the blinds and sweeping past the pool table. The eight ball suddenly dropped neatly into the pocket. As the onlookers cheered, Sister Agatha's knees nearly buckled with relief.

The biker shook his head, muttered a curse, then laughed. "First time I've ever seen that happen. Guess I should be glad it was divine wind, and not lightning. Your victory, Sister." He went to settle Celia's tab.

Sister Agatha decided that she'd better leave now while the going was good, so she grabbed the postulant by the hand and hurried outside.

"Thank you, Mother Mistress, but I'm not going back," Celia said firmly, refusing to get on the bike.

Sister Agatha wanted to throttle Celia, but somehow kept from losing her temper. "Let's go for a short ride, then. There's a secularized adobe church—one the Church sold a long time ago—not far from here. We can take shelter there and talk."

Celia hesitated, but then got on the bike and petted Pax, who, having hunkered down in the sidecar to keep out of the rain, seemed happy to see her.

They rode in silence, the headlight cutting through the darkness. When they arrived, Sister tried the heavy wooden doors and found they weren't locked. The building had become a community project and it was slowly being restored through volunteer labor. Eventually, it would be a community art gallery and meeting hall.

Sister pulled the motorcycle inside with her, a feat which was possible thanks to double doors and low front steps. "No sense in calling attention to the fact we're here. This place is dark, and it's very late now."

They took a seat on a low windowsill and Pax came over and rested his head on Sister Agatha's lap. She stroked his massive head absently, glad he'd come with her. It was good to have a guardian on a stormy night this far from home.

"You shouldn't have come after me, Mother Mistress. I can't go back," Celia said quietly.

"You have no money. What were you planning to do, go back to your mother's house?"

"No. I'd never be able to bring myself to go back there," Celia said firmly.

Sister Agatha nodded slowly. "So what are your plans?"

"I'll think of something. All I know now is that I'm bringing chaos to the monastery, and I can't let that continue. During recreation I overheard Sister Ignatius and Reverend Mother talking. Reverend Mother was saying that the spirit of the monastery would live on in the nuns, no matter where they went. But I could tell that she was really worried about the possibility that our monastery would be closed down. It seems we've had too many bills at the same time support from our benefactors is waning. And don't you see? I'm the reason donations aren't coming in. I'm single-handedly destroying the monastery."

"I hope you didn't repeat Reverend Mother's conversation to any of the other nuns."

"I kept it to myself—that is, until now. But I knew then what I had to do. I love the Life, Mother Mistress, and I've given it my heart and soul. But what kind of nun could I ever hope to be if I disregarded the Rule? It's very specific about never judging what's better for oneself over what's good for the monastery."

Sister Agatha fell into a long silence. Celia would make an excellent nun someday, but if that was ever to happen, the next few moments and hours would have to be handled very carefully. "What you've said is true. Our monastery is founded on Christian charity and that's something we all practice and value. But charity doesn't flow just one way—the nuns extend that to you as well. The monastery needs you, Celia, just as you need us. What the sheriff has done is beyond your control, and God never holds us accountable for the actions of others. You have to trust in God now—not partly but all the way. Don't tell God how you think things should be handled. Trust Him to handle it for you in the right way."

Celia took a deep breath. "In some ways, that's even harder."

"Yes, I know."

"But even if I wanted to return, I don't think I can do that now. I've left the monastery without permission."

"No one else knows you're gone. For now, let's get you back. We'll figure out the rest tomorrow. But I promise I'll speak to Reverend Mother on your behalf."

With Celia holding on tight and Pax peeking happily around the windscreen, Sister drove quickly back to the monastery. The rain had stopped, and with luck, she'd still get an hour or so of sleep before having to rise. No one had ever accused her of being perky in the mornings, but on days when she didn't get enough sleep, she could be decidedly grouchy. Tomorrow she'd have to work hard to avoid giving new meaning to that word.

Before she reached the gates Sister Agatha turned off the engine and they coasted in. She locked the gates behind them, parked the motorcycle, then hurried to the door of the monastery, Celia and Pax beside her. Cautioning Celia with a gesture to remain totally silent, she led the way inside. Maybe, if God smiled, they'd both make it to their cells without waking anyone else.

They'd made their way down the corridor and were just going around the corner when Sister Agatha suddenly noticed Reverend Mother. The abbess had pulled up a chair, and was sitting right outside Celia's door, a small oil vigil lamp on the floor beside her and a rosary in her hands.

Sister Agatha stood there in muted shock. The Great Silence couldn't be broken except in dire emergencies, but perhaps Mother would consider finding out where they'd been such an emergency.

Celia stared first at Reverend Mother, then at Sister Agatha, her eyes wide with alarm. But, mercifully, she didn't break silence either.

Reverend Mother stood then, and with a nod of her head that spoke volumes about what tomorrow would bring, went wordlessly down the corridor. Moments later, they heard her door close softly.

Sister Agatha's knees almost buckled. Taking a deep breath, she gestured for Celia to go into her cell, and then hurried inside her own, Pax trailing behind her.

Removing her veil and cincture, she lay down. *St. Michael, glorious Prince, be mindful of us. . . . St. Raphael, guide us daily.* Tomorrow, when she faced Reverend Mother, she'd need all the help she could get. It couldn't hurt to try to get a few angels on her side.

Sister Bernarda woke her a few minutes before the Matins bells. Sister Agatha felt every joint in her body creak and groan as she made her bed and quickly left her cell.

More awake than she'd dreamed she could be at that hour after her exertions of the night before, she hurried to prepare for what would undoubtedly be a very trying day.

As Sister Agatha stepped out of her room, Sister Eugenia appeared at the door, two pills in her hand and a small glass of milk in the other. She refused to budge until Sister Agatha had taken the medication. Then, wordlessly, she hurried back down the darkened hall toward the chapel.

After breakfast Sister Agatha went directly to Reverend Mothher's office. The prioress had a right to an explanation, but all things considered, Sister Agatha would rather have been stomped on by a herd of cattle than have to be the one to explain the events of last night.

Sister Agatha stopped outside Mother's office, took a deep breath, and knocked.

As expected, she found Mother waiting for her. Visions of a firing squad came to her mind, but she pushed them back quickly.

Without preamble, she recounted everything that had happened the night before. "Mother, you've entrusted me with this postulant, and I've taken that responsibility very seriously. What she did was misguided, but her intentions were good. I truly believe that Celia has the heart of a nun. She belongs with us. She'll have to pay a penalty for leaving, of course. Her postulancy will have to be extended now, but I think we should allow her to return to us."

Reverend Mother nodded. "I tend to agree, but before I say more I'd like to speak to her myself."

"Yes, Mother. Shall I send for her now?"

"Yes, but before you do, what are *your* plans for today? We still need answers, maybe even more than we did before. Will you be going to town?"

"Mother, I—" She stopped abruptly, uncertain of how much to say.

"Tell me what's on your mind, child," Reverend Mother said softly.

"I'm convinced that the answers I need now are here, Mother, not in town."

"Then you believe, as the sheriff does, that it's one of us? Whom do you suspect?" Reverend Mother asked.

She hesitated, but gathering her courage, answered. "Sister Mary Lazarus—though her motive still isn't clear to me," she said, and explained fully. "But, Mother, what I have is based on conjecture and hearsay—it's certainly not something I can share with the sheriff. I have no proof."

"All right. Follow your instincts, child. But be careful."

"Yes, Mother."

Sister Agatha went directly to the scriptorium and, as she walked inside, saw Frank was there already working at a carrel with Mary Lazarus. Sister Bernarda was watching them. She said nothing, but the look on her face worried Sister Agatha.

"I have bad news, Mother Mistress," Sister Mary Lazarus said, looking up and seeing her. "I started to use the computer with the library collection when I came in this morning, but it crashed again. I had most of my work on disks so I transferred it all to the other computer, the one that you've been using. But then it crashed too. I tried to reload your work into another computer, but it seems your backup disks are all corrupted and won't reload. All your work . . ." She couldn't bring herself to say more.

"The scanning work is lost?" Sister Agatha's heart dropped to her stomach.

"We won't know until I get this beast up and running again, but it may be," Frank said.

Weeks of hard work, gone, just like that. Sister Agatha bit back tears of frustration. "We can't afford to lose that work—or that computer. Do whatever you have to."

Sister Bernarda joined her. "I'd like a word with you, Your Charity."

As they stepped out into the hall leaving the door open so that their visitor would not be within the enclosure unsupervised, Sister Bernarda glanced back inside the room. Satisfied no one would hear them, she continued. "I have a very serious matter to discuss with you."

"What's happened?"

"We'd made a great deal of progress last night. This morning when Celia and I came in all the computers were working fine, and everything was in order. Then, when Sister Mary Lazarus joined us a few minutes later, first the computer she was working on crashed—that's almost normal around here—but we couldn't get it to boot up again. She wanted to call Frank immediately, but I held back. I wanted to take a look at it myself and see if maybe I could fix it. Then, in order not to lose more time, Sister Mary Lazarus tried to work on the one you've been using, but it crashed too."

"Are you saying that you think she found a way to make them crash on purpose? But why?"

"I think she wanted to see Frank, Sister. And when Frank came—which he did almost right away—he insisted on having her help him."

"Insisted?"

"Politely, but there it was. He said that he knew I was needed to supervise the postulant's work and that Mary Lazarus could give him a hand more easily than I could. That was true, of course, but so is the fact that he really wanted to work with her."

"Do you think they have feelings for each other?"

Sister Bernarda glanced at Pax, who had just come padding down the hall and, finding Sister Agatha, lay down by her feet. "I don't know. But there's something going on and, as I was watching them, a thought occurred to me. What if Sister Mary Lazarus has been meeting Frank after hours? We know she wanders about at night. Maybe she hasn't been sleepwalking every time. And if she's been leaving the door open when she wanders, almost anyone could have come into our monastery." Sister Bernarda took a deep breath. "But now that I've said it, I feel guilty about having such uncharitable thoughts."

"Leads are often nothing more than hunches played through. Don't feel guilty. Just remember that we're all fighting for the same thing—our monastery."

When they stepped back into the scriptorium, Sister Agatha sat down across from Frank and Mary Lazarus. She said nothing, she simply watched them. Under her gaze, Frank managed to get one computer going in record time. The second computer followed a short time later. To everyone's relief, no data had been lost.

"A memory problem," Frank said as she walked him outside. "Will you make your deadline, Sister?"

"I think so," she answered, "particularly since you were able to resuscitate the computers."

"That's good. I know you've all been working very hard and putting in all the time you can. Sister Mary Lazarus mentioned it to me."

"I'd like to talk to you about Sister Mary Lazarus. This is a very difficult time for her. She is about to make some very important decisions about her future." She paused then, meeting his gaze, and added, "Do you think she'll stay with us, Frank? I know you two were close once." Although she watched him carefully she couldn't see any reaction to her comment or her question. He hid his thoughts well.

"She's at a crossroads, as you say. But I think she'll stay. Don't you?"

He'd turned it right around on her. "I guess we'll all just have to wait and see."

After he'd left, Sister Agatha returned to the scriptorium. The phones wouldn't be manned this morning. Nor would the monastery door be opened. It wasn't a free day—one where no one worked— but Reverend Mother had given the externs and their team her blessing to work nonstop in the scriptorium. The money made on the quilt had gone to make the overdue loan payment for work done on the monastery and for a partial payment for work on the An- tichrysler, but the fees they'd collect for their scriptorium work were now needed to help them catch up on other bills.

Today they would stop to observe the liturgical hours but for nothing else. Such progress would come at a price to Sister Agatha's joints, but by the end of the day, there was no doubt in anyone's mind that, barring some fresh disaster, they'd make deadline on all scriptorium projects.

During recreation that evening, Sister Agatha found it hard to keep her eyes open. She was exhausted, but using the discipline she'd learned in more than a decade as a nun, she refused to give in to her weariness. One couldn't command one's own body by giving in to it. She sat on one of the benches outside and watched as Mary Lazarus went off on a walk by herself.

Sister Bernarda came up to join her. "I know you're tired. Feel free to close your eyes. I'll watch our novice for you."

"If I close my eyes, I won't wake up before morning," she an- swered with a weary smile. "But there's no need to keep really close tabs on Mary Lazarus anymore. If I know generally where she's gone,

I can still track her. I made a mark on her shoes," she said, and explained further.

"Then I'll talk to you so you can stay alert. There's something on my mind I need to discuss."

Sister Bernarda leaned down to stroke Pax's massive head. "Do you remember last April, when Reverend Mother assigned us all our spring work duties? Sister Mary Lazarus specifically asked that she be allowed to continue caring for the flower beds."

"Yes, I remember that well. It was a surprise to everyone after that terrible allergic reaction she'd had her first day in the gardens." She stood, realizing that she'd lost sight of Mary Lazarus, and began walking around casually with Sister Bernarda, hoping to spot her again.

"The thought that occurred to me was this—what if it wasn't an ordinary allergic reaction at all? What if she'd been handling monkshood? The toxicity of the plant itself might have caused the symptoms we saw."

"You think she planted the monkshood?"

"Not necessarily. She might have simply found it accidentally, and only decided to take advantage of its properties later."

Sister Agatha considered that possibility for several moments. "Celia pointed out some time ago that the monkshood on the alb was most likely intended to affect me, not Father Anselm. I just can't see Sister Mary Lazarus wanting to harm me for any reason, can you?"

"Did she ever get particularly angry with you about something, or resent a task you'd asked her to do?"

Sister Agatha considered it carefully. "Not that I remember. Novice Mistresses can seem exacting, I know, but I really haven't been hard on either of them."

They continued walking and searching for the novice while trying to appear uninterested in everything but their own conversation. "There she is," Sister Bernarda said at last, "on the far side of Sister Clothilde's vegetable garden, near the wall."

"What on earth is she doing back there? I better go have a look around there later. For right now, let's head back. She's turning this way, and I don't want her to know she's being observed."

As Sister Bernarda fell into step again beside Sister Agatha, her silence spoke of her concerns more effectively than words could have. "What do we do next?" she asked at last. "How can I help?"

"Once recreation is over, take Celia and Mary Lazarus with you to Compline. I'll stay out here for a bit longer and make use of the daylight that's left."

"To do what?"

"I want to check out the route Mary Lazarus walks during recreation. After last night's rain, the ground should be soft enough to show the marks on the soles of her shoes."

A half hour later, the bells rang for Compline. Sister Agatha saw Sister Bernarda signal for the novice and postulant to follow her as the nuns headed to chapel.

As arranged, Sister Agatha lagged behind. Then, while the nuns' voices rose from choir, she made her way around the building to the spot by the wall where they'd seen Mary Lazarus. She searched the ground carefully, but there was no evidence of monkshood, not even any upturned earth that might have indicated someone had uprooted some plants recently.

Frustration and disappointment washed over her. She'd been so sure. . . .

Unwilling to give up, she followed the novice's tracks on the soft, sandy earth. At one point, from what she could see, the novice had gone around the building and in through the kitchen doors.

Tracking her on brick floors was impossible, so Sister looked around the kitchen, hoping to figure out what had brought Mary Lazarus back here.

Mary Lazarus had always seemed to head for the kitchen whenever she'd had her sleepwalking episodes—with the exception of the other night when Sister Agatha had seen her outside. Maybe she'd done that simply to mislead them—especially if her sleepwalking had been a ruse all along.

Lord, open my eyes. She wandered around the kitchen slowly searching for a clue. Then she saw it. There were several tiny clumps of wet sand on Sister Clothilde's otherwise spotless floor, inches from the basement door.

21

A S SISTER AGATHA STARTED TO GO DOWN THE STEPS, PAX
appeared at the door. Without waiting for an invitation, he
went down ahead of her into the darkness.

The descent consisted of only seven steps, but there was no
railing to hold on to and the light was at the bottom of the steps.
The basement of the old farmhouse had been built as a larder mostly,
to store canned and dried food. It had a hard dirt floor, which was
somewhat uneven.

When she reached the basement, she switched on the lightbulb
that hung from a cord in the middle of the room.

The basement was stark, mostly stuccoed in the gray scratch
coat, with one brick supporting wall. It had a dungeonlike feel that
made her think of the catacombs used during the early days of Chris-
tianity. She hated coming down here, and most of the other nuns
did as well. Sister Clothilde had categorically refused to store food
down here. Janitorial supplies were the only things kept in the basement, except during winter when some of the garden tools were
brought down as well.

As she looked at the ground, Sister Agatha clearly saw Mary
Lazarus's tracks imprinted on the dusty earth floor, mingled with a
surprising number of other tracks. The marked heel tracks stopped

before a solid-looking eight-foot-wide brick wall that served as a support for the building above.

Sister Agatha looked up at the wall, perplexed. Why was Mary Lazarus coming down here to stare at the wall? Had she fashioned her own penance?

Stymied, she went across the small room and sat down on the last step, Pax beside her. For several minutes she stared at an indeterminate spot on the wall, lost in thought. Celia wasn't the only one who realized that when something didn't make sense, you needed to change your perspective.

She thought about everything she'd learned, arranging and rearranging the bits of information as one would the pieces of a puzzle. There was no monastery duty that could have brought Mary Lazarus down here. That left personal reasons. But the only personal interest Mary Lazarus had these days, apparently, was Frank Walters.

Pax stood, shook himself, then walked over and sniffed the corner where the brick wall met the concrete pillar of the monastery's foundation. Picturing old movies and television shows about haunted houses, Sister tried pushing several bricks to see if they would move. Maybe the old farmhouse had been built with a secret passageway of sorts. She tried every section of the wall, especially those areas with bricks that seemed to have less mortar between their joints, but the wall seemed solid.

At long last, Sister Agatha made her way back up the stairs. This was getting her nowhere. She'd try a new tack. Even if Mary Lazarus had either found or planted monkshood, to be guilty of the crime that had been committed, she would have had to make a concentration of the herb. For that, she would have needed some of the supplies in the infirmary.

From what she'd learned, monkshood had to be dissolved and concentrated, but it couldn't be heated. Mary Lazarus would have had to soak the herb in water or some form of alcohol, leaving the bottle open so that the liquid would evaporate a bit, then repeat the process until she'd amassed the toxic preparation that had been used on the alb.

During the Great Silence, the house stood quiet. Only the incessant hum of the night insects marred the stillness. Trying to be as quiet as her surroundings, Sister Agatha slipped into the infirmary and checked the supplies in the inventory book. Everything had to be carefully accounted for, and any discrepancies, however small, had to be noted.

Sister Eugenia's record keeping was flawless as Sister Agatha had expected, and everything the infirmary had on hand was listed, down to each and every aspirin. The less perishable supplies were listed as well, and one small medicine bottle with a dropper lid had turned up missing in early June. Sister Eugenia had left a note to herself in the margin to continue to look for it, but from what Sister Agatha could see, the bottle had never been found.

Placing the book back on the desk, she looked around, noting the careful way everything from pills to Band-Aids had been stored inside the dispensary. She knew without being told that the missing bottle had driven Sister crazy. She'd have to talk to Sister Eugenia about it tomorrow.

After Lauds the following morning, as everyone went to the refectory, Sister Agatha managed to catch up to Sister Eugenia.

"Do you need some of your pills, Your Charity?" Sister Eugenia asked quickly as Sister Agatha joined her.

"No. My joints seem to be doing much better. Maybe it's because I've had something else on my mind." She smiled. "No room for pain, you see."

Sister Eugenia smiled. "It works like that sometimes."

"Sister Eugenia, I'm sure you're aware that Reverend Mother has asked me to look into Father Anselm's tragic death."

She nodded. "All the sisters are praying for you. I know Celia has a perpetual novena going on your behalf, as do Sister Ignatius and myself."

"I appreciate that, but I need something more material from you now."

"Name it, Sister Agatha."

"I'd like you to tell me about the dispensary. I specifically need to know about anything that's turned up missing lately—even if only temporarily." She already knew about the dropper, of course, but she needed to find out if there had been any other items.

"Sister, you know how careful I am with everything that's in my charge. An infirmarian must be precise, and willing to serve the monastery as she would Our Lord Himself. But several weeks ago, during an inventory, I realized that one amber glass dropper bottle was missing. I looked everywhere for it. I even asked each of the nuns who had been assigned to help me in the infirmary if they'd had occasion to use it, and broken or lost it. Sometimes they'll take something and forget to tell me in perfect innocence. But, in this case, the bottle never turned up. I'm still searching for it."

"Are you able to pinpoint exactly when it disappeared?"

"No, that would be almost impossible, because I didn't use it to dispense medication. If I had, I would have noted it. It could have disappeared anytime between my regular monthly inventories."

"Should you find it suddenly, please don't touch it. Just let me know."

"All right," she said. "Do you think the monkshood used to kill Father was stored in that bottle?"

"I don't know for certain, but there's a good chance that it was."

When Sister Eugenia bowed her head to utter a prayer, Sister Agatha joined her.

After Divine Office, Sister Agatha took the novice and postulant aside. "For the next few days, you will work exclusively in the scriptorium. That will be your second highest priority." She knew she didn't have to explain what their first priority was. That part came as naturally as breathing to a nun.

"Mother Mistress, if you don't mind my saying so, the real problem is that you and Sister Bernarda are the only ones who work on the manuscripts that need to be scanned into the computer. That's the most important job on the schedule now, and it's way behind. If only you would let me help with that, I know we could catch up. I don't need as much sleep as some of the others, so I could come in at night. If you'd give me the combination to the safe, I'd be happy to work while others are resting or asleep."

Sister Agatha stared at Sister Mary Lazarus, a new realization dawning. She'd been searching for a motive all this time, and maybe she'd finally found it. The manuscripts in the safe were extremely valuable and some collectors, she was sure, would gladly look the other way about how they were acquired in exchange for the thrill of possessing them. Mary Lazarus might have hoped that with her out of commission from contact with the monkshood, she'd be given access to them.

"That's a generous offer. I'll consult with Sister Bernarda and let you know."

"Mother Mistress, Sister Mary Lazarus is right," Celia added. "If both of us were to able to start work on those manuscripts when you were out, or when Sister Bernarda had portress duty, we could get that job done on deadline without any problem. And there's no reason you can't trust us to lock up afterwards."

"I don't understand why those manuscripts are kept locked up anyway. It's not like we work in a public place," Sister Mary Lazarus said. "The scriptorium is within the enclosure."

"Our insurance carrier requires that all the books and documents we work on be kept in a fireproof safe," Sister Agatha answered.

"Oh—in case of fire?" Sister Mary Lazarus nodded slowly. "I guess that makes sense." She paused, then added, "But Mother Mistress, consider our offer of help. There's no reason why we shouldn't pitch in. Celia and I *are* part of this monastery."

"I'll speak to Sister Bernarda and Reverend Mother, then let you know. In the meanwhile, it's time for you to get to work."

After her two charges left for the scriptorium, Sister Agatha went to the parlor and called Lenora Martinez, the school secretary at St. Charles Academy. By the time she hung up ten minutes later, many of her suspicions concerning Frank Walters and Sister Mary Lazarus had been confirmed. Her spirit was heavy now. The truth was revealing a story not of greed but of hopes lost and desperate acts. Evil was easy to condemn—human frailty was not.

Maybe if she worked quickly and God was with her, she could get evidence that Tom would accept and that would put him on the right path.

Somehow, she'd have to prove that Mary Lazarus hadn't been sleepwalking—that she'd been meeting with Frank somewhere inside the monastery. Though the kids she'd had searching for monkshood had found the plant growing in several places throughout the community, she was certain it had been grown either on monastery grounds or very close by. Maybe Frank had provided it and Mary Lazarus had stolen the missing bottle to make the extract. The way things were shaping up, for the intruder theory to have any validity she'd have to demonstrate that the intruder had inside help.

All along, she and Tom had considered this as a strictly inside *or* outside perpetrator, but now it seemed likely it was both. What she still needed to do was find out how it had been done, and locate the source of the monkshood Tom had been told to find.

Sister Agatha stared at the rosary attached to her belt. Prayers crowded her mind, and she reached out in desperation to the One who was always with her and she knew she could count on. A moment later she was suffused with the knowledge that the Lord was not only in her heart but also in her head.

Slowly an idea came to her. What she needed to do was talk to one of the seniors who had lived in the area all his or her life—someone whose roots and heart had always been here in Bernalillo. Someone who knew all the secrets that got forgotten over the years, including the gossip and history about places like the monastery.

Then Sister Agatha remembered elderly Elena Serna. At one time, the woman had lived north of the river not too far from the farmhouse that became the monastery. Churches in town had labeled her a witch, and she'd endured persecution for many years. Though those days were over it was no secret that Elena particularly hated Catholics. But Sister Agatha knew she had no other choice now. Her best chance lay in getting Elena to talk to her.

22

SISTER AGATHA DROVE ACROSS THE RAILROAD TRACKS TO the eastern outskirts of town, farther from the river and close to the interstate. The roads were almost exclusively dirt tracks out here, and the gravel from the nearby mountains was much coarser, making travel bumpy except when the road was crossed by a sandy wash.

She went around a bend, having run out of street signs long ago, and just as she was about to conclude that she was hopelessly lost, a low adobe house appeared before her in a gravel-filled flat spot beside a small spring. Several goats inside a split-log pen fifty feet from the house browsed on small tufts of grass.

"You leave her livestock alone, Pax," Sister Agatha said sternly, catching him eyeing the creatures as she parked. A curtain moved in the house, indicating that the distinctive sound of the motorcycle had drawn the occupant's attention.

Pax whined, obviously in the mood for a goat chase.

"You heard me, boy. This is important. I want you on your best behavior."

He sighed loudly as if he'd understood.

A few moments later she stepped up to the front door with Pax on a leash and knocked. The doorbell was just that, a bell, but there was no cord or clapper, and the slightest tap would have probably sent the precariously mounted device plummeting to the earth. Looking down, she saw the clapper and remnant of string on the ground below the bell.

An elderly lady in a shawl opened the door a few inches, looked at her and the dog, then spoke. "Go away."

"Please. I just need to talk to you for a few minutes. You've lived in this area a long time, and I'm hoping you can tell me something about the history of the house that is now our monastery," she said, sticking her foot in the door. "I'm Sister Agatha, from Our Lady of Hope. I grew up in Bernalillo, and my name was Mary Naughton then."

The woman looked at Pax, then turned back to her. "Don't remember you. And the dog? What's his purpose? You're not blind."

"No, I'm not. Pax is my companion and guardian when I'm away from home," she answered.

They stood face-to-face for a moment, and Sister Agatha forced herself to remain smiling, despite the woman's suspicious scrutiny. Then finally, Elena Serna moved aside. "Come in, but if I hear one word out of your mouth that sounds like you want to sprinkle me with holy water or convert me, that'll be the end of our talk."

"Fair enough."

Elena gestured for Sister Agatha to sit on the couch.

Sister Agatha made herself comfortable on the old sofa then looked around casually. There were candles everywhere and cryptic symbols drawn on the concrete floor. They made her uneasy.

"You're free to leave if my decorative touches disturb you," Elena said, noticing her anxiety.

Sister Agatha took a deep breath. "Just because you and I have different beliefs doesn't mean we can't get along with each other. Neither of us has anything to prove to anyone. We both know who we are."

"Many of *your* faith are capable of unspeakable acts of violence against those who don't share your beliefs."

"The sisters in our monastery follow a rule of charity and love. Violence and hatred have no place in our lives. Pax and I are no threat to you. I think you know that, or you wouldn't have invited us in."

Pax came over to the old woman and placed his head on her lap. The elderly woman looked surprised but not fearful, and reached out to stroke him gently, her hand steady and sure.

Looking up, Elena met Sister Agatha's gaze with a direct one of her own. "Why, exactly, did you come here? What is it that you need from me?"

"I know that you've lived in this town practically all of your life. What can you tell me about the farmhouse that is now our monastery and its former tenants?"

"I think I know why you're asking me that question. I've heard about the trouble you all had." She pointed to a stack of recent newspapers beside a well-used woodstove, then took a deep breath. "That farmhouse has seen more than its share of trouble. I always thought it was an odd place for nuns to establish a monastery."

"Why do you say that?" Sister Agatha asked, leaning forward.

Elena offered Sister a cookie from a platter on the table before her, gave one to Pax, and took one for herself. The cookies were freshly baked and tasted of rich peanut butter. "The original owner of the place was Francisco Vargas. He built the farmhouse before I came to Bernalillo. Don Francisco apparently had a good head for business and was well respected. But his son, Daniel, who was ten years my senior, was completely the opposite of his father. A few years after Don Francisco died, during World War One, Daniel managed to bankrupt both his father's fine farm and his Mexican import business. Daniel, who'd never been poor in his life, found himself penniless.

"Then Prohibition started. Daniel, who was in desperate straits, became a moonshiner. Every cop around these parts knew him and what he was doing, but no one could ever catch him at it. The police would raid the farmhouse on a regular basis, but they'd always come out empty-handed. I know this and remember it well because, at the time, my husband, Carlos, worked for Daniel. We lived right on the farm—in an adobe building on the north side."

From the description, she realized it was what they now called

St. Francis' Pantry. "But that's barely more than a room—a narrow one at that."

"Oh, it seemed a grand honeymoon cottage for Carlos and me at the time. It had everything we needed, and the adobe kept us cool in the summer and warm in the winter, with some help from the little potbelly stove we had."

"Did your husband help with Daniel's moonshining business?"

"Yes, he did. I never approved, but I knew that poor people had to survive either by their wits, if they had any, or by the sweat of their brow. At that time, with the influence of the drought, even growing a few vegetables in the garden was a tricky proposition. Many went hungry in the valley, but the people who worked for Daniel were always able to put food on the table for their families."

"How did Daniel get away with it if he was being raided often? Did he pay off the cops?"

"I'm sure there was some of that, but the truth is that while Daniel might not have inherited his father's business sense, he was as crafty as a fox. He had a secret passageway built inside the property. Only a handful of specially selected men who'd worked on it knew its location. Those men comprised Daniel's inner circle and were mostly people who were in the country illegally or had family in that situation, so they had as much to fear from the police as Daniel did. But even with that precaution, Daniel always kept a close eye on everyone who worked for him. If he suspected someone was becoming a risk, they were dealt with—violently and mercilessly. If a man threatened to talk, he'd show up dead with his tongue cut out as a warning to others not to wag theirs. But, as ruthless as Daniel was to his enemies, he could also be a strong, dependable friend. Many of his people would have been willing to die for him."

"I know the monastery well. It's our home. But I don't know of any secret rooms."

"Not rooms—just a passageway. And, for all I know, it was sealed off permanently a long time ago. After Prohibition was repealed, Daniel, who'd made his fortune by then, moved away to Denver and built a mansion there, I'm told. The property here passed from owner to owner after that, but no one ever stayed long. Then,

World War Two came, the house needed repairs, and the land itself was more of a detriment than an asset with no farm hands available to work it. For a few years it stood empty and all but abandoned. Then a man who'd made a lot of money making airplanes during the war retired and moved out here with his family so they'd have a place for the kids to run and ride horses. They fixed up the place, and were happy there for many years. But then the husband died, and the woman moved back East to live near her grandchildren. It was empty for another few years, then the nuns were given the property."

"Where is the passageway? Can you give me any idea?"

Elena Serna shook her head. "I don't know. You have to understand that things were different for women back then. The men didn't confide in us—they protected us. Well, at least that was the excuse they used for keeping us in the dark about nearly everything," she added with a wry smile.

"Thank you for taking time to talk to me. Next time Sister Clothilde bakes cookies, I'll save some for you and bring them over."

"I'd like that. I've heard about her cookies—Cloister Clusters they're calling them now in the newspaper." Elena smiled as she walked with Sister Agatha to the door. "You'll be welcome if you return, and the dog, too."

Due to her age, a visit would be considered a sign of charity and brotherly love. "I think you can count on it."

After saying good-bye to Elena, Sister Agatha and Pax drove back to the monastery. All the way there Agatha investigated every corner and path inside her home in her mind. She knew the monastery like the back of her hand. And maybe that was the problem. Once things became familiar, it was easy to overlook details.

As she neared the monastery's gates, she came up with a new strategy, and pulled over. Maybe she'd have better luck finding this secret passage from the outside, a place less familiar to her.

She glanced around. They'd already searched close to the wall and found nothing, so perhaps the entrance—or exit, depending on how one looked at it—was farther away. She drove back down the road another fifty feet, then pulled over and parked. An old road, long deserted, ran parallel to the river just to the west. Overgrown with plants common to the flood plain, the ground there was largely sand beneath a thin layer of sediment, and probably not a good place to begin a tunnel. Farther to the north, she could see a dilapidated farmhouse and the outline of an old field, now overgrown with brush and small trees.

Chances were that the field had been under cultivation fifty years ago. The soil in this area was a mixture of fine sediment and clay, and now hard packed. "Come on, Pax. Let's take a look around."

Ahead, giant tumbleweeds mingled with sagebrush the size of sheep. She pulled her skirt up as the prickly bushes tugged on the serge fabric of her habit.

Hearing something scamper into the brush, Pax shot ahead. In a flash, he disappeared into a thicket. Sister Agatha looked around, trying to spot him, but she couldn't see him anywhere, despite his light color. "Pax, come!"

She waited for a moment, but the dog didn't return. Muttering under her breath, she went to find him. It was her fault for letting him run off the leash. It was too much to expect that he wouldn't find an occasional jackrabbit irresistible.

"Pax!"

She forced her way through the clusters of sage and tumbleweeds, but the dog still failed to appear. As she stopped to catch her breath, she looked up and saw an electrical transformer ahead, the same one that was visible from the monastery gate. The small electricity-boosting station had a tall wire fence around it, and big electrical lines extending from the top to overhead power lines, almost like those in the Frankenstein pictures she'd seen as a kid. She looked at the well-protected utility, lost in thought.

That fenced-in area would have been the perfect place to grow something you didn't want others to see or examine. People tended to avoid going anyplace that was filled with cables that carried high-voltage charges and had warning signs posted all around.

She went toward the fence, deciding to check it out. If the fence was secure, she'd turn back and go find the dog, but if not, she wanted to take a look around.

When she got really close to the twenty-by-twenty-foot fenced enclosure, she saw no obvious signs that anyone had trespassed. Weeds nearly as tall as she was grew around the fence, and it was difficult to see beyond them. She walked completely around the enclosure, checking the fence carefully. Then, on the side opposite the narrow padlocked gate, she saw a section of fencing that had been cut loose from its post, then reattached with what looked like several pieces of aluminum wire twisted loosely in place. It wasn't obvious until you looked very closely, but she could see that slipping under that portion of the fence by untwisting a few of the wires wouldn't have been difficult.

She removed the lowest three wires, pulled part of the fencing back, and ducked inside the small enclosure. Then, from out of no-where, Pax crashed through the brush and appeared right behind her, on the other side of the fence.

"Pax, you moron! You startled me."

The dog slipped under the new gap in the fence and went up to the large green transformer, which was humming at a low pitch, but was probably carrying enough current to electrocute them both easily.

"Stay back, Pax."

He lowered his head, sniffing the ground, and started pawing the dirt at a spot where water erosion had dug a narrow ditch about eight inches deep and a foot wide.

The weeds were nearly as thick in the small enclosure as they were outside the fence, so she pushed her way past them slowly. But she still didn't see anything unusual. When she turned around to look for Pax, she realized that he was still pawing at the spot that had intrigued him before.

"Pax, come here."

The dog kept digging, and sniffing the ground.

"All right, you prairie dog. That's enough."

As she went to grasp him by the collar, something shiny on the ground caught her eye. "What have you uncovered?"

In the wall of the tiny ditch that meandered through the area, probably leading to the river, she saw the sun glinting on an amber bottle that had been buried, then exposed by the last rainfall. There was still a bit of pale liquid inside it.

She went to reach for it, but then stopped. The last thing she wanted to do was tamper with evidence. The bottle would have to be left in place for the sheriff to recover. She started to back away when she heard the roll of thunder. Looking up, she saw the skies were thick with clouds. If it rained, it was possible the bottle would get washed away and never be found again. It was already exposed, and it wouldn't take much water in the ditch to dislodge it from the soil.

Sister Agatha felt a few drops of rain on her face. Then a slight breeze began, evidence of the storm approaching.

"Okay—decision made. I'll take it with us." To protect any fingerprints that may have been on it, she picked up the bottle at the bottom using the small handkerchief she carried and put the container in her pocket. Then she found two sticks and stuck them in the ground so they formed an X marking the spot.

Making a split-second decision, she decided to search the immediate area before leaving. Mixed in with a generous crop of weeds, she found several monkshood plants that had been pulled up, their roots harvested.

"Let's go, Pax. It's time we paid Sheriff Green a visit."

By the time she reached the motorcycle, she realized that the rain had eased, and the momentary breeze had already diminished. She glanced around. Above her was the haze of virga, rain that was evaporating in the warm air without ever reaching the ground.

"Let's hope the weather will hold a little longer so Tom can process this scene properly. But if it doesn't, he'll at least have the bottle, and whatever evidence can be gotten from it, in police custody."

As the monastery's bells chimed in the distance, calling the nuns for None, the canonical hour that commemorated the ninth hour when Christ died, Sister Agatha said a brief prayer—for herself, for Father Anselm, and for the monastery.

23

SISTER SAT ACROSS FROM SHERIFF GREEN AS SHE TOLD HIM everything. Fortunately, their luck had held and the rain had been marginal. A team was searching the site as they spoke, but the sheriff had sent them in a borrowed utility vehicle, and they had been ordered to keep a low profile to avoid attracting any attention from the monastery. The bottle she'd brought in had now been tagged and labeled and it was on its way to the state crime lab.

"We'll process the dropper bottle for prints and have what's left of the liquid analyzed," he said.

"I really don't think we should wait for the results. I'm sure that Frank Walters and Mary Lazarus are behind what's happened, and I don't think they're going to stick around forever."

"If Mary Lazarus wants to leave the monastery, why doesn't she just go?" Tom asked, trying to understand everything she'd told him.

"Look at it from her perspective. She's devoted several years of her life to the monastery, and now she has realized it's just not for her. She may feel her years with us should be worth something, and that we owe her. She's essentially penniless now. But, most important of all, I believe she really loves Frank. He's desperately in need of money and I think the temptation the manuscripts posed became too much for her to resist. Women have done worse things than steal in the name of love, and remember, they never intended to kill anyone."

"So you think Frank and Mary Lazarus formed an alliance in order to steal the manuscripts?"

"Yes, I do. It's the only thing that makes sense. What else does our monastery have that's worth so much money? I realize I have little proof, but the bottle we found may change that. The case against Mary Lazarus and Frank is already far stronger than any case you had against Celia, and you were ready to arrest her. What I need now is for you to help me protect the monastery and make sure neither she nor Frank do any more damage. I have a plan that might work, but let me go talk to Reverend Mother first before I share it with you. I have to run it past her because this directly involves the monastery." She stood to leave, reaching into her pocket for the keys to the Harley.

"Okay, though I won't commit myself until I hear your plan in detail. But before you go, there's something I need to tell you— something you have a right to know." He paused, avoiding her gaze and looking decidedly uncomfortable. "You had someone shove a note in your pocket during the Fourth of July fair, didn't you?"

"Yes, but how did you know that?" she asked surprised.

"It was Gloria," he said, exhaling softly.

"Your wife? But why?"

He took a deep breath. "She was also the person who followed you in the sedan. I put a stop to that as soon as I found out, but I learned about the note yesterday during our session with a marriage counselor. I thought I'd better let you know and assure you that she won't be bothering you again. She's really sorry about all that, and so am I."

She shook her head. "I don't get it."

Tom met her gaze. "To her, you've always been a threat. She's very possessive of me, and when she found out that we were working together, she couldn't handle it." He paused for several moments. "Gloria is a good woman, but she's never quite realized that I love her. We have some issues of trust to work out and my job doesn't help. I'm away at all hours of the day and night. But we're working things out. What we have is real, you know? I would never leave her."

"I'm very glad to hear that. You have a family to protect, Tom. I'll ask the sisters to pray for you and Gloria, and I'll start a novena for both of you myself."

"Does that mean you'll forgive me and her for what's happened? I know I should have told you . . ."

"Don't give it another thought. The matter is forgiven and behind all of us now."

"Thanks," he answered. Before he could say anything else, one of the deputies called him from inside the building. "I better go."

Moments later, she and Pax were under way. As they left the station behind them, Sister Agatha thought about what Tom had said about his life—and his love for his family. She felt the same way about the sisters and their monastery. Both of them had been led down the right path. Each of them were where they belonged.

She headed home, feeling at peace with herself and God.

Forty minutes later, she sat in Reverend Mother's office. The abbess looked tired and somber.

"Is there any chance you're wrong about Sister Mary Lazarus?"

"A chance, yes, but not a big one, Mother. For the first time, the pieces all fit together."

The abbess considered the matter for several minutes before looking up again. "We'll go with your plan, then. This has to be settled once and for all."

Bowing her head, Sister Agatha hurried out of Mother's office and down the hall. She had to make a call to an old friend now, but it was imperative that no one overhear her.

As she passed the scriptorium, she saw Mary Lazarus scanning one of the valuable manuscripts using the thin white gloves that would protect the original. Sister Gertrude was right beside her as she worked.

She smiled, thinking that Mary Lazarus had finally gotten what she'd wanted, only not quite in the way she'd wanted it.

When she entered the parlor a moment later, Sister Bernarda looked up at her hopefully. "Can you take over for me, Sister Agatha? I've left Sister Gertrude in charge of the scriptorium, but I've been wanting to go and check on things there."

"Go, Your Charity. I'll handle things here." As a matter of fact, that was just what she'd been hoping for, privacy to make a phone call.

Once she was alone, Sister Agatha picked up the phone and dialed an old friend, the librarian at the university library's special collections room. It was time to set her plan in motion. The scriptorium had done work for her on several occasions, and over the years, Louise Knight and she had become friends.

Shortly after Vespers, Sister Agatha met with Sister Bernarda and filled her in on the details of her emerging plan.

"Are you sure about this?"

"It's the only way," Sister Agatha answered.

"All right then. Collation is taken in silence except for the readings, but we'll have plenty of time to publicize the manuscript's arrival after that during recreation."

"Reverend Mother will help, too. I believe she plans to make an announcement after dinner."

"Are you sure you're up to the rest?"

She nodded. "The critical part of this plan is going to take Oscar-winning acting skills. I hope I can pull it off. The part that I really hate is that I know I'll be worrying some of the older nuns. I wish there was some way for me to avoid that."

"Could they be told ahead of time?"

She shook her head. "It's possible their reactions might not be credible then," she said sadly, "and we can't take a chance Mary Lazarus will catch on."

"Then let's get on with it. I want the monastery back the way it was before all this happened. I miss the peace, you know?"

"I sure do," Sister Agatha nodded.

They walked in silence to the refectory and ate as the reader read a selection from Thomas Merton, and then the martyrology.

As the meal came to an end, Reverend Mother made the announcement that their monastery had been entrusted with the original *Ben Hur* manuscript, written by Lew Wallace in 1880 while he was governor of New Mexico. Work scanning it into digital format would begin the following morning and continue nonstop until the entire manuscript was scanned. The work would have to be done in one day, but would bring in a handsome fee from the state library.

Sister Bernarda elaborated, explaining that their monastery had been selected from among several private companies who'd competed for the honor of working on that manuscript. Our Lady of Hope's reputation for accuracy and careful handling of fragile documents had won them the job.

As they went to recreation, Sister Agatha kept close tabs on Mary Lazarus. She had no doubt that the news had gotten her attention. What they'd seemingly presented her with was a once-in-a-lifetime opportunity.

Seeing a car drive up, Sister Agatha went out to open the monastery gate and greet Louise Knight. Aware that the other nuns were watching her, she made a big deal out of receiving the manuscript and then hurried with Louise into the parlor.

"I really appreciate this, Louise," Sister Agatha said.

"No problem, but I want to hear the whole story as soon as you can talk."

"You've got it."

After seeing Louise out, and locking the gate behind her, Sister Agatha locked up the parlor. She then walked outside and met Sister Bernarda, Mary Lazarus, and Celia. "I hate to take you all away from recreation, but I need your help. For the work on the manuscript to be finished on time, we'll all have to take turns working on it in shifts."

She led them to the scriptorium, then set the manuscript down so they could all see it. "It's fragile—not to mention one of a kind."

According to plan, Sister Agatha picked it up again and carried it to her carrel. "I'll set up the computer and get things started. Mary

Lazarus, your shift will begin after Compline and end at midnight. Celia, you'll follow for four hours, then Sister Bernarda will take over for you. I'll take the shift after that. We'll rotate often so we can stay alert and get it done. Of course if either of you have any problems, come get Sister Bernarda or me immediately. Are we all agreed?"

Before they could answer, Sister Agatha sat down heavily and took several deep breaths.

"Are you all right?" Sister Bernarda asked, playing along.

"Yes . . . No, not really. My chest feels tight—" She doubled up, feigning a heart attack. Having seen two elderly nuns who'd died of heart failure, she was pretty confident she'd faked the symptoms well.

Reverend Mother came in then, having heard the commotion. She immediately began helping Sister Bernarda.

"We have to take her to the infirmary," she said quickly.

Sister Bernarda glanced at Sister Mary Lazarus and Celia. "Put the manuscript into the safe and then lock it," she ordered.

As they made their way down the hall, Sister Agatha caught a glimpse of Sister Gertrude's face and saw her mouthing Hail Mary's through trembling lips.

"Sister, don't worry," Sister Agatha said, unable to stand the look on her face. "It's just the new medication I'm taking. I think I took the wrong dose. I'll be fine. My heart is beating overtime, but it's strong." At least that latter part was true.

Once in the infirmary, Sister Eugenia was waiting. She'd made a bed ready, and now took over for the others. Sister Bernarda quickly ushered Sister Gertrude back out, reassuring her all the way and then closed the door behind them.

"You've been told what's going on, I hope, Sister Eugenia?" Sister Agatha whispered.

She nodded. "But I must say you were so convincing I was worried you were really ill."

Reverend Mother looked toward the door then back at Sister Agatha. "And now we wait?"

Sister Agatha nodded, then looked at Sister Eugenia. "It's very important that the nuns believe I'm here, so the door will have to remain closed and no one must be allowed to come in—unless of course there's an emergency."

"I'll handle it, rest assured, Your Charity."

As the bells for Compline rang, the nuns left to join the others in the chapel. Sister Eugenia had agreed to recite the Divine Office from her post in the infirmary, to make sure everything went according to plan.

After the nuns were inside the chapel and their chant filled the corridors, Sister Agatha slipped out of the infirmary and hurried to the scriptorium. Once there, she took a position between Sister Bernarda's carrel and the large armoire where they kept all the scriptorium supplies, such as paper, toner, and storage media. As soon as the lights were turned off, only moonlight filtering through the windows illuminated the room. The black serge habit was an enormous advantage, helping her blend with the darkness.

After Compline ended, Sister Bernarda returned with Mary Lazarus, took the manuscript out of the safe, then with a nod left Mary Lazarus alone to work.

Then, to Sister Agatha's surprise, Pax came into the scriptorium, looking for her. For some reason, she'd forgotten to factor him into her plan! She froze in place, hoping he'd simply go to her cell and wait. He sometimes did that when he couldn't find her at night. But in a heartbeat Sister Bernarda appeared and, grabbing him by the collar, led him away.

Mary Lazarus waited at her carrel until the nuns had retreated down the hall to their cells. Then, silently, she hurried down the hall.

Sister Agatha moved quickly to the door and saw Mary Lazarus going into the parlor. Moving forward quietly, she heard the novice making a call.

Sister Agatha didn't wait. She'd heard Mary Lazarus mention Frank's name and that was enough. She now knew that Mary Lazarus had taken the bait. Hurrying, she went back to her hiding place.

Moments later, Mary Lazarus came in, picked up the bound manuscript, and walked out of the scriptorium.

Sister Agatha followed her as she made her way to the kitchen. The problem with the Great Silence was that there was no other noise to mask the sounds of her own movements. She held on tightly to her rosary so the beads wouldn't click as she walked, and gave thanks that she didn't have to follow closely, knowing already where the thief was headed.

Sister Mary Lazarus suddenly stopped by the basement door and turned her head, looking behind her, waiting and listening. Sister Agatha ducked back into the shadows and stayed impossibly still, holding her breath until she heard the novice open the squeaky door and go downstairs.

As soon as the novice disappeared from her view, Sister Agatha hurried forward. Then, making sure not to touch the already open door and risk another squeak, she slipped in. She felt her way step by step down the stairs, using the dim moonlight washing through the kitchen windows above her to light her way.

As she reached the bottom, she ducked back behind a support beam and watched Mary Lazarus switch on a small flashlight she'd taken from the shelf. Holding the manuscript and flashlight under one arm, she pressed two bricks in the wall at the same time. With a soft swooshing sound, the wall swung out a few inches.

Sister Agatha could see only darkness beyond the opening, but the subtle breeze that came through and filled the basement attested to the presence of a passageway.

Sister Mary Lazarus stepped into the opening and disappeared from view. A moment later, the wall closed behind her.

24

B Y THE TIME SISTER AGATHA REACHED THE WALL, THE OPEN-
ing had completely vanished.

Sister Agatha reached into her pocket for the small flashlight she'd brought along, then touched the same bricks she'd seen
Mary Lazarus press. As soon as she did, a portion of the brick wall
opened. Quickly, she switched off her own flashlight, and stepped
through the opening.

Inside, Sister Agatha realized she was standing in a six-foot-high
tunnel carved from the earth and shored up by railroad ties. She
hugged the wall, taking one sideways step at a time and trying to be
as silent as death itself. For a moment all she saw was Mary Lazarus
standing twenty feet inside the tunnel with her flashlight, then she
heard the sound of heavy footsteps.

"It's about time, Frank," Mary Lazarus said, as the tall businessman appeared in the beam of her flashlight from farther down the
tunnel. If Frank had a flashlight, it wasn't on.

Mary Lazarus joined up with Frank, who was forced to walk with
his head ducked slightly, and handed him the thick *Ben Hur* manuscript. "Here. This is my ticket out. Now let's go. I hope I never
see this place again."

"That's one thing you can count on." Sheriff Green's voice

boomed out, as a bright light appeared from behind Frank, illuminating him and Mary Lazarus.

Frank reacted instantly. Swinging Mary Lazarus around to face Tom and using her as a shield, he pulled out a small pistol.

"Drop your gun, Sheriff, or I'll shoot her. I swear."

"Don't get excited, Frank. If I drop my weapon, it could go off accidentally and injure someone. I'm going to place it back in the holster," he said.

Frank released Mary Lazarus then, and she backed away from him.

Sister Agatha crept forward, wondering if she could get close enough to conk Frank in the head with her flashlight—or if she should even try.

Annoyed that the sheriff was once again shining the beam of his flashlight into his eyes, Frank waved his pistol at him. "Shine that light on your pistol, Sheriff, so I can see that it remains in the holster. Otherwise, I'll assume you're pulling something and start shooting."

In that split second while Frank's attention was on Tom, Sister Agatha stepped up and grabbed Mary Lazarus by the arm, yanking her out of the line of fire.

Mary Lazarus yelped and Frank spun around. Seeing it was Sister Agatha, he pointed the gun at her chest.

Suddenly a white streak came flying past Tom Green.

Pax clamped down on Frank's gun arm with his jaws, swinging them both around in the narrow space from the momentum of the attack. Frank howled, bounced off the side of the tunnel, and dropped his gun on the ground.

Sister Agatha let go of Mary Lazarus and scooped up the pistol, jumping back out of Frank's reach as he tried to regain his footing and ward off Pax, who was holding on to him with a death grip.

Tom Green stepped up just then, his gun back in his hand and his flashlight illuminating the tunnel. "Rex, out!" he ordered sharply.

The dog complied instantly, releasing Frank, but remaining in front of him, growling.

"I wouldn't move if I were you," the sheriff warned, reaching for his handcuffs with his free hand.

Less than ten seconds later, two deputies came up from the outside end of the tunnel and joined them. Sister Mary Lazarus was handcuffed as Sheriff Green turned Frank over to a deputy.

"Get them out of here the same way you came in," Green said, then turned to Sister Agatha. "Are you okay?" he asked, taking Frank's gun from her hand.

"Yeah," she said in a thin voice. "I'm sure I'll stop shaking real soon, too, like maybe around Christmas."

Tom laughed. "You'll be fine. You're tough—for a nun."

"All nuns are tough. Don't you remember Catholic school?"

She'd started to walk out with him, but before they'd gone more than a few feet, he stopped in midstride and looked at her. "You'd be better off going back the way you came in. The weeds and thick brush around the concealed opening are pretty rough on the skin, and it's tricky with all the goatheads and cockleburs there. I think Frank planted those himself to keep anyone from finding the end of the tunnel. If I hadn't been watching him, I'd have never seen it myself."

"How did you get Pax through them?" she asked.

He glanced down at the dog, who was by her side. "He'd apparently discovered his own way in—a narrow path he'd used before. I saw his prints all over the ground."

"Looks like he had more than one way in and out of our monastery."

"Go ahead and take him back with you now. He's done a good day's work as far as I'm concerned."

"I'm glad you feel that way. Be sure to bring him a special treat next time you come see us."

Tom laughed. "I'll do that."

When Sister Agatha emerged from the tunnel into the basement with Pax—the wall opened with just a push—Reverend Mother was waiting, and now the light was on. Sister Agatha nodded reassuringly, letting Mother know everything was all right. Pax barked and wagged his tail. Mother looked at him sternly, then at Sister Agatha, and held up one finger to her lips signifying that the Great Silence was not to be broken now that the emergency was past. Smiling, she gave Sister Agatha a hug, and scratched Pax behind the ears vigorously.

It was a welcome home, and a testament to the peace that had just been won. Their victory had come at a cost, but now they could all go on.

The following morning as the bells rang for Terce at eight, Sister Bernarda came to the parlor, but Sister Agatha was already there.

"Go join the sisters in chapel, Your Charity," Sister Agatha said. "You've been portress almost exclusively for far too long without anyone to help you."

"God reward you, Sister. It feels good to get back to our regular schedules," Sister Bernarda said with a sigh. "Maybe now we can finally begin the process of healing."

Sister Agatha looked down at the dog by her feet and smiled. "Some blessings came out of all that heartbreak and sorrow, too. It wasn't all bad."

Sister Bernarda watched her pensively. "You sound almost sorry that things will be returning to normal now."

"No, that's not it." Sister Agatha took a deep breath. "It's just that I'll miss the challenges that come with investigative work. For a long time investigative reporting was my passion, you see."

"It's time to let go, Your Charity. We all need to get back to our lives and our duties here," she said firmly.

After Sister Bernarda left, Sister Agatha picked up a rag and began dusting as she said her Pater Nosters. She loved their monastery and the company of the sisters and she loved God—above everything else. Although she'd had an exciting taste of her former life, it was now time to close that door. Bernarda was right. As the nuns' voices rose in choir, an indescribable peace settled over her.

She'd just finished cleaning the parlor when she heard a knock at the door. Sister Agatha opened it, and saw Sheriff Tom Green standing on the stone steps. "Come in. What can we do for you today?" Although she knew the investigation was over, she couldn't quite make herself stop hoping that, somehow, things would take a new and challenging turn that would require her involvement.

"I wanted to give Reverend Mother an update."

"Is everything okay?"

"Everything's fine. The investigation is now closed."

She nodded. "All right. Make yourself comfortable. I'll go get Mother."

As the nuns came out of the chapel, Sister saw Reverend Mother walking down the hall and went to meet her halfway.

Sister Agatha quickly explained that the Sheriff was waiting in the parlor to speak to her. "He said the investigation is closed," she added, not wanting her to worry.

"Praised be Jesus Christ," Reverend Mother said, relief evident on her face.

"Now and forever," Sister Agatha answered.

Reverend Mother went to the grille as Sister Agatha returned to the other side of the parlor where Tom was waiting.

"I wanted to update you," Tom said, looking at Reverend Mother first, then Sister Agatha. "Anita Linney—the nun you knew as Sister Mary Lazarus—has made a full confession in exchange for reduced charges. She was about to leave the order, and got pulled into Frank's scheme because she was in love. She felt it was the only way she had of holding on to him. He was almost broke after paying off his son's gambling debts, and his business was losing money."

"What about Frank?"

"He's still not saying much. I think he's hoping to cut a deal for himself. But he'll come around. I've been through this before."

"What are the charges against Anita?" Sister Agatha asked. "I know she never meant to kill Father Anselm."

"We're charging her with involuntary manslaughter. Apparently she'd originally found the monkshood here on monastery grounds while weeding the rose beds. When her hands swelled up and she got sick, she read up on the plants and learned that the toxic chemicals in monkshood could be absorbed through the skin. Later, when Frank hatched up his scheme to steal the manuscripts to fund their future, she suggested he get some monkshood plants, like the ones she'd pulled up, and cultivate them in the patch near the transformer, which was only a few feet away from where the passageway ended. Then she could have access to it. She'd hoped that after you got sick and were sidelined that she'd be given the work you were doing. But if not, she was confident that she'd be able to open the safe once she had time alone in the scriptorium. She'd managed to learn all but one number."

"And then what, did they already have a buyer?" Sister Agatha asked.

He shook his head. "They'd hoped to sell the manuscript back to the insurance company through a broker. They figured the insurance company would rather buy it back with no questions asked than take the loss and have to honor the claim. They weren't expecting to be millionaires. They just wanted enough of a nest egg to start anew."

"How anyone could think they could get a fresh start with that hanging over them is beyond me," Sister Agatha said.

"I wish things had turned out differently," Reverend Mother said.

Sheriff Green nodded, then looked at Sister Agatha. "You know that the person who tried to run you off the road in the pickup was Don Malcolm. But I thought you'd like to know that he finally admitted that much to us. He said he was just trying to rattle you, but that won't lessen the severity of the other charges against him."

"Good. I hope it'll help keep him from corrupting any more young men." She paused, then added, "What about the manuscript Anita took with her? When will I be able to get it back?" Sister Agatha asked. "I know it's just a good forgery that still embarrasses the library, but they'd like it back eventually."

"It's evidence now, but once the trial is over, it'll be returned to you, and you can give it back to your librarian friend. In the meantime, don't worry. We'll take good care of it," he said, and glanced at his watch. "Well, I better be going. There's a lot of paperwork waiting for me at my office."

"Thank you for coming by, Sheriff. We appreciate that," Reverend Mother said.

Tom gave her a nod, then looked at Sister Agatha. "By the way, Sister, you'll have to begin training with Pax and his former handler, Deputy Ralph Ortiz, soon. Changing the dog's name isn't enough. In his heart, he's still a cop," he said with a tiny smile.

"I'll give your deputy a call tomorrow," Sister Agatha said.

As the heavy door closed behind Sheriff Green with a massive, final thud, Sister Agatha glanced at Reverend Mother. "I guess it's time for me to start working full-time again in the service of the Lord."

"Child, you never stopped," Reverend Mother said quietly.